Linda MacDonald was born and brought up in Cockermouth, Cumbria. She was educated at the local grammar school and later at Goldsmiths', University of London where she studied for a BA in psychology and then a PGCE in biology and science. She taught in a secondary school in Croydon for eleven years before taking some time out to write and paint. In 1990 she returned to teaching at a sixth form college in south-east London where she taught psychology. For over twenty-five years she was also a visiting tutor in the psychology department at Goldsmiths'. She has now given up teaching to focus fully on writing.

Her first published novel *Meeting Lydia* is a prequel to *A Meeting of a Different Kind* but either book can be read independently. Meeting Lydia tells of the effects of bullying on later life from the perspective of a woman in turmoil. It also examines midlife crises and internet relationships.

A Meeting of a Different Kind

Linda MacDonald

Matador
9 Priory Business Park,
Wistow Road, Kibworth Beauchamp,
Leicestershire. LE8 0RX
Tel: (+44) 116 279 2299
Fax: (+44) 116 279 2277
Email: books@troubador.co.uk
Web: www.troubador.co.uk/matador

ISBN 978 1780883 250

British Library Cataloguing in Publication Data.
A catalogue record for this book is available from the British Library.

Typeset by Troubador Publishing Ltd, Leicester, UK

Matador is an imprint of Troubador Publishing Ltd

Printed in Great Britain by the MPG Books Group,
Bodmin and King's Lynn

To Emily, Cameron and Fraser

Acknowledgements

The publication of this sequel to *Meeting Lydia* has only been possible because of the support for its predecessor.

I should like to thank Brian Hurn for critical comments on the first draft and my sister-in-law Lindsey MacDonald for invaluable advice on the opening chapters. Also grateful thanks to Matthew Fall McKenzie for inspired and painstaking interpretation of my brief for cover artwork and to Kit Domino for editorial expertise and professionalism. I am especially grateful to the late Patricia Bullard who advised Broadclyst village as a suitable place for Edward Harvey to live. I had no idea at the time what an unusual and interesting location this would turn out to be.

The team at Troubador have once again provided excellent service and support, especially Amy and Sarah. I am indebted to several people who have helped with research queries: Dr Suzanne Conboy-Hill for clinical expertise and input regarding psychotherapy; Jo Barlow, poultry consultant; Helen Trebble on the workings of the Killerton estate; Alasdair Moore for Tresco tree identification; Rachel Davies for sharing her experiences of apple-packing and Martyn Clayton who pointed me in the right direction on the practice of wassailing.

Finally I would like to say a special thank you to friends and family who have offered encouragement and practical help, and without whom this novel would not have been completed.

The University of Devon and Stancliffe University in London are fictional institutions at the time of writing, as are Blackbrook High and Cedarwood schools. The maze discovered by Edward Harvey at Troy Town on St Agnes is fictional, but it is not without possibility that there might have been a maze much earlier than the one found dating back to the 18th century. The characters are fictitious with the exception of the owners of the Parsonage in Chapter 25.

L.M.

Flower of this purple dye,
Hit with Cupid's archery,
Sink in apple of his eye.

William Shakespeare
A Midsummer Night's Dream

1

Edward Harvey is not the philandering type, so it would surprise him to know that soon there will be two significant 'other' women in his life. At the moment there is only one woman occupying his thoughts, his wife Felicity, but for the first time there are ripples on the matrimonial lake and these thoughts have become disquieting. He might even call them qualms.

It is March 2003 and the family is having breakfast; Edward, Felicity, four children, two springer spaniels and a cat. They are scattered in their newly extended, newly fitted, modern chrome kitchen, with the longed-for double hob, the pine table, the French windows leading out onto the patio, the breakfast bar and the central work station. Pans of various sizes, a fish kettle and two woks hang on the wall and glint in the morning sun. This is a serious kitchen for serious cooks.

Felicity is bustling about grilling bacon, frying eggs, unloading the dishwasher, watering herbs, an expert at multitasking. She says, 'By the way, Ted, I shall be giving up my job at the end of the term. I've handed in my resignation.'

No discussion, just a statement of fact.

'Are you sure about this,' says Edward, who is sitting at the table and stops reading his newspaper mid paragraph. A wave of something that others would interpret as panic passes over him. He is not used to being out of control of his life. The qualms multiply in seconds; the ripples on the lake become waves.

'It's the only way I'll have time to carry through my plans,' says Felicity, basting eggs with a fish slice.

1

My plans, thinks Edward. *Not our plans.*

'Things have changed because of Mummy's money; I want to put it to good use. Okay so the plans are a tad more ambitious than they were, but a restaurant is what I've always wanted, and the children will help. They'll love it.'

'I think we should discuss it fully before you do anything hasty.' Edward hopes that she will listen to his fears and exercise some caution, but he knows that it is not in Felicity's nature to be cautious. If she had been, they would never have got together in the first place.

'You're never here at the time when discussion might be appropriate, Ted. My career has been on hold since we met.'

That's two Teds already, thinks Edward. *And it's only just gone eight. Bad sign!* 'That's not strictly true,' he says.

The children sit on stools around the breakfast bar. James, eighteen, the Brooding Intellectual; Rachel, sixteen, the Sensible One; Harriet, fourteen, the Feisty One ... Oh yes, they were very regimented about family planning until Christopher, ten, Red Wine Mistake. Felicity insisted on Edward having a vasectomy after that.

The spaniels, dark-chocolate, Clint and Gryke, five, trot between the table and the bar, hoping for crumbs, awaiting their first morning walk with Edward.

'The fattest one of us here is Mum,' says Christopher from the breakfast bar, oblivious of his parents' conversation.

More incendiary words.

Edward's attention flips. *Felicity ... Fat ...*

'Chris!' says Rachel accusingly. Rachel is going on thirty-five.

Christopher is attempting to eat his third Shredded Wheat and his comment is in response to a jibe by Harriet. Edward waits for a huffy repost from his wife.

Felicity turns and glares at her youngest son. 'With charm

like that, you may have difficulty getting a girlfriend.'

Ouch! That was a good strike Flick, but harsh. He's only ten. He didn't mean to be unkind.

Edward had never before thought of Felicity as fat and wouldn't have mentioned it, diplomacy always being wisest in matters of personal attributes. But the idea bothers him, and he is annoyed that it bothers him, preferring to believe that he is higher up the evolutionary scale than those whose decisions about the merits of women are governed by aesthetics.

These thoughts take milliseconds and there are swift reactions from the rest of the children whose seniority relative to Christopher has graced them with considerable tact when dealing with parents, though not, alas, with each other.

'Oh duh, moron,' says Harriet, adding, 'I wonder if Dad's Fanclub is fat?'

'Mum is *so* not fat,' says Rachel. 'Curvy is the new thin.'

'What's "curvy"?' asks Christopher.

'You'll understand in a year or two,' says James.

Felicity stalks over to Edward and puts the plate of bacon and eggs firmly in front of him, clattering it against the fork. Her mouth is tightly closed and her eyes are steely blue.

'What's up with her?' whispers James, smoothing his long, wavy brown hair and nibbling a piece of toast.

'I am here,' says Felicity. 'If you must talk about me, can you save it for later when I'm out of earshot?' She removes the tea towel that's wrapped around her waist, covering her skirt. Edward catches her eye and tries a smile, but she turns away.

'Who's Dad's fan club?' asks Christopher, eyes wide behind dark-rimmed spectacles.

'Dad's fan club is called Fanclub,' says Harriet.

Edward gives a sweeping warning glance across the kitchen, briefly scanning each of his children, trying to avert a crisis, but saying nothing. He is conscious of their proximity, but with the distance between the table and the bar, he has a sense of being in another room with a clear partition between himself and the rest of the family. Teenage babble in the mornings mostly goes over his head as lightweight chatter unworthy of attention, but this observation about Felicity has found a place in his brain to lodge and make itself comfortable. He is aware of it stretching out and yawning, surveying the habitat for other similarly disquieting thoughts with which to mingle. And there are companions nowadays where there never used to be.

Gradually the teenagers melt away from the bar and there is much to-ing and fro-ing and gathering of bags and books, and yelps when needed things cannot be found. During the mayhem Edward returns to the newspaper and Felicity shoos her children in the same way as she shoos her hens, tidying in their wake until James, Rachel and Harriet are out of the front door, heading for the bus that will take them to their school in Exeter, and Christopher is on his way, walking to the primary school at the other end of their village.

Both Felicity and Edward work at the University of Devon, situated on the other side of the M5 from the city, just off the Honiton road and less than five miles from where they live on the edge of Broadclyst. While Felicity aims to arrive at her administrative post by eight-fifty, Edward, as head of the archaeology department, has a more flexible schedule. This is why they need two cars and have an unnecessarily large fuel bill. Edward knows it is a sore point with Felicity who is adding to her green credentials on a daily basis and feels he should travel in early with her.

'Are you in this evening?' she asks as she winds her long hair into a rope with practised dexterity, loops it under itself a couple of times and secures it with a large slide.

Edward thinks she sounds different this morning. She is

4

often brisk, but usually with him there is a warmth about her eyes that means he never takes it personally.

'Yes, but I've work to do on the maze lecture.'

Felicity gives him a knowing look, and when she leaves, he thinks she closes the door with a little more force than usual.

Something is definitely not right.

It is hard to be precise about when the not rightness occurred for it moved into the house as stealthily as the spiders, lying low, undiscovered until the tell-tale signs of gossamer. It might have been when Felicity's mother died a few weeks earlier and the inevitable emotional fallout, but he suspects it was before that. He is aware of being marginalised by both his wife and the children; as if he matters less; as if his widely recognised discovery on the Isles of Scilly last summer, is inconsequential to his family. This is a new feeling. Normally Felicity is full of admiration for his achievements and he has to restrain her from shouting from the rooftops. Not this time. When he said he had been invited to contribute to the forthcoming Maze exhibition at the British Museum and that a model of his discovery was going to be included, she said somewhat disparagingly, 'I expect you said "Yes", like you always do?' And when he added that he would be giving presentations, necessitating frequent visits to London, she had added, 'I suppose I will have to cope, as usual.'

It wasn't like her to complain.

A large inheritance from the deceased mother is making him feel redundant. Of course they have not seen any of it yet, but Felicity is already spending it and scheming. He is also aware that he is not being consulted about any of her plans. The new kitchen is merely the start.

He begins stacking the breakfast things in the dishwasher. It is one of his jobs on the days he is working locally and not lecturing at some distant university or historical society. It is his penance for leaving the house later than the others; for refusing to part with one of the cars.

Three days ago Felicity questioned the energy consumption of the dishwasher and speculated that they might all take turns in doing the washing up and drying on a rota system as they had before the kitchen arrived with its gleaming appliances. Edward said it was ludicrous to buy the machine if it was going to stand idle.

Felicity said, 'We can use it when we need to; when we have people over. Not as a regular thing.'

James, who was following in his mother's footsteps as far as environmentalism was concerned, added, 'Our form tutor said it costs about ten pence per cycle.'

'Peanuts,' said Harriet.

James climbed aboard his hobby-horse. 'It's not the money; it's the unnecessary waste and the carbon footprint. It's all the little things added together that can make the biggest difference. Light bulbs, stand-by buttons, over-filling the kettle. And dishwashers. Together, yeah, that's a whole load of wasted energy.'

Edward fears that soon his morning task of merely moving dishes from one location to another might take on an altogether more unpleasant complexion.

His other morning jobs are letting the three hens out of their coop, collecting the eggs, walking Clint and Gryke, and checking the goats in the paddock haven't eaten anything they shouldn't during the night as is their tendency. Rachel feeds the rabbit and the cat, and if Edward is especially nice to her, she will do the hens as well.

Walking the dogs is a joy he only swaps when he has to, and it is during such strolls down the country lanes bordering their property that he can ruminate on his forthcoming lectures and construct earth-shatteringly complex sentences with which to impress his students.

But this past week, disquieting thoughts – *the qualms* – have interfered with his intellectualising.

The question of sex is one. The lack of sex. The ceasing of the weekend ritual that needs no effort or initiation. For twenty-five years it has never been an issue. Now he hesitates to approach for fear of rebuff.

Conrad Vaughan, friend and colleague for almost twenty years and a self-acclaimed authority on women, said, 'It'll be the change, mate. Hate to tell you, but it happens to them all and when it happens they go weird. My Sandra suddenly didn't want to know, and she was always red hot. When a marriage is on the rocks, mate, the bed's where the rocks are. We lead separate lives now. She does her thing, I do mine.' Conrad is forty-nine, two years older than Edward, bearded and ponytailed, a typically 1970s lecherous lecturer.

And Marianne Hayward, Edward's Fanclub according to the girls, is another disquieting thought. The two thoughts are as yet not linked, but he fears the possibility, especially when Conrad voices his opinion about Marianne's intentions.

2

On the other side of the country, in a tree-lined road in the London suburb of Beckenham, a small angry woman stands outside her front door, lit by the glow of a street lamp, creating a scene worthy of a soap opera.

'And you can take your fucking Scrabble with you!' she yells, flinging a flat dark green box into the air whereupon it makes a parabolic arc like a giant square Frisbee before landing on its edge on the pavement and shedding the contents. Dozens of little cream tiles bounce onto the road and into the shadows.

The recipient of the flying box is Marc, with a 'c', a man of muscular build wearing a leather jacket and jeans. He has very dark hair and a suspiciously orange complexion considering it is early March – although this is barely discernible in the darkness. Had he been Mark-with-a-k, he might have been be-suited with v-necked pullover, sporting a late-winter pallor. He bends down and starts picking up the tiles. 'You stupid bitch! There's no need for that.'

It is probable that a few curtains twitch in Coppercone Lane.

The woman, whose name is Taryn Danielli, stalks down the path to where Marc is scooping up the pieces and purposely jabs at a tile with her stiletto, hoping it is the Z. 'I always said you were a bastard. I hoped I was wrong.'

When angry, she is a firecracker in a small neat package, always immaculately dressed and with a short, dark hairstyle, moussed and blow-dried into spiky filament fronds that frame her face. She is petite, pint-sized, gamine, elfin. She is also very attractive which gives her a distinct advantage when dealing with men. No-one she meets for the first time guesses she is in her mid forties.

'You *are* wrong,' says Marc, still shuffling tiles.

'You said you'd changed,' she accuses.

'I have. I wouldn't have moved in with you if I hadn't changed. It was a bloody text. I'm not crawling into bed with her.'

'There's no such thing as an innocent text exchange with an ex-girlfriend. Texts are inherently flirtatious.'

'What's flirtatious about *How r u*?'

'*Luv Marc,*' says Taryn. 'Luv.'

'It's just a word.' He straightens up, holding the box like a barrier between them.

'Texts are only innocent if you're making arrangements. Anything else with the opposite sex is flirtatious.'

'These are Mad Rules invented by Taryn. Other people text all the time. It means nothing. It's how we connect in the modern world. You're showing your age. I can text who I wanna bloody text.'

'Which is why our relationship can't possibly sustain.' Taryn faces him with hands on hips and a resolute gleam in her eyes.

'Oh gerrof yer high horse, woman!'

When Marc drives off down the road with a screech of tyres on the tarmac, Taryn dusts off her hands in a gesture of good-riddance, throws back her shoulders and struts back into the ground-floor flat with much wiggling of hips and her head held high, glaring at Mrs Bream from next door who is watching the action through the window with a cat in her arms.

Inside she discards her shoes and makes some effort to tidy up the trail of her own clothes and belongings that have tried to escape along with Marc's, all the while replaying their acidic confrontation and rewriting her own lines with more venomous impact.

She first met Marc a couple of years earlier and was charmed by his Latin good looks, his six-pack and the fact he was four years younger than her. When he tried to be masterful and protective she said to him, 'Don't underestimate me just because I'm small. I am large inside. I am enormous. I have strength and energy and determination. I don't do *Little Girl Lost*. What you see is not what you get.'

He had been an on and off relationship ever since.

He ran a flat rental business of dubious repute and was a smidgen away from being a south London geezer. But he was good in bed and played a mean game of Scrabble. She also told her best friend Marianne that he was well-endowed in the lunch-box department, which as far as she was concerned, was important. What he was not was kind, sensitive or faithful. She knew this but it didn't put her off. It was familiar. Indeed, it might have been part of the attraction. She felt comfortable with bastards; she knew the scripts and the rules by which to play the game.

But living with such a man was another thing altogether and she had resisted the temptation throughout her life, preferring solitude and independence. A moment of weakness, of unaccustomed loneliness, of being forty-six, had brought about the suggestion that she and Marc co-habit.

From the start there were rows about big things, little things and freedom. There was a jockeying for position; an attempt to establish a pecking order.

'I'd rather you didn't spend so many evenings at the pub with your mates,' said Taryn. What she didn't want was a repeat of her father.

'Thought you were an independent woman who liked space,' said Marc, sarcastically.

'Space, yes. Not knowing when you're coming home or in what state you'll be in – no. This isn't a hotel.'

'That's what my mum used to say!'

Taryn was not going to accept a life of subservience and three paces behind, and despite enjoying funky music, Marc was a traditionalist when it came to sex roles. They were doomed from the moment his overnight bag became a suitcase and his slippers found a home under the bed.

'You've been too long on your own,' said Marc. 'You're not normal. There's no level of tolerance with you.'

'And you think I should tolerate your leaving pubic hairs in the bath?'

'It's hardly a crime—'

'And the fact that you never clean the loo, or pick up your clothes, or cook the supper, or—'

'Bollocks, Taryn! This is real life. Okay, I'm not perfect, but nor are you. I like to be left alone in the mornings but you witter and whinge. You're obsessed with cleaning and tidiness. You have far too many disinfectants and bleaches. Mess is relaxing. I don't want to live in an antiseptic environment and get asthma. It's amazing you're so good at sex. No wonder you insist on condoms—'

'That is just being sensible.'

'Being paranoid.'

'With your track record?'

'You're in no position to be judgmental.'

But it was when she caught him sending texts to an exgirlfriend that she finally exploded irretrievably and decided sharing a flat with him was not for her.

'You think you can live here with all the benefits, yet still carry on life as a single man.'

'I've only been here a few weeks; it takes time to adjust.'

'I don't want to be the one doing all the adjusting,' said Taryn firmly.

And half an hour later, following an escalation of the argument into personal areas such as Taryn's refusal to have sex during her period; Taryn's nagging when he wanted to have a long lie in at the weekend; Marc's beery breath and lack of hygiene after a night out with the lads; Marc's appropriation of the TV remote control whenever they were together and his irritating habit of flicking through the channels without asking her if there was anything she might like to watch …

'But it's a man thing,' he said in his defence.

'Well it's not a man thing I want in my flat.'

'*Your* flat!'

'It is my flat. That's a fact. I pay the mortgage; I pay the maintenance.'

'Fuck you, Taryn.'

'Fuck yourself, Marc.'

And shortly after, there was much scurrying around, flinging clothes out of drawers and wardrobes; CDs and DVDs from their various scattered resting places and into carrier bags; a slamming of doors, and Marc making a stomping, crashing, snarling, hissing exit down the path to his BMW, followed by Taryn with the Scrabble box.

What a palaver, she thinks as she finally flops into her favourite chair; the chair that for the past few weeks has been commandeered by Marc. She fishes the remote from under the *Radio Times* and with a gleeful smile on her face, turns on the TV. It is *Match of the Day* and the pundits are deep in analysing the finer points of some debatable penalty. *Smug, opinionated bastards!* Marc would love this. With great delight, and an exaggerated flourish of the remote, Taryn switches over to BBC2.

3

Edward is driving to the university, wondering where the last ten years have gone. The '90s seem to have escaped him. It is as if he has been pleasantly sleeping and has woken to find a new era has dawned. His once small children are now quite suddenly almost adults and he listens to their opinions as much as he expects them to listen to his. His eldest son, James, is over six feet in height and it is unsettling no longer being the tallest in the family.

When did it happen? When did he grow from the child into the man?

At an intellectual level there has been some vying for position, but so far Edward feels his supremacy is unchallenged. He is still the alpha male. Soon James will go to university to read biological sciences. He will come home full of new confidence, new arguments, new strategies for undermining his father's position, but at least it may distract him from Kylie, the air-head girlfriend who he has been seeing for most of his upper sixth year. Kylie, with the mechanically straightened bottle-blonde hair, who thinks a guava is a type of bird, believes Cumbria is in South America, and wears skimpy vests in all weathers, displaying an uncomfortable amount of toned midriff bejewelled with a belly-button ring. Edward thinks she is a little too free with her sexuality and when he remarked on this James said, 'Dad, lighten up, we're not going to get married.' Still, it isn't a bad thing to sow a few wild oats. Edward missed out on that.

Now the children are growing up, courtship rituals are played out daily in front of his eyes, mostly by Rachel and

James. He envies their confidence and regrets lost opportunity in his youth. Meanwhile Harriet flaunts the latest crazy fashions in clothes and vocabulary, and Christopher, habitually treated as the baby of the family, is now on the verge of adolescence.

His children are a constant source of fascination; the way they have each developed; their individual quirks despite essentially similar upbringing. He has always been an advocate of the *Nature* argument and enjoys engaging in playful repartee with the behaviourists in the psychology department.

James and Rachel look like Felicity with their sensuous mouths and tumbling light-brown hair. This goes against the notion of Conrad Vaughan's that first children, particularly first girls, take after their fathers to avoid any doubts about paternity.

'How is that possible?' said Edward. 'How can an egg know that it's the first one to be fertilised and how can it allow the male genes to dominate?'

'Search me,' said Conrad. 'But that's what they say.'

'There's a fifty-fifty chance of looking like either parent anyway,' continued Edward. 'Is it not just that the focus of attention has been on those children that support the theory rather than those that don't?'

Harriet and Christopher, third and fourth out of the womb, both look like Edward with dark hair and brown eyes. Yet they are impulsive and opinionated like Felicity, while Rachel and James are placid and industrious like Edward. He marvels at how the cards have been dealt; how the dice have been cast; how the genes have been mixed.

Conrad has another theory that if both parents are at least reasonably attractive, then children who take after their same sex parent will also be attractive, while children who take after their opposite sex parent may not be; attractive features on one sex being less so on the other.

'Look at this hooter,' said Conrad by way of explanation, patting the side of his sizeable nose and sniffing. 'Gives me an aristocratic air, doesn't it? A touch of class? But stick it on a woman and she'd be first in line for a nose job. This is why I would hate to have daughters. This is why some of the beautiful people have bog-standard children and, conversely, why Mr and Mrs Average sometimes produce the occasional stunner.'

Edward had shaken his head. Conrad's turn of phrase often left him speechless, but when he went home that night and looked across the supper table at his family, he had to acknowledge that Conrad might be right, Christopher and Rachel being significantly better looking than James and Harriet. But that could just be coincidence.

He wondered what Marianne would think of this theory of Conrad's. Marianne is a psychology teacher in a sixth-form college and is always writing to him about some strange notion or other. He hesitated to explain it to her in case it made him sound chauvinistic and arrogant – both attributes that he tries to avoid though he knows he is sometimes guilty of the latter when in the company of fools. Edward doesn't suffer fools, but has endless patience with anyone in whom he sees a glimmer of hope.

The University of Devon is one of the so-called *new* universities, the former Devon Polytechnic that underwent a change of description in 1992. Under Edward's leadership, the archaeology department has acquired a reputation to rival some of the best in the country and although he has sometimes contemplated moving to a more prestigious institution – and has had several tempting offers – the convenience of the location, the age of the children and the fact that the Dean allows him considerable flexibility to lecture elsewhere, has meant that he has been perfectly content to stay.

Indeed, the previous summer he had taken a team of

archaeologists and students to do fieldwork on St Agnes, one of the smallest of the inhabited Isles of Scilly. There he had uncovered the original Troy Town maze – far pre-dating any others that had been found or even speculated about, and instrumental in him being involved with the exhibition at the British Museum.

He arrives at the university car park and slots his Volvo into its regular space between Conrad's white sports car and Gemma Saborey's Fiat Uno. Gemma is the departmental administrator: single, fortyish, efficient and keen to please. She clucks around him like a mother hen and seems to know what he wants almost before he realises it himself. She also protects him from tiresome staff and bothersome students, inventing meetings in which he is unavoidably delayed and doing the best she can to field their questions with sensible replies. On a good day, he thinks of her as Miss Moneypenny to his James Bond, wondering what goes on beneath her clean and pressed exterior. It seems only a year or two since she was twenty-three and he and Conrad arrived as equals on the bottom rung of the departmental ladder. On a bad day she is a simpering Miss Jones and he is Reggie Perrin.

The University of Devon campus is an undulating landscaped garden of delights, fiercely competing with Exeter University for the prize of the institution with the most scenic grounds. Edward never tires of watching the changing seasons, perhaps eating a sandwich or a slice of pizza, sitting on a wooden bench by one of the lawns while casting a practised eye over his forthcoming lecture notes. The azaleas remind him of Amen Corner at the Augusta National.

He and Conrad are occasional golfing partners; occasional because Edward is always busy, and golf is a sport that cannot be rushed. It is during these games that Conrad offloads about his latest sexual encounters, and about his concerns that his wife Sandra might put a stop to his shenanigans, even though they are separated in all respects other than name and address. Edward and he are unlikely friends, but once Conrad was extraordinarily kind and he has never forgotten it.

This morning he feels distracted and is oblivious to the fact that it is unseasonally warm with a bright blue sky. He should be thinking about his ten o'clock lecture on dendrochronology. He takes his briefcase out of the boot and walks absently towards a rectangular block with its large blue-tinged panes of non-reflective glass, the Scattwood Building, where the archaeology department is based.

The problem is Felicity, his once beautiful Felicity. Following Chris's observation at the breakfast table, he saw her as if for the first time and it shocked him how much she had changed, both in size and in her manner towards him. He thought, *is this my wife; the woman I married?*

Then he thought, *is this still me?* And he felt his own stomach in an exploratory way, still relatively flat – for a man of forty-seven – the product of much walking and an aversion to pastries. It must be true what Conrad said about middle-aged women laying down stores for the hard years ahead.

Edward was twenty-two when he first met Felicity.

He was sitting alone at one of the large tables in the student refectory at University College, London, browsing through an archaeological paper on Roman artefacts, when he was aware of the presence of someone slipping onto the chair opposite. He glanced up from his reading. It was meant to be a momentary glance, a millisecond scan, just in case it was someone he knew. But no one who saw Felicity Mayfield at close quarters could ever resist lingering on her face for a little more time than was polite. Not that she minded, he later learned.

'Hi,' she said.

Thankful for a reason to stare, Edward smiled and nodded, absorbing the waves of 1970s brown hair, touching her bare elbows, parted in the centre, one side tucked casually behind an ear. She wore blue denim jeans, and a black vest clung tightly to her breasts. There was a heavy silver chain around her neck and her lips looked shiny and inviting. It was a look that was deliberately casual, yet somehow glamorous.

She was, he thought, a goddess.

Edward wasn't used to goddesses saying 'Hi'.

'I'm Felicity,' said the goddess.

'Edward,' said Edward.

'I know,' she continued. 'Edward Harvey, archaeology department, post-grad, silent and mysterious, almost permanent resident of the library. No-one seems to know anything much about you.'

'I like my privacy,' said Edward, smiling in a welcoming way nonetheless.

'We've never seen you without your glasses before.' She nodded towards a nearby table at which two other similarly styled, but not so pretty, students were sitting watching them intently.

'You have fabulous eyes,' she continued in her sultry voice that reminded him of serious-minded presenters of *The Book Programme* on Radio 4. 'The kindest eyes I've ever seen. I had to tell you. Like a horse's eyes. Not that you look like a horse.' She blushed.

Edward detected a slightly plummy accent.

'I've just discovered I don't need glasses any more. Had them since I was six. Whatever was wrong has righted itself. I now have twenty-twenty vision, they say.'

'How amazing! Just think, I might have spoken to you before.'

Edward was slightly annoyed that his wearing glasses should make such a difference. It wasn't something he had analysed. Perhaps she was joking. 'I haven't changed as a person since last week, as far as I'm aware.'

'I didn't think you would be my type. I know it sounds shallow to say that.'

So she wasn't joking. 'The studious bespectacled stereotype, you mean?'

'We don't see you with women,' she added.

It was a statement requiring an answer.

'I'm too busy for women.'

'Are you gay?'

'No!'

'Are you too busy to take me out for a drink?'

'Is this some kind of dare?' said Edward, shooting a glance towards the friends on the neighbouring table and noting that they were staring and open-mouthed.

'I'm between boyfriends,' said Felicity. 'And I'm done with the Jack-the-Lads. Time for something different. I've been watching you for some time – even with the glasses. I like what I see.'

Edward was disarmed by her directness. Too often he was confused by women and the games they played. He didn't have time to learn all the rules: that *yes* sometimes means *no*; that *maybe* usually means *yes*; that when they ignored you, they might be interested, and so forth. He agreed to meet her in the union bar for a drink the following lunchtime.

It transpired that Felicity was a biology undergraduate in her final year. She had taken a gap year before starting college and was the same age as Edward.

When he asked her about her ambitions, she said, 'A country house with some land for livestock. Children, and perhaps a restaurant eventually. At heart I'm an old fashioned girl.'

'Why biology?'

'I'm good at it. It's interesting. If I'm going to keep animals and grow plants, then I want to know how they work. And that includes children.' She laughed.

'Shouldn't you be in pursuit of a farmer then?'

'I don't see many of those in London. In any case, I'm also searching for sparkling repartee.' She looked at him coyly, then averted her gaze.

Edward was transfixed. 'Have you always been so clear about what you want your life to be?'

'Of course. Haven't you?'

'Haven't thought much beyond the completion of my PhD – perhaps three years down the line.'

'Do you want to remain in academia? To continue to do research? To lecture?'

'Probably.'

'And do you want to have a family? A wife and children?'

'I think so.'

'And do you like animals?'

'Er, yes.' Edward wondered where this was leading.

'Then your future is decided. That wasn't hard, was it?'

Then she looked him in the eye, a long lingering, seductive glance that made him feel hot. 'You, Edward Harvey, are different and special, and I think we might have chemistry.'

'What makes you think that?' said Edward, still unsure whether this was a wind-up. 'You just said no-one knows anything about me. You don't know me at all.'

'Oh, that was just something to say; an introductory remark. I know you,' said Felicity, with such certainty that he felt a tingling sensation snaking down his backbone. 'And I think you could use some help while you achieve your goals. You must get lonely doing all that research.'

She might just as well have said, *I want to be the woman behind the man.*

Many men would have fled at such obvious pursuit, but Edward, who didn't have time for women in the ordinary sense, thought that a woman, this woman, this goddess, who was pretty, intelligent and confident, and unashamedly volunteering to help to further his career, might be a chance to be snatched and decided that it was time to embark on a journey into the unknown and see if she was right.

And it was. It was perfect.

Meeting Felicity transformed him. He was the type of person who didn't seek out opportunities but always threw himself wholeheartedly into any that came his way. Felicity had a wide social circle and her friends became his. It was an effortless way to meet people and left him plenty of time to pursue his research.

While he spent the next three years fine tuning his PhD, she completed her degree, gaining an upper second, and then worked in the university library and in a local café. During the first year, sometimes they stayed at her place, a house shared with three other girls, and sometimes they stayed in his rented housing association flat. When Edward's flat-mate moved out, Felicity said, 'I think you will be lonely on your own,' and the next day she arrived in a taxi with two suitcases and set about building a home for both of them.

After completion of his thesis, Edward secured a lectureship at the University of Devon and while waiting for him to take up his position, they spent the summer back-packing round Europe.

On returning they moved to the West Country and acquired a small terraced house in Exeter. Felicity continued to boost their income with any odd hours of part-time work she could find, often with a loosely biological or food related theme, first at a wet fish shop and then at an apple packing establishment where she spent hours grading for quality and learning about all the different varieties.

It was from here that they decided to get married, in secret, in a no-fuss, economical kind of way, and where the first three children were born in relatively quick succession. In 1989, starved of space, they moved to the Deer Orchard on the edge of Broadclyst. It was a ramshackle old stone farmhouse with a barn and outbuildings, a garden covered with weeds, a substantial but overgrown orchard and a decent-sized paddock.

'It has much potential,' said Felicity, and Edward, who had largely forgotten what she had said when they first met about wanting a smallholding, agreed that it did. Over the years it was modernised by degrees and a few animals acquired in the shape of three hens, a cat, two spaniels, a rabbit and, more recently, two goats: Margo and Barbara.

Edward climbed up the ranks at work and has been in his current position for more than ten years. He is also joint author of a widely used basic text in landscape archaeology and often gives lectures to various ancient history society gatherings around the country. When he asked Felicity if she minded him being away from home so much, she patted him on the back and said, 'Go and entertain those serious-faced men and women in anoraks with your eloquent prose.'

Meanwhile, when Christopher started nursery, she secured a small part-time job at the university in the admissions department, gradually increasing her hours as the children became more independent. It wasn't what she wanted, but she said that she didn't have time to keep chasing work and at least this job was permanent, part-time and flexible; ideally suited to the needs of the family.

Edward imagined that this is what it would be like for the forseeable future. Of course he has recently had the odd doubt about whether he wants to be doing the same thing for the rest of his working life, but they are wispy doubts that melt as soon as he becomes involved in anything archaeological. And as

Felicity rarely mentioned her restaurant dream, he assumed that her early desires had subsided, or would at least wait until they both retired.

But then her mother died.

Felicity's Surrey-based parents had been reasonably well off but considered their only daughter should make her own way in the first instance. With Felicity on the other side of the country, they feared ending their lives being put out to graze in a residential home and decided that their money should be kept for that eventuality, rather than passed on to Felicity in the interim. But they did help out with carpets for the first house and were always generous with presents for the children.

Felicity's father died in 1998, but her mother had remained in good health and refused to downsize from their palatial home until just before Christmas when a massive stroke had led to her needing nursing care. She only survived a further week. The house was rapidly sold and even after death duties, Felicity as the only child would soon inherit the best part of a million pounds.

'You could give up work,' she said to Edward. 'We could travel Europe again – or even the world – but in more luxury this time.'

'I don't want to give up work,' said Edward. 'I know I grumble from time to time, but work is important to me; it's who I am. And who would look after the animals?'

'The Molwings would be only too happy. A few extra would be nothing to them. We could do a luxury cruise.'

The Molwings ran a mixed farm next door. Edward said nothing.

'You could become a counsellor. You always said it was money that stopped you from retraining.'

'That was just a whim.'

Felicity gave him a doubtful glance. 'Well, so long as you

don't object to me doing a few things.' She had seemed deliberately vague.

'It's your money,' he said, suspecting she was thinking about the restaurant again.

She didn't contradict him. Perhaps he should have been forewarned.

4

Taryn was an abused child. This is why she is the way she is with men. This is at the root of her failure to settle, her cynicism, her singledom, her almost pathological independence. Now Marc is history, she carries on in much the same way as she did when he was living with her. She does not grieve or work her way through a box of tissues, eating tons of chocolate and moping, as others might. Nor does she spend hours on the phone to her friend Marianne, desperate for consolation, reassurance that it will be all right in the end; that nothing is absolute; that he might come back begging for forgiveness, promising to change. In fact she hasn't yet told Marianne of the split.

'Why waste emotion,' she says to Kimberley Edge, with whom she works as a teacher in the English department at Blackbrook High School on the edge of Beckenham. They are standing in the playground doing break-time duty, alert to signs of bullying, surreptitious smoking, the passing of drugs. Kimberley is twenty-three, smallish, mousy-haired and doe-eyed. She has a steady boyfriend called Jason and has yet to understand the treacherous nature of men. She is Taryn's project for conversion.

'He's a commitment-phobic,' says Taryn. 'And so am I. There was no love involved, and there lay the problem – for both of us.'

'I don't know how you can be so calm. I'd be in pieces if Jase an' me broke up.'

'I don't cry,' says Taryn matter-of-factly. 'Though I did once when I was ten and my hamster died.'

Kimberley blinks, shivering in a short skirt and pulling her fuchsia angora cardigan tightly across her pert chest. 'I cry at the drop of a hat. I get upset even if Jase looks at me in a cross way. I'm like a tap.'

Clearly Taryn has her work cut out.

It wasn't sexual abuse, as far as she can remember, but she knows all about the possibility of repression and how hypnotherapists can regress a patient back through their life – and sometimes even further into previous lives – to uncover unpleasant truths. She doesn't think they'd find anything, and she won't take the risk of any planting of false memories. In any case, if it had been sexual, she doesn't want to be reminded. What she remembers with luminous clarity is being hit, often and for no apparent reason, by a father she began life adoring, but who began drinking seriously when she was eight and who, when drunk, became a maniacal mad-man that had she and her mother screaming for mercy.

Carlo Danielli came to England just after the war. He was slight of build but didn't allow this to get in the way of his dreams. Indeed it is his words about being big inside that Taryn echoes whenever she feels disadvantaged by her diminutive size.

Carlo was enterprising, hard-working and full of Italian charm. He started out with an ice cream van in Leeds, finding a chime that played 'On Ilkla Moor Baht 'at', which endeared him to the locals and steered him onto the road of prosperity. Soon he set up a shop and café in the city centre, introducing Yorkshire to pizza and pasta the way his mother used to make them. He had the foresight to marry a local girl, Daisy, who was personable with customers and happy to work all hours while the business was becoming established. The name Danielli, emblazoned in pink lettering across the shop's black façade, became synonymous with daytime café culture and with their delicious ice cream.

He was a success and the money rolled in. Taryn was born – named by Daisy after Tyrone Power's daughter, and pronounced with a Yorkshire short 'a'. In true Italian style, Carlo insisted that Daisy gave up work to look after the family. Two years later Louisa was born and they lived a comfortable life from the proceeds of the café and the van. Indeed, they could have moved to a bigger house, but instead they sent little Taryn and her sister to private schools.

All was well until Gino Gambero appeared on the scene and opened a rival business in a nearby street. Gino undercut Carlo's prices and lured some of his clientele.

'He know' nothing about cooking,' said Carlo to Daisy. 'I wouldn't feed his pizza to animal. He jumped-up-start.'

'Take no notice,' said Daisy in Cleckheaton tones, aware that her husband didn't like the competition after years of being revered for his exotic originality. 'We're fine. We have trouble finding space for all our sit-down customers. There's enough business for both of us, and there's nowt we can do but get on with it.'

But Carlo was territorial and disillusioned. He became lazy and depressed. Sometimes the girls came home from school and found him drinking. And if he was out, he was down at the pub. When he came back their mother would be nervous, hardly seeming to dare to speak because anything she said seemed to set him off into a rage that echoed around their little house. The girls escaped upstairs and hid in their room, listening to the shouting and the crashes and bangs as their mother was knocked into the furniture.

But Taryn was a spirited child and one night when she was nearly nine, she decided to stay downstairs and challenge him. She was his darling; he wouldn't hurt her. This way she could protect her mother.

'Don't be mad, Babbo,' she pleaded.

'Who you think you speaking to?' yelled Carlo, eyes raging. 'You nothing but snotty little kid. I am your father. You no too old to put cross my knee.' And he slapped her hard across the face.

Taryn reeled backwards with the force from the blow and hit her head on the edge of the door.

Her mother ran forwards and started punching him.

'You bring up brat,' shouted her father to Daisy, throwing her off balance. '*Si*. A monster. She try tell me what to do in my own home. I no have it.'

Taryn crawled behind her mother's long nightdress, shaking in terror at the change in her father towards her. Blood trickled down her face from the cut on her head and in that instant she was disillusioned.

Next day it was as if nothing had happened.

'*Buonjourno, Bella*. How my little Hun-bunch? We no take notice of Babbo's bad moods, *si*?' And he ruffled her hair like he always did, causing her to wince when she felt his fingers on the bruise.

Little Taryn's eyes stared coldly back. She'd witnessed these day-after apologies to her mother many times and knew that they meant nothing; it would all happen again.

That night was the first and last time she cried because of a man. From that moment she began the process of de-loving her father and distancing her emotions. It was hard at first; hard to walk away from the cuddles that had been the norm. She developed a shell; she ignored him. She knew this inflamed him even more, but she didn't care.

'I no send you to posh school to be stuck up and look down your nose on your father. I send you for you get good education; go to university.'

'Stop drinking then. Stop shouting at Mum. Stop hitting

us. I don't like you when you're drunk. I want you to be like you used to be.'

For a couple of days he would make an effort, struggling with his own demons, but he was too far down the road and as the withdrawal symptoms became unbearable, he reached for the bottle again.

'He's not a bad man,' said her mother. 'He doesn't mean it. He's sick. Don't drive a wedge between you that you'll regret.'

'He hits me, Mum. He hits you. Soon it will be Louisa too. He's a drunken pig. Why don't you leave him?' She knew she couldn't wait to get away from the arguments, the violence, the uncertainty, the whisky-laced spit that sprayed from his lips when he was shouting, the stench of vomit in the bathroom, and sometimes even on the stairs when he hadn't made it in time.

'Where would we go?' said Daisy seeming suddenly old and tired. 'What would happen to him? He'd end up in the gutter. I still love him.'

One night he fell down the stairs and lay motionless at the bottom. Taryn heard the crash and flew out of her room, first on the scene. She thought he was dead and it was with some disappointment that she registered the twitch of his eyelids and the licking of his lips. Daisy was soon beside them with frightened eyes, her blonde curls in disarray. When they established with some difficulty that there were no bones broken, they left him there to sleep it off.

'So drunk, he lands like a cat,' said Daisy.

The teenage years were predictably problematic with Carlo being moody and controlling, and Taryn oscillating between wild tantrums and dark depressions. When she escaped to Birmingham to study English, she heaved a sigh of relief and without the spying eyes of her father upon her, she accepted every social invitation, revelling in the attention she was paid by men, yet full of cynicism, all the time on guard. She was wary of getting too close; of caring. She knew the way they could turn; she knew the dangers of drink. Not for her a cosy romance culminating in a couple of children, a white picket fence and a cat.

'Oh, aren't you small,' they said patronisingly.

Fuck off, thought Taryn, but she usually gave them a tight smile and waited for the chat-up line.

Men seemed to want to protect her, like her father once had. They opened doors and carried the shopping. She went to the gym; she developed muscles; she jogged. She didn't want protecting; she knew it wouldn't last.

In 1978, while she was studying for her PGCE at the London Institute, she met Roberto, son of an Italian millionaire and with money almost bursting out of every pocket. He had charisma and wild, dark eyes, was a member of Mensa and drove around fast in a silver Lancia, so proud of his parallel parking skills that he would search for the smallest possible space rather than the largest or even the most convenient. His mother approved of him dating someone with Italian blood who could feed him as she had on home-made pasta.

Taryn saw him as a challenge, and she liked challenges. He was an actor and he sucked her into his glamorous, theatrical world of luvvies and late night dining in town. She had always been a night-bird and the antisocial hours suited the rhythms of her life.

One night they went to see *Carmen* at The Coliseum, and afterwards, following some frogs' legs in a bistro frequented by his thespian friends, he took her left hand in his, produced from his pocket a solitaire diamond ring of almost ice cube proportions and began sliding it down her third finger.

No warning, no preamble, no suggestion of marriage.

It was an extravagant gesture of possession and Taryn

snatched her hand away with such speed that the ring fell to the floor.

While Roberto was on his hands and knees under the table, partially hidden by the red checked tablecloth, Taryn leapt to her feet and protested.

'What are you doing, Rob? I thought we were having fun. This is way, way too much.'

By the time he emerged red-faced, clutching the ring, half the restaurant was staring at him.

'I wanted to show you how much you mattered to me.'

'With help from dear Babbo's bank account?'

'Ace bitch,' he said, glaring at her, deeply humiliated, the passion gone. Then he marched off and apart from a cool exchange of loaned books and vinyl records, was never seen again.

New best friend Marianne, from her education class, said, 'Oh my God! How could you refuse? I wish someone would give me a diamond ring and say they'll love me forever.'

Taryn had shrugged. 'Well that's the point. Love doesn't come into it. Oh, he's said it often enough. Mere words. I was tempted for two seconds. But it meant nothing. He wouldn't have married me. He is totally fickle when it comes to women. Only months before me, he was supposedly madly in love with a chemist who worked at the Science Museum. Now I hear he's already dating one of the leading ladies in *La Ronde* at the Aldwych.'

'But you could have always kept the ring,' said Marianne mischievously.

'You'd have to know Roberto to believe it was real. The folks we knock around with would think it was cubic zircons.'

After Roberto, in a slightly manic episode, Taryn hacked two feet off her long brown hair and scissored it into a new short style. Inspired by Ziggy Stardust, she began persuading it to defy gravity. Now it is her trademark, changing colour with the seasons. At the moment it is almost black with subtle claret highlights.

Also after Roberto, she developed an early warning system for signs of commitment and backed away before it became embarrassing. She bought a converted flat on the ground floor of a detached house in Beckenham's tree-lined Coppercone Lane and revelled in the independent life, determined that marriage was not for her. Even when Marianne snared the handsome Johnny and set about playing happy families, she wasn't tempted in the slightest. And when after twenty-odd years of bliss Marianne started having problems, it confirmed Taryn's suspicions that even the most idyllic relationship could be thrown askew by alcohol and in this case, the added burden of jealousy brought about by another woman on the sidelines. She suspected infidelity, but didn't tell Marianne. With Marianne she was the perfect friend, constantly reassuring her that Johnny wasn't that kind of man. Deep down she didn't believe it, and it was something of a surprise when Johnny cut down on his drinking, apologised in the form of a romantic, old-fashioned letter, and the other woman disappeared from their lives. Marianne appeared to be happy again.

But Taryn doesn't think it will last.

5

For a very long time, the significant people in Edward Harvey's circle had remained largely constant: a collection of colleagues at the university, academics from across the globe, Felicity's friends, neighbours in the village, immediate family, an old school friend and his publishing agent. Then one winter's evening some sixteen months earlier, he had received via Friends Reunited a totally unexpected email from someone he hadn't seen since or heard of since he was eleven; someone he shared a class with for three years when as a child he attended the Lakeland prep school, Brocklebank Hall.

The classmate was Marianne Hayward, one of just a handful of girls in the school, and the email was unexpected because he had not added himself to the Brocklebank page of Friends Reunited, but only to that of his secondary school, Waterside Grammar. As he was listed as Ted Harvey (a contraction he has lived with reluctantly since then), Marianne's first email had been speculative and brief.

If you are who I think you are, she had written, *I knew you as Edward and also as …*

Ah yes, a reference to his character in the school play. He remembers being amused by this. It grabbed his attention, he was intrigued, he wanted to know more and perhaps his response was a little over-enthusiastic, mailing her by return and asking questions. The following day, having established that he was the Edward Harvey whom she knew, she wrote to him in more detail and again he replied immediately. To be honest he had little recollection of Marianne Hayward other than as someone who used to challenge him for the form prize and sometimes beat him in spelling tests, but her lengthy and frequent emails over the next couple of weeks soon filled in the details, and when she wrote that she too had been in the school play, and that they had shared a scene together, a picture formed in his mind.

The picture was of a fairly non-descript individual with dark plaits. Still, she was married now; she was in her mid forties; she would have changed.

Marianne's emails reminded him of a life long forgotten, and such was the detail of her memories that he was transported back to the austere grey house that had been his home during term times for three years from the age of nine. He remembered the masses of rhododendron bushes and their vibrant blossoms, the woods where he and his friends had a den, the cricket field, the sports days and the camaraderie. He had mixed emotions of that time. There were fights and squabbles with other boys, and bullying from Barnaby Sproat and his gang. At times there was heart wrenching loneliness at being a boarder away from his family for three months at a time. He missed the hugs and the emotional warmth, recalling sadness and fear when the days at school seemed long and cold and the next holidays stretched over the horizon, far out of reach. But gradually new friendships were formed and new adventures counterbalanced the pain.

Marianne was a day girl, the only girl in his class for a while, and it appeared from what she said that she had been traumatised by bullying. He couldn't remember.

When he and the family went off to Sydney, Pitcairn Island and New Zealand for a month, less than three weeks from her first email, it would have been easy to let the new contact drift, but she had intimated that it would be nice to keep in touch,

34

and because he was curious by nature, and curious to know where this re-acquaintance might lead, once settled back in England, he sent her a brief email and waited to see if she responded.

She did, and mailing became a regular thing until a few weeks back when the family crisis of Felicity's mother dying precluded all but essential communication. Every weekend, either he drove Felicity down to Surrey to clear the house or he stayed at home to look after the children. He hardly had a moment to breathe.

After that his computer hard-drive packed in completely and he lost all his email addresses. He was too wrapped-up with family concerns to worry about losing touch with Marianne.

Eventually he received an email from her, concerned by his uncommon silence, which touched him and troubled him in equal measures. She thanked him for helping her to move on from the bullying that had apparently lurked in the background for most of her life, and said that he had reminded her of the good times at Brocklebank. While quietly pleased to have had such an effect, in his reply he brushed it aside as a mere nothing. He reassured her that he was still alive, excused his lack of contact by explaining about Felicity's mother and the computer, and promised he would write again when he returned from Norway where he has just been to meet with Henrik Selgelid, the maze expert in charge of setting up the exhibition at the British Museum.

His computer is housed in the privacy of an upstairs room that he uses as an office. Many times the girls have tried to commandeer it as a bedroom so that they don't have to share, but Edward is adamant that he needs a space for uninterrupted writing, and it is difficult for the rest of the family to mount any reasonable justification for a change of use.

From: Edward Harvey
To: Marianne Hayward
Date: 11th March 2003, 21.33
Subject: Re: Is there anybody out there?

Dear Marianne,

At last a proper update ...

Great time in Norway looking at remains of mazes around Oslo, including an incredible and scary boat trip to the island of Tisler. Weather turned while we were on our way back!!

They call such mazes Trojaborgs in Norway. Like Troy Town ... Also trekked to the Sunnmøre region to see den Julianske borg (the Julian castle) high up on a plateau. So rough, remote and inaccessible compared with St Agnes. But the maze is believed to be perhaps 3000 years old – which fits in nicely with the find in Scilly.

Felicity is on the verge of becoming a very wealthy woman. Should be pleased; am pleased, but feel a sense of redundancy looming. Felicity has plans connected with her restaurant dream. She said I could change things too, but all the things I thought I wanted now seem less attractive propositions. Contemplating giving up the archaeology has made it all the more precious – especially since the discovery! Have been invited to join in with maze exhibition soon to start at BM as they want to include the St Agnes find. Currently in processes of helping to set up with Henrik Selgelid – Norwegian authority on labyrinths!

Dashing as usual.

Best wishes,

Edward

He thought about putting *Love Edward,* a new development started by Marianne in her last email. But although he had responded in kind at the time, it made him uncomfortable to continue the trend when they hadn't even met.

From: Marianne Hayward
To: Edward Harvey
Date: 12th March 2003, 18.52
Subject: Re: Is there anybody out there?

Dear Edward,
I had to get the atlas out! My knowledge of Norwegian geography is not good!
I am sorry to hear about Felicity's mum. Times like this are very hard. I know we must all face such losses. I am scared for the future.
Perhaps when the dust has settled she will re-think the restaurant dream. They say we shouldn't make big changes to our lives in times of crisis; that we should wait until we have adjusted before putting the wild schemes into action.
Do tell me more about this exhibition.
Best wishes,
Marianne

Marianne Hayward is a teacher of psychology so advice from her, he construes, is from a reliable source. He will tell Felicity to put the brakes on.

From: Edward Harvey
To: Marianne Hayward
Date: 15th March 2003, 22.35
Subject: Re: Is there anybody out there?

Exhibition is of mazes throughout the world, but particularly in Scandinavia. Henrik's speciality is of those in the liminal zone. He is less sceptical than I am about the supernatural aspects – though I may have mentioned already that my experiences in Scilly made me think again. The exhibition had been arranged before St Agnes discovery but the BM thought it should be included and that I could do a lecture. Thought it would just be one, but it now seems to have expanded to alternate weeks for the run of the exhibition. Henrik will lecture too, but more generally. Perhaps you would like to come? There would probably be time for us to meet either before or after …

Edward

Marianne's emails range from the reassuringly sensible to the slightly crazed. She is inclined to write to him at length about all kinds of things, sometimes bordering on the weird. Usually he doesn't have time to reply in detail but he taps out a few sentences in response and this seems to keep the contact flowing.

He tells Felicity, because he tells her everything. There is nothing to hide. Marianne is married to Johnny and seems content. She doesn't tread beyond the boundaries of respectability when she writes. Her only daughter left home for university shortly before she found him on Friends Reunited. He deduced she was lonely with no child to care for. Rachel and Harriet decided she must have had a crush on him at school and they tease him endlessly. It was Harriet who coined the name 'Fanclub'. He laughs it off in a good humoured way, but wonders if it was true.

And he wonders what she is really like. With Felicity's sudden lack of interest in his career, the idea of another woman being enthusiastic is comforting.

Marianne ... Marianne ... Who is she now?

From: Marianne Hayward
To: Edward Harvey
Date: 17th March 2003, 20.29
Subject: Maze Matters

Dear Edward,
What is the liminal zone?
If you give me the details of when you're at the
exhibition, I'll see what I can do.
Marianne

From: Edward Harvey
To: Marianne Hayward
Date: 17th March 2003, 23.01
Subject: Re: Maze Matters

The liminal zone is a border between one state and
another. Coasts fit into that category. Hence labyrinths
being generally found close to the sea – particularly
along Baltic coasts of Sweden and Finland. If you come
to the lecture, you will find out more! The exhibition
starts next week on 24th March, and the first lecture I'm
giving is on Thursday 27th at 6.30. It's an open lecture ...
Hope to be able to see you ... At last!!
Edward

To: Edward Harvey
From: Marianne Hayward
Date: 18th March 2003, 21.13
Subject: Tagged by Aliens

Dear Edward,

I was watching a wildlife programme this evening and am concerned that trapping and tagging an at-risk species is not humane. I know it is done in the name of conservation, but in the not-too-distant-future we may become an endangered species, visited by extraterrestrials who cause us stress by trapping us, weighing and measuring us, piercing us with some implement to extract body fluids and tissues, then sticking some irremovable antenna in a conspicuous place and then a pat on the back, an 'off you go into the yonder' (no longer wild and blue!). Aliens happy; human pretty pissed off, perhaps because this damned object means they can't lie on their backs any more, or wash their hair without it getting caught up in the plug-hole. Or perhaps it bleeps irritatingly when the Aliens' tracking device is switched on. In the world of desirable attributes, this appendage would score low. Then what? Human reproductive strategy now seriously inconvenienced; no mate; no offspring. But will the Aliens care? Not a bit. They've discovered we traipse up mountains for no reason (aren't they an odd bunch?); we fly to hot places and lie in the sun for hours which they know is A Very Unwise Thing to Do; we sit in traffic jams further exacerbating Global Warming. They call it erratic migration. They've learnt lots about us from their tracking devices, but what if it was you who had the stress of being chased and caught and stripped and subjected to humiliating testing? What if it was you with the undesirable attachment? And it doesn't stop there. The Aliens would worry about us and our continuing declining numbers and decide more drastic solutions were necessary. They'd send a working party down to Earth to capture a few specimens to take back to their zoo-equivalent where they might begin a breeding programme just in case we go extinct in the wild.

Sharon from Essex (still with tracking device stuck on her head) is put in a cage with Rupert Bilberry-Fforbes. The Aliens feed them well and anxiously await developments. Nothing happens. Mostly they don't speak to each other. The only time there was a moment that had the Alien researchers in a frenzy of excitement was when Rupert put his hand on Sharon's leg. She screamed, *'Piss off ya poncy wanker, what the hell d'ya think ya doin'! Are you 'avin' a giraffe? We're bein' watched, you know. See them little spy holes in the corners? There's a camera behind every one. I'm not taking part in any porno movie so they can get their rocks off!'*

Just thought I'd share this with you!

I shall be at your lecture unless some other currently unidentifiable circumstance forces otherwise! Third time lucky! Will try to catch you before if I'm early, but otherwise shall see you after.

Marianne

This is one of Marianne's crazy emails. One of the craziest. At times like this Edward wonders if she is totally sane. Yet it makes him smile; makes him think about things from a different perspective. He likes that. But it isn't like her to use bad language. Perhaps she is practising for the novel she is trying to write; a novel she says is inspired by memories of Brocklebank Hall and by her re-acquaintance with him. He frowns and wonders how to respond. Brevity is generally the best policy.

To: Marianne Hayward
From: Edward Harvey
Date: 19th March 2003, 22.47
Subject: Re: Tagged by Aliens

Dear Marianne,
So this is where we went wrong with Chi Chi and An
An?!
Hope to meet you soon!
Dashing …
Edward

Edward sighs. They had tried to meet a couple of times before but first some boyfriend of her daughter's was killed in an accident, and the second time it snowed so badly the trains weren't running properly and there were problems on the tube. Or that's what she said. Perhaps this time will be hitch-free and he will know whether or not he is dealing with someone who, as his Australian friend Glen Rushworth might say, 'has a kangaroo loose in the top paddock'. If so he will have to engineer a swift but diplomatic retreat.

On hearing the news of an imminent meeting, Conrad Vaughan is suspicious. 'Don't tell me you haven't thought about giving her one?'

They were standing between the tea urn and photocopier in a square waiting area between the two rows of archaeology offices; a place where most university gossip unfolded.

Edward hadn't thought any such thing until Conrad uttered these words, but now he can't erase them. It disturbs him. He has firm principles about marriage and forsaking all others. Even mental infidelity is something he has always resisted. But his unsettled state has made him vulnerable and until he knows for certain that she has evolved into a middle-aged woman of no particular merit, he can imagine possibilities that Felicity won't entertain and it keeps him amused during these times of unusual drought bedroom-wise.

Conrad says, 'I wonder what her ulterior motives are?'

'Why should there be any? She had a tough time at school. She said finding me healed the wounds. No, that's not quite it. What she actually said was that the emailing reminded her of the good times; laid the ghosts to rest.'

'*Laid!* There you have it,' says Conrad. 'I told you she was up to something. Remember she's a psychologist; planting such thoughts in your mind.'

'Bloody hell, Conrad!'

6

Eventually Taryn decides she will tell Marianne about Marc. She knows Marianne will think *I told you so,* even though she won't say it. Her eyes will flash and narrow and her lips will twitch as if she would like to speak, but thinks better of it. Marianne and she have been friends since the beginning of their teacher training days at the Institute and know each other inside out. Or they each think they do, but Taryn always keeps some things to herself. Quite a lot of things, some would say. For a start, Marianne doesn't know about Taryn's childhood, her violent father and the true extent of her mood swings. Marianne has an over-developed super ego (her words) and doesn't approve of half the things Taryn tells her, never mind those she doesn't divulge.

Despite the chilly late March weather, they meet up for a game of tennis at the local club as they do occasionally in school holidays or at the weekend. Taryn emerges from the locker rooms looking like an advertisement in a Wimbledon programme, in a fashionable white tennis dress, white track-suit top, wrist sweat bands and a Nike headband like Roger Federer's. Her spiked hair sticks out every which way, but chicly so. She is always on the lookout for male distraction and the tennis club is awash with her kind of men. She must appear at her best, just in case. Marianne is more casually attired in a blue skirt and top, her dark hair caught up in a ponytail.

While they play there is little time for chatter as both of them take their workout seriously and being evenly matched, there is always a competitive edge. They keep an ongoing record of who has won the most games. Taryn can run faster, but Marianne is taller and has the longer reach. Taryn excels around the net, while Marianne has a lethal two-handed backhand with built-in spin that she uses effectively from the baseline.

Today Taryn wins. She is pleased. This will give her the advantage when she reveals the Marc story. As they leave the court she removes her headband and shakes her spiked hair at one of the coaches with whom she had a dalliance a few years previously.

She begins to tell the Marc tale while they are showering, hoping that when Marianne first hears of the split, she will be too preoccupied to react in a way that will make Taryn feel stupid.

Afterwards they sit in the bar drinking mineral water and catching up on the gossip. It has begun to rain and droplets patter on the window. Taryn likes rain, *such gentle pain,* and for a moment she is distracted.

'So what sparked it off in the first place?' prompts Marianne.

'I caught him texting his young ex-floosy. In the living room, in front of me, while I was watching *Coronation Street.* Imagine that! So I snatched his phone and reading between the lines, there was something going on. And that was on top of all the little niggles we'd been having; some of which were just as much my fault as his. Best to cut and run before I got too used to him being there. Don't know what possessed me to invite him to move in. Must be an age thing. I'm losing it.'

Marianne nods sympathetically, but there is the tell-tale twitch of her mouth and Taryn knows that her friend thinks she is an impulsive fool. Then she explains how she flung the Scrabble down the path and they both dissolve into giggles, attracting stern looks from the more senior club members.

45

'Now he's gone and I'm fine and ready to move on. I'm thinking about joining a dating agency.' She isn't really thinking any such thing, but throws out the comment and waits for Marianne's disapproval.

Marianne merely raises her eyebrows.

Taryn continues, 'How are you and Johnny?'

'We're back on track and everything's pretty good. We're doing things together, he's cooking again and he's cut right down on the drinking. Of course I still have moments of slippage; moments of insecurity. But the trick is not to be discouraged. At a deeper level, I feel more confident and capable and it's just when the mad hormones kick in and I'm not thinking straight that I'm temporarily thrown off track.'

Taryn secretly covets Johnny but tells herself she has sufficient scruples to leave well alone although she does flirt with him in a half-hearted way, while he disdainfully resists. Taryn believes she could lure him into bed if she really wanted to, but has chosen not to.

'And the Cow-Charmaine has gone?'

'Vamoosed with someone else's husband,' says Marianne triumphantly.

The Cow-Charmaine is a woman with whom Marianne suspected Johnny was having an affair. She was a colleague in his geography and geology department at Cedarwood High who, it seemed, was throwing herself at him in a big way, going drinking with him down the local and telling him about all her problems. Johnny claimed he was merely being supportive, but Taryn isn't sure. She sympathised with Marianne because it was the thing to do with friends, but she feels rather hypocritical because she is not above throwing herself at the odd husband who takes her fancy.

'And,' continues Marianne in softer tones, 'since we last spoke, Edward has written at last. Several times, in fact. We're back to having mail conversations. I'm so relieved. I honestly thought he was dead, but it transpired that his wife's mother died and then his computer went on the blink—'

'For three months?' Taryn has her own thoughts about Edward's sudden silence and most of these are to do with him backing off in the face of a barrage of emails from Marianne, who since becoming menopausal, has reverted to obsessing and fantasising like a teenager about the object of her first crush.

'Wife's mother lived in Surrey so they had to go there every weekend to sort the house. He had a lot of catching up to do. I'm not that important, I guess. But he did suggest again that we try to meet. Next week!' Marianne's eyes light up and she flushes.

Taryn grins. Perhaps she was wrong about him backing off. 'Be careful,' she warns and gives a little shiver that is meant to convey excitement.

'I think he might be having a few problems at home. Felicity's inherited stackloads of money and seems to be turning the place into a bit of a farm.'

Taryn's ears prick. *Mr Perfect perhaps not so perfect after all.* 'You said he was happily married.'

'Well, he was. Is. I don't know. There was just something different about his tone. He sounded overwhelmed. He's also been asked to be involved with an exhibition of mazes at the British Museum.' Marianne blushes again and starts to fiddle with the ends of her dark hair now released from the ponytail and touching her shoulders.

'That rats run through? That sounds more like your kind of thing.'

'Turf and stone mazes. Or labyrinths. Archeologically, they're very significant. He and some Scandinavian expert are putting on weekly lectures, and I'm invited.'

'Thrillsville,' says Taryn, unimpressed. History is not one of her best subjects. She finds the past dark and depressing and prefers chrome and glass to wood and stone.

'Actually, it's a very interesting subject. You shouldn't mock.'

'I don't understand how anyone can get so excited about such things.'

'Edward is clearly passionate about them.'

'And you?'

'I shall be passionate about them next week. Actually I am interested. There's a mystical quality about them and I like that. I want to know more.'

'Well, at least it gives you another chance to meet, though it sounds a little public.' Taryn supposes that Edward doesn't want to risk a one-to-one encounter until he is sure it's safe and that Marianne isn't a nut-case.

'What do you think I should wear? Boho chic or classic smart?'

'He'll be in a suit, I s'pose, so classic might fit in better.'

'But Boho chic is perhaps more archaeological?'

'Boho chic is more you.'

'I think he's quite conservative.'

'Classic then.' Taryn is frequently exasperated by Marianne's indecisiveness about trivial things.

'I'm nervous, but not quite like I was last time we tried to meet. Since Johnny apologised, I've been thinking perhaps I was a bit extreme over Edward. I spent too much time thinking about him and turning him into a fantasy object. I blame the hormones. And I needed to be distracted because of the Charmaine business. But I've put it all into perspective now. I'm still excited though. I can't wait to have a proper conversation with him; find out what he's really like—'

'Find out if he's sexy like Pierce Brosnan.' Taryn grins, exposing perfect white teeth, the result of several sessions of orthodontics during her teens and early adulthood.

'That was Holly's suggestion.'

Holly is Marianne's daughter, in the middle of her law degree at Sussex. Taryn was not pleased when she came on the scene and pushed her into the background. She wasn't keen on babies and didn't want to become involved, yet she resented Marianne's unavailability.

'I hope you're not disappointed.'

'I hope he's not disappointed.'

'How could he be?'

Marianne has high cheekbones and a subtle French beauty that comes from her maternal grandmother. The fact that she doesn't realise it makes her all the more alluring. She also has a heart; something that Taryn lost the day her father first hit her. Taryn is secretly envious of Marianne's natural attractiveness, her height and her husband, but she never says. She likes people to believe she is in control of her life; happy to be short, happy to be single, to use men as play-things. She hides her jealousy well. Marianne is the only longstanding friend in her circle, others coming and going and seldom remaining for more than a few years at a time; sometimes only months. They come because of her wit and magnetism and her ability to make them feel that they are the most important person she knows. They go because she gets bored easily and finds someone new to woo; or because she takes offence at something many would see as inconsequential, exploding venomously and accusing the friend of disloyalty. This is then followed by a pulling away during which she acts the hurt victim, and the perpetrator retreats in shocked bemusement.

It is a miracle that she and Marianne have never had more than the occasional brief spat, possibly because Marianne has Johnny and isn't possessive about her friends, or probably because she is very forgiving of Taryn's inclination towards uppityness. Either way they have supported each other through the good and bad times for over twenty-five years.

'What will you do now Marc is gone?' asks Marianne as they stand by their respective cars ready to go their separate ways. 'Have you someone lined up to take his place?'

'I've had enough of men for a while,' says Taryn disingenuously.

But during a quiet moment later at home in her immaculate flat now happily restored to its Marc-free state, Taryn thinks about Mr Perfect Edward Harvey and the news that he will be visiting London several times over the next few weeks. Marianne keeps saying he isn't the philandering type; that she feels totally secure in emailing him because there is no hidden agenda. Taryn doesn't believe a word of it. There isn't a man alive in her opinion who doesn't have the potential to philander, given the right material to philander with. Taryn firmly believes she is that material; or was. But her on-and-off relationship with Marc has left her deflated and on the downward slope to fifty. She wonders if she could still play the temptress as before, or is she now on the slush pile?

7

Felicity and Edward are in bed, reading. The room has a low ceiling and exposed beams, fitted oak wardrobes and a large dressing table. It is cosy, wallpapered and carpeted, colours a mix of turquoise and raspberry, inspired by an article in an interior design magazine.

Edward is engrossed in *The Kite Runner* and Felicity has a book open about hen husbandry, but doesn't seem to be turning the pages. There is a faraway look in her eyes.

'Are you in the mood to talk more about my plans?' says Felicity.

Edward places his book face down on the duvet. 'Marianne says it's unwise to make big changes too soon after a traumatic event.'

'You've discussed this with her?' Accusatory tone.

'Only mentioned in passing.' He tries to avert an argument, keep his voice casual.

'It's not as if I haven't been thinking about this for years, Ted. It's not a whim. I just wasn't sure that I'd be able to do it without your financial input. And that would have had to wait till the children finished uni and were self-sufficient – always assuming you would've backed me.' She pauses as if waiting for an answer but Edward remains silent, staring at a small spider marching across the corner of the ceiling.

'I intend to have everything in place by the time I'm fifty,' continues Felicity, closing her book and putting it on the bedside table. 'No time to waste. The older I am, the harder it'll be. Hugh says that energy and drive are required. I have those now – but for how much longer?'

Felicity's guru is Hugh Fernley-Whittingstall and she watches his *River Cottage* and its spin-offs with the zealousness of an Open University student, taking prolific notes and then filing them in a green ring binder that she keeps in the kitchen on a shelf with her vast number of recipe books. Now all of her new ideas seem to be prefixed with 'Hugh says ...'

'Your ideas will have massive impact on the family. I should have been consulted before you resigned.'

'For over twenty-five years, it's been about *your* ambitions. I'm not complaining, Ted, but it was part of the agreement that when the kids were older, there would be time for me to do what I wanted.'

'Christopher is only ten.'

'He starts secondary soon. Another couple of years and there'll only be Christopher and Harriet at home. A rapidly emptying nest as of this September. I don't want to be unprepared. You have your job ...'

'*You* have a job.'

'That's exactly it. It's a job – not a career. It's always been just a job. I have a degree in biology. People used to tell me I was clever. But what have I done with my brain? Zilch. And we did agree—'

'I don't remember this agreement.'

'Okay maybe not in words of one syllable. Unwritten. Unspoken, even. But implicit. I wasn't a fool, Ted, even at twenty-two. You needed my support first; then the children. Now it's my turn. When I mentioned the restaurant the other day, it sounded to me like you were saying you wanted nothing to do with it. I'd like your approval, but I don't need it. It won't cramp your style, I promise.' She hesitates, relaxes, becomes almost flirtatious. 'I'm very determined, honey, and when I'm determined you know I'll always get my way in the end.' She leans over and kisses him on the cheek and for a moment he thinks his luck is in. But then she pulls away.

'We'll talk about it tomorrow,' he says, closing his book, reaching for his light switch above the bed, resigned.

Later in the night, when Edward is still restless from an overactive mind imagining the following day's conversation with Felicity, he hears her mutter, 'God, I'm hot,' and throw off her side of the duvet.

When tomorrow comes she corners him after breakfast, while he is in the middle of fulfilling dishwasher duties and the three oldest children have gone to school. Christopher is outside with the rabbit.

'Lou-Lou and Lexi think it's a great idea.'

'So you saw fit to discuss this with your friends even before mentioning it to me?'

'And you saw fit to discuss it with Marianne Hayward. Anyway, Lou-Lou and Lexi are *our* friends,' she corrects.

Olivia is Felicity's friend from pottery classes at the community centre and Alexander is her husband. They call each other Lou-Lou and Lexi when in the company of friends, but it has never been suggested that the friends do likewise, although Felicity and Edward do so in private. They live in a large, modern red-brick house in the centre of the village, show-home tidy and with all the latest gadgets. Edward finds them intensely irritating, but it is more than his life's worth to say so. Olivia 'paws' him at every available opportunity. Felicity says it is because she fancies him and he ought to be flattered. From childhood, Edward remembers his father being similarly annoyed by such women. His father was kind and patient; more patient than he considers himself to be. Olivia has thick red hair, so stiff with lacquer that it reminds him of something constructed by a weaver bird. Her teeth are large and blindingly white since she had some fancy new dental treatment that required going to bed with a tray of gunk clamped in her

53

mouth. She is a snob, a name-dropper; everything he detests. Alexander is long-suffering and means well, but although he has a diverse job working for the Killerton Estate, he is about as interesting as a bag of flour.

Edward pauses with a plate in hand. 'Don't you think you should wait a little; think it through properly. Do all the research; a cost analysis.'

'Cost analysis! Darling, I've been thinking about this since I was seventeen when Mummy let me host my first dinner party for my friends. I remember talking about menus with her and then helping with the cooking. It was a real buzz. In two or three years' time there'll only be you and Christopher to cook for – and you're often elsewhere.' Felicity rushes around as she speaks, tidying stray oddments, gathering bits and pieces for her day at work.

'It's an enormous undertaking.' Edward wishes she would keep still and concentrate on the seriousness of what he is saying.

'I have researched the market. There's a real need for a small, intimate restaurant in this area, where the focus is on quality rather than quantity. With the Ronsons selling up, there will soon be a gap.'

The Ronsons own and run Heliotrope, a popular eatery and bar near the post office in the centre of the village. They have decided to retire to Milton Keynes to be closer to their daughter and grandchildren.

'If you're planning what I think, that's a huge commitment,' says Edward, sitting at the table and gesturing towards an empty chair for Felicity to join him.

'I'm not chasing big profits. I don't want to be run ragged. The Ronsons have a regular client base and I merely want to build on that. This will be no ordinary restaurant,' she persists. 'I also want to cater for people with special dietary requirements. You know how awkward it is for James with his nut allergy. There are thousands of people like him for whom eating out is a nightmare. I will put ingredients on the menus and make sure wherever possible that there are alternatives for diabetics, coeliacs and people who want dairy free. Needs have moved on since vegetarianism and nut cutlets, but the catering industry has largely ignored them – unless people make special requests in advance. And even then some places can't seem to manage Flora instead of butter, or your decaf tea. You shouldn't have to ask for such things and be made to feel like a freak. They should come as standard options on the menu or, in the case of margarine, on the table.'

Edward has to admit that this is a novel idea.

'You can hardly ever find soup without butter or cream, yet "Soup of the Day" with a roll is a lunchtime basic. People don't always like to ask what's in things. It draws attention. So they avoid going out. Go to a posh hotel or restaurant and the puddings are likely to be anti-health time-bombs, packed full of calories, sugar and cream. The only alternative is usually a fresh fruit salad. But I can do dairy free pastries and cakes, poached fruit in wine – and more. And I'm also thinking of offering two choices of portion size. That's another thing that hacks me off in restaurants. You never know whether you're going to be given a miserly portion of veg or half a plateful. And sometimes people would like a half size steak, or a half size pudding – so long as they are paying less. Wouldn't have to be half the price, just two thirds, perhaps. It would save waste. There's a market out there waiting to be wooed. I know there is. You say I should research. I have – albeit in a casual fashion. And my friends and colleagues say they would support me and spread the word. And as long as it pays for itself.'

'There are no guarantees of that. I'm sure there are sound

economic reasons why most other restaurants don't offer such choice.'

'I intend to turn more of the garden over to vegetables; probably buy in some help with the heavy work. Do some farmers' markets for getting rid of surplus, for selling added-value products – and for publicity and free advertising. And I'll hire a chef, even though I will cook too. I might even start producing more pottery. It could be on sale at the restaurant.'

'You'll need more than just a chef. There's cleaning, dishes, front of house, waitressing.'

'I've always been good at multitasking.'

'Don't be flippant – I'm being serious.'

'So am I.' Felicity gives him one of her hard stares. 'And the children will help.'

'Don't bank on it.'

'They've already promised. The girls want to be waitresses and earn some holiday money. James is as keen as anything to help with markets and selling. He even said Kylie could be roped in. She's got experience in catering.'

'A Saturday job at McDonalds is hardly the experience you want.'

Edward listens with growing apprehension. They were all ganging up on him. It is true that there is little about which he can object. Her enthusiasm is evident and she does seem to have a clear strategy. The financial risk is minimal because even if it all goes wrong, they will be no worse off than they are now. So why the gnawing feeling of doubt? It is as if the rug is being pulled from under him and his controlled existence is being put under threat.

The following day the livestock at the Deer Orchard fluctuate in numbers. First it is the arrival of more hens; five pairs of different breeds plus a buff Orpington cockerel.

'As I'm only keeping small numbers of everything, they

need to be special,' says Felicity, showing Edward the new hen-friendly, multilevel real estate that was erected in the paddock that afternoon by local chap called Rick Rissington, who is a rangy fellow of about thirty-five, known in the village for being able to turn his hand to anything practical and also to the odd bored housewife. He lives alone in an old property near the church and has always been the subject of much tittle-tattle and speculation.

'Hugh says that giving them optimal living conditions for the breed will increase egg yield and ultimately chickens.'

'We're going to eat them?' Edward hasn't anticipated this.

'Of course we are! James has already been over to the Molwings for a lesson in Humane Chicken Dispatch.'

Edward grimaces and pushes the side of the hen coop in an exploratory way, rather hoping that Rick's handiwork is less sturdy than it looks and that it might collapse. It remains firm and immovable. 'If that cockerel wakes me up in the morning, he's not staying.'

'You won't hear him through the double glazing. And I'm calling him Cyril.'

The hens are apparently silver laced Wyandottes, black Orpingtons, speckled Sussex, Welsummers and Australorps. Felicity tells him this proudly and then proceeds to explain which breed prefers to live at which level and how such attention to detail can lead to happier hens and improved productivity. 'The perches inside are also at staggered heights. This reflects their pecking order – higher being safer and so forth.'

The three existing hens, Helen, Amy and Sarah, also buff Orpingtons, do not look pleased and watch the new arrivals from the far end of the paddock.

'If the old hens are not happy, they will have to go,' says Felicity.

'That's very harsh,' says Edward. 'The girls love those hens. They have personalities; you can't send them away.'

Meanwhile the two goats, Margo and Barbara, look on with interest.

'And we need to get those two in kid for next spring. There's a growing interest in goat meat and it will be a useful product for the farmers' markets and the restaurant. We could even do milk and cheese.'

Edward shuts his ears to the bombardment of threatened changes.

Two days later, a bundle of black and white fluff arrives, greeting him with wagging tail when he comes home from work.

'Felicity!' shouts Edward, throwing down his briefcase and storming round the house until he finds her extracting washing from the laundry basket in the bathroom. 'We already have two dogs.'

'So no problem with walks. And soon I won't be working at the college, so she won't be alone for long. Remember how Clint and Gryke used to chew your pyjamas when they were drying on the radiators? You won't know she's here. You can't possibly object. She is called Meg as befits a working Border collie.'

'How do you mean "working"?'

'You know the field just across the lane? Beyond the paddock? I'm in the processes of negotiating a deal with the Molwings. If it goes through, then we will have a few sheep. Just think: fresh, home-reared, organic lamb.'

'Yesterday you said restaurant. You didn't say farm as well.'

Felicity takes a deep breath. 'Restaurant ... Farm ... Whatever.'

'When do you do all this negotiating?'

'When you are shut away in your study writing your papers

and lectures and all the things you do that you don't share with me.'

'Tell me at mealtimes.'

'But you aren't interested.'

'How do you know?' Edward opens his mouth to say something else, but realises it is pointless. Only his lack of enthusiasm displays his unease. Felicity is on a roll and there is no stopping her. It was just like when they first met and she began planning their future together, only that time he had been more than willing to have her take the lead. He visualises a steam-roller hurtling towards him. At such times it is best to get out of the way. And privately he thinks Meg is adorable.

But Eric the cat is not amused and stalks around territorially while Meg bounds and wags and tries to catch his tail.

To: Edward Harvey
From: Marianne Hayward
Date: 25th March 2003, 20.03
Subject: Meeting

Dear Edward,
Everything is still okay for coming to your lecture on Thursday.
Marianne

To: Marianne Hayward
From: Edward Harvey
Date: 25th March 2003, 22.28
Subject: Re: Meeting

Dear Marianne,
Felicity is dead set on pursuing agricultural objectives in addition to opening a restaurant.

We have a puppy, Meg. Very sweet! Felicity says we
mustn't pet her too much or she won't work. This
means sheep are on the menu – in more ways than one!
See you in two days!!
Edward

Are they really going to meet at last after thirty-four years?
What will they say? What will she look like? Will he (or she) be
disappointed? Might she stop writing to him? He sighs. This
meeting matters in ways he hadn't appreciated. His world is
taking on a new complexion and the only constant at the
moment is Marianne.

8

Taryn lies on her cream leather sofa, staring at the ceiling in her minimalist living room, the only concession against this being a Llewellyn-Bowen inspired *tromp d'oeil* opposite the window. It is of a garden viewed from between two pillars which has the effect of making the room seem larger, as well as being a conversation piece. She has a rectangular glass dining table in the corner and four wrought iron chairs. Near the bay window on one side is the new flat screen television and on the other side a white-painted workstation with computer. Taryn dislikes wood and only allows it in the flat if it is painted in coordinating shades, or in white. The walls and carpets are cream throughout and outdoor shoes are left at the entrance to encourage visitors to do the same. The pale colours are supposed to maximise light and ward off depression.

Not so successfully today.

She is thinking about Marianne and Edward, and wishing it was her feeling the thrill of meeting a long-lost crush. When she was young and still at school, she listened to her friends describing the stomach churning butterflies of passion, and failed to equate her lack of similar response with the fact that since her emotional estrangement from her father, she had chosen not to love. She used the adrenalin rush of the chase as a substitute and became addicted to that instead, wanting it again and again and leading to a string of lovers, sometimes two by two, Noah's ark style, though not in the same time dimension.

Edward Harvey …

Although Taryn considers Marianne to be her best friend,

this is more because she has known her for such a long time; a friendship that has endured where many have failed. Being single, and often solitary, she has always had a wide circle upon whom to call to share various activities. Marianne has Johnny so there is a limit to the amount of time she can spare. She also has her beloved daughter Holly, who as a baby took virtually all of Marianne's time and attention. Within twenty-four hours Marianne transformed from being nearly always there for Taryn, to being never there. She was forever feeding, changing, sleeping, eating, washing, cleaning. *'Such a baby bore,'* Taryn used to say to anyone who would listen. When they did meet, Marianne looked pale and tired, hair straggly, clothes shapeless; no longer fashion conscious and manicured. *Uggh!* thought Taryn at the time. *I don't want to go there. And the smell of nappies and sick.* When she arrived home after a visit, she was compelled to bathe, to wash her hair and clothes. Had anyone known this, it would have alerted them to her fragile psychology.

To avoid feeling jealous or resentful, Taryn collected a selection of acquaintances in much the same way as one might collect a set of commemorative plates; one for every month of the year; one for every occasion. Most have drifted or moved, but as one leaves, she is adept at securing another, often by attending a local evening class for a few weeks. If she chooses, she is nectar to bees as far as friends are concerned. Women worship her humour and wit; men worship her sexuality. She has an honours degree in making people feel special – if she chooses.

If she chooses …

Currently she has Vickie for trips to the cinema; Rosemary for musicals and theatre; Ray for sporting events that don't interest Marianne, like Ascot or soccer (Ray is an ex who is now married to Tupperware Tina, *poor soul*); Dan who is gay, for pop concerts, the pub and escorting her to parties; and Isabelle for advice at any time of the day or night when it comes to men. Marianne doesn't know about Isabelle; someone else of whom she wouldn't approve. Marianne thinks she is the only person who advises Taryn in matters of passion.

And then there's faithful Neil, Head of History in her school, who idolises her since his wife left him for a man who came to lay more than the carpet in the living room.

'Good-looking, sort-of, if you like rugby thighs. Solvent, yes,' said Taryn to Marianne. 'Funny, kind and intelligent. Checklist perfect. Almost. But a name like Neil is oh so, well, you know. He's got an allotment and a Yorkshire accent. Too close to home. And too nice; too nice. Don't want to mess with him when he's already messed.'

'Unlike you to be so thoughtful,' said Marianne.

'Not thoughtful, selfish. You know me. He has long-term good friend potential and will do anything for me, with nothing expected in return. And his vegetables are divine. Courgettes that have flavour beyond flavour and ruby chard the like of which you will never taste from the supermarkets, not even the best.'

'So you're using him,' said Marianne.

'No more than anyone uses anyone else. I make him pasta every now and then to keep him sweet. And every couple of months he suggests a proper date and I turn him down. All good-humoured stuff. It's become a kind of ritual.'

Having a wide circle means she can keep her mood swings well-hidden, because the assumption when she is unavailable will always be that she is out socialising with somebody else. Even Marianne doesn't know the extent of her psychological reactivity. Marc had a fair idea, but was too self-centred to give it much thought.

It is to Isabelle that she turns now. Isabelle is a flamboyant thirty-something who works for the BBC as a researcher. She epitomises the phrase 'footloose and fancy-free', and although she has been having an affair for three years with one of the

63

dentists at her local practice, she also enjoys clubbing and speed dating and usually has a temporary boyfriend with whom to go places when Leo, the dentist, is unavailable.

In the life she leads, she reminds Taryn of herself about ten years ago, but without the dark angst that lay behind her own *modus operandi*. Isabelle likes men, but hasn't ever wanted to settle down and have children. Leo suits her purposes. She also lives in a flat a little further down Coppercone Lane, so is very conveniently located for brief visits.

Taryn takes a stroll on this bright spring Sunday morning, down her street in which the horse chestnut trees send fingers of bright green bursting from their sticky buds. A white van driver nods his head towards her and grins as she sashays along the pavement in her skin-tight jeans and a mini padded jacket. She gives him a sideways glance and a half smile before turning down the path to Isabelle's and buzzing the entryphone. She takes the stairs instead of the lift.

Up on the third floor Isabelle opens the door and beams.

'Hi Is!'

'Hullo, darling.' Isabelle is blonde and shiny with a botoxed face and a chest that seems to grow a cup size every year or so.

'Advice needed,' says Taryn walking into the square living room and noting the new Turkish rug on the laminated floor.

'Who is he?'

'An eminent archaeologist with a midlife wife and a tedious amount of sprogs.'

'Why?' Isabelle struts into her adjoining kitchen and switches the kettle on.

Taryn sinks onto the sofa among a pile of ethnic cushions and eyes her nails critically. 'Distraction … Because I want to know if I still can.'

'Of course you can,' says Isabelle over the noise of the agitation within the electric kettle.

'Thanks, but I need to prove it with someone who reputedly doesn't see every woman as a shag.'

Isabelle returns with two mugs of coffee and flops into a chair. If she was able, she would have a furrowed brow but her face is impassive. 'What's he like?'

Taryn carefully omits to say she hasn't met him or even seen a photo. The previous evening she had tried Google images, but none seemed to be of the right Edward Harvey. Even the university website had a curiously blank space where a picture could have been. 'The general opinion seems to be that he is exceptionally nice. Winning him over would be a significant achievement.' She has already decided that if he's not her type, she can cut and run.

'I'm not one to talk, in my position, but isn't it a tad extreme?'

'Extreme is good. I like extreme.'

'And how do you come to know him?'

This was tricky. She didn't want to mention Marianne.

'I don't know him, exactly. But I know of him, and I'd like to know more.'

'Weirder and weirder,' says Isabelle.

Yes, of course it is. It is Taryn in a manic phase, full of wild thoughts that seem sensible to her at the time. Only afterwards will she reflect on the sense; usually when it's too late. Marianne would say, '*Stop and Think. Wait twenty-four hours and then some.*' Marianne was her braking mechanism. But this time Marianne didn't know and Isabelle was a poor substitute, being inclined to fan the flames rather than provide the ice-cold bucket of water that such impulsiveness requires. Taryn launches into an explanation of the maze lectures and the opportunity for an encounter at the British Museum.

'I admire your cheek,' says Isabelle.

This is all the encouragement Taryn needs.

9

The British Museum is one of the most impressive spaces in the world, with its Greek styled facade of Ionic columns and, most recently, its spectacular Great Court. Light streams in through the glass and steel roof and onto the latest exhibition, the display of many different labyrinths and mazes, largely of European origin. Some are depicted by enormous colour aerial photographs, some are black and white drawings, but there are four life-size replica mazes on the floor that can be walked through, including the star attraction, a copy of the original Troy Town maze of St Agnes, Scilly, uncovered by Edward and his team from the University of Devon the previous summer.

In one of the lecture theatres, Edward has been talking about the Scilly discovery and mazes in general to a group of about sixty people. Most are academics and historians, an earnest, grey-haired and bespectacled bunch that follow the London lecture circuit of anything that smacks of antiquity. There is also a small band of New Age types with their long hair and retro hippy style. These are the worshipers of the summer solstice at Stonehenge: Druids, dowsers, and mystics. And some are the interested general public who are passing through and have heard rumours of Edward's captivating eloquence. Even the occasional tourist, with ubiquitous camera slung round the neck or over a shoulder, has dropped in for some intellectual stimulation.

It was originally intended that Henrik would lecture just once or twice during the run of the exhibition, but such was the interest when the Scilly addition was first announced and

Edward joined the team, that one or other of them is now scheduled to speak every week at variable times during the evening. It seems that maze-fever has gripped the nation, perhaps in part due to the appearance on breakfast television by a woman called Jennifer Wimsley who is convinced that walking the Troy Town maze on St Agnes is directly responsible for her conceiving twins after four failed attempts at IVF. It is no coincidence that labyrinths were often used in fertility rites. During the programme two women sent in emails claiming similar conceptions had happened to them after walking mazes in Sweden, and a man wrote to say he believed that his chronic sinus problems had been alleviated by spending a couple of hours reading a novel in the vicinity of the St Agnes maze.

Edward is gathering up his notes and waiting for the predictable couple of shy people to approach with a question they haven't liked to ask in front of the assembled group. So far, he has not seen Marianne so either she didn't make it, or she has been listening to him all along, *in cognito*. It has been so long since he has seen her and he doesn't know what to expect; doesn't know if she is pretty or plain; fat or thin.

When he sees a smartly dressed woman coming towards him with a big smile on her face, he doesn't realise at first it is her. This woman is the type who sits watching the French Open tennis at Roland Garros. A woman whom the cameras seek out and linger on; dark, smooth, shoulder-length hair, parted at the side and flicked up at the ends, sophisticated and attractively mature in a pink lace top and plum-coloured suit.

She stops in front of him. 'Edward,' she says, extending her hand. He waits for her to say she is some European expert on mazes. And then it dawns on him.

'It's been an awfully long time,' she continues.

'And you haven't changed a bit!' says Edward, jesting, smiling back, trying to assume an expression that says he recognised her straight away. He kisses her on the cheek in case it is expected, catching a subtle scent of perfume, of hair spray, of woman, and feeling his heart jump a little in a not altogether unpleasant way.

So this is Marianne Hayward. At last. Thirty-plus years since they last shared a classroom and eighteen months since her first unexpected email.

His initial impression is that she doesn't seem in the least bit crazy. He absorbs information without appearing to scan, relying on peripheral vision as she holds his eyes with her own. She looks younger and more stylish than he expected. Her off-the-wall emails led him to imagine an eccentric character with layers of home-made knits and a large patchwork bag.

'I really enjoyed the lecture,' she says. 'Pitched at the right level for a non-archaeologist like me. Just got here in time. Sorry I didn't see you before you started. I was delayed at work by a crisis with one of my tutor group. But this time at least I made it.' This, a reference to the previous time they tried to meet, when the trains were disrupted by snow; when he was hoping that at last he would meet the woman behind the often convoluted emails; when he had experienced a shoulder-dropping sense of disappointment when she didn't show.

'I've some slides to sort out, and I must deal with—' He waves his arm at the small group of people waiting to ask questions. 'Perhaps a tea or a coffee?' He finds himself drawn towards looking at her intently, gazing deep into her green eyes, monitoring her face for recognisable features. She is staring back at him too, but it isn't uncomfortable.

'Whatever is best for you. Lecturing is tiring, I know.'

Marianne stands back and Edward fields a few more questions; one from an elderly gentleman in a Columbo mac who is convinced that mazes ward off evil spirits and another from a plain young woman with a stud in her nose like Harriet. He answers with practised skill, making each person feel that their question is the most important one in the world, thoughts of Marianne pushed temporarily aside.

Eventually they sit opposite each other in the Great Court Café, Marianne with a coffee, and he with a decaffeinated tea, catching up, reminiscing and pouring out name after name of the Brocklebank pupils, the occasional snippet of grapevine news. Edward is transported back to those three years of mixed emotions when he sometimes felt abandoned by his parents yet at others revelled in the camaraderie of gangs.

'Well … well … Marianne Hayward,' says Edward, during a pause.

'I am no longer the Marianne you knew at Brocklebank. In some ways I was until I found you again. That scared little girl was still within me. But now I see her as a separate being. I have moved on. I'm not sure that I would have recognised you, if I didn't know.'

He smiles, momentarily self-conscious. 'Even my children don't recognise me from the old photos.' He shakes his head from side to side in the way that people do when they are both amazed and almost speechless.

Marianne continues, 'Now you must tell me about you. Tell me about your family. Properly. Email just scratches the surface. Window dressing.'

Relieved, Edward fishes out his most recent photograph.

'Rachel is like Felicity. Like Felicity was when she was young and thin. Harriet is more like me, poor kid, but she makes up for it with bags of style. They are both clever, but Rachel is industrious and Harriet wings it. Just goes to disprove the environmentalists.'

'Even if they are close in age, you won't have treated them exactly the same.'

'Not differently enough to be the cause of such contrasting personalities. Don't tell me you're a behaviourist?'

'I thought you would have gathered that from my emails,' says Marianne, teasingly. 'What about James?'

'James is already a talented scientist and will go far. He applied to Oxford but didn't get in. Their loss. We expect him to go to UCL.'

'Is this Christopher? He's just like I remember you at that age.'

'Spoilt rotten, being the baby of the family.'

Marianne says, 'I can't imagine having four to deal with. One teenager plus friends took up so much space.'

'Apart from being a taxi service and homework advisor, I've got off lightly, considering. Felicity has always done most of the domestic stuff. And they entertain each other. I expect with one, you have to take that role.'

Marianne nods.

'Did you ever think of having another? Sorry … Personal … Shouldn't have asked.'

'I had a miscarriage once. A very early miscarriage. Nobody knew I was pregnant. Johnny still doesn't know. After that it just never happened.'

'I'm sorry.'

'We were happy enough with Holly.'

All the time Edward watches her intently. He notices her manicured nails that are varnished in the same plum colour as her suit. A simple silver chain of Celtic design hangs round her neck and a matching bracelet on her wrist. Is this what she always wears to work or has she made a special effort for this meeting?

'The girls think your book is about me,' he fishes, changing the subject.

Marianne flushes ever so slightly and he is aware of hesitation before she answers. 'Not about you exactly, but

70

inspired by you. The children in the story – Adam and Maya – have many of the experiences we had at Brocklebank, but the adults are fiction. I don't want any libel suits,' she laughs.

'And how much have you written? So often people say they are writing a book but then they give up after the first few chapters, unable to sustain the necessary discipline, or to develop a plotline worthy of a full-blown novel.'

'About ninety thousand words so far. The first draft's nearly finished.'

Edward is impressed.

'But, hey, I'm writing it because I need to write it. Expectations of publication are low. You know how almost impossible it is for new authors to get published.'

'Have you thought of self-publishing?'

'Maybe as a last resort. It's becoming cheaper. Perhaps it will eventually become more acceptable.'

Edward nods sympathetically, then quite without forethought, he finds himself telling her more of the detail about Felicity's plan.

'I wonder if this need to do something different is age-related? You writing; Felicity and the restaurant. Does it affect women more than men?'

'Are you suggesting a hormonal link?'

'Flick's been behind me every step of the way since college and although she mentioned this when I first knew her, she seems to have gone completely bonkers, rushing things into place as if time is running out.'

'It is. That's how we women suddenly feel when we get to a certain age.'

'It seems churlish of me to resent what she's doing, yet if she does open this restaurant, it is bound to impact on our lives. I know it's fair that she has a crack at doing what she's always wanted, but—'

'It may be fair, but you are entitled to feel uneasy. It changes the balance; the control.'

'What do I do?'

'What *can* you do?'

'Psychologists are supposed to have answers.'

'No. Psychologists have questions to help you find answers.'

'Be a friend then, not a psychologist.'

Marianne's eyes flicker and she opens and shuts her mouth as if to speak. Then she breathes in deeply. He can almost see the cog wheels of her brain turning. Is he being too presumptuous of their relationship? Still she fixes him with those green eyes.

'As a friend, I will tell you to be patient and see what happens; to practise Taoist philosophy.'

'I don't know much about Taoism.'

'Don't paint legs on the snake.'

'Crystal clear,' he laughs. 'Explain.'

'Don't make things worse than they are. Don't have catastrophising thoughts. You don't yet know what the new life will be. It may not be as bad as you imagine.'

'I didn't know you were into philosophy.'

She continues, 'And when you meet an obstruction in your path, be like the river when it meets a boulder; find a way round, and as you do so, sing. Felicity's plan is the boulder …'

'Are you saying that I won't be able to change her mind, but I have to change the way I think about it?'

'I am. Softness conquers hardness. The opposite of how we usually react in the West. You have to do it differently. It will save you a lot of grief in the long run – not that I'm very good at practising what I preach, but it is the best way to cope with difficult situations.'

'But it won't stop Felicity from doing what she wants, will it?'

'From what you say, nothing will stop her. You might as well accept it. And looking at it objectively, it is fair. It sounds to me like you've got away with a lot over the past twenty years. Go with the flow.'

'What if the flow is no longer compatible with my life?'

'Now you are painting legs on the snake again.'

Edward grins, wondering if she is teasing him. He doesn't mind if she is. All around the buzz of the café has faded into the background, his full attention is on her, noticing details that he never usually notices with women; the way she fiddles with her necklace and then stops as if aware that she is betraying a lack of confidence.

The conversation drifts pleasantly along for the next half hour while Edward eats a sandwich and Marianne a slice of apple pie. They reminisce some more about Brocklebank, and catch up about the rest of their schooldays. It is as if they really are old friends reuniting and not just classmates who barely knew each other as children.

Then, reluctantly, Edward says he must speak with Henrik before catching his train.

A shake of the hand, a half-hug, a kiss on the cheek and she begins to leave.

'We must do this again sometime,' he hears himself saying. 'I'll give you a tour of the exhibition.'

'I'd like that!' She calls across the yards that now separate them.

As she walks away, she turns ever so slightly and gives him a little wave. He feels the urge to follow her. To say, *Don't leave yet … it's been such a long time …'* The healing balm that surrounded him while she was there is dissipating fast. She understands. Oh what a relief to find someone who empathises with his plight. She has given him strategies. He must listen. He must go with the flow. This is anathema to him; he who has plotted every move since leaving school.

'So what's Fanclub like?' asks Harriet in stripy pyjamas, as soon as Edward walks through the front door. He had hoped they would all be asleep in bed and he could avoid any discussions. All the way home on the train he had thought of Marianne and the conversations they might have in future.

'Is she pretty?' asks Rachel. 'Is she mad?'

'Must be if she likes Dad,' says Harriet.

'Is she like you remember?'

'Is she fat?'

'Is she writing a book about you?'

Edward brushes these comments aside and, after dropping his bag and jacket on the chair at the bottom of the stairs, he works his way to the kitchen, the two girls following in his wake. It is after ten o'clock and he is hungry and tired.

'Where's your mother?' Usually after a late evening lecture, Felicity waits for him with sandwiches or a hot snack and a glass of wine.

Rachel says, 'Oh, she's having a bath and then she's going to bed. We said we'd wait up for you 'cos we're dead curious to know about Fanclub. She said not to wake her if she's asleep when you get in.'

Edward is disappointed that Felicity has abdicated her caring role.

'James is out with the dogs,' adds Harriet, 'and Chris is in bed.'

'Which is where you two should be with school tomorrow,' says Edward. 'Marianne is very nice and she's not mad – or fat. Nor, as I keep telling you, is she writing a book about me. That's all I have to say on the matter.' He roots around the fridge for something to put in a sandwich.

Rachel and Harriet shrug and disappear up stairs.

When James returns with the dogs, he says, 'Mum said to

tell you the sheep are coming on Saturday morning and would you make sure you're free to do the shopping.'

Edward is normally extremely patient where his family are concerned and although he is sometimes brisk and likes to get on with things, he rarely loses his cool. He stops in mid-mouthful, thinking hostile thoughts.

Sheep! Already! 'Nobody tells me anything any more,' he says sharply.

'I'm only the messenger,' says James, throwing up his hands and backing out of the kitchen.

All Marianne's words about flow and snakes and boulders seep away.

The next day at work Edward arrives early and walks in the grounds before his morning lecture with the second years. The spring blossoms on dozens of trees catch his attention. His mood is lighter following a reasonably convivial conversation with Felicity over breakfast during which diplomacy was to the fore and sheep were not mentioned. Felicity had been curious to know about Marianne and he found himself being deliberately vague and casual as if she didn't matter at all. In truth, when he wasn't thinking of the imminent invasion by woolly creatures, Marianne was constantly on his mind.

When he bumps into Conrad by the photocopier, he casually tells him that he has finally met Marianne and that she didn't try to seduce him or haul him off to bed.

'*Quel dommage*,' says Conrad, adjusting his ponytail and scooping a large pile of handouts from the tray. 'I was hoping for some juicy bits to prove that you are of this planet; to tarnish your reputation.'

The reputation to which Conrad is referring is that Dr Edward Harvey is unseducable, as evidenced by the failed attempts of many a drunken archaeology student during departmental social events over the past twenty years. In days of old the young girls were captivated by him because he was lithe and good-looking – even if a little conventional for the typical student taste. His natural reserve presented a challenge and each one of them wanted to be the first to melt the iceberg. They lined the corridor outside his office, hoping for a word about an essay; they invited him to parties and plied him with extra-strong home-made wine (most of which he passed on to Conrad when they weren't looking); they wore low-cut t-shirts and push-up bras and sat on the front row at his lectures chewing gum, trying to catch his eye, asking an occasional intelligent question with fluttering eyes and pouting lips.

Edward acquired a technique of placing an invisible barrier between him and them. Always courteous, always polite, but surrounded by a force field that said, *'You can look, but you can't touch'.* This drove them to deeper levels of obsession and cunning ploys. They sent him mysterious Valentine cards with cryptic messages; they wrote poetry about him in the college magazine and they turned up early for his seminars, hoping for a word alone before the class arrived.

Now a dwindling number of generally mature students fall in love with his mind and his avuncular manner but are too sensible to plot and scheme. The corridor outside his office is quiet and only Gemma Saborey, the departmental administrator, still carries an obvious torch that makes him smile.

'She's turned into a very lovely woman,' continues Edward in measured tones, preoccupied with punching instructions into the photocopier to hide his embarrassment. 'And perfectly sane.'

'Dimensions?'

'Bloody hell, Conrad!'

In the evening, while Felicity and James are visiting the Molwings to discuss sheep welfare, Edward catches up on his emails.

To: Edward Harvey
From: Marianne Hayward
Date: 28th March 2003, 22.02
Subject: Meeting

Dear Edward,
It was such a joy to meet you after all these years! And
to find there were things to say beyond our Brocklebank
memories. Loved your lecture too! Hope you got home
okay and weren't too tired.
Do keep in touch!
love
Marianne

Love Marianne ... She had written 'love' at the end of one email
before, the email when she thought him lost. But she had
signed it with the name of the character of the play they were
in, which made it more remote. And he had done the same in
reply. *Love Marianne ...* Were they friends now? A warm feeling
settles in his soul, followed almost immediately by unease. It is
wrong that his emotions are being affected by another woman.
They never have before. He begins a reply of equal enthusiasm,
and then worries at the implications of the words and clicks
delete. He must calm down, rid himself of this distracting
nonsense; focus on understanding his wife and ever-expanding
menagerie at the Deer Orchard. But a picture of the unsent
email sails around his head like an unsinkable boat on a voyage
of discovery. Maybe tomorrow.

10

When Taryn was twenty-one, her mother died from a brain haemorrhage. Since then she has denied the existence of her father. She blames him for her mother's high blood pressure and untimely death; she blames him for everything that has gone wrong since she was nine. After her mother's funeral she thought, *only Louisa left and then there will be no one else of importance to leave me; to hurt me.* She was determined not to love anyone new. Love always brought pain; first her dad, then her mum. It is one of the reasons she won't even have a cat.

She thinks Marianne is far too sentimental for her own good, verging on the hysterical when her husband befriended his colleague, Charmaine, and plunged into a ridiculous level of despair when Edward Harvey stopped emailing her for three months. Okay, if she was being generous she could just about understand being upset when the marriage was under threat, but Marianne hadn't been in contact with Edward Harvey for thirty-odd years, so getting in a state about him was definitely beyond the reasonable, especially when she hadn't even met him – unless, of course, there is something Marianne is not telling her. She had wanted to give her a good shake; to say, *'For God's sake, get a grip,'* but Marianne was in hormonal meltdown and unlikely to listen. Taryn didn't want tears. She couldn't abide tears, so she had played along, offering sympathy regarding Charmaine and fanning the flames of the long-lost crush regarding Edward. It is a relief to know that Marianne has calmed down. Her guilt is somewhat assuaged, but she awaits the news of their re-acquaintance with more than a little interest.

In the meantime she busies herself with a little retail therapy online. If she wants to impress, she needs the right tools. New shoes would be good; black courts with sexy high heels.

Rouge Vibration lipstick from Yves St Laurent, with just the right amount of shine and staying power.

And a little black suit with a nipped-in waist and short skirt.

Perhaps a new bra too; black, with lace; and wiring to maximise thrust and cleavage. And matching knickers, because she just has to match her underwear; and suspenders because it will make her feel good knowing she is wearing stockings.

Sexy! So, so sexy! She can imagine it all like a film flickering before her eyes. If he lives up to her hopes and is worth the pursuit, he won't stand a chance.

Click … Click … Click … Money flies from her debit account. Next week the post person will be busy. With a low mortgage and no children, Taryn can afford plenty of treats.

'So how was the event of the New Millennium?' asks Taryn of Marianne over a Saturday morning coffee at her flat in Coppercone Lane. Marianne dropped by unexpectedly on her way back from grocery shopping. Taryn doesn't like being taken unawares, and one or two things are not as pristine as she likes them to be when visitors arrive, old friend or no.

They are sitting in the multipurpose front room with its high ceiling and elaborate cornice.

'It was absolutely perfect,' says Marianne excitedly, perched on the edge of her seat because she said she can't stay long as she is on her way home with some smoked salmon and avocados that husband Johnny needs for preparing the lunch.

Sometimes Taryn wishes she could find a husband who would prepare an edible lunch, but all her men have displayed as much culinary skill as a ferret, preferring to sit back with their feet up and a beer in their hand while Taryn scurries around the kitchen concocting something quick and Italian, usually pasta.

Marianne continues, 'It went better than I dared hope. Edward is as charismatic as ever – in an almost indescribable way.' She shakes her head. 'He's competent and confident, but not arrogant. Not in the least bit intellectually remote and much more down to earth than I expected. He doesn't use complicated, jargon-ridden sentences if there's a simple alternative. It was a brilliantly interesting lecture with just the right level of humour, and then afterwards we went to the café for tea and a chat. He was so sweet, so friendly and, well, normal. I felt just like I did when I was ten – innocent admiration; nothing more. And I came back smiling.'

Taryn detects teenage sparkle in her friend and is envious. It has been a few years since she has felt the *frissant* of delight when someone new and significant enters the romantic sphere. Not that there's anything romantic between Marianne and Edward – or so she has been led to believe.

'What did you talk about?'

'Mostly reminiscing. There wasn't a lot of time because he had to speak to Henrik before he caught his train.'

'Did you get on okay?'

'I think so. He's sooo nice. And it's genuine too. You know how you can tell if someone's just putting it on? Well he isn't. He oozes niceness.'

'Imagine that!'

'But there was nowhere near enough time for everything. I came away with a thousand unasked questions.' Marianne starts to fiddle with her necklace. Taryn thinks she looks younger since the meeting. More girlish.

'Did you tell Johnny?'

'The censored version. Don't want him to feel insecure after all we've been through.'

'Is there any reason why he should?'

'Of course not!'

'Not fanciable then?' Taryn wants to know if he is her type.

'Not the Pierce Brosnan look-alike that Holly thought he might've evolved into when she saw our school photograph. Actually, he's more like an older version of Carlos Ramos, the tennis umpire, only taller. Edward has the same ruffled hair that looks as if an effort hasn't been made with it even though it probably has. But greyer. Not very grey though … Yet … No beard, no ponytail, no additional wildlife in occupancy.'

Taryn laughs. 'So quite fanciable?'

'Taryn!'

'Just curious to know whether he lived up to expectations.'

'I expect he was very fanciable when he was younger. Objectively, he's still quite fanciable, but it's a non-sexual thing between him and me. Must be something to do with liking him when I was so young – before the hormones kicked in.' Marianne grins. 'And now the hormones are being kicked out, I suppose it's just the same.'

Methinks she doth protest too much. Taryn doesn't believe Marianne would be so excited about the meeting if there wasn't an element of physical attraction, but she decides not to push it. 'And did he tell you any more about what's-her-name Felicity? Did you get any inclin' as to whether all is well?' She also doesn't believe that anybody's marriage is as perfect as Edward's purports to be.

'Yes,' says Marianne. 'But I don't feel at liberty to divulge.'

Taryn is a shade annoyed. She has listened to Marianne's endless speculations prior to meeting Edward. The least she can do is share the juicy bits. But it is typical of her to keep secrets, particularly those of other people.

'Will you see each other again? Will he be doing any more lectures?'

'He said he and Henrik are each lecturing on alternate Thursdays, but the times vary. I sent him an email to say how much I enjoyed meeting him, but he hasn't replied yet. Which is a little odd. It's not like him to be discourteous. I mean, even if he didn't feel as enthusiastic as me, he would still say something, don't you think?'

'It's only Saturday,' says Taryn.

When Marianne has gone, Taryn fixes herself a microwavable snack consisting of something Chinese with rice, and takes it with a fork in hand over to her computer in the corner of the living room. She is thoughtful. First she finds the page for the British Museum, and the dates and times of all Edward's and Henrik's scheduled lectures. Then she types *Mazes Edward Harvey* into Google and a hundred links line up invitingly for searching. She finds the paper that Marianne told her about from the *Antiquity* magazine – the paper Edward wrote on the discovery of the original Troy Town maze – and prints it off. Homework!

An hour later, after reading it three times in between mouthfuls of Oriental Spicy Prawns, and making a few scribbled notes, she puts the paper down and pours herself a glass of wine, stretching out on her sofa like a cat, enjoying her Marc-free space.

Can she pass herself off as an archaeologist? That would be fun. She can feel the excitement already. But what will be her reason for tracking him down at the BM? A lecturer at a university? Leeds perhaps? Her home town. Surprised he hasn't heard of her? Would he mind very much if they had a chat over coffee?

Then she will tell him the truth – a partial truth that she is not an archaeologist. Cast the line, make the play; get him to talk about himself, his marriage; reveal the midlife angst. Then she will attempt to leave. He will ask her not to go just yet because she will have dazzled him, flattered him, made him want to know more, the hook gently tweaking. Time will pass. Trains will be missed. Perhaps he would like to stay in her spare room? *No ... No! Definitely no ... Too fast ... Too fast!* Edward Harvey is not the type to be rash. The hook will have to embed itself more firmly before she pulls the line. And then ... Then he won't be able to resist, and she will wind him in like a trout. Will she tell him about her connection to Marianne? Eventually, but not immediately, because he might have scruples. And when it is too late for scruples to get in the way, she will tell him and hope that he won't tell Marianne about her.

Marianne would be furious if she knew what she was planning, but Taryn thinks this is hardly fair. She has no exclusive rights to Mr Perfect. After all, she is married to sex-god Johnny (which is how Taryn always thinks of him), and she says all is well between them after their turbulent year. A small doubt the size of a grain of sand lodges in her conscience for a second but it is swiftly dismissed as irrelevant. Tracking down Edward would be such an exciting challenge, such a buzz; it would cheer her up and make her feel young again. It would help to eradicate Marc. It would be worth the risk.

'Darling Neil,' she coos into her phone in her dusky voice, leaning back into the cushions on her sofa, neat legs stretched out with ankles crossed. 'Fancy popping round for a bite of pasta tomorrow night – and a little chat about archaeology?'

Taryn, you're brilliant!

11

It is early Saturday morning, nine days since the meeting with Marianne. Edward has just woken up and is disorientated by a dream he had last night about her. She came to meet him at the Deer Orchard, but it was his parents' house and not his, and his children were teenagers despite him being only about twenty-three. There was no sign of Felicity. Marianne was also young, bounding exuberantly, curvaceous and beautiful with flowing hair; a fantasy version of the real woman. He kept suggesting that they go to Wolverhampton and she kept fretting about missing her train home. They walked in blazing sunshine down a beautiful Broadclyst country lane with summer-long verges of clover, marguerites, meadowsweet and poppies. They were talking as friends not lovers, yet being physically close and almost intimate. At one point he placed his arm high around her back and under her arm, his hand over her breast. She didn't seem to mind. He could feel the soft resilience and when he woke he wanted to go back into the dream to see what happened.

He reasons that he is sexually frustrated and wonders if he should make more of an attempt to seduce Felicity, instead of being deterred by her reluctance. It is difficult learning new strategies when he has been so used to her taking the lead. Tonight, perhaps …

He still hasn't replied to Marianne's message after the meeting. He feels guilty, but all his attempts look trite. He has heard about email relationships drifting into territory that is below-board and although on the one hand with Felicity being the way she is, this seems rather a pleasant prospect, on the other, he has never yet ventured into a dangerous liaison and even the thought makes him distinctly uncomfortable. Besides which, Marianne is happily married and the most they can hope to be is friends. He wants his reply to convey his enthusiasm for friendship, yet not be misconstrued as anything more.

Felicity stirs, yawns and disturbs his reverie. 'I've decided to change the name of the restaurant to the Retreat. It has a country feel without sounding like a pub.'

Edward realises by her tone that this is yet another thing about which she has made up her mind to a point where it won't be shifted no matter what he says. 'And will it be expensive?' he asks flatly.

'We have to lure people in with reasonable prices, but we don't want the riff-raff element spoiling the enjoyment of others. And I need to cover costs. If the ingredients are more expensive, then obviously that will bump up the price. Once my vegetables get going, that will help the profit margins.'

'They say restaurants go out of business every week.'

'Bad restaurants might. This one won't be bad. We've eaten out enough over the years to know exactly what's needed in a place like this. I've put in an offer on Heliotrope.'

'You never said—'

'It's already got newly refurbished kitchens and all we will have to change is the ambiance in the restaurant itself. It's small and ideally located. They are prepared to rent it to me once the contracts have been signed – so we won't have to wait until the sale is completed. There's also a flat upstairs which they said I can sub-let. Possibly to Gianni.'

'Who's Gianni?'

'My chef – I hope! He's been working in one of Rick Stein's kitchens in Padstow, so he knows what he's doing and can cope with the idea of simple but good food. He wants more independence before eventually branching out on his own. He's coming round later to discuss terms.'

'Won't he be expensive if he's been trained by Stein?'

'You get what you pay for in this world.'

Broadclyst is quite large for a village, having a population not far short of three thousand. It is unusual in that scattered throughout are many distinctive yellow-rendered cottages making them identifiable as being owned by the National Trust and part of the Killerton Estate, covering an area of over six thousand acres in eastern Devon. Many of the cottages are thatched, notably one of the visitors' attractions, Marker's Cottage, a medieval cob house with tall chimneys and smoke-blackened timbers inside. The Deer Orchard is located at the southern end of the village, accessed by a lane that leads to the Molwings' farm.

Edward is driving back from the supermarket on the edge of Exeter, the boot of the car bursting with bags of groceries. He is in a bad mood, not least because he acknowledges that Felicity goes through this hell every week and he feels guilty. Feeding a family of six is a major undertaking.

He is now on his way to Killerton House shop to buy special Clyston Mill flour which is grown and milled by the Estate and makes the most delicious scones. Felicity won't use anything else and despite his protests that he has much to do, she insisted that she needs it today. While he is there, he buys some of their home-made and ever popular cider and, by way of late elevenses, he treats himself to tea, cake and ice cream at the Killerton Kitchen which overlooks the grounds. The magnolias are already beginning to flower in the spring sunshine and soon the ancient rhododendrons will create a magnificent display.

It has taken him most of the morning to do what Felicity does in a couple of hours. Usually on a Saturday, while she shops, he walks the dogs further than during the week and then settles in his office to do some writing and preparation so that he can have the rest of the weekend free if he wishes. He hopes that today's arrangement isn't another taste of his future.

Arriving back home, there is a commotion behind the house. Len Molwing's Land Rover and trailer are parked on the gravel and he and his son Peter are talking to Felicity.

The Molwings are tenants on one of Killerton Estate's twenty-odd farms. Len is a small wiry man in his fifties, with beady eyes, a hooked nose and a weather beaten face under a checked cap. His son Peter is tall and solid, bearing no resemblance to his father. As his wife Anne is also small, Edward suspects the work of an external gene pool and surmises that Mrs Molwing may have seen some action in one of the hay barns while her husband was out in the fields. There are no other children to support or refute his theory.

The sheep are in a trailer, six woolly backed Cotswold ewes, roundly pregnant with new spring lambs. They have been fetched by Peter Molwing from a farm near Stow-on-the-Wold and are ready to be taken round to the field beyond the orchard and paddock. One of the many old out-buildings has been turned into a lambing pen by Rick, and James and Felicity promise they will deal with the labour, working shifts through the night if necessary.

After they've gone, Edward starts fetching the groceries from the car.

'Why the face?' asks Felicity.

'Watching a few episodes of *Vets in Practice* doesn't mean you'll be able to do this on your own,' he says, with undisguised scepticism. They are in the kitchen unpacking the carrier bags.

'We shall go to the Molwings and see how it's done. Some

of their ewes will lamb earlier than ours,' says Felicity, methodically putting things in cupboards and in the fridge.

'And what if we end up with a pet lamb?'

'We will all take turns with the feeds.'

'By *all*, I hope you're not including me.'

'You're turning into such a grouch.'

In the afternoon, Gianni arrives by taxi looking very suave, dark and Italian. Edward overhears Felicity in the kitchen where she is finalising details. 'One thing I forgot to mention at the interview …'

What interview? he thinks. Yet more happenings behind his back. He hovers in the passageway.

'I want to cater for people who can't eat certain things: dairy, lactose, wheat, diabetic. I want to provide as many diet sensitive ways of cooking the same dish as possible.'

'It will be cost,' says Gianni, with a strong accent. 'It will be complicated. Sauce is sauce. You want best, you not mess round with ingredients.'

'This is not negotiable, Gianni.'

Edward wonders if he's going to be temperamental. Perhaps Felicity has been so overcome by his dazzling good looks that she has failed to identify him as potentially awkward.

'What is negotiable mean?'

'It is going to happen irrespective of what you say.'

'What is this "irrespective"? *Non capisco.*'

Edward hears Felicity take a deep breath and he is quietly pleased that her patience is being tested.

'It will happen. This is the way it will be done. *Capite? Si?* I won't be too ambitious to start with – you will be able to manage. Then you'll see how the bookings flood in.'

'What is "flood in"?'

Edward grins.

'If we are busy.'

'If they "flood in", I will need help.'

'I will help,' says Felicity. 'I have done courses in *Cordon Bleu* and my risottos are legendary in these parts. If things get really busy, you will have a sous chef – someone for you to train.'

Edward marvels at Felicity's cunning. It is how she has manipulated him over the years, but it is only now that he is beginning to appreciate the true extent of her guile. He wishes he could play her the way she plays him.

He can't bear to listen to any more and goes upstairs to his study, ostensibly to mark some essays. Instead he checks his emails again, hoping for another one from Marianne – which is silly when it is his turn to write to her.

To: Marianne Hayward
From: Edward Harvey
Date: 5th April 2003, 15.11
Subject: Re: Meeting

Dear Marianne,
Sorry for delay in response to your email. It was good to meet you too!

Understatement of the year, he thinks.

Extremely busy with all this travelling to London. Even had to do shopping this morning due to arrival of sheep! Felicity usually does the weekly shop so took me twice as long as I didn't know where anything was. Shameful!
love,
Edward

Mostly he sends his replies to Marianne without a second glance. This time he re-reads, looking for spelling errors or potential misunderstandings. He deletes the 'love', thinking this will bring things back to a safe, friendly formality. Then after he has sent it, he immediately regrets his coolness.

To: Edward Harvey
From: Marianne Hayward
Date: 5th April 2003, 15.20
Subject: Re: Meeting

Hi Edward,
Didn't you once say you were a metrosexual man?
Shopping should hold few fears!
I have been hearing rumours that Bavarian beavers are going to be reintroduced to Britain. There is opposition from those who fear destruction of habitat and damming of watercourses. Why is it that we so-called developed humans, who are the most destructive creatures on the planet, are so set against our fellow wildlife?
Busy writing.
Hope sheep settle in well.
Marianne

Drat! Now she's stopped writing 'love'. Is she offended? Such a little word to have such heavy connotations … Unusually short message from her … She must be working on her book …

To: Marianne Hayward
From: Edward Harvey
Date: 5th April 2003, 15.35
Subject: Re: Meeting

Hi Marianne,
It was Felicity who said I was metrosexual. At the

moment she may have changed her mind!

Seems a pity to evict the beavers from Bavaria.

Sheep expectant; Meg excited, but too young to be let loose on them.

Hope the writing goes well.

love,

Edward

To: Edward Harvey
From: Marianne Hayward
Date: 5th April 2003, 15.51
Subject: The Potato Theory

Dear Edward,

I've recently been pondering the thought that potatoes might be dangerous(!). This thought began when contemplating that the Mediterranean diet is healthier than ours. Perhaps it's not the olive oil and fish – as opposed to the animal fats and red meat – that makes the difference, but the difference between pasta and potatoes. (Also Chinese and Japanese incidence of cancer and heart disease relatively low compared with the West.)

My HoD Pandrea Kinnear (for whom I'm currently Acting as she's on maternity leave), believes that anything related to deadly nightshade must be viewed with suspicion. When potatoes go green or develop shoots, then the solanine in them increases to dangerous levels, so why not suppose that if you eat enough of the normal ones, they may also cause some sort of toxicity over a period of time? Tomatoes, aubergines and peppers are also solanaceae and apparently if these and potatoes are cut out of the diet,

91

then arthritis sufferers have reduced symptoms!
I am thinking of having a potato free week to see what
happens. But I am so potato dependent this is going to
be very difficult. Johnny is also taking a dim view!
Must dash.
love,
Marianne

This is more like the old Marianne. The pre-meeting Marianne whom he sometimes thought might be crazy. He wishes she wouldn't mention Johnny. It reminds him that she is unavailable. But so is he. And he mentions Felicity …

His thoughts are random, wispy and illogical. His quiet family life is threatened by intruders who seem to know more than he does about things that matter to his wife.

Out in the back garden, Rick is turning over one of the lawns with view to planting potatoes. *Wonder what Marianne would say about that!* Edward can see him from the window of his office, wielding a spade with youthful ease. He wonders if Rick knows all this stuff about solanaceae and whether Felicity will offer potato alternatives. He will make the suggestion; try to show interest. She is out there too, waving her arms around, issuing instructions, always the great organiser. She has warned him that Rick will be doing a lot of work transforming the garden, clearing the orchard and doing some of the structural alterations to bring the out-buildings back into use. He feels a twinge of jealousy and a dull ache, remembering lost youth and vigour.

To: Marianne Hayward
From: Edward Harvey
Date: 5th April 2003, 16.21
Subject: Re: The Potato Theory

Dear Marianne,

Aren't tomatoes supposed to contain lycopenes that reduce cancer risk? Also peppers and aubergines feature heavily in Mediterranean diet. I take your point about arthritis, but other Western diseases surely cannot be blamed on these members of the nightshade family. Unless as you suspect potatoes are the culprits, the lycopenes in the other plants outweighing the solanines. Felicity plans to grow our own this coming summer.

love

Edward

Alexander and Olivia come to see the sheep. Edward hides in his office for as long as he can without appearing rude. When he emerges, he wanders through the paddock and feigns surprise at seeing them.

'Hello! How long have you two been here? Have you had a coffee?'

Olivia, dripping in gold jewellery, flashes him a big-toothed smile. 'Felicity's been showing us your new arrivals. Aren't they darlings. Such cutesy faces.'

'Totally dim, though,' says Edward, thinking uncharitably that this characteristic would also describe Lou-Lou and her daft husband.

The sheep are in the field on the other side of the lane that borders the paddock, lazily surveying their new territory between mouthfuls of grass.

'Felicity tells us your exhibition is going well,' says Alexander. He is a short, muscular man with an alarmingly large amount of black hair spreading from his open shirt and up his neck. 'We thought we might pop along and have a look. I got lost in Hampton Court maze once. Had to be rescued.'

'You won't get lost in ours,' says Edward, wondering how

Felicity knows about the relative success of the exhibition when she has shown such little interest. 'They're pebble and rock mazes – close to the ground. They're also unicursal. You just follow the path; no decisions to make.'

'So what's the point of them?' asks Olivia.

'Many theories,' says Edward patiently. 'The coastal ones were possibly to help protect those at sea. It was believed that unwelcome winds would get caught up in the coils of the labyrinth. Some believe they were important in fertility rites.'

'Oooh, better be careful then.' Olivia gives her husband a knowing look.

'We'll be glad to see you,' says Edward charitably.

'We can fit it in with a show. Lou-Lou loves Andy Lloyd-Webber. She's got all the CDs.'

Edward smiles quietly to himself.

After supper Felicity is watching the television, sprawled along the length of the sofa, one leg dangling over the edge and an arm behind her head. Her old jeans and sweater aren't exactly inviting romance, but he has made up his mind to be bold, and her tousled part-pinned 'Not tonight Josephine' hair does have a certain *je ne sais quoi*.

'Fancy an early night?' he asks hopefully, perching on the arm of the nearby chair with a tea towel over his shoulder.

Felicity reclaims her limbs from their casual pose and stiffens. 'What's brought this on so suddenly?'

'We've been neglecting our Saturday night ritual.'

'Rituals are so tedious, don't you think?'

'All these years and you never said. But they do save brain work and effort after the busy working week.'

'There's so much going on,' says Felicity, hesitating. 'I'm exhausted.'

'I miss you.'

'If you are looking for truth,' says Felicity, who has always spoken her mind, 'I've not been much in the mood lately.'

'Could we not try to create the mood? It apparently takes twenty-seven minutes of foreplay for women to—'

'Have you been reading magazines?' she accuses.

'No! One of Conrad's pieces of wisdom.'

'It never used to take me twenty-seven minutes.'

'Come on, Flick. Use it or lose it, they say.'

'So romantic!'

'I'm not going to beg,' he says and walks off.

Half an hour later they are both lying on their backs naked in bed. An uncomfortable silence has fallen. Felicity's half-hearted gesture at passion has left him cold and unaroused. He is about to reach for his book when Felicity speaks.

'Everything has always been about you, Ted. First the PhD, then the job. Even the children were produced in accordance with your work schedule.'

'Not Christopher.'

'I've been behind you all the way.'

'Exactly. I discussed everything with you and you agreed. You never said you wanted children earlier or later—'

'Because I could see the sense of having them when we did.'

'No regrets?'

'No regrets.'

'So you were happy to go along with my plans?'

'Yes.'

He turns towards her. 'Well I'm not happy going along with all of this. It's happening too fast. I don't feel part of the decision making process.'

'I'm not going to run this business like your archaeology department. None of that strategic planning stuff. I'm for looseness and flexibility.'

'Neither of which make good business sense.'

'I can afford to do it the way I want.'

Not 'we' thinks Edward crossly. 'Is this a row?' he asks.

'I think so.'

'We hardly ever row.'

'Welcome to the real world.'

Edward doesn't want things to get out of hand. He tries an alternative strategy, a change of tack; a peace-offering of a sort. 'We haven't been out for ages. You could come and meet me in London after my lecture and we could go to a play like we used to do. The kids are old enough to cope.'

'And that's supposed to help me feel less tired?'

Edward goes silent, returning to a supine position. This has been a day when his world has been turned upside down. Shopping and sheep, Gianni and Rick … Apart from emailing, he's hardly done any writing. He remembers Marianne's words about softness conquering hardness and about finding a way round the boulder. Sure as hell Felicity isn't going to budge, so he will have to adopt a survival strategy. His comfortable life is under threat, and it seems there is no going back.

12

Two weeks after the meeting with Marianne, Edward is once again about to deliver his maze lecture at the British Museum. He is tired. The fortnightly visits to London in addition to his lecturing load at the university would normally be of little consequence, but he has been sleeping uncommonly badly and with all the comings and goings at home, fatigue is beginning to set in.

He had tried to sleep on the train to Paddington, but just as he was drifting off, the train manager appeared to check his ticket and having been disturbed, he couldn't find the relaxed mood again.

He wishes it was like last time when he was looking forward to impressing Marianne and to meeting her. And now that he has met her, he wishes she might be there again so they could have another conversation where she would advise him about Felicity – about not painting legs on snakes and about boulders and rivers – and he could gaze once more into those steadfast green eyes that spoke to him with compassion and gave him hope.

He is just about to address the gathered audience of about thirty people when he notices a little woman in a black suit with a hair-do that reminds him of the time when the class at his school were being acquainted with a Van de Graaff Generator. She has bright red lipstick and dark-rimmed rectangular glasses. He thinks she looks fierce and not like an archaeologist. Perhaps she is a reporter of some sort. He clears his throat and relaxes his shoulders; he had better put on a good show.

★

Taryn settles herself down in the middle of the lecture theatre with its raked seating, four rows from the front and between two dull-looking over-sixties in cardigans, between whom she hopes she will be extra conspicuous.

When she arrived at the museum, early, she went to have a look at the mazes. These had been recreated with natural stones in what looked like large flat sand pits. She tottered round the narrow paths of the Troy Town replica and wondered what she was supposed to feel. She became aware of a man near the opening explaining something about the displays to a small gathering of people, and she smiled at him when she finished the walk.

'Well done,' he said, turning towards her as the group dispersed.

With round glasses and pointed features, he reminded her of an insect and for a moment of disappointment, she thought it was Edward.

Then he said, 'Quite an achievement on those heels.'

And the way he pronounced his S's made her realise with relief that he must be Sacandinavian.

'Henrik Selgelid,' he said as if reading her mind. 'I am involved in setting up this exhibition with Dr Edward Harvey. He lectures soon, if you are interested.'

'I expected these mazes to be much bigger. What are they for?' she said, pretending ignorance.

'In Finland, we know the shepherds walked the maze to protect from wild animals, also to trap evil spirits and trolls who follow the shepherd in, but cannot get out themselves. The lecture will tell more.'

Now in the lecture theatre, she opens a folder in which she has clipped a few sheets of A4 lined paper. The top sheet is covered with scribblings from her supper with Neil, with

98

added sub-headings of her own acting as crib notes for the train journey into town. Neil had been most forthcoming about Taryn's speculative interest in mazes and even brought a few downloads from selected websites. She can now bluff her way across Scilly and round the Oslo region and the Baltic. After pasta and a couple of glasses of wine, he had asked baldly whether this interest in archaeology should give him hope that she might now consider a romantic involvement with him.

'Don't do romance, as well you know,' Taryn had laughed, and Neil had laughed too.

'But you are up to something, I can tell,' said Neil. 'What's he called?'

'You read me so well,' said Taryn, but refused to be drawn further.

Now she takes a pencil from her handbag and prepares to make notes on Edward's lecture with view to asking a question or two at the end.

She feels his gaze lingering a shade longer on her as he scans the group prior to beginning, and she smiles slightly and lowers her eyes briefly in what she has been told many times is a come-hither and sexy way.

He looks very relaxed and at home, she thinks. *It is his territory, surrounded by history and artefacts and familiarity. And he's rather cute, if a little tired-looking. Navy with royal blue aren't his best colours. He should wear a black suit with a crisp white shirt, and a monochrome tie with a hint of colour. Or grey with a lilac shirt; but perhaps he's not the lilac type.*

Taryn knows a thing or two about fashion.

She is brought back to reality by a ripple of laughter. She smiles. She missed the introductory joke; she must concentrate. She hopes he didn't notice. *Not very flattering to lose a listener after less than thirty seconds!*

Little does Edward know that his familiar world is about to

become even more unsettled. As is customary at the end of his lectures, the shy ones hover as he gathers up his papers and retrieves his PowerPoint presentation from the PC. He recognises one girl who has been following him around for years, turning up in different parts of the country whenever he is speaking. She is a lumpy individual with greasy skin, lank ginger hair and spots. Clever though, judging by the questions she asks. Sometimes he wonders if she should be classed as a stalker, but she seems harmless and makes no contact except at public lectures. It might just be that she's interested in field archaeology and has a lot of spare time.

He glances up and notices the Van de Graaff Generator woman is waiting in line, clutching a folder to her chest. She is tiny. If it wasn't for the inches added by her hair and high-heeled shoes, he reckons she might be little over five feet tall; or short. One by one he deals patiently with the questions. Yes, he does believe that labyrinth mazes have a mystical quality, but whether they really do aid fertility is anyone's guess. It could be that the belief that they do is all it takes to bring about the magical fusion.

'So it's all in the mind?' asks the questioner, an anxious-looking woman of indiscernible age.

'Maybe,' says Edward. 'But does that matter if it works?'

The woman in black stands before him and holds out her hand. 'Taryn Danielli,' she says, in a voice that is surprisingly low for such a small person and with a tone that implies he should know who she is.

'Leeds,' she adds.

Edward can't recall a Taryn Danielli from his last visit to the archaeology department at Leeds University, but the thought passes him by.

'I am particularly interested in what you were saying about … mazes of the liminal zone, and also about ley-lines. I wondered if we could discuss it further – over a coffee perhaps? You must be thirsty after such a performance. I expected you to be good and you didn't disappoint.'

He smiles at the flattery. She is business-like and unthreatening, yet with an expectation of an affirmative answer. He is instantly reminded of his first encounter with Felicity.

'If you're happy to watch me eat as well,' he says. 'I'm starving.'

He gestures for her to wait while he deals with one final question and then with briefcase in hand, he strides towards the exit, Taryn at his shoulder.

When they are suitably settled in the café, Edward with some pasta and Taryn with a salad, she asks him about Swedish mazes.

Edward asks her where her interest in mazes began.

'I'm not an archaeologist,' she says.

Edward is surprised. 'You know a remarkable amount about mazes.'

'A little bedtime reading, that's all.'

'You said Leeds,' said Edward. 'What's your subject?'

'I'm not at the university. I was born in Leeds.'

Edward is puzzled and sits back a little in his chair. 'I must've misunderstood. So who are you then?' He wonders if his first instincts were correct, that she is a reporter, a journalist.

'I am a woman who is interested in knowing more about mazes from the world authority that is Edward Harvey.'

'Henrik Selgelid is more of a world authority than I shall ever be.'

'But – forgive me – Henrik hasn't quite the same charm as you.'

'You've met?'

'Just before your lecture.'

Edward is baffled. 'Do I get the feeling that I'm being targeted for some purpose?'

'Targeted, yes. Purpose, debatable.' She flashes him one of her brilliant smiles, then looks away.

'I'm intrigued,' says Edward, thinking this is one of the most bizarre meetings he has ever had and wondering what is going to happen next. He focuses on the tagliatelli, winding expert forkfuls, waiting for her next surprise.

'Be intrigued, but don't be worried.'

'You're a journalist, then? You want to interview me?' Since Scilly, he has become used to journalists.

'God, no!' says Taryn, leaning forward in a conspiratorial way.

He catches a glimpse of black lace and cleavage. He suspects she isn't wearing anything under her jacket except a bra. Not like most of the archaeologists in the University of Devon!

It is all going to plan and he is better looking than she expected. She noted immediately the way his eyes crinkle when he smiles, emanating warmth and honesty. What started out as fantasy is beginning to take on some realism. She begins to want him, or at least want him to want her.

He is leaning into her space; he is gazing into her eyes; he doesn't flinch when she lays a hand on his arm in sympathetic response to his bemoaning the problems surrounding widening participation in universities, the burgeoning size of the student intake and the reduction in time for research. She can't believe how well she remembered the history supplied by Neil and the mythology dredged from her schooldays.

But she knows the rules of the game too well from snaring a dozen men and more. Without warning she looks at her watch and stands up. 'Cripes! Is that the time! Oh lordy ...' She feigns sadness. 'I am so, so sorry. And I was enjoying our conversation so much. But I'm going to have to dash.'

'Must you?' says Edward, sounding taken aback. 'You still haven't told me why I've been targeted.'

'I must go.' Taryn pauses. 'I have things to do.' She always has to be the one to leave first. She knows the effect this has on men, on their pride. 'Targeted? Did I say that?' She assumes a look of surprise.

'You did.'

'With all this intellectual stimulation, I've quite lost track.'

'So? Are you going to tell me?'

'Oh, you don't really want to know. It's a mere nothing. Inconsequential.' Taryn fixes her gaze on one of his eyes and then moves it to the other. This strategy is supposed to have a hypnotic effect; supposed to draw men in. Whether this is the reason for her past successes, she can't say.

'Now I'm even more intrigued.'

'And I'm going to be late if I don't fly.' Taryn leaps to her feet and gathers up her bag.

Edward also stands and holds out his hand. 'It's been interesting to meet you, Miss Danielli. But I feel that there's something you're not telling me.'

'Well I could ... no ... no ... I couldn't. You would think it mad. I mean we hardly know each other.'

'Go on.'

'Hmmm. I would really like to continue our discussion. Mazes are such a fascinating subject and the more you find out, the more you realise there is to discover. And you make the topic so very interesting, so accessible, so much more than a few rocks in concentric circles. But I can't.'

'What?' says Edward. 'Go on. Tell.'

'Well I was going to suggest that I meet you again next time you come – if you're here again. We could finish our conversation. I don't like to rush off.'

'I'm here the Thursday after next—' Edward stops, pauses,

looks hesitant. 'Might you divulge the nature of your interest, if we meet again?'

'I might,' says Taryn, teasing, knowing she has aroused his curiosity and that he is trying not to sound too eager.

'Then I shall look forward to it.'

'Ciao!' And with that she leaves, taking little running steps in her high-heeled shoes until she is out of the museum and heading towards the Holborn tube station. Only then does she slow down.

Yes, she thinks, *Marianne is right. He does possess a certain something that makes you want to dance.*

13

On his way to the university the day after meeting Taryn, Edward stops off at the bank to move some money from one account to another. Until Felicity's cheque comes through from her mother's estate, he has to pay the bills resulting from her schemes. What with the vet's bills and supplementary feed, six pregnant sheep are more expensive than he anticipated. While he is waiting in a queue of funereal slowness, he watches a youngish couple who are engaged in lengthy and convoluted transactions at one of the nearby windows. It is they who are responsible for the delay.

The young woman has shiny, shoulder length russet hair, streaked with strawberry blonde, and flicked up at the ends. When she turns, he notices her large nose and freckles. She is quite plain apart from her hair, and wears no make-up. The man she is with is small and narrow shouldered with close-cropped brown hair. He looks like a plumber. Edward and his children play a game where they categorise people by imagined occupation. They have discovered that almost all British professional golfers can be grouped into builders, plumbers and electricians.

The couple stand so close they seem fused, and every few moments while the bank clerk is tapping details into the computer, the woman gives the man a hug and a kiss or ruffles his hair. Sexual energy radiates from them and it is as if they are in their own little private space and not being watched by a dozen or so impatient customers. Edward wonders if they are arranging a mortgage; perhaps setting out on the life-journey of living together. They are clearly very excited. Maybe they are going on a special holiday, to an exotic land with palm trees and blue seas. He and Felicity haven't arranged a holiday this year. Not since their wonderful trip to Australasia at the end of 2001.

Again he feels the pang of nostalgia, for times now gone when he and Felicity planned their future with such emotion-charged zeal (though generally they drew the line at such public displays of affection). He was so happy then, and beyond, but all in the space of three months, since Felicity knew she would inherit such a large sum of money, the happiness has dissolved like aeroplane trails into the vastness of a bright blue morning sky. He wonders if this is what happens to some lottery winners.

He feels a restlessness he has never known in his married life and his thoughts surge between worries about himself and Felicity, and fantasies about Marianne. He is becoming more adept at these with practice, and they are now taking on a more erotic complexity involving showers, mirrors and wet lacy underwear. He blames Conrad. Then there's that weird occurrence yesterday with the diminutive and slightly scary Taryn. What was that about? Who exactly is she? Will she turn up again as she promised?

He tells Conrad about Taryn in the late afternoon, after their departmental meeting. They are in Edward's office, a long airy room, painted white with a window looking out over one of the many expanses of grass and trees. Edward's desk and computer are at one end along with a couple of easy chairs. At the other end are a large round table and two filing cabinets. Books line one of the walls from top to bottom apart from a second door leading into Gemma Saborey's office. Assorted green plants, mostly cacti and aloes, are on the window sill; appreciated by Edward, but cared for by Gemma.

'Sounds like you're well-in there,' says Conrad, slapping Edward on the back before making himself comfortable in one of the chairs. 'Don't know how you do it, mate. Spoilt for choice.'

'They just try it on because they know I'm unobtainable,' says Edward modestly. 'If I responded, they'd be off in a flash.'

They all try it on except Marianne, he thinks. *But what would I do if she did?*

'Gemma'd have you, you know. Drop of a hat. She's been lusting from behind that door ever since you met.'

'Shhh! Poor Gemma. I don't lead her on.'

'Don't let her get wind of the pursuit by the Van de Graaff Generator. I reckon things could turn nasty if she found out. Not a hundred per cent certain that our Gemma is totally stable. Gotta watch these nervy types. Keep the knives under lock and key. She's very protective of you, you know.'

'I shan't be telling anyone apart from you. I'm only telling you because you're more, huh, experienced in these matters than I am.' Edward gives a wry smile and picks a thick elastic band from his in-tray.

'Is that a compliment? If you don't want her, send her my way. She sounds like a handful and I like masterful women. Nice for a bit of a romp between the sheets. And they know how to be discrete.' Conrad winks.

There's a gentle tap on the door and Gemma walks in with some letters to sign. Edward thinks she is very sweet but lacking in sex-appeal. She is mousy, prim and wears a lot of beige and brown with sensible tan shoes. He remembers Felicity telling him once that it is impossible to be sexy in brown. She beams at both men. Edward is aware of her slightly cloying perfume and high-collared blouse.

'Treat him gently, Gem,' says Conrad, heading towards the door and winking again at Edward as he leaves.

Gemma appears to notice the wink and looks quizzically at Edward, but he doesn't offer an explanation.

'Why gently? Are you ill?'

'Conrad's little joke.'

'Dick's next door. He would like a word,' she says.

Dick Fieldbrace is the Dean of the Faculty of Social and Historical Sciences.

'What does he want?' asks Edward.

'No idea,' says Gemma.

Dick appears in the doorway. He is a squarely built man in his mid fifties, with thick salt and pepper hair and a matching close cropped beard and moustache. He has an immovable quality about him; legs set wide and large feet; the type of physique that would be advantageous in a tropical storm.

'Ted! Just passing by. Do you have a moment just now?' He has a gentle Edinburgh accent masking a steely personality.

Edward gestures him in and Gemma reverses back into her office.

Dick settles himself in a comfortable chair and scratches his beard. 'Are you happy here, Ted?'

Odd question to ask after almost twenty years.

'I am,' says Edward tentatively.

'Good … good …' Dick pauses and surveys the room, his eyes alighting on each one of Gemma's carefully tended plants. 'I don't know if I should be saying anything, but I was in London earlier in the week – at a conference at Stancliffe. The word is, there will be a new chair for the archaeology department. The HoD is retiring and they're looking to expand. The vision of some benefactor, and there's a lot of money being thrown at it with the intention of recruiting some of the best young guns in the archaeological world. They've already snapped up Robert Ivastrope from UCL and Julia Bannon from Durham – but they need someone with experience and reputation to lead the new team. There's talk of approaching you to see if you'd be interested. Everybody's excited about the Troy Town maze, and the lectures you've been giving at the BM are going down a storm. Patrick Shrubsole says they want somebody with a high profile who's experienced in landscape archaeology.'

Stancliffe University is in London, not far from the Natural History Museum. It is one of the lesser known universities gathered under the umbrella of the University of London, originally specialising in teacher training, but in recent years expanding its humanities departments and acquiring something of a reputation for being dynamic and forward thinking. Patrick Shrubsole is a leading historian and Dean of Humanities and Social Sciences at Stancliffe, with a CV of publications that stretches to several pages and legendary status since he presented a Channel 4 series on British henges. Edward is flattered and alarmed at the same time.

Dick continues, 'I said I didn't know whether you'd be prepared to up sticks, with the family being settled here. But you could always commute. People do. Of course we'd be mortified to lose you, but it's an opportunity that's unlikely to happen here, and having the Prof status is always handy when you publish.'

'I'm surprised. Speechless.'

'You'd deserve it more than most. This is off the record, by the way. Keep schtum. Act surprised if anyone makes an approach. And I say *if*. It was all speculative. No guarantees.'

When Edward is driving home he remembers the couple in the bank and how affectionate the russet haired woman had been towards her partner. Felicity would never have ruffled his own hair like that in public. She wasn't the soft and warm lovey-dovey type at all, but she had been passionate in her youth and had made him feel a million dollars because she said she wanted him.

But what did she want me for?

An unsettling thought occurs. Did Felicity ever really love him at a deep, all-consuming level, or was it all a ploy; a devious charade to lure him into paternity.

Yet they got on well enough. Very well ... They shared the same likes and dislikes about music and the arts; the same political leanings; the same taste in holidays. Or did she just pretend to like the things he did? Was he just a meal ticket, a sperm donor, a supplier of genes for intelligence and niceness? Had she surveyed her options as one might survey a horse in the sale ring; checking teeth, condition and temperament? Was he just someone to provide the comfortable life; someone who wouldn't stray?

He has never shared her dream about self-sufficiency, and even though they lived in a property that was ideally suited to growing-your-own and keeping animals, while they were both so busy with work and the children, there was never time to explore its potential and the fallen fruit in the orchard was mostly left to the wildlife.

He hears an echo from their first meeting: *'I didn't think you would be my type ... I'm done with Jack-the-Lads ... You have kind eyes like a horse ...'*

Like a horse! Bloody hell!

Now he has started on this destructive line, the thought won't go away. He is questioning Felicity's motives from way back; doubting her love, recognising her lack of compassion. When he was young and healthy and full of optimism and certainty about his future, he didn't need compassion. Now he's not so sure.

And would any of this matter if they were still having sex on a regular basis? Probably not. Presence of sex is very much taken for granted, but an absence is like missing meals; starvation of the soul.

As soon as he arrives home, he parks the Volvo on the gravel at the front of the house and walks around to the back to establish the whereabouts of the different members of the family. Since the advent of Felicity's plan, they are more likely to be outside than inside.

The first person he sees is Rick who is hammering planks of wood and seems to be making raised beds on what was once a second lawn. They nod to each other, but do not speak. Edward is irritated by the way in which Rick seems to come and go without a word and to virtually ignore him, all his dealings being done with Felicity. When he is with her, or the girls, or even with Christopher, he is vocal and animated. *Strange,* thinks Edward. A new medium-sized greenhouse has suddenly appeared at the bottom end of the garden, bordering the paddock. Rachel and Harriet seem to be doing something within. Edward makes a detour past it and peers inside, the warm and humid earthy smells immediately envelope him.

'Runner beans, broad beans and peas,' says Rachel, popping seeds into trays.

'Lettuces, radishes and carrots,' says Harriet, doing likewise. 'Rick says we are stars.'

Wouldn't he just! He leaves them to it and closes the door.

James and Kylie are leaning on the paddock fence watching the hens.

'How d'you think they're doing?' says Edward, trying to show interest.

'Helen, Amy and Sarah aren't very happy,' says James, nodding at the three original buff Orpingtons who peck and scratch some distance away from the others. 'Cyril keeps trying to round them up, and when he's not looking, they sneak away again. It's so funny. We're taking some of the eggs down to Silverton market on Sunday. Peter Molwing's selling veg and says we can join him and get a feel for how the market works. Kylie's going to help and as soon as Mum's stuff grows, we'll have our own stall. Rick's been showing us how to start things off in the greenhouse. Yetti and Rach are sowing legumes, salad stuff and carrots. We're a bit late and disorganised this year, but—'

'Don't let it get in the way of your schoolwork. This is an important time,' says Edward, hearing his son's enthusiasm and worrying that he will be distracted.

'Don't worry Dad.'

Kylie smiles, but says nothing.

Edward doesn't think she has uttered an interesting word since James first brought her home. But she's pretty enough. *Wallpaper,* he thinks.

Edward can see Felicity in the field beyond, checking the new sheep. He waves, but she doesn't see him so he returns to the house, says hello to the dogs, grabs a slice of bread and hunk of cheese and darts upstairs to his PC to check his emails.

Marianne!

Of course he can check them from college, but it is against his principles to mix work and pleasure except when his home PC is down.

Marianne often writes on a Friday …

To: Edward Harvey
From: Marianne Hayward
Date: 11th April 2003, 19.20
Subject: Potatoes, Prostates and Panic Attacks!

Dear Edward,
I think not eating potatoes might be making me more lively!

Edward for a moment drifts into his shower fantasy, where the thought of an even livelier Marianne makes him hot. So far he has allowed himself to look, but not touch. It seems more respectful and less incriminating to keep her at arms' length, even in his dreams. He is concerned that things may get out of hand if he moves the boundaries.

He shakes his head and continues to read.

In addition to plum tomatoes (and I'm hesitant about mentioning this in an email!) Johnny says sex is good for the prostate, though I believe the research on this is mixed!

God! She's not making this easy!

It's been a difficult week at college. One of my students had a panic attack in class. She was in such a state – crying and saying she couldn't breathe; frightened because of tingling sensations in her arms. Classic symptoms, but I've never seen anyone in such a bad way. Even though I told her all the right things for controlling her breathing, it took one of our experts in yoga and first aid to calm her down. (Breathe in through the nose, deeply, and then more slowly, out through the mouth! Apparently the focus on the technique removes the focus from the negative symptoms!) When we talked afterwards I realised she was drowning under a mountain of pressure. I found myself telling her to stop worrying about work; that health is more important; that essays and deadlines could wait. Then I felt such a hypocrite, because in the next lesson, I was the one piling on the pressure, setting tests, demanding that targets should be met.
Do you remember when we were at Brocklebank and we had exams every summer? We were so young. It was the same miserable annual ritual until I finished my

degree. I remember the first summer of no exams and feeling so free. What do we do to our children? I know exams demonstrate a certain level of capability, but most of what we learn for them is lost.

There must be an easier way.

If I think this, should I be doing the job any more?

Best wishes,

Marianne

Best wishes?? A mistake or deliberate re-setting of boundaries?

To: Marianne Hayward
From: Edward Harvey:
Date: 12nd April 2003, 23.10
Subject: Re: Potatoes, Prostates and Panic Attacks!

Dear Marianne,

Perhaps I ought to give up potatoes too!! Felicity has procured the services of a local man called Rick and when I see him digging trenches, lopping trees and generally bounding around the place like one of our dogs, I feel old. I want to support her, but I'm not sure in what ways I can without becoming too involved.

The child-friendly alternatives to exams are continuous assessment and coursework. But people cheat – students, parents, even some teachers. And the internet has opened up a minefield for subterfuge. Exams may cause stress – and I agree there are too many of them – but at least they are objective.

Am sure your charges appreciate the efforts you make in the long run.

love

Edward

In the evening, after supper, when the children have melted away from the table, Felicity asks Edward what kind of day he's had. It is now the Easter holidays – late this year – but while Felicity is now a free woman, he still goes into work on odd days, not least to escape feeling guilty when he sees all that Rick is doing. He decides not to tell her about the possibility of being headhunted by Stancliffe University. Nothing may come of it; nothing can come of it.

Before he has finished giving her the censored version of his manoeuvres, she interrupts. 'Gianni's moved in above the Retreat and we're starting evening service three days a week after the weekend: Tuesdays, Thursdays and Saturdays, allowing plenty of time for planning in between. You will have to fend for yourself on those days – or wait for leftovers. We'll open more frequently when we're settled into a routine – including lunches. Also, I've ordered an incubator for hatching eggs, and a kiln.' She says this last part in the same tone that one might use for announcing that a new cooker is on the way.

'They're both going to be in the old milking parlour,' she continues. 'It means we'll soon have home-reared chickens and I can mass produce my pottery without having to rely on the community centre for firing.'

'Do you really think you'll make enough and sell enough to warrant the expense?'

'I've always wanted a kiln,' snaps Felicity. 'If I hadn't done a biology degree, I would have gone into the arts. But Mummy and Daddy said it was too risky and pushed me into the sciences. Time to speculate before I'm too old. There's the restaurant outlet and also the markets. Some have crafts as well as produce. And I can still use eBay for the odd piece. Olivia will use it as well. She would like to make stuff for Christmas presents and her vases are quite nice even if not in the same league as mine. Rick will do most of the re-build. He's so versatile.'

Edward again feels the twinge in an imprecise place that he is beginning to realise is jealousy. He detects a note of criticism in her voice. He imagines her telling Olivia, *'Rick can turn his hand to anything. Not like Ted. Ted has spent all his life in academia and the practical world is anathema to him. I have to deal with all the minor electrical and plumbing tasks, never mind the hoovering. When Ted puts up a shelf, I hide the valuables. But Rick is so versatile ...'* And Olivia will nod and simper and shake her bird's nest hair because she hangs on to every word of Felicity's.

'And,' adds Felicity, 'while Rick's doing the alterations, there's space enough for me to have an office as well.'

'Hope you haven't forgotten Killerton has National Trust covenants over all properties within the Estate.'

'When I applied to the Trust about the kitchen after Mummy died, I put in proposals for everything else as well. The rural surveyor has been very understanding and supportive. I just keep her informed about any adjustments to the plans. Most of the work is actually internal and they are only too happy that we are bringing the out-buildings into productive use that will ultimately benefit the community.'

'And council planning permission?'

'Granted.'

Edward considers telling her what he thinks of such devious underhand tactics but doesn't want the inevitable disagreement. Even if she had told him what she was doing – even if he had objected – he knows she would have gone ahead anyway. Interesting that he hasn't seen any of the notices or letters. She must've kept them hidden. Perhaps he was too wrapped up in his work. Perhaps he always has been and her independence is his creation.

Later in bed, he lies awake until the early hours, musing that perhaps he should be thinking of changing his life too.

Eventually he falls into a sleep of sorts, but it is the wrong sort of sleep for refreshing the body and he wakes wondering if he has been to sleep at all. He tosses and sighs, hoping perhaps Felicity will hear him, register that he is troubled and ask him what's wrong. But she remains soundly asleep, breathing deeply.

Towards dawn he has a dream in which he is at a social gathering in the grounds of an enormous dark stone house, with many pointed grey-tiled roofs, castellated turrets and a Gothic facade. He is young again – perhaps late teens or twenties – and Marianne is there, also fresh and young, thinner than when he saw her at the museum, and with longer hair. She weaves among elderly be-suited businessmen, in jeans and a t-shirt and although he tries to catch up with her, she is elusive. Trestle tables covered with white plates and stacked high with greasy-looking pastries are on a huge lawn backed by tall dark green pine trees, yet nobody is eating.

He follows her into the house where she appears seated on a sofa with chintzy covers in a fusty old-fashioned living room. It is dark and gloomy, full of old furniture and floral rugs. He doesn't speak to her, but thumps down beside her, squashing in between the arm of the sofa and her left hip. She shifts slightly to let him in, but keeps her upper arm in contact with his. He shivers and picks up a newspaper, aware of his breathing, aware of the closeness, of increasing passion.

Suddenly he throws down the paper and lunges at her with adolescent fervour, touching her face with his hand, feeling its youthful softness and then kissing her on the mouth. He is amazed when she responds, but then he panics as if this is something he shouldn't be doing; as if Felicity is somewhere in his life, though not present at the party.

'Mother might see us,' he says and pulls away.

Marianne stares into his eyes and says, 'You have nothing to fear from me.'

He wonders what she means, embraces her again, mumbles

about his mother catching them, that he will see her later; knowing that later means at night when he is sure she will welcome him into her four-poster bed with its crisp cotton sheets. She releases him, rises, glances over her shoulder as she walks away; a temptress.

He wakes, savours the dream for a second and tries unsuccessfully to return to its promise for the night.

Minutes pass and his mind begins to whir and click, all hope of slumber gone. *You have nothing to fear from me.* What did she mean by that? What did his subconscious want her to mean?

He analyses: might the house represent Brocklebank Hall? The schoolhouse was quite old and the cricket pitch was backed by fir trees. Did he wish to be young again? Did he wish he had known Marianne when she was young? Maybe, yes. But he wouldn't have known what to do with her even if he had, and she didn't seem the type to take the lead – except in dreams.

To Edward Harvey
From: Marianne Hayward
Date: 13th April 2003, 21.51
Subject: Re: Potatoes, Prostates and Panic Attacks!

Dear Edward,
Don't let this Rick guy get you down …
Think wine!
Marianne

Wine? Ah, wine! If only it were true.

14

Taryn is in a rush.

She has bolted home from her three-fifteen finish at school and left a trail of coat and books, bag and shoes on her way to the bedroom. There she opens the window to freshen the air and changes the double bed, bundling the old duvet cover and sheet straight into the washing machine and replacing them with crisp, freshly washed and ironed magenta bed linen. She plumps the pillows, shakes the duvet so it lies neatly, and arranges matching cushions on the top. Then she scurries around with a duster and an aerosol spray of polish.

In the living room she lights an oil burner on the glass dining table in the corner, adds some water and then a couple of drops each of ylang ylang, sandalwood and rose essential oil; a fool-proof mixture for relaxation and sexiness.

On the kitchen windowsill is the plant she uses as a prop when teaching *A Midsummer Night's Dream.* It is the wild pansy, *Love-in-idleness,* and she is pleased to see it is already blooming on her sunny windowsill:

> *Fetch me that flower; the herb I shew'd thee once;*
> *The juice of it on sleeping eye-lids laid,*
> *Will make or man or woman madly dote*
> *Upon the next live creature that it sees.*

'And with the juice of this I'll streak his eyes,' she murmurs, cutting a few delicate green sprigs and purple flowers and pounding them in a pestle and mortar. Then she adds water, and leaves it

on the side. She knows this is silly and extreme, but she revels in drama and the possibility of magic.

Then she dashes into a hot shower with liberal amounts of scented, soapy gels and a razor. *(Should have gone for a waxing session!)* But for all that she is vain, she is also reluctant to spend money in salons.

With wet hair wrapped in a towel turban, she changes into a matching set of black lacy underwear and ten denier stockings. *(Spare pair in hand-bag to be on the safe side.)* Then a little black dress with a low scoop neck, cut just below the knee, and high-heeled shoes, *(spiky stilettos – no pain, no gain)*. A simple gold chain and her favourite unicorn earrings complete the look. She is clearly on a mission.

Sitting in front of her dressing table mirror, she cleanses her face and applies make-up for the night time, even though it is only four o'clock. Primer, followed by brush on minerals foundation; then dark, smoky eyes with lashings of mascara and holly berry glossed lips. She makes a few artistic strokes with an expensive concealer stick, hiding lines and shadows that betray her age.

Then mousse on her hair, and with head upside down, she sets about drying with a very fierce hair dryer. She is well-practised in creating her trademark spiky halo.

Finally, the all-important temptress perfume which she sprays into the room, and then walks through, adding extra dabs behind her ears.

A quick flurry removing untidy items, a light-weight black velvet jacket to finish her outfit, and she is off.

Off for an assignation that has the potential to affect several lives, in addition to her own.

This week Edward is doing an earlier five-thirty session and when she arrives at the British Museum after a couple of train delays, she is too late to go in without causing a disturbance. But she never said she would go to the lecture anyway, just that she would meet him. This will give her time to have something to eat and to compose herself.

Forty minutes later, she is hovering outside the lecture theatre, pretending to study a picture on the wall. Eventually his audience begins to trail out, excitedly chattering about what they have seen and heard. It is some minutes before he appears, his hair a little more ruffled than she remembers, a rather sexy evening shadow darkening his jaw.

'As promised,' she says, springing out at him from behind a group of Americans.

'I thought you weren't coming,' he says, smiling.

'Do you need to eat?' She thinks he looks pleased to see her and notes that this time his shirt is white and his suit is grey. *Much better!*

'I ate earlier,' he smiles again.

'In that case, I know a wine bar near here.' She grins and leads the way down staircases, through the Great Court and out of the building, glancing over her shoulder, excitement in her eyes.

Edward follows meekly.

In the wine bar they find a quiet corner. The room is decorated in green and dark red and the lighting is subdued and flattering. A cross-section of ages and cultures, some smart and some casual, line the bar and sit chattering at the wooden circular tables with wrought iron legs. A juke box in the corner plays popular songs and the atmosphere is lively.

'So,' says Edward, settling down with a glass of red wine, 'are you going to reveal the mystery?'

'What mystery?' asks Taryn innocently.

'"*Targeted, yes; purpose debatable*," I believe were the words you used.'

'You remembered.' She plays for time.

121

'Hardly something one would forget.'

'I had to come up with something intriguing to attract your attention,' she says. 'After all, you meet loads of people in your job – why should you want to talk to me?'

'Why indeed.'

'If I said that I am a mystic and feel you have a troubled soul, would I be right?'

Edward gives her a long stare before looking away, embarrassed. 'That's a shade personal considering we've only just met.' He shifts slightly in his seat.

'Okay, I'm not a mystic.' Taryn detects his unease. *Gently ... Gently ...*

'So how do you know, then?'

'I'm a woman; I feel things.'

'So you know my wife's having a midlife crisis and turning our house into a small farm?' There is bitterness in Edward's voice and he looks almost surprised at the way in which he has spoken.

'I guessed as much,' says Taryn. 'About the crisis – not the farm.'

'Because you're a woman or a mystic?'

'You have the classic symptoms of a man whose wife has become less attentive.'

'"Less attentive" is an understatement. I have almost ceased to exist. I suspect she may be going menopausal, but she hasn't said, and I don't like to ask in case she takes it as criticism.'

'I'm a good listener,' says Taryn as compassionately as her acting ability allows, amazed by his candour after everything Marianne has said about him. *Just another man who can't wait to off-load onto anyone who's willing to listen.* She wonders that perhaps he isn't so different after all.

Edward pours out his woes about Felicity.

So this is what Marianne wasn't going to tell me, thinks Taryn as he tells of mother-in-law popping her clogs, the dosh and the restaurant, the zoo, and even the hints that all is not well in the bedroom. She feels smug and nods in an understanding way in all the right places.

'I'm sorry, I shouldn't burden you with all this. I don't know why I'm telling you. It's sometimes easier telling a stranger than people closer to home. People tell me all kinds of secrets when I'm travelling on trains.'

'Is that what we are? Strangers?'

'Virtual.'

'Do you normally join strangers for drinks in wine bars?'

'No.'

'We must at least be acquaintances, then.'

'Perhaps.'

'Imagine that!'

'Bizarre,' says Edward, laughing.

'Have you told anybody else how you feel about Felicity and her plans? Anyone you can get on your side who might have influence? Close friends of the family, perhaps?' Oh she is so clever, so cunning; so good at fishing that she always lands the fish she wants.

Edward pauses, breathes audibly, takes a drink and pauses again, licking his lips, staring at her as if he is unsure whether or not to say more. 'A special friend,' he says at last.

'What sort of special?'

'She's married too.'

'Ah-ha.'

'It's all perfectly above board.'

'Would you wish it otherwise?' Taryn probes, wanting to know if she has a rival.

'It's not my style.'

'Are we quite sure about that?' She takes a sip of wine and gazes at him over the rim of the glass, her eyes holding his.

'We are.'

Every cell in Taryn's brain is on the alert, processing each word and movement, stalking her prey with the subtlety of a cat; inching closer, freezing, watching, waiting for the moment to pounce.

'Does she know Felicity?'

'No.'

'What did she say?'

'To be patient. To find a different way of being ...'

Typical Marianne! So philosophical. So sensible when giving advice to others. Useless when applying it to herself. Was this it? The moment she should seize? 'Could meeting me be the different way?'

'It's certainly different.'

'In a good way?'

Edward smiles, but doesn't answer. 'Enough about me. What about your life story? You must have a story too or I don't suppose you would be here either.'

Taryn is disarmed. The pounce that was going to happen ends instead with an embarrassed pause, energy dissipated. The cat turns its head and swishes its tail at the lost opportunity. She must wait. She hadn't planned to reveal her past, but something about Edward's vulnerability makes her break her long vow of silence and she tells him about her violent father.

Edward has surprised himself: *following her to the bar like some fluffy gosling behind its mother.* He went because he was curious and because she has the same commanding tone as Felicity; a tone demanding compliance. He chose to ignore the faint alarm bells, aware the alcohol was loosening his reserve; that he had already said far more than he should. Even when the warning lights flashed, they were so far away, he barely noticed them. He knew the conversation was heading into dangerous territory, but he is an expert at dealing with flirting and is confident that his tossing the ball onto her side of the net will ensure safe passage.

He listens with the attentiveness of a good therapist, making no judgements, frowning slightly, shaking his head at the moments of crisis. He cannot help but be moved by her story. She tells it so well that he sees a sweet little girl brought to her knees by the force of her father's slaps; sees her pleading with him to leave her mother alone; sees her crying with distress as she experiences the conflicting emotions of love and hate.

Time moves on. People come and go from the wine bar but Edward and Taryn keep on talking, liberal amounts of wine freeing their inhibitions, months of resentment in Edward's case, and years in Taryn's, tumbling and gushing from their mouths in unstoppable torrents.

Eventually Edward sits back, takes a deep breath and gives a long sigh. 'Unless I catch the eight-thirty-five from Paddington, I won't be home until the early hours of the morning. Much as I am enjoying our conversation, I shall have to dash.'

He feels the beat of time, but doesn't attempt to fill the silence.

Taryn pauses and looks down, innocently. 'Well, you could always come back to my flat and stay the night. I have a spare room. If Felicity wouldn't mind ... Sadly I haven't a husband to make it seem more respectable.'

Edward is dimly aware of a fast beating heart and of paths diverging; choices to make. This is it; the moment when a small action may transform the future in a significant way. The moment when, if lost, may never occur again. The noise of the people in the bar, the rhythms of the music from the juke box, the alcohol in his bloodstream, all create an incendiary bomb in his head. Even if Taryn isn't Marianne, she is still drop dead gorgeous – to use one of Conrad's sayings. He wishes it was

Marianne. Marianne has crept under his skin. He is comfortable at the thought of Marianne, but apprehensive – scared even – by Taryn. And Marianne is an impossibility. He is captivated by Taryn, but the response is physical and not emotional.

He is tired and a little drunk. What would he do if he were sober? He would run away, that's what. He would thank her for the offer and say how much he had enjoyed talking to her. He would give her the impression that nothing 'extra-curricular' had entered his head and both of them could leave without losing face.

But still he hesitates. The thought of not having to trek across London is very appealing. He is hurt by Felicity's disinterestedness, frustrated by abstinence, charmed by Marianne who isn't here; aroused by this tiny stranger with the amazing hair, whose manner reminds him of Felicity; the Felicity who wanted him. It felt so long ago.

He looks at his watch. It is already late. He has drunk too much and will have to get a taxi home from Exeter station. He will probably miss his train and the last one won't get him home until after two so he will have to find somewhere to crash in town. Why not go back with Taryn? He can stay in the spare room, sleep, leave very early, catch the seven-thirty from Paddington, and arrive at the university in time for his eleven o'clock lecture. No hassle; no harm done.

But he knows accepting her invitation will send the wrong message and the sensible voice that had carried him through most of his life says, *you don't know who she is. She could be dangerous.*

Yet there is something about the way she speaks to him that makes him feel as if she has known him for years. She is Felicity in a different package; so direct. If he said no, he'd probably never see her again; never get another chance like this. He was always being careful; making the right decision where other women were concerned.

'Okay,' says his mouth. 'Felicity's used to me staying over after lectures. I'll phone her.'

Taryn gives him one of her biggest smiles.

When they walk towards the underground, she takes his arm and he doesn't flinch. When she leans close while seated next to him on the train from Victoria, he is drawn into her web.

Once back at the flat, Taryn lights candles and the oil burner, and puts music on the CD player. She opens a bottle of red wine, pours two glasses and hands one to Edward. He hovers and then sits on the sofa while Taryn perches on the arm of a chair, seeming not quite settled. He nods towards the *trompe l'oeil*. 'Unusual,' he says.

Pulp's 'Disco 2000' plays and Edward closes his eyes, the exertions of the day catching up with him. Taryn at first doesn't interrupt his reverie, but he is conscious of her slipping down beside him and leaning close.

He listens to the words with more concentration than he has ever done before and memories of school and university dance in his brain and he is swept along with the nostalgia. Next comes Sony and Cher belting out 'I Got You Babe' and then 'Days' by the Kinks.

'Happy tunes,' whispers Taryn. 'Guaranteed to lighten the heart.'

'But strange bedfellows,' says Edward, still with his eyes closed.

'Like us.'

'Bedfellows?'

'If you like.'

His muscles tense; his eyes open. Of course he must've guessed what she was planning, but now it is becoming a reality, he panics. 'You said you had a spare room.'

'I have – but I was just giving you the options. Trying not to seem too forward.'

He looks around the room. On the wall is a silver picture frame containing a silhouette of the top half of a naked woman with small pointed breasts and Van de Graff Generator hair. *Such confidence!*

'I also have a certificate for aromatherapy massage,' says Taryn, filling the pause. 'Very good for de-stressing.'

'Is this another option you're offering me?'

'I'm an options kind of woman. Another option is a mug of cocoa and a slice of toast. Why don't you think about the options while I go and change?'

'I'm very tired,' he says, suddenly aware that he is.

'Have a snooze, I won't be long.'

Edward thinks about her taking off her dress and revealing the black lacy bra that he glimpsed on their first meeting and again tonight. He is quickly aroused, but these days he is used to ignoring it. Would he like to? *Yes!*

Then he closes his eyes again and drifts. He can hear the music, but part of his mind has escaped onto another plane, the beginnings of sleep. He is brought back to wakefulness by something cold on his eyelids. His eyes snap open; he is groggy and can't focus properly. But there is Taryn leaning over him in a long, slinky, red crushed velvet dress that reaches to the floor.

'Thought this might seem less intimidating,' she says, smoothing the dress with her hands. 'Perhaps you would like to remove your jacket and tie as a similar gesture of good will.'

Edward obliges.

Taryn twirls round the room and swings her hips in rhythm to the music. Cockney Rebel's 'Make Me Smile' is now playing. She touches her neck flirtatiously; stares him in the eye; says nothing.

He looks at her, transfixed. *Is this what it's like at a lap-dancing club?*

She holds out her hands to him, inviting him to join her;

she smiles, she teases, she beckons until he finds himself propelled from the sofa, taking her hands and gradually being drawn in closer, being wrapped by her tiny arms, expert fingers sliding over his neck, his hair, his back and then ...

One by one his shirt buttons are being undone; the heat of her hand against his skin; how good it feels to be caressed, to be wanted again.

And then she moves below and he is helpless.

In the middle of the night, Edward is woken by a police siren. He wonders where he is; wonders why he feels sick. Beside him there is an almost circular mound under the duvet and a few fronds of hair sprouting upward towards the pillow. The mound seems to be asleep and he tries not to wake her when he goes to the bathroom, tripping on a high-heeled shoe, slipping slightly on a satin underskirt, feeling his way in the half-light, unsure of where he is going. Trying one door, a cupboard, and then another. *Bloody hell ... What have I done? Mad fool ... Felicity ... Felicity. Oh God! Idiot!*

He recalls the night before; the fumbling with the condom that Taryn insisted on even though he'd had the snip. He hadn't used one for years. They ended up laughing. He remembers how it was and there is also a sense of achievement, of deep sexual satisfaction; of new experiences beyond the realms of his usual predictable conservatism. But now his thoughts are of his headache and of how he is going to extract himself from what suddenly seems a very awkward situation. Guilt is already making its presence felt. He wishes he had said no; wishes he were at home.

In the bedroom, Taryn has also been woken by the siren and she hears Edward leave the room and then return. She doesn't stir. She reflects and analyses. She too has experienced something different. Gentleness and kindness; vulnerability, selflessness. Never traits in any of her previous conquests, because she always chose men like her father, men she couldn't love; experienced men who were used to getting their way without an emotional connection. She wriggles her toes as if checking she is awake and alive. Her arm has gone numb, but she dare not move. The dark hours might lead to doubts; to reflections she doesn't want to see.

In the morning the alarm goes off very early so Edward can catch the train back to Exeter in time for his lecture.

They speak little as they each shower then dress. Taryn decides she must break the news she's been withholding. Any later and there is a danger of a diplomatic incident with her best friend. If he told Marianne about Felicity, he might also tell her about this night of passion. She is sitting at her dressing table with her back to him, but she keeps catching glimpses in the mirror.

'Oh, by the way,' she says, lightly patting her hair to check it is appropriately electrified, 'I know I should have told you last night – but I didn't want to interrupt the flow, and then it just slipped my mind – but we have a friend in common. Marianne. Marianne Hayward. I believe she's an old classmate of yours?' She makes it sound unimportant, like forgetting to put the rubbish out.

Edward is sitting on the bed and stops dead in the middle of tying his shoelaces. The colour appears to drain from him and he looks at Taryn with disbelief.

'Marianne? Hayward? You know Marianne?' He sounds aghast.

'Yes. We're best friends.' She turns and stands in front of him, hands on hips, daring him to be angry.

His face darkens. 'My God! So all of this? Does she know?'

'She knows nothing.'

Edward makes a wild gesture with his hands. He looks utterly perplexed. 'Then why, Taryn? Why?'

'She said you were wonderful. I wanted to check. Is that a crime?'

Edward gives a rueful smile. 'Did you know I was referring to her last night when I said I had told someone else about Felicity and me?' A sharpness has entered his usually gentle voice.

'Yes.'

'So why didn't you say something then?'

'Because I would have had to justify myself – like now.'

'She's your best friend. Had I known that, I wouldn't be here.'

'Just think what you'd have missed.' Taryn is hurt, she sits beside him on the bed, changing with the speed of a chameleon from the dominant to the submissive.

'The way I'm feeling now, perhaps it is too big a price.'

'She won't hear about it from me, if that's what's worrying you.'

'I have … feelings for her,' he says.

Taryn is startled and jealous. Marianne already has a doting husband. She doesn't need someone else thinking about her in that kind of way. It is greedy. 'You hardly know her.'

'I know her … better than I know you. But that's something else you mustn't divulge. It's at an intellectual level.'

'Pretentious crap,' said Taryn, privately thinking that this is almost how Marianne describes her feelings for Edward.

'Call it what you will, but it's true.'

'I don't think you know what you think or feel at the moment. You've been so rattled by Felicity's apparent defection that you've lost your sense of self.'

'So all this was part of some plan, then?'

'Guilty as charged,' says Taryn, deciding that there's no point in making excuses.

'What a fool I've been.'

'Lighten up, Edward. It was just a night of fun. Nobody died.'

'I am not a "Nights of Fun" type of person.'

'Then perhaps you *are* a fool,' says Taryn crossly. 'If it was okay last night, it's okay this morning. Me knowing Marianne is irrelevant.'

'Did Marianne tell you about Felicity? Is that how you knew we were having problems? Nothing to do with being a woman or a mystic? Did you think I was fair game?'

'Marianne wouldn't tell me anything. She's good at keeping secrets. She won't break a confidence.'

'She has more integrity than you then.'

'You could say.'

'Last night you told me about the betrayal by your father? D'you remember what that felt like? How d'you think Marianne would feel if she knew you'd gone behind her back like this?'

'It's no worse than you and Felicity.'

'I'm not proud of that, believe me. But it's not the same thing at all.'

'Or you and Marianne? I don't suppose Felicity would be too pleased to know you have feelings for another woman.'

Edward is silenced by this.

Taryn feels the tide has turned; that she has just scored some points. 'Sex is just sex, after all. Love is much more of a threat.'

'I didn't say "love".'

'Whatever,' says Taryn, intending to provoke.

'Look, I haven't time for this. I'm going to have to go. Have you any juice? I'll grab something to eat at the station. And thanks for putting me up for the night. For your hospitality.' Edward is as ever courteous, but there is a touch of sarcasm in his voice. He puts on his jacket and makes for the kitchen.

'Will I see you again?' asks Taryn, following him, pouring two glasses of cranberry juice from the carton in the fridge.

'I doubt it.'

'We had a good time.'

'We did,' he says without emotion.

'You still have a few more lectures in London.'

'Things are different now.'

'Marianne?'

'Marianne. Not only Marianne – I have a wife. This isn't me. I don't do this.'

'You just did. And I'd like to—'

'Taryn, my head's in a mess and I really have to go.'

'Forgive my deception. I meant no harm.'

Edward raises his eyebrows.

'I've lent you a bed for the night, that's all.'

'Bye, Taryn. Let's just leave it at that.'

And he walks down the path, heading down Coppercone Lane to Beckenham Junction.

'I hope you get back in time for your lecture,' Taryn hears herself whispering, but her words are lost on the spring breeze. She shudders and turns back to get ready for school.

The flat seems strangely empty. Emptier than it has ever felt before. She is uneasy. Edward isn't like the others guys.

I'm a crap friend.

His words hurt.

Later, on the seven-thirty from Paddington, Edward is trying to catch up on sleep. He has eaten a bacon sandwich, drunk a cup of decaffeinated tea, mentally run through the things he needs to do at college before his lecture. But even though he is so tired, the precious sleep won't come. Round and round his thoughts churn, tangled like clothes in a washing machine.

Over and over again he plays the scene with Taryn, furious with himself and agonising over the moments when different decisions would have freed him from his current torment.

And what was all that stuff he said about Marianne? He wasn't even aware he had those sorts of feelings for her. It must surely be that he had overplayed his interest to try to deter Taryn. Either way, he cannot stop thinking about her; romanticising her; allowing her to divert him from concerns about Felicity. He cannot let this go on.

Hollowness settles in his heart, not only the guilt at betraying his wife for the first time, but now the precious fantasy has been tainted too.

15

When Edward arrives back home on Friday afternoon after his eventful trip to London, he finds Felicity in the orchard with Rick, setting up a couple of bee hives by the hawthorn hedge that runs down the side bordering the paddock. For a moment, guilt dissipates. He takes a deep breath and stops to prepare his reaction. *Bloody bees now, for God's sake!* How many more things are going to materialise without warning? Is she doing this to provoke him? He suspects not, but it riles him all the same.

He is confused. He likes bees. He admires their community spirit, co-operation and industry. He even likes the idea of bees in hives and luscious dripping golden honey oozing from the waxen hexagons and onto thick slices of wholemeal toast at breakfast time. It is bees without consultation that he doesn't like; bees without a by your leave.

Rick is holding a hammer and some nails and he and Felicity converse for a moment or two, glancing up at the sun and then at the fruit trees, before adjusting the positions of the hives.

He's so bloody versatile he can even make fucking beehives!

When Felicity sees Edward, she stops and comes towards him, grasping a few strands of escaped hair and trying to secure them with a clip. She greets him with a beaming smile, hitching up her old denim jeans that are now too small for her.

'Aren't these just great? Rick's been so busy.'

A 'How are you?' would be nice, he thinks. *A hug, a kiss, a promise for the weekend. A guarantee of touch and warmth; a reminder of the important things in life; an erasure of all the week's hassles; an apology for the bees.* He keeps his displeasure within.

'I'm impressed,' he says truthfully. 'Our own Deer Orchard Honey.'

'And not just that. Bees are having a bad time at the moment. The environmental consequence of being without them is enormous. Their value to the economy is huge. I like the idea of doing a bit to help.'

Edward also feels he is having a bad time and wishes her concerns were closer to home.

'Hugh says they make a massive difference to the fruit crop.'

'Won't it be a bit late for this year?' asks Edward, surveying the pink and white blossom on the trees, reminding him of a Monet painting.

'This first year is bound to be a bit out of synch while I get everything together. It's bad luck to buy bees so we have to wait until a swarm becomes available. I've been in touch with the local co-ordinator at Silverton and we should have at least one within the month. I've also signed up for a course.' Felicity is clearly brimming with excitement.

'What's the likelihood of being stung?'

'Very likely – even with all the space suit gear – but apparently you become immune in time. You just have to be careful not to antagonise them.'

'Hope you do a better job on them than you're doing on me then.' The displeasure creeps out before he can smother it.

Felicity looks at him in shock and gives him a furious glare that is usually reserved only for the children.

'I'll take the dogs out,' he says hurriedly, backing off before she can say anything.

At the house the children are scattered. James and Rachel are doing homework in their rooms. Harriet is carefully ironing a sparkly top in the kitchen and Christopher is playing with Meg. The spaniels, Clint and Gryke, are asleep on the rug in the living room, but when they hear Edward, they greet him with wagging tails and hopeful expressions.

Glad someone is pleased to see me!

'Dad,' says Harriet in wheedling 'I-want-something' tones. 'Would you take me to Beth's tonight?'

'Have you asked your mother?' Edward feels impossibly tired and after his walk, wants to have a bath and settle down for a quiet evening with a glass of wine.

'Mum says she'll pick me up, but to ask you to take me. She says she has menus to write after she's seen Gianni.'

'James?'

'James is taking Kylie to see a film.'

'He can take you on the way.'

'Dad!'

'Your mum wants us to save energy. It's wasteful making two trips when one will suffice.'

'Dad! Please!'

'No, Yetti. Not tonight. I need to rest.'

Harriet scowls, unused to her father saying no.

Usually when he's at home he is completely accommodating when it comes to lifts. He feels guilty that his teenagers are away from the hubbub of a town or city. They don't complain, but that might be because he and Felicity provide such a reliable taxi service.

He puts Meg on a lead because she is still too small to be trusted, whistles for the other two dogs and sets out down the garden and across the paddock where the goats graze and the hens scratch. He climbs over the stile at the bottom that leads into the lane, and then through a gate to the fields beyond. The Molwings have given permission to walk the dogs on their land as long as they are put on leads if the fields contain animals. It means that for the most part, the dogs can run free which gives them more exercise and takes less time.

It is a glorious spring evening and the gently rolling Devon countryside looks lush and green. With only the dogs for company, Edward is able to muse on the happenings of the previous forty-eight hours.

When he stepped off the train at Exeter station that morning, he decided to think of the experience with Taryn as a strange dream and to try to forget about it. Extensive analysis during the journey had only made him feel worse.

But when he retrieved his emails after his lecture, Taryn's name appeared in the inbox. He had thought about deleting it straight away, but curiosity got the better of him.

Cunning bitch must've looked me up on the university website, he thought.

To: Edward Harvey
From: Taryn Danielli
Date: 25th April 2003, 8.15
Subject: Thank you!

Hello Edward! Caro mio!
Hope u r ok!
Worry not! Best night I've had 4 years!
Hope 2 c u again.
Taryn
xxx

He had read it twice; felt momentary self-satisfaction at the compliment, quickly replaced by guilt at his unaccustomed infidelity. He read it a third time, was irritated by the text-speak, angered again by Taryn's failure to tell him exactly who she was, and annoyed that he had allowed such a thing to happen. He was also distinctly uneasy at the possibility that Marianne might find out. He deleted it. He would not reply.

At least she doesn't have my phone numbers or my home email address.

Then Gemma had appeared in their common doorway with a pile of letters in her hand. She seemed to have put blonde stripes in her hair since he last saw her, perhaps in an effort to be more modern. They were overly obvious and not in keeping with her mode of dress. He decided not to comment.

'You were late this morning,' she said lightly. 'Not like you.'

He was feeling tetchy and hadn't wanted any questions. 'Have there been any calls while I've been away?'

She recomposed her face into seriousness. 'A Patrick Shrubsole from Stancliffe, London, and he said he'd call again next week, and it was nothing urgent.'

Must be about the chair.

Then Edward had picked up Conrad on his way for some lunch at the staff canteen. Much as he would like to have Conrad's take on his eternal quadrangle, he couldn't risk anyone at the university knowing the truth. Okay, so he had told Conrad about Taryn's existence and what she'd said, but he never believed he would be seduced, despite Conrad's teasing. After all, he is unseducable; everybody says so. He had acted out of character, and after all the years of finding it easy to resist temptation, he can't understand his transgression. But then he had never been unhappy before. There may lay the difference. He remembered the Franklin quotation: *'Three may keep a secret if two of them are dead.'* Only he must know about Taryn.

So when over a fish pie, Conrad asked, 'Did that Van de Graaff bird turn up then?' Edward had shaken his head in an ambiguous way and said, 'I don't suppose I'll ever see her again, but it was weird at the time.'

'Such a waste,' said Conrad jokily. 'That's two you've let slip through your hands in almost as many weeks. You must be losing it, mate.'

Now walking the familiar paths across the fields, he wishes he could turn the clock back; wishes it felt the same as it had last week; that he didn't have this horrible sick feeling. He also wishes he could talk to Marianne. She would give him good advice. She told him to find a different way. Could Taryn have been the different way? Of course Marianne wouldn't approve of that. What she didn't say was go and fuck my best friend. Would she have minded if it was someone else? He realises he wants her to mind.

She said you were wonderful … Was that true, or a Tarynism; an exaggeration? He doesn't feel so wonderful now.

And as if there wasn't enough to worry about, now he'd annoyed Felicity. The thought of bees being antagonised makes him smile. He couldn't resist the jibe. *Such perfectly timed sarcasm.*

Yet he isn't generally sarcastic.

After his walk, and establishing that James is going to take Harriet to her friend's, he runs a hot bath and pours in something turquoise of Rachel's that contains lavender and says it is good for de-stressing. He doesn't usually take early evening baths either. Indeed, he prefers the speed and immediacy of showers. But anything to keep away from Felicity. She's meeting with Gianni, but will be back soon to prepare supper. There will be consequences from his daring to speak to her in such a way.

It's true he shouldn't have said anything in front of Rick, but he probably didn't hear as they were a few paces away from him and he had his head in a hive.

The foam rises in peaks like lightly beaten egg white and he steps in, appreciating the cool soft bubbles and then the hot water. It is almost too hot, but he bears the pain like a hair shirt, keeping still until it is comfortable enough to move.

He begins talking to Felicity in his head, justifying his actions, his words, even though it is a conversation of truths that will never be said.

Connection ... That's what's missing. We don't connect any more. Mentally or physically. One of those would be nice. Is two being greedy? For so long I loved you Felicity. I still do. You don't extinguish twenty years with a few months of alienation.

You spend more time with Rick than you do with me. Is it his muscles that turn you on? Or the fact that he can talk 'plant and sheep and hen and bee' like Hugh? Are you bored with bones and artefacts and mazes? Were you ever interested in my work, or did you just pretend to be because you knew it was the way to win me over? You're a clever woman, Felicity, you can talk the talk of any subject if you so wish. I've heard you with our friends over dinner, stroking egos till the men are all puffed up like cock pheasants shaking their flamboyant tails at you. I've heard them make flirtatious comments and then say to me, 'You're a lucky man Ted; you've a good woman there.' I've been so proud to have you as my wife and I knew you wouldn't stray.

This life of ours has suited you fine for twenty years, but now this money's turned your head. You don't need me any more ...

'You don't need me any more,' he breathes the words aloud, a sudden realisation of a most disturbing kind, and he sinks down low in the water until all but his face is submerged.

After his bath, he sits at his computer, dealing with the daily flood of emails; reminders about family birthdays from his mother, suggestions from his agent about a maze book, messages from his publisher who has also been in touch with his agent, and a request from the Isles of Scilly Museum that he might consider a short lecture tour round the islands during the summer holidays at the peak of the tourist season. That looks interesting. He flags the message.

Nothing from Marianne this weekend. He is disappointed and concerned. Usually he waits for her to send an email first, to initiate a conversation. It is the lazy way, he knows. But he is so busy ... And he finds it difficult to think of new and interesting things to say. She has no problem with that. He can't tell her about Taryn; can't tell her about the possibility of being headhunted because he is sworn to secrecy. *I wonder if she knows anything about bees?*

To: Marianne Hayward
From: Edward Harvey
Date: 25th April 2003, 18.42
Subject: Bees

Dear Marianne,
Felicity has set up two bee hives in the orchard and we are awaiting a swarm as soon as one becomes available. Felicity says one should never buy bees. (Not quite sure why!) I don't know where all this is going to stop. Every time I come home there seem to be more animals! Am trying not to be confrontational – to go with the flow – as you suggested, but it is against my nature not to be proactive about matters concerning the house and land, so am finding it difficult. Have intimated that she is antagonising me and have taken refuge. A confrontation looks likely. This was not meant to happen.
Hope you are well.
love
Edward

He waits until Rachel calls before going downstairs to supper. If the children are present, it is unlikely Felicity will make any reference to the Orchard Incident.

They sit round the dining room table in uncommon silence considering Edward is there. Usually all manner of topics are hotly debated when he is at home for a family meal in the evening. Felicity casts him an occasional pointed glance which he chooses to ignore and Harriet alternately sulks and scowls. Rachel tries to talk about Gianni upon whom she seems to be developing a crush and Christopher tucks into the chicken cacciatore with gusto, oblivious to the atmosphere.

At length, Edward speaks. 'This is tasty.'

'Gianni's version,' says Felicity. 'I told you he was good.'

This seems to restore normality.

'Rachel, are you still seeing that geek Damien or Daniel?' says Harriet.

'I like geeks. At least they talk about stuff other than themselves,' says Rachel.

'But you wouldn't marry one,' pushes Harriet, as if wanting a reaction. Edward thinks her acerbic nature masks jealousy of her sister's attractiveness.

'Why not?'

'So embarrassing.'

'How, "embarrassing"?' asks James. 'Specify … Details … How are they more embarrassing than you?'

Harriet bristles, touches the stud in her nose and then fingers the little dark plaits that cover her head, as if in silent recognition of what James is alluding to. 'Moi, embarrassing? At least I'm not dating a plank.'

'Your dad was a geek when I met him,' says Felicity. 'A good-looking geek, but a geek nonetheless. Geeks are very marriageable.'

Edward hears his name. Not Ted this time, but his other name. *Dad.* He's sure she uses it more than she used to, placing him in the role of father rather than husband; desexualising him. 'Marriageable?' he says, imagining being on a list of those

143

who are and those who are not, hurt by the geek reference – no doubt a pay-back for the comment in the orchard.

'Whatever,' says Felicity in the tone of her teenage daughters.

'What's wrong with geeks, Yetti?' continues Edward.

'Geeks are so not cool.' Harriet glares at him, presumably still annoyed that he won't give her a lift after supper. She has been called Yetti since she was born. It is a term of endearment, but now she is almost fifteen it is a source of huge irritation.

'What she means,' says Rachel, 'is that geeks don't listen to her kind of music or have piercings and tattoos.'

'I wonder if Dad's Fanclub is a geek,' says Harriet, now deliberately provocative.

'She's a girl, idiot,' says James.

'Woman,' says Felicity.

'From what I know, she is not a geek,' says Edward.

'You can be a girl-geek,' says Rachel. 'Michael Bobbinton's sister and her friends have started a girl-geek club at school. Only they don't call it that. Officially they're *The Feminist Computer Society.*'

'Surely they don't allow something so blatantly discriminatory?' says Edward.

Rachel says, 'It's not official. It's an underground society. In any case, if it wasn't for the discrimination, there'd be no need for the society.'

Afterwards Edward escapes once more to his computer, this time to write another article on mazes, and also in the optimistic hope that Marianne has replied to his email.

She hasn't, and unease ripples through him.

'So,' says Felicity when he is in bed and she comes into the room and he can't avoid being alone with her any more. 'It's no good pretending to be asleep. What was that all about, before, in the orchard? I'm antagonising you, did you say?' She sounds cross. Edward now knows what the children must feel like when she goes into one.

He emerges slowly from the warmth of the duvet, pretending not to hear. 'What, Flick? I'm so knackered. Can't it wait until morning?'

'No. It – can – *not* – wait!' she says in staccato, pausing by the bed with hands on hips. 'Explain! How am I antagonising you?' She begins the process of undressing, methodically removing jumper and jeans and folding them over a chair.

'Oh God, Flick, it's all these changes. The animals … It's happening too quickly for me. You don't ask if it's okay with me; you just do it.'

'But you like animals.'

He hesitates. This is true. 'Okay, it's not just the animals. It's everything. The restaurant, the kiln, you giving up your job so suddenly, the beehives, the garden makeover, Rick, Gianni.'

'No point in bothering you unnecessarily. I don't need you to help me decide what to do. None of it will get in your way, so I don't see why you would object.'

'You seem less available. We don't connect any more,' he adds, remembering his thoughts in the bath.

'Ah! So now we're getting somewhere. You object to me having the life that I've always wanted.' She takes her blue towelling dressing gown from the back of the door and puts it over her underwear, tying the belt with sharp, determined movements.

'I never knew this was what you wanted.'

Felicity disappears to the bathroom. Edward can hear the familiar order in which she goes through her nightly ablution ritual. Electric toothbrush, lavatory flush, shower. At least she doesn't come to bed smelling of sheep and compost.

'We talked about the restaurant almost from when we first

met,' she says, reappearing after a few minutes looking damp and glowing.

'Yes, but a distant dream and not all this extra stuff tagged on.'

'It wouldn't have been possible without Mummy's money. There was no point in having impossible dreams before.' She sits at her dressing table, unpins her hair and begins to comb out the snags from a day in the wind.

Edward can see her face looking back at him from the mirror, still pretty, especially with all the fresh air. 'I thought we were a partnership.'

'We are.'

'Partners discuss. We've always discussed everything. Now you're always discussing things with Rick.'

'Rick is working for me.' Felicity says, taking a brush to the dappling waves of brown and grey.

For me, not us, thinks Edward. 'You don't have to spend so much time talking to him.'

'And when do you have time to talk to me about my plans? You've just made it clear you're not interested.'

'That's unfair.'

'Are you jealous of Rick?'

Felicity climbs into bed and Edward momentarily thinks about Taryn's enthusiasm and feels his stomach contract. It wasn't long since Felicity would slither towards him for a cuddle and a kiss before they went to sleep. 'Why should I be jealous – he's almost half your age.'

'Not true, actually.' She turns towards him, eyes ablaze. 'Are you saying I'm getting too old to attract the likes of Rick?'

The warning lights blink, but still he continues. 'He has a reputation.'

'I can look after myself.'

'And the girls?'

'He wouldn't dare.'

Edward isn't so sure, but this is getting way out of hand. He's not used to quarrelling with Felicity. Maybe sometime in their early years he learnt not to because he knew the way she could be when provoked. He decides to change tack.

'Aren't you interested in what *I* do any more?'

'Don't be so childish.'

'Felicity,' he says as calmly as he can. 'I think you're getting too carried away too quickly. Why not wait and see how one of your enterprises works out before embarking on another?'

'They are all interlinked,' she says firmly, taking her book from the bedside table to indicate the termination of the conversation. 'I'm not getting any younger – as you so diplomatically imply – and you're a long time dead.'

Later in the night his mind loops and dives, visiting images from the time with Taryn; images that are forbidden when he is wide awake and alert. Taryn has an extensive sexual repertoire, much of which she ran by him during their 'romping between the sheets'. He hadn't appreciated that such things were possible. Felicity was never too keen on oral sex. There was plenty of passion between them when they were young, but she wasn't adventurous, and once the kids arrived, sex became perfunctory. But he hadn't minded because he loved her and she loved him and alternatives never entered his head.

Now the alternatives won't go away. They appear like video images, a little blurry at the edges, but he is uncomfortable with Taryn in the leading role. Gradually he morphs her into someone else. Morphs her into someone taller with dark shoulder-length hair and green eyes; someone for whom he says he has feelings; someone called Marianne.

16

'Pea is not a good colour on Caucasians,' says Taryn to Marianne as they stroll round the local park in bright spring sunshine. It is Sunday and they have decided to have a picnic lunch after playing tennis. 'I know you'd rather I said what I think. Makes the skin look pallid and blancmangy.'

'Thanks a bunch,' says Marianne, visibly shrinking in her green cardigan.

'It's not that you can't wear green, it's just the wrong shade. People seem to think that they either can or can't wear a particular colour, when in fact in most cases it's the shade that's the crucial factor. One of my school friends had an aunt in Hexham. We went for tea one day and she said in her Geordie accent, *"I can't wear black next to my face, Pet,"* and you know what – she had dyed jet-black hair. We nearly had a fit trying not to laugh. She also had the most enormous spiky cactus in her upstairs loo.'

Marianne grins.

Taryn knows that her humour often diffuses the situation when she has been tactless, especially with Marianne who is on the same wavelength when it comes to seeing the funny side of things.

They walk down some roughly crafted steps to the point where the lake becomes a stream. Young silver birch trees offer some protection from the sun and cast dappled light onto the water. They sit on one of the seats on the bank and unwrap some sandwiches, quiche and nibbles which they lay on a cloth between them.

'What's the latest on the Edward front?' Taryn asks, trying to sound casual while focused on cutting the quiche.

'He's emailed first for a change. Usually he only writes first when he wants information about something.'

'What did he say?' Taryn senses she is about to blush and turns away to admire some baby moorhens.

'Felicity is going to acquire some bees.'

'Bees? Imagine that! Have you replied?'

'Not yet. D'you think he wants advice, even though he didn't ask? I'm never sure with men.'

'Advice about bees, or advice about Felicity acquiring them?'

'Either or both.'

Taryn is niggled by the knowledge that Edward has written to Marianne when he hasn't yet replied to her email. She knows he must have read it because he said he was going straight to the university. She also believes he's the type of person to reply out of politeness because Marianne has told her as much. Marianne has also said how zealous he is in responding even if he doesn't have time to write at length. Perhaps he is still cross about her deception? Still, once he is used to the idea, she is confident that he will be unable to resist her charms. They did, after all, have some fabulous sex and she is used to men wanting to come back for more.

'Do you know anything about bees?' Taryn thinks it would be safer to keep Marianne away from discussing relationships.

'A little. My aunt told me some of the myths about them.'

'Tell him those then.' Taryn now wants to be the only one to advise about Felicity. Marianne playing counsellor is likely to mess up her plans. 'Aren't the stings supposed to help with arthritis? I'm sure I read that somewhere.'

'The thing about Edward,' says Marianne, 'is that he's breathtakingly clever – and you can tell that from his lectures, his writing, his speed of perception, his wit – but he doesn't shove it in your face like some people do. He's not weird or eccentric or boring. He's quite happy to talk about normal things. Yes, he likes to analyse – in fact he's a bit of a psychologist on the quiet, which is probably why we get on.'

'I wouldn't have thought you knew him well enough to make such sweeping judgements,' says Taryn, even though her own brief acquaintance with him corroborates this assessment.

'I've known him nearly all my life, in a way. When you've known someone as a child, you know things about them that can never be acquired at a later time by meeting, hearsay or anecdote. The adult may be a different incarnation, but behind the poise, the composure, you will always remember the developing person, the uncut rock.'

Taryn is annoyed. This assumption means Marianne will always be one step ahead. It is another reason for her to feel she has overstepped the mark.

After the picnic, they go back in Taryn's Golf convertible to Marianne's house in Beechview Close, just off one of the roads leading from Beckenham to Bromley. Husband Johnny has been on one of his outings to the country where he likes to walk for miles and looks for fossils. Taryn is hoping to find him still out, but no such luck.

'Hi, Johnny,' she says, hovering in the kitchen while Marianne puts the kettle on.

She knows Johnny disapproves of her; thinks she's a bad influence on Marianne. She is under the impression he secretly desires her and his standoffish manner is a defence mechanism to ensure the truth doesn't show. Despite her apparent cavalier attitude to friendship when it comes to Edward, she draws the line at her best friend's husband even though she thinks he's sexy.

'So what's the latest in the world of rocks and fossils?' she asks.

Johnny Ingleton gives her a half smile which she knows too well means: *you are always so flippant, Taryn, why can't you be serious for a change.* He is tall and lean with chiselled features, longish brown hair and a casual sartorial style. At weekends he often doesn't shave so Taryn invariably sees him with designer stubble. In sunshine, with added sunglasses he looks like a film star.

'Do you really want to know, or are you just being polite?' he asks jokily.

'I'm always keen to learn new things,' she says.

'In March, a group of palaeontologists found a skeleton near Barcelona that they believe to be the last common ancestor to living great apes, including man. They have nicknamed it *Pau* – Catalan for Peace – which is somewhat ironic as they found it at the time the war started in Iraq.'

'And it's not a hoax?'

'So cynical,' says Johnny, running a hand through his hair.

Taryn and Marianne take their drinks out onto the patio. Johnny disappears and Marianne once more externalises her thoughts about Edward. Taryn finds it hard to hear of their developing friendship and common interests. She wants to tell her to shut up, but how can she when she has spent the past year eagerly awaiting the next chapter of their email relationship.

'It is as if all the hopes I had that we could be friends – seemingly impossible hopes – are now being realised. After almost thirty-five years. Now that we've met, I can hear the voice in the emails and it's so much friendlier than it was. He is real, and just about everything I hoped he would be, but didn't think possible.'

'Yet you don't fancy him,' said Taryn, searching again for anything that might add to her guilt.

'I can't afford to fancy him. Johnny and I are sorted and all I want from Edward is friendship. I'm comforted to feel I have that now. Like having a hot water bottle on a cold night.'

Taryn is not sure how Edward would feel about being compared to a hot water bottle. Her romantic emotions have been stirred for the first time and the feelings that she has for Edward seem to outweigh any guilt about betraying her best friend. *All's fair in love and war,* she thinks.

It is to Isabelle's that Taryn goes on her way back from Marianne and Johnny's. She needs someone to talk to about her dilemma.

'You're not falling in love with him, are you?' says Isabelle, appearing with mugs of tea. She wears her blonde hair in a loose plait, slung over one shoulder.

'I don't do *love*,' says Taryn. 'I believe we choose whom we love, and I choose not to.'

'Sometimes love chooses us,' says Isabelle. 'Takes us unaware. Sounds to me like this Edward guy has sneaked through your defences.'

'Hardly. We've met just the once, for a matter of hours.'

'Very intense hours, from what you say.'

'It was meant to be a casual fling; a bit of fun. Marianne said he wasn't a philanderer. I saw him as a challenge; nothing more. He's not my type.'

'And there may lie the problem. Perhaps your so-called type is the wrong type for you.'

Such a simple idea, so obvious, but until today, Taryn has never considered it. *Your so-called type is the wrong type ...* Isabelle's words worm through her brain and she begins a desperate self-analysis that plunges her once more into depression.

When she arrives back home she lies curled up on her bed with catatonic stillness. She is unsettled and out of balance. She wants to cry, but dare not. She is frightened of tears and their association with her past. Tears mean weakness and vulnerability; the risk of being like her mother. Last week she had no trouble in keeping tears from her eyes. What is different about this week; about now?

Her heart has never before been touched by Cupid's arrow. She has never endured its piercing pain. Never been where most young girls go in adolescence; where knees are weak and pulses are set racing by the smallest glimpse of *him*. She was always the one with a heart of steel, picking out the arrogant boys who thought they were God's gift to women. The loud boys, cracking jokes and strutting their stuff; boys who knew they were beautiful because Mummy said so and all the girls had been swooning at their feet since Kiss Chase at primary school. These were boys that played the field; that said they loved you, then moved on to the next girl. They two-timed, three-timed, drew attention with their loud sexy voices; performed to gathered throngs and practised their chat-up lines from store to store with the check-out girls.

They were boys like her father and she despised them. They sweet-talked their way to the back row of the local flicks, where under cover of semi-darkness they tested the water with wet slobby kisses, then fumbled under t-shirts and groped at breasts. They took their fill and then spat you out, broken and bleeding on the floor. Taryn watched from the sidelines at first, a late-developer, watching her friends be enthralled then hurt. She vowed when it was her time, she would be one step ahead with the *I love you's*; she would lead the way.

Of course she acquired something of a reputation, but she didn't care. When they called her a slag, she said, 'Slag, *chi io*? Do you mean me? That's rich coming from a boy who's shagged half our class and then some. Don't give me that double standard crap. If I'm a slag, what does that make you?'

She knew they called her names because they couldn't have

her. They protected their egos with insults. Said she was *'Star Bitch'*, and worse.

Of course she had been brought up a Catholic, and the nuns at her independent school warned of many things that Taryn chose to ignore.

'Don't wear patent leather shoes,' they said, 'or boys will see the reflection of your knickers.' And, 'Should you ever have to sit on a boy's knee, always put a magazine between you to stop him from getting excited. They are evil creatures, these young boys and are likely to lead you into Sin.' And as far as evil creatures were concerned, Taryn agreed, though she couldn't be doing with the notion of sin.

When she went to university in Birmingham, she left her tarnished reputation in Leeds and although she played the same game, she was far more selective about whom she dated. She became known as something of a mystery woman.

So all her life she has steered clear of men like Edward; the nice men who show reserve with women; the quiet and the shy. Nice men can be friends but not lovers. She has never felt the touch of selflessness until last Thursday night. Is it really only three days ago? Already she aches for Edward's closeness. He has tapped into some primal need for comfort that she didn't know she possessed. She can't let go; she must have him again. If he isn't going to respond to her email, she will have to hatch another plan.

17

It is Sunday evening, three days after Taryn, and Edward's computer is busy receiving its usual vast quantity of emails, mostly from universities across the world, but also from colleagues, his agent and his publisher. The notion of a book about mazes is gathering momentum and there will be decisions to be made, possibly a joint authorship with Henrik, based on their respective lectures.

He sits waiting patiently for the process to complete, tired after a weekend marking third year essays coupled with lack of sleep. *Please may there be an email from Marianne.* He's never doubted her before, but before was a time when his hectic life had a comfortable level of predictability. He knew what Felicity was likely to think and do and he knew himself. Now Felicity has adopted a Fernley-Whittingstall regime and is championing the causes of organics, self sufficiency and saving the planet. And he finds he cannot trust himself with women. His world has most definitely gone mad.

He scans the list of about twenty-five names. Near the bottom, he sees what he wants to see. At last her name graces his inbox again. It has only been two days since he wrote, but it feels like much longer. *Surely all is well? May nothing have changed; may she remain in ignorance of his indiscretion; may she still be the fantasy …*

He deals with all his other emails first, prolonging the hope.

To: Edward Harvey
From: Marianne Hayward

Date: 27th April 2003, 16.34
Subject: Re: Bees

Dear Edward,

Bees are wonderful!

If it wasn't for bees our apple growers would be in trouble. Do you have apple trees? If so, how many? I heard that for a successful fruit crop, they should come in groups of three to ensure full cross-pollination.

And there are lots of old country superstitions surrounding bees which is why you must never buy them. My aunt used to say, 'When anyone dies, you must tell the bees.' And you are supposed to inform them of births and marriages too!

A more scientific use of social insects comes in the form of ants ... which I have read are helping to solve complex routing problems in telecommunications networks!!

You say you have only just returned from London ... Did you stay overnight? If ever you need a bed, you'd be most welcome to stay here. Johnny wouldn't mind. We rattle about the house during term time when Holly is away – and we have a spare room with a bed, even though it doubles as an office.

As to the confrontation to which you refer ... I hope it wasn't as bad as you expected. It's better that you talk than keep avoiding the issue. If you say nothing you will feel dreadful resentment. She may carry on in happy oblivion, but in the long term, if you suffer so will she.

love,

Marianne

I wonder if bees should also be told if a marriage is dying?

First the relief that she doesn't know about Taryn, then the guilt, the wave of nausea, the heightened breathing. He sighs; he blinks. She must never know. And the offer of a bed … To stay with her would mean they could talk again. It wouldn't be the same with Johnny there, but it would be interesting to meet him.

To: Marianne Hayward
From: Edward Harvey
Date: 27th April 2003, 22.17
Subject: Re: Bees

Dear Marianne,
We have twelve apple trees – three each of Bramley, and Cox, and the old English varieties Star of Devon and Morgan Sweet (very good for cider!), so someone must've known what they were doing. We also have two pear, two plum, a damson and a couple of cherries. There are so many fruit trees in these parts that there will be plenty of cross-pollination. Felicity is already excited at the prospect of an autumn when she can make full use of the produce. She's planning to press our own apple juice too – using a hand-cranked contraption she bought off eBay!
Will inform her about 'telling the bees' – not that we've got any to confide in, yet! We did talk, and there's no danger of happy oblivion. She knows what I think, but is as immovable as the rock in the river to which you referred. I shall have to follow your advice of trying to find a different way round the obstruction!
Have heard something about ant colony optimisation … they are incredibly efficient …
Thanks for the offer of a bed! May yet take you up on it.

Coming to London so frequently in the evenings is
sapping my energy. Wouldn't be so bad if the trains were
reliable.
love,
Edward

To: Edward Harvey
From: Marianne Hayward
Date: 27th April 2003, 23.12
Subject: Re: Bees

Dear Edward
I am much better at giving advice than following it
myself. When in the centre of emotional turmoil, it is
difficult to see the whole picture and act rationally. I
speak from having had a turbulent couple of years! It is
all sorted now, but at the time, I said and did many
unwise things. My midlife madness, I call it now.
love,
Marianne

Turbulent couple of years … How turbulent? Why turbulent? He
never would have guessed from her emails.

To: Marianne Hayward
From: Edward Harvey
Date: 28th April 2003, 21.21
Subject: Re: Bees and Sheep

Dear Marianne,
Last night was incredible! One of the sheep gave birth
prematurely to twins, but the first one was stuck. Felicity
knew what to do, but wasn't strong enough to pull it

out. She dragged me out of the deepest sleep and I
followed her instructions, yanked the poor little blighter
out and swung it round like a bucket for a few seconds.
It gave a pitiful little bleat whereupon we rubbed it
vigorously with hay until it started to breathe properly.
Mum and twins now doing well!
It was a great feeling.
Edward

As he writes this, he is reminded of the night before; of the
earthy, country smells of sheep and hay. It had been such an
emotional experience that, buoyed up by euphoria, he and
Felicity had returned to the house together, showered, giggled
in the bathroom together like teenagers, and then once back
under the duvet they had made love with, he thought,
something like their old intimacy.

To: Edward Harvey
From: Marianne Hayward
Date: 28th April 2003, 22.03
Subject: Re: Bees and Sheep

Look out James Herriot!!
Perhaps this will help you to feel more involved.
Marianne

To: Marianne Hayward
From: Edward Harvey
Date: 28th April 2003, 22.32
Subject: Re: Bees and Sheep

Trouble is I don't particularly want to be involved. This
was fine as a one-off but we haven't enough sheep for an

event like this to be a regular occurrence. Animals are very time consuming. If I start showing any sort of interest, Felicity will expect me to do all sorts of stuff like Farmers' Markets and taking lambs to auction etc. Work takes all my time and I'm not interested enough to make it a career.

Bees have arrived! Took over two hours to walk up a ramp from their box into the hive. Thought you could just shake them in, but apparently not!

Hens causing problems. Old hens don't like being rounded up by new cockerel! He's now adopting more aggressive tactics …

Edward

Felicity's benevolence does not sustain beyond the single act of passion. The next day when he tries to hug her, she brushes him away and he wonders if her apparent enthusiasm was a gesture merely to reward him for his veterinary-style intervention.

A phone call to Patrick Shrubsole on Tuesday afternoon results in an invitation to 'have a chat' at Stancliffe on Friday morning. He won't tell Felicity exactly what it's about yet, just that he has to attend a meeting. She is so used to him disappearing to some university or other that she won't ask questions. Then a call from Henrik on Tuesday evening complicates matters further, saying he is unwell and could Edward do his Thursday session at the museum.

To: Marianne Hayward
From: Edward Harvey
Date: 29th April 2003, 20.14
Subject: Hotel Reservation?

Dear Marianne,

If you receive this in time … I've just had a call from Henrik saying he is ill. This means I'm coming to do this week's Thursday lecture instead of him. I've also been asked down to a meeting at Stancliffe, late on Friday morning. Is it possible to take you up on your kind offer of a bed? Short notice I know, but I'm very tired at the moment and don't feel like making two journeys if one will suffice. If you can't, don't worry … I have other options or can stay in a hotel.

Edward

Almost by return Marianne replies saying that of course he may come and stay over, and gives him mobile and landline contact numbers. She also says he will need to make his way to Beckenham Junction; that she will pick him up when he knows which train he is catching, and offers him supper or sandwiches.

A hopeful sensation of opportunity washes over him. Opportunity for consolidating friendship. He refuses the offer of supper as he expects already to have eaten, but adds that breakfast on Friday would be most welcome.

Breakfast at Marianne's, he thinks. It has a certain ring to it. But then all things have a certain ring when they are associated with the beginnings of love.

18

When Taryn receives a phone call from an excitable Marianne telling her that Edward (now Taryn's Edward) is going to spend the night at Beechview Close, she is consumed by an unpleasant and unfamiliar feeling that she vaguely recognises as jealousy. It is not an emotion that she generally suffers from, most people in her opinion being replaceable, but she remembers a time at school when she was very small and she came back from absence to find her best friend linking arms with another. Half a lifetime later, she is aware of similar sensations.

She collapses with the phone onto the sofa in the living room, lifting her neat stockinged legs onto the cushions and crossing her ankles. A wave of indignation washes over her. *Why Marianne's?* Why doesn't he come to her instead? Is he deliberately avoiding her? The thoughts tumble over one another, a cacophony of sound, making her head hurt. She frowns, and hisses within, dimly aware of Marianne's voice in the background. She cannot believe he still hasn't called her since they met. She had hoped for, or even expected, flowers. He seemed a flowers type of guy. Even Marc-with-a-'c' gave her flowers. She had imagined the extravagant bouquet of pink or white lilies, and washed her large vase in anticipation. But there were no flowers and no emails. Not even a 'thank-you'. This isn't the usual response from men after they have spent the night with her, especially not such a night as that. She shivers excitedly at the thought and her stomach lurches in a way that is new to her.

Is it because he's married? Is it because I know Marianne? Is it because he doesn't like me? Is it because he's not the philandering type?

She is in denial about their conversation the morning after; his anger, his supposed feelings for Marianne, the speed of his departure. She wants answers, not least to the question of whether she's mistaken in thinking him special; whether she's wasting emotional energy on someone who on further acquaintance would prove a bastard like all the rest.

Marianne is gushing in the background about something that has happened at work. Taryn hasn't been listening; she makes non-specific noises of agreement hoping they will suffice; she needs to steer the conversation back to Edward.

'Listen, darling, tell me more about Edward. I mean why he's coming? You must be so excited.' *Lucky bitch!*

'Like I said, he's doing an extra session for Henrik this Thursday evening, and he's got some bloke at Stancliffe uni to see on Friday morning.'

No reason at all why he can't come to me and have wild passionate sex as before. She is hurt. She wants to know what is going on in his mind. She needs to see him. To say, *'Caro Edward, cos'è successo?* What's happened? *C'è qualcosa che non va?* Is there something wrong?' Often her second language of Italian coming to the fore during times of emotional stress.

She sits up and twiddles her hair. She tries to get an invite.

'Marianne, why not ask me over too? Make it a foursome? Balance the table. I'd so love to meet the guy after everything you've said.' She thinks that at least if she meets him legitimately, then she won't feel so bad when Marianne talks about him. And then when their relationship progresses, she can tell Marianne that it all started there and then, on that evening; can even blame Marianne for it happening. Assuming she tells her at all …

But I jump ahead … I go too fast …

At the moment it is Relationship Nil. But if she can only see him it will jog his memory about their night together. Surely if she is there, in the flesh, with a delicately low cut top and just a hint of cleavage, a splash of the same perfume she wore the other night, he will find it impossible to resist? And it will be such a buzz being together knowing what they both know, but not being able to say.

For a moment she is sitting opposite him having supper, kicking off her shoe and inching her toes up his trouser leg; Johnny to the side banging on about fossils and Marianne doing her Delia impression, far too flustered about impressing Edward's stomach to worry about what was going on under the table. *Imagine that!*

'He's not coming for supper. A sandwich at most. And it will look a bit odd if you suddenly turn up,' says Marianne, breaking the reverie. 'Like I was trying to pair you up.'

What irony!

'Marianne, don't be such a bore. People don't think like that these days. He's a married man, for God's sake.'

'A married man who will be dead tired. I expect he'll just want to go to bed.'

Yes please!

'How about I just drop round on spec to borrow something? I won't stay.' *Not as sure-fire as the foot up the trousers, but an opportunity to say hello and gauge his reaction.*

'How about you keep your curiosity to yourself. I'll give you the low-down when I next speak to you. It's not as if I've yet had much opportunity to chat to him face to face. It'll be bad enough with Johnny there. I don't particularly want the meeting to be hijacked by someone else as well.'

'That's very possessive of you,' Taryn says crossly, yet recognising in Marianne's reaction, a reflection of herself.

'Taryn! You of all people should understand.'

Should, but don't.

'There's not much chance I'll ever get to see the guy, then.'

'So?'

'You've made him sound such a star. I'd love to meet him.' She tries the little girl voice, higher in pitch, that she rarely shows to boyfriends; the one that used to get round her father in the days before he hit her. 'How do I know you're not seeing him through rose-tinted glasses? I might be able lend some objectivity to the situation, burst your bubbles, if they need bursting.'

'I don't want my bubbles bursting.'

'Maybe I want some bubbles of my own.' A dangerous thing to say, but it slipped out. She tries to retract. 'Don't take any notice of me, I'm only teasing.'

'He's not your type, Taryn.' Now Marianne sounds cross.

'I'm reviewing my type since the Marc thing.' What she really means is that she is reviewing her type since the night with Edward.

'All the more reason to keep Edward at arms' length.'

She's blown it. Aroused Marianne's suspicions about her intentions. 'Is there nothing I can say to make you change your mind on this?'

'Nothing.'

She puts down the phone, breathing quickly, eyes darting left and right. She grabs a cushion to her chest and begins to rock.

I will not lose control …

She suddenly cannot bear the thought of not having him again; of him being just down the road with her friend when he could be in bed with her. Lightness of being fades just as it has done so many times before when she does not get what she wants; when people stand up to her; when people say '*No*'. She wants to scream out loud, but instead she screams inside.

I will not lose control.

They said she has hypomania. It was when she was nineteen and at college and curious to know more about her state of mind. It was one of her other psychology friends that first suggested it (curious that she gravitated towards that type of person; not only Marianne). At the time she laughed it off, but she knew there was something not quite normal about her moods. She traced it back to the onset of puberty when for her, teenage volatility raged out of control like the fiercest waterfall splashing down from on high, with gleaming rainbow refractions in the glittering streams.

Her mother said it was because of her father, and Taryn believed her.

Now she thinks it was a biological time bomb that just needed the hormonal trigger of adolescence to explode. Her maternal grandmother had referred to her as 'spirited' for as long as she could remember. And looking back, Carlo showed all the signs of bipolar disorder.

Without telling anyone, during term-time at university, she made an appointment to lie on the couch of a clinician and have a chat. Dr Henry Woodcock said it was not quite full blown manic-depression, but on the continuum of mental wellness and illness, she was a silken thread from the latter. That was all she wanted to know.

Like many, she enjoys the roller coaster of the hypo-manic episodes; the creativity, the need for little sleep, the wild ideas, the danger and excitement of the risky situations to which she is inexorably drawn.

But the flip side is the darkness, the heavy moods and the depression. It doesn't take much to send the graph in a downward plunge; a difficult week at work, a row with a boyfriend, cloudy days, or someone saying 'No'. Sometimes it is nothing specific at all, hormone fluctuations or neurotransmitter irregularities in the brain. She could have it treated if she wants, with lithium salts. But she doesn't want, because the highs are worth more than champagne and sunsets and Christmas bells all rolled into one. She loves her slightly manic self and knows that others do too. Her success as a teacher owes much to her energy and eccentricity in the classroom. Her success with men – in catching men – is because they've never met anyone else like her before who can be witty all night long and argue with the best, before rolling over like a pussy-cat for playtime.

I will not lose control.

Edward has blown her ship off course. She must, absolutely must, see him again. She will have to have a plan that beats all other plans.

In her spare room, she has a table on which are scattered the various accoutrements of an artist: a couple of rags streaked with colours, a jar of brushes, assorted tubes of gouache and watercolour, mixing palette, paper and various half-finished paintings of some lurid abstracts and self portraits, and some contrastingly subtle landscapes with delicate pastel shades and gentle impressionistic lines.

She takes a large sheet of paper, already stretched, and with a wet brush heavily loaded with a mixture of crimson and cobalt blue, she begins making extravagant sweeps. To an observer, she appears to be fully absorbed in what she is doing, but on the inside part of her mind is plotting and scheming and working on the plan to entrap Edward Harvey again.

After barely an hour she sits back satisfied with a thunderous sky before her. The dark demons have left her. She has a new mission, and with it, new hope.

19

On Thursday morning Edward wakes with a sense of optimism and anticipation. He has told Felicity that he will be staying overnight in London again and her only reservation was regarding the lambing.

'Let's hope there's not another breech birth,' she said.

Edward is increasingly of the opinion that with each new animal acquisition, his place in the family hierarchy of importance slips a notch. Playing second fiddle to sheep was not something he ever anticipated when he first married.

Today he intends not to worry about such things. Even the nagging anxiety from the Taryn aftermath has been successfully banished for now at least. The sun is shining, it is distinctly warm, and in a bright white room in the archaeology wing at the university, he gives an inspired lecture on geophysics to the second years.

There are thirty-three in the year group, a mixture of young men and women, several of them serious and introverted souls who will ultimately spend their lives in quiet reverential employment cataloguing artefacts in museums around the world. Bringing such personalities to life can sometimes be a chore and as many archaeology students prefer hands on methods of discovery, he often finds eyes beginning to glaze over during a lecture such as this.

Although generally known for being self-contained, when Edward has an audience he comes to life. Today he has decided to draw on his acting talents to woo them. Talents first discovered at the age of eleven when he was in the school play at Brocklebank Hall; the school where he shared a classroom for three years with Marianne, only vaguely aware of her presence as someone else who could spell, do Latin and excel in tests and exams.

He arrives a few minutes before the start time and in between scanning his notes and checking his PowerPoint presentation, he casts an eye over the rapidly assembling group. Every year, they seem to be looking younger and require a more paternal approach.

Gary Cornhill has a perpetually vibrating leg and sits in the middle at the front next to one of the more outgoing girls with pink streaks in her long black hair. And there's Vincent MacBraine who seems unfortunately named as he always asks daft questions at the most inconvenient times. Georgina and Judith are mature students in their mid twenties who sit at the back looking superior and interested, scribbling vast quantities of notes, and regularly asking for further references.

When the lecture begins, Edward struts from one side to the other on the slightly raised platform at the front, adopting the delivery of a somewhat eccentric scientist for whom all things geophysical mean excitement and a reason to get up in the morning.

Some days this approach works better than others, but today he flies, witty asides come to him effortlessly. He tells the students that geophysics may not be about digging holes in the ground, but the techniques used for discovering what lies under the surface are just as interesting. He explains about resistivity meters for detecting the amount of moisture in the soil, he informs them about magnetometers for measuring magnetic field strength, and ground penetrating radar to indicate the depth of objects by showing changes in stratigraphy. He has the students spellbound not so much by the content of what he is saying, but by the way in which it is said.

At the end Ruth Reid, an earnest looking girl with freckles and a basin haircut, seated in isolation to the side at the front, spontaneously begins to clap, stopping abruptly when she remembers where she is and a snort erupts from Vincent MacBraine.

'Thank you,' says Edward, nodding at Ruth. 'Mostly the difference between acting and lecturing is that we rarely get to hear the applause. I will remember this moment.'

Suddenly there is a spattering noise from the middle of the audience which rapidly gathers momentum until the whole group is clapping and banging the tables, whooping and whistling.

Edward waves at them to stop and takes a flourishing bow. 'Does anyone have any questions?'

Afterwards he finds Conrad who on hearing about the pending visit to Marianne's says, 'Which one is she? Remind me? Stalker or Fanclub?'

They are by the rack of staff pigeonholes near the main departmental office. 'Hush! Fanclub – if you must use that term.'

'Another bite of the cherry, mate,' says Conrad, taking a gulp of coffee from the polystyrene cup in his hand.

'Her husband will be there.'

'But perhaps not all the time.'

'Perhaps not.' Edward hopes not, but for different reasons than Conrad has in mind. It is always more difficult to have meaningful personal conversation with friends if the spouse is present. Felicity told him this when they were first married and usually tried to shoo him out of the way when her female friends came round. Usually he was glad to be shooed.

'There's nothing quite like a fuck with a desperate woman. They really try to please,' continues Conrad.

'Who says she's desperate?'

'Is she over forty?'

'Yes.'

'There you go, then.'

'Don't judge everyone by the women you meet.'

'If I had as many opportunities as seem to come your way, I'd be exhausted.'

Edward shakes his head and grins. If it wasn't for his natural tendency to be loyal and for Conrad having helped him at an incredibly crucial moment in the past, he wouldn't be listening to all this. Probably wouldn't give him the time of day.

He remembers it vividly, the time when Rachel was born a week early and snow lay on the ground like a thick layer of meringue, whipped up as it had been by the wind into peaks that had become frozen sharp. He was at work and in the middle of a lecture. Peggy Streeter from next door rang the department and said it was all systems go on the baby front but he was not to worry. The ambulance had taken Felicity to hospital and she wanted him there as quickly as possible; that things were happening fast; that little whoever couldn't wait. Peggy said she and her husband would look after young James for as long as it took.

That was in the days before they moved to the Deer Orchard. Thank God for good old fashioned neighbourliness.

He had belted from his office without grabbing his coat, fumbling for his keys which then struggled to unlock his old Cortina. Of all the days to have a flat battery, this must have been one of the worst. Felicity had told him to get a new one before the winter – just in case. They had practised the hospital run at various times of day and night, thinking they had covered every eventuality. But when he turned the key in the ignition there was barely a groan. When he turned it a second time, there was an ominous silence. He panicked, then took a few deep breaths. Felicity would be furious if he didn't make it in time. He would get a taxi. He raced back to the departmental office, nearly knocking Gemma over as she appeared in the doorway with a tray.

'Taxi, Gemma, please. Urgently.'

The taxi firm said the soonest they could be there was twenty minutes as the snow had brought on a rush and they were short of drivers. Gemma said she would take him herself if she had a car and could drive.

'What about Conrad?' she had said.

Edward didn't know Conrad very well at the time and thought him a stereotypically scruffy archaeologist with a rather brash outspoken manner.

'I'll see if he's in, and while I'm doing that, you get your coat and scarf or you'll catch your death.' Gemma looked at him protectively, picked up the phone and called through to Conrad's office.

Conrad appeared in seconds with his keys in hand. 'Always wanted to do a mercy dash,' he had said cheerfully and they both headed for the car park at a swift jog.

Edward just got to the delivery room as little Rachel's head was beginning to show and Felicity was howling like a wild wolf. With James she had sung 'La Donna è Mobile' at the top of her voice through all the contractions and pain. He wasn't sure which was the most embarrassing, but he wouldn't have wanted to have missed the birth for anything and has never forgotten Conrad's willingness to help, including his offering to pick him up from the hospital as soon as he was ready to leave.

When Edward arrived back at the university, he found Conrad had been in touch with the AA on his behalf and a new battery had been fitted. The car was ready to go.

'I owe you one,' said Edward. He valued kindness above many things and thought it an increasingly rare characteristic. His father was kind …

'How about a pint to wet the baby's head?'

And off they went to the union bar where they spent a convivial hour and discovered their completely differing attitudes regarding matters of fidelity. Since then, Edward forgives him everything.

Edward finds himself at Beechview Close just before nine in the evening. Marianne picked him up from Beckenham Junction following his phone call from Victoria and drove him the half mile or so to her house.

In the car they had talked rather stiltedly about their respective days at work and Edward's covering of Henrik's lecture. Now he sits in the living room awaiting a beer that husband Johnny has gone to get from the kitchen, and the sandwiches that Marianne has offered. He had supper of sorts in the form of pasta before his lecture, but that was several hours ago and he is quite hungry. He is also exhausted. He sits on the edge of the armchair and looks around him.

The room is light with pale cream walls and two uplighters casting a flattering glow. He is envious of the lack of clutter and realises that having four children makes such impossible at the Deer Orchard. On a shelf near the television is a photograph in a silver frame of a pretty young smiling teenager with long dark brown hair. At first he thinks it is Marianne, but then realises it must be her daughter Holly. Marianne must have looked very similar when she was twenty and he feels a tremor of loss that he never knew her at that time.

Johnny reappears and hands Edward a pint. 'Make yourself comfortable. Mari'll be through in a sec.'

Mari, thinks Edward. *How intimate that sounds ...* He takes a long gulp of beer, makes noises to register his approval and wonders what to say. He has few pre-conceived ideas about Johnny as Marianne writes little about him. He knows they had originally been to the same grammar school, but they hadn't become romantically involved until some years later. He also knows he is a teacher of geology at a local comprehensive. Felicity would be amused as she's not overly fond of the school-teaching fraternity and regularly grumbles about their long holidays and left-wing tendencies. He has no idea about Marianne's political leanings. He suspects her background is Conservative because her dad was an architect and she started out being privately educated. But their emails and conversations have steered well away from politics.

'It's Sneck Lifter,' says Johnny referring to the beer. 'From Jennings' Brewery in Cockermouth. Whenever we go up to the lakes, I bring back a stash of their speciality brews. You can't usually get it round here and it's nice to be able to give people something different.'

'I'm not a Real Ale connoisseur,' says Edward. 'But I do appreciate it when it's there.'

'I have this picture of archaeologists trooping into old country pubs while they're excavating.' Johnny settles himself in the second armchair and runs a hand through his impressively thick hair. Edward thinks he looks like an artist.

'Indeed we do.'

'Marianne tells me you discovered the original Troy Town maze on St Agnes. We've been there a couple of times. Even walked the maze. Great little place. Great people.'

'Been asked to do a lecture tour of the islands this summer,' says Edward.

'Oh, when?' asks Marianne, appearing with a platter of sandwiches which she places on a table near Edward. 'Have as many as you like. I've made a few extra so we can keep you company, but it's not long since we've eaten.' She passes him a plate, shiny white like Felicity's restaurant crockery.

'Early August when the tourist season is in full swing.'

Edward helps himself to a variety of the sandwiches on offer, noting that each has at least two ingredients: prawn and lettuce with Marie Rose sauce; egg and tomato with watercress; smoked salmon and cucumber. She has made an effort – unless they are from M & S, but he thinks not.

'Where will you be staying?' says Marianne, settling herself on the sofa.

'On St Agnes to start with. Last year we all camped at Troytown Farm, but this time I'll B and B at the Parsonage for one night. I've been there before – self-catering with Felicity and Christopher. Didn't you say that's where you stayed once?' He glances at Marianne, seeing that she's dressed more casually than when she came to his lecture, in a green floral printed dress and a cardigan. Her hair is clipped back in a slide, and she wears very long, beaded silver earrings that glint when the light catches them. He wonders if this is her real style, in which case it is closer to his original assumptions about her.

'Also self-catering,' says Marianne. 'In the summer of 2000. It was the first holiday we had on our own since Holly was born. Fabulous.'

Edward notes the intimate way she looks at Johnny and the way he looks back. 'Then I'm off to Tresco. Still to finalise the itinerary but I'll be doing lectures on a couple of evenings and leading groups to the maze every morning.'

Both Marianne and Johnny are very enthusiastic about Scilly and they talk animatedly for some minutes about the peacefulness, the rock formations and the Scillonian ways.

Afterwards, Johnny takes Edward to see his rock and fossil collection.

'I'm not an obsessive collector, you understand,' says Johnny, 'but if I happen to see something when I'm out walking, I bring it home. If it's of particular significance, it usually finds its way to a museum, if not it comes back here. I suppose it's like your archaeology in many respects.'

'Where do you walk?'

'The Jurassic Coast.'

'Nearer me than you, I should think.'

'You should join me sometime. Occasionally I take a caravan in Dorset for a weekend. Haven't for a while, though.'

'On your own?'

'Mari used to come with Holly many years ago, but now I'm usually on my tod.'

Johnny shows Edward an enormous ammonite. 'This is one of the biggest I've found,' he says proudly.

They discuss several more of the specimens before Johnny says he's going to have an early night and suggests Edward might like to return downstairs to talk to Marianne.

Edward is pleased by this suggestion and even though he is welcoming a chance to sleep, he is also keen to speak to Marianne alone.

He finds her watching News 24, curled up on the sofa. She has kicked off her shoes and her legs are hidden under her dress. He also notices that she has removed the slide from her hair and now it flops loosely on her shoulders. There is a vulnerable quality about her that makes him feel protective. She waves him over to a chair and smiles.

'Johnny loves showing off his collection. Especially if there's half a chance it will be appreciated.'

'So how's the book coming on?' He still isn't sure whether or not he is pleased that she is writing a story based on their childhood at Brocklebank Hall and their meeting through Friends Reunited.

'Quite rapidly. Second draft is well underway. I'd like you to look over some of the early Brocklebank-inspired chapters before I offer them for publication. Just to make sure you're happy about what I've said. Did I say the children are based on us? Of course it's just my perception of you at that time. It might not be true. And I've had to spice things up a bit. Literary licence.' She flushes.

'How do you mean, "spice things up"?' Edward is worried.

Marianne grins girlishly. 'I'm not sure I should tell you this, but I used to think you were so wonderful when I was ten. You had a brain and you weren't horrible to me like the others were. So I've just exaggerated it a little.'

Edward isn't sure how to respond to this, so just smiles.

'I still think you're wonderful.' She says it in such a way that he's not sure whether she is teasing. Her eyes flash and she grins. 'Be flattered, but don't be alarmed.'

'I'm not alarmed,' he reassures, feeling hot. This is, after all, just confirming what Taryn said. He is somewhat concerned about the type of relationship that her adult characters may have – fiction being fiction – but cannot bring himself to ask.

'So what's happening at Stancliffe?' says Marianne.

Edward hesitates before telling her. 'And please don't mention it to anyone. Whatever it is, I can't imagine leaving Devon.'

Then Marianne suggests he might like to turn in and arranges to give him a knock at seven-thirty.

Lying in the remarkably comfortable spare double bed, Edward stretches out on his back, trying to relax in preparation for sleep. He is so very tired, but the adrenaline from both the morning and evening lectures has carried him through the day and his mind will not be stilled.

He is surprised and pleased that he likes Johnny. He's good-looking too. No danger of Marianne's head being turned. Maybe he should take up the offer of a fossil hunt along the Jurassic coast. He could do with expanding his geological knowledge. Then his thoughts drift to Felicity. Normally he phones when he stays away overnight. It is too late now.

Over breakfast and in the absence of Johnny who has gone to work, Edward raises the subject of Felicity.

'I think I've already told you about Rick. He does the garden, builds hen houses and bee hives. Now he's turning the old milking parlour into a kiln and office. Gets to know things before I do. I think Felicity fancies him. She definitely flirts with him.' He takes another slice of wholemeal toast and spreads it with Flora and then liberally with strawberry jam.

'Women of our age do that with younger men. Just to see if we get a response. It makes us feel better if they flirt back. But it doesn't mean anything. I wouldn't worry about him.'

He wants to grab her hand as it rests so close to his across the table. But he resists. It wouldn't do to spoil the moment. Instead he says, 'Your friendship is very important to me. Felicity was once the only female friend I thought I'd ever need, but when you want to talk about that relationship … who else is there?'

'I used to think that about Johnny,' says Marianne. 'Last year, I had a crisis of confidence; a few months before I found you on the internet. I think it was because I started to feel middle-aged and all the insecurities from when I was a kid suddenly raised themselves up from the depths. It was like they'd been asleep throughout the first twenty years with Johnny. I never doubted his love for me before.

'Then I looked in the mirror one day, as you do, and thought *who am I?* And I came home from work and found this gorgeous young – comparatively young – woman sitting here where we are now, chatting to Johnny as if she owned the place.' She pauses. 'It's not the same as a Rick situation. A younger woman is a very real threat. There's plenty of evidence to make one wary.'

Edward holds his breath.

'I thought: why would he want me when he could have her with her pneumatic chest and her cascade of blonde hair? All the things I know about men's biology and psychology – how they are driven towards procreation, which is why beauty and youth are everything – all those things made me feel hopeless and jealous.'

Edward is reminded of how he has noticed Felicity's ageing and feels guilty.

Marianne continues, 'I imagined he must be having an affair, and the more cross I got, the worse our relationship became. Finding you helped me to deal with the past and move on. It took a while to sort it all out, but we did and it's fine now.'

'That's how I feel about Rick.'

'But women are not driven by the same impulses as men. Felicity is probably just enjoying the flattery.'

'She's gone off sex. She's gone of sex with me.'

'It's unlikely she'll be looking elsewhere. She might come back to it. It's hard being a woman when the hormones pack their bags. Be patient.'

'I hope you're right. I wish we'd met up sooner. Talked properly. All those emails ...' He shook his head, not lost for words, but concerned that all the words he wants to say would be misinterpreted. He wants to tell her that she seems so familiar despite their thirty-four years of separation; that knowledge of her as a child, however inconsequential to him at the time, somehow gives their relationship a foundation of depth and substance that he has never found with other adult friendships.

And there are many other things he wants to tell her, but knows he never can.

20

Taryn found herself transported into the world of education almost by accident. As a teenager she desperately wanted to become a journalist, perhaps working on an upmarket women's magazine like *Vogue* or *Cosmopolitan*, but indecision during her English literature degree at Birmingham forced her into a postgraduate teaching certificate at the Institute in London, supposedly while she made up her mind. Here she first met Marianne, both specialising in secondary English, although Marianne's background had been in psychology. It was while on teaching practice in a pleasant girls' school in Orpington that she discovered she had quite a talent for imparting knowledge and bringing her subject to life.

To her surprise, she even found she liked children, especially the eleven and twelve year olds, fresh from junior school and mostly unspoilt by hormones. If ever she had any maternal instincts, it was on these youngsters that she exercised them during the snowy winter of 1979, when icicles hung from the guttering and prompted one of her colleagues, who was giving her a lift home, to speculate on these as weapons for the perfect murder.

As the years passed and she gained experience and confidence, she became more and more innovative. Perhaps to add a sense of presence to her diminutive stature, she frequently stood on top of desks, even before Mr Keating became known for this in *Dead Poets' Society*. She also wore dark-rimmed glasses she didn't need, and never smiled at a new class until after the first Christmas.

The children by turns hated her, respected her then adored her, eventually rushing eagerly to her lessons, wondering what lay in store.

She practised the Rex Gibson method of teaching Shakespeare, ahead of his revolutionary project in 1986, emphasising the dramatic approach, and using performance to find ways into understanding character. Often she took her younger classes to the school hall, handing out a long soliloquy cut up into individual lines. Each child would be given one line and told to walk around speaking it or shouting it, playing with different methods of delivery until its meaning was found and the line was learned. Then the class would regroup and the speech would be delivered in its entirety in a way that could never have happened merely by sitting in class and reading from the text.

Her Head of Department, Josh Redley, was sceptical. He had sandy hair, a purple alcohol-induced face, wore tweed jackets and was a traditionalist by nature. 'Filling them with all this drama nonsense isn't going to help our exam results,' he would say frequently. 'Leave the poncing about to Miss Pringle and the Drama shebang. I would prefer it if you would stick to our scheme of work.'

Taryn ignored him, and her class exam results confirmed her own suspicions that this method of bringing the play to life was vastly superior to a more class-based approach. Josh was most probably jealous of her success, but chose to belittle her at every opportunity.

'You are a belligerent know-all,' he said once when Taryn justified her theatrical approach to Shakespeare in the face of yet more criticism. The Head, it seemed, was questioning the number of lessons for which she booked the hall, and Josh had apprehended her in her classroom during a break.

A few years later when Dr Gibson began publishing articles

and writing books advocating the very same practices, Josh did a remarkable u-turn and suggested she give a presentation on the technique during one of their departmental Inset days. But he never apologised.

Hypocrite, thought Taryn, and she threw her colleagues knowing looks, but remained silent. Once she had cascaded the technique to the rest of the department, it became increasingly difficult for anyone to book a slot in the hall and in the summer she often resorted to the playground.

Many of the best teachers of young children are caricatures, and Taryn is all too aware that she has become one. Entering the classroom, she shrugs her shoulders as if taking on a second skin. She becomes Ms Danielli: unpredictable, slightly off-the-wall, even a little scary at times, but good at her job.

She likes where she is in terms of pecking order and status. She has a range of classes of all ages and as second in the department, enough responsibility to keep her enthusiasm, but not so much as to cramp her extra-curricular style. It is important to her that she has a life beyond the classroom, and she is sure that any further climbing of the professional ladder would most certainly lead to personal sacrifices that she isn't prepared to make. A couple of classes of lower school art extend her repertoire and prevent her from being bored.

Today she is preparing her face for one of its most important missions. Devoid of make-up she still looks relatively young and innocent, but she knows that over the next twenty-five years this face of forty-six must somehow metamorphose into a virtually unrecognisable face of seventy.

How will I turn into the grandmother figure with twin-set and pearls? Will it happen in fits and starts like a staircase, or will the deterioration be smooth, an almost imperceptible slide into the world of zimmers? Will I start calling people 'Pet' and 'Dear', like the women on the check-outs at supermarkets, and will they use the same form of address to me?

She has had several conversations with Marianne about such things.

Marianne ... She abandons the thought.

She brushes her face with her minerals foundation, circular strokes that the make-up specialist at Bluewater showed her how to do. Her skin is still quite resilient and free from lines. She wonders if that's due to good genes, obsessive sun protection, or the bizarre facial exercises she sometimes does when watching television.

She wonders about having a facelift in due course. In many ways it is against her principles, but she sees the benefits on some of the celebrities. On others she thinks it is a mistake as they appear to become ever more startled with each phase of surgery. Likewise, the Botox option. She likes to be expressive and she fears the long-term consequences of using a drug that causes muscle paralysis. It's also against her principles to mess with nature; to suffer pain because of society's current obsession with youthfulness. Yet conversely, she is considering HRT when the time comes, primarily because she can't bear the thought of losing her desire for sex.

But for now she intends to use this face while she can. She completes her eye make-up a little more subtly than usual, adds pale pink lipstick and lip gloss, and puts small gold hoops through her ears. Then with a final glance in the mirror, she dons some high-heeled cream sandals, grabs her bag, leaves the flat, and sets off purposefully down Coppercone Lane for Beckenham Junction station. Her destination is the British Museum.

It is three weeks since Edward's visit to stay at Marianne's. The intervening time has been spent in much contemplation of the meeting with Patrick Shrubsole, which despite his original thoughts that any change of job would be out of the question, has left him in a serious quandary.

They had met in a modern and spacious office which Patrick said would be given over to the recipient of the new archaeology chair. Edward outlined Felicity's enterprises (surprising himself at how exciting they sounded) and said he couldn't envisage a move at present.

'Commute,' said Patrick unhesitatingly. He was a thin and nervy type with hollow cheeks and fair hair, probably in his early forties and very public school. Edward had always thought him intense and a shade foppish. 'It's two hours to Exeter from Paddington. Come up Monday mornings and be timetabled for teaching between Monday afternoon and Thursday. You can work from home on Fridays so nothing lost from your weekend. Travelling time would also be part of your working week. Loads of people commute here from Oxford. We even have an economics lecturer who lives in Wales.' Patrick had looked at him, daring him to refuse.

'I'd have to find somewhere to stay.'

'Travelodge. Or you might even find a spot in suburbia if you prefer.'

'I'd miss being at home during the week.'

'My understanding is that you're often away giving talks – many of them in London.'

Edward said he'd think about it and Patrick said that the job wouldn't start until January so there was plenty of time.

The crux of it all lies in the fact that they want him and are prepared to manufacture an offer he finds hard to resist. His reputation for the smooth running of the department in Devon is known throughout academic archaeological circles, and if the department at Stancliffe wants to carry on being one of the flagships of London University, he would be an ideal figurehead to continue its reputation on the highest rungs of the archaeological ladder. From Edward's perspective, the added kudos that goes with being a professor would be very useful for helping to sell his books. Also, it might lead to the TV work he has long desired.

Now he is back again in London showing Olivia and Alexander around the maze exhibition. As promised they have come up to see a show and decided to drop in at the museum beforehand, catching Edward as he was coming out of his lecture. Edward is sure they are just being polite and he takes them from maze to maze, keeping his explanations as concise and simple as possible.

They have just walked through the Troy Town replica, with Olivia asking inane questions about *'the teensy-weensy rocks'*, when he becomes aware of a presence. It is Taryn. Wellbeing drains from him in an instant. He freezes. From what she said, this isn't her style. He assumed if he didn't contact her, then that would be that.

'Might we have a word?' she says without smiling, gesturing away from Olivia and Alexander.

'It's not exactly convenient,' says Edward quietly, his heartbeat cranking up in speed and the now familiar waves of guilt once more sweeping over him. He is seized with a feeling of doom. He hates scenes. Could she really be a stalker, or worse? He excuses himself and leads Taryn into a space a few metres away.

Taryn raises her eyebrows and whispers, 'I didn't have you compartmentalised as ungracious.'

'Meaning?'

'A reply to my email would have been courteous.'

'I honestly didn't know what to say.'

'*"Thanks,"* would have been a start.'

'You're a friend of Marianne's. You should've told me. It was underhand.'

'Guilty as charged. Look, can we have a coffee or something? A chat? I don't like to part on bad terms.'

Edward's heart sinks but he rejects lines of escape, desperate to put a lid on this sorry affair. 'You think a chat will make a difference?'

'Of course.' Taryn looks at him innocently.

Edward notices that her hair is not as vertical as usual and she has less obvious make-up, dissipating some of her power, giving her a girlish look. A short summer frock shows off her legs. He tries not to drop his gaze. Instead he nods at her by way of assent. He doesn't like parting on bad terms either.

'This isn't a good time,' he says, nodding at Olivia who is staring at them both.

'I'll meet you at the café, same one as last time,' says Taryn. 'As soon as you can. Don't let me down.'

Edward shrugs and turns to make his excuses while Taryn struts off in the direction of the cafeteria.

'Who was that miniscule woman?' said Olivia. 'She didn't look very pleased.'

Edward struggles to find words, then remembers what Taryn first told him. 'She's from Leeds and has a particular interest in mazes. I need to see her about an issue with a paper I wrote.' He hopes that Alexander and Olivia are as dim as he has always supposed and that they won't ask any further questions.

'Well, we'll let you go and catch you anon,' says Alexander.

'Enjoy *Phantom*.' Edward's heart continues to pound as he tries to block all thoughts of anything other than a polite termination of his acquaintance with Taryn.

After a few minutes, he joins her with a decaf tea.

'How are you?' says Taryn lightly, sitting at right-angles to Edward.

Edward wonders whether being honest will lessen his

position, but who else can he tell? 'Sleeping badly. Since … I don't know who I am any more. It wasn't me. It was a dream. I'd rather pretend it didn't happen.'

'Such flattery. I can assure you it was you,' says Taryn, giving him a sexy pout.

'I am wracked by guilt. All the things I despise in others apply to me now.' His voice is sad.

'It seems to me that you've been restrained for far too long. Felicity can't expect to have it all ways; to keep her distance and expect you to do the same.'

Edward sighs, clutching his tea cup with both hands, feeling the comforting heat. 'I'm sure it's just a temporary blip.'

'Most evidence would suggest otherwise,' says Taryn. 'Hate to tell you but women are only driven towards sex because of a biological need to procreate. Once that goes, desire soon follows.'

Is she offering herself as an antidote to the midlife tunnel towards despair? Edward remembers what Marianne said about hormones. He is hanging onto the hope that once Felicity has got used to the idea of menopause, she will want him again. 'You're generalising, Taryn. Not all women feel that way. It's too soon to give up hope. We've been married for over twenty years. We've strong foundations. I'm not used to things being bad between us.'

'People have problems all the time. Marianne and Johnny were on the slippery slope this past year,' says Taryn, 'Due to the cunning wiles of a woman called Charmaine.'

'Yes, Marianne told me, and as you mention cunning wiles, the words *pot* and *kettle* spring to mind,' says Edward.

'Hey!' She gives him a friendly punch from which he recoils. 'I am not trying to break up a marriage. Charmaine was.'

Edward stares at her, searching for the truth. 'And now

Marianne and Johnny seem fine. Things do turn round. I need to be patient with Felicity. I don't want to jeopardise a possible – or even probable – return to normality by behaving like a complete arse.'

It's a game of verbal tennis between two champions of repartee.

'You were Marianne's distraction,' counters Taryn. 'She claimed that having obliterated the ghosts from her childhood, she was less threatened by the scheming cow. I hoped I could be your distraction while Felicity sorts herself out.'

'That's a noble sentiment, but I'm not convinced either that you mean it, or that it would have worked.' Edward is buoyed by the notion that he matters to Marianne, but he will not cave in under pressure. His resolve is clear. He made a mistake. Nothing she can say will throw him off balance. He is skilled in dodging amorous advances. He's been doing it for years in the corridors of the university. Christ, he could have had medals for out-manoeuvring obsessed undergraduates who were anything but subtle.

Taryn fishes in her bag. 'Look, here's my card. I won't phone you, text you or come here. You needn't see me ever again. But I would like to see you – even if just a couple more times while your exhibition is finishing its run.'

'Why? What's in it for you? It's not going anywhere.'

'I like you. You've restored my faith in men.' She places the card in his hand, and as she does so, she clasps his hand between both of her own.

'And in the process, I've lost faith in myself.' He withdraws his hand clumsily, dropping the card onto the table.

'You're not a bastard, Edward. You were provoked. By Felicity and by me. You never went looking. It happened. These things do.'

'Not to me, they don't.'

'Can you deny that we had a good time?'

'No.'

'The best time?'

'In recent years. If I'm honest.' He doesn't want to leave her feeling bad about herself. He is still the gentleman.

'How can you regret that?' Again she rests her hand on his arm.

'It was just sex, Taryn, Nothing more. And that's not something I do. I wouldn't regret it quite so much if it wasn't for you knowing Marianne. And the fact you kept it from me. You knew I'd say no if you had. Now when I see her, I feel there are secrets.'

'And that's worse than betraying Felicity?'

'Different.'

Edward looks up to consider what he might say next. Then his blood seems to stop in its veins for the second time, for standing behind Taryn, in a long, dusky pink, dip-dyed summer dress is Marianne, gawping at them with a shocked look in her eyes. He experiences an unpleasant swimming sensation just underneath his ribcage. At first he thinks he is seeing things. Then a rush of heat and joy, followed by acute embarrassment at the predicament in which she has caught him.

Marianne stares, open-mouthed, then turns and walks away.

Taryn says, 'God! I wonder how much she heard. I'd better go after her.' She pushes her chair backwards and nearly spills her coffee in the process.

Edward is frozen and alarmed on several levels. He looks round wildly. This surely has to be almost as bad as Felicity finding out.

Taryn's thoughts move fast. Is honesty the best policy? Does she assume from the look on her face that Marianne has presumed the worst; guessed the truth? She will have to hope she is in a forgiving mood. Impeded by high heels, she is struggling to keep Marianne in sight.

Marianne in flat sandals moves swiftly downstairs, through the masses of visitors, slowing only when she nears the exit.

'Wait,' says Taryn, catching up with her just outside the entrance at the top of the steps.

Marianne stops. She looks flushed and her eyes are over-full with tears.

'I'm sorry,' says Taryn breathlessly.

'It is what I think it is, isn't it?' Marianne is also panting a little.

'I'm sorry,' says Taryn again.

'You mean you're sorry you were caught.'

The enormous stone columns loom beside them. Marianne sinks down onto the top step, smoothing her hair, tears falling, wiping her eyes. Taryn joins her. The evening sun is warm and bright, casting long shadows.

'Yes, but not for the reasons you think.'

'Don't presume to know what I think!' says Marianne. 'Just how long has this been going on? Weeks? Months? I feel such a fool.'

'The trouble with putting people on pedestals is that it doesn't take much to knock them off with an accompanying crashing and smashing of preconceived ideas. What you thought was reality turns out not to be so.' Taryn knows that Marianne will be devastated. 'Please hear me out.' She tries to be kind. 'It's not like it looks. Well, it was, but it isn't now. We won't be seeing each other any more. We had a one night fling. That's all.' The reality has sunk in even if she was pretending it hadn't. Even if she was stringing Edward along with reason after reason to see her again, she knew it was hopeless. He wasn't the philandering type. She'd always known it.

'You had a one night fling? Oh great!'

'It was nothing more.'

'How did you come to meet? You must've planned this.' Marianne's face darkens with incredulity. She takes a tissue from her bag and wipes under her eyes, smudging the mascara, making her look sultry.

'You were right about things not being great Felicity-wise. I was curious about everything you'd said. I took a chance. I found him here. It was my fault. Marc fallout. Madness. Wanting to prove that I could still attract someone – particularly someone who so plainly wasn't the type to stray.'

'So you did plan it. Not a word to me. I've told you virtually every thought I've had about Edward. How could you poach on my territory?'

'I don't recall sex being on the menu in your territory,' says Taryn a little crossly.

'That's not the point,' says Marianne. 'He's *my* friend.'

'Friends are not exclusive.'

'Have you talked about *me*?'

'He didn't know I was a friend of yours until afterwards.'

'Did you talk about me?' Marianne is insistent.

'Yes, but in a good way. He likes you very much and sometimes there comes a point in a man's life when he wonders what he's missed; especially someone like Edward who didn't play the field before he met Felicity. If it hadn't been me, it would probably have been someone else.'

'That's a typical guilt-assuaging excuse.'

'Better me than someone who's going to get involved and make a scene.'

'Edward wouldn't have gone looking for it. You know he wouldn't.'

'It might have been you. But you're married.'

'Is that what he said?'

'No.'

'Well, then.'

'Implied.'

'He's not the man I thought he was.'

'He is. He really is. In most ways. But he's human. You know what I'm like.'

'Yeah, too right. Not so different from the Cow-Charmaine.'

'I wasn't trying to split up his marriage, and I wasn't going to get clingy. Very different from the Cow-Charmaine.'

'You're not the friend I thought you were.'

Taryn is hurt. All this is true and reality is dawning. Her manic phase begins to crash and she sees herself as Marianne must see her and is ashamed. 'No, I'm not. I was selfish and got carried away. It started out as a challenge, a game, and it got out of hand. Edward is who you thought he was. Very nearly. He's suffered more than anyone I've ever known. He's been riddled with guilt. About Felicity, about him and you, about me and you.'

'So why, then?'

'Because he's a man. Because he's heading towards fifty. Because I was there and made it so easy.'

'I will never forgive you for this,' says Marianne vehemently. 'The ultimate betrayal is between women. We think we are the same and so we trust. Yes, I know you're no saint and that you've played around in ways you've never said. I know why you don't tell me. I don't want you to tell me because I don't want to be judgemental. You're my friend. Were. That was enough. I trusted you would never make a play for Johnny—'

'I wouldn't have. Ever. I'd draw the line—'

'So why Edward? I may not be married to him, but you knew how I felt. You've stolen him from me as a friend.'

'He's still your friend. There's no restriction on friendship.'

'But he kept you secret. He deceived me.'

'Not his fault. He had no choice.'

'Last week when he came over, it seemed so special. I thought we'd be friends forever.'

'You can be. Come back with me. Come and talk to him.'

'I've nothing to say any more.'

'I'll leave you alone together.'

'No.'

'Please.'

'No.'

'I won't see him ever again. I promise.' Was this true. Did she promise? What if he came to her again? What if he wanted her? He was so sweet. But he doesn't. He wouldn't. Hope was lost of ever having him as a lover. She might as well try to salvage her relationship with her friend. 'I promise,' she says again, this time meaning it.

'No,' says Marianne, standing up and brushing her dress with her hands. She looks like a wounded animal that is almost too weak to run. 'Tell him I won't see him ever again either.' Tears are starting to trickle beneath her eyes again and with a final shake of her head, she walks away.

Taryn finds Edward coming towards her.

'Shall I go after her?' he says.

'No. She's in a state. Leave her to calm down. She'll come round in a day or two.' Taryn feels the words sticking in her throat. She doesn't believe them and nor by the look on his face does Edward. He looks so vulnerable and her once-ice heart is a liquid pool, making up for over forty years of Arctic chill.

They look at each other hopelessly.

'It's not my fault,' says Taryn. 'Blame her, not me. I didn't know she was going to come today.'

Edward appears angry. 'I was opting for damage limitation. It's you who shouldn't have come today. There's no more to be said.' He turns away and heads back into the museum.

Taryn is left on the steps, a small deflated figure. She remembers his gentleness and closeness with a poignancy she never thought was possible. Seeing him again has overwhelmed her with emotional thoughts of their night together. She is mortified that he hates her so when all she wants is love. Yes, love. She cannot believe how much she cares and is wondering how she could have got it all so wrong.

21

Edward arrives back at the Deer Orchard, late, cold and tired. He leaves the car in the driveway and closes the door with care, as if he is embarrassed to indicate his presence. The sky is clear and a peppermint moon is high over the trees. The night is warm and smells of animals and grass, and he can hear an owl calling evocatively from the stand of oaks on the Molwings' land. He has loved this place for fifteen wonderful years of watching the children grow; a haven away from the bustle of his work. It is home, yet it no longer welcomes him as it used to do and his heart aches for the joyous times now lost.

He yawns as he puts the key in the back door. Sleep eluded him on the train, images of Marianne looking shocked and then running away, playing before his eyes like a reel of film; a horror film. *If only I hadn't gone for a chat with Taryn, then how different things would have been.* But he isn't one to play the 'if only' game and he had squashed the thought before the train reached Slough. He could not change the past, but he wondered what he might say to salvage the future.

The house is silent and he creeps around the kitchen fending off the dogs who bound and whimper in the hope of a late snack or even a walk. He finds some leftover chicken and mushroom pie, with instructions on a pink Post-it note from Felicity including information that all the children are in bed. He pops the pie in the microwave, cuts a hunk of bread and pours a glass of red wine from the half-empty bottle on the kitchen table.

Then he notices a large high-sided cardboard box by the

radiator. Inside there is a hen; one of the original buff Orpingtons. He gently lifts her out and takes her over to a chair where he sits with her on his knee. She doesn't object.

'And what's up with you, Helen Hen?' he says, noticing one of her eyes is swollen and closed. He strokes her feathers and she settles down contentedly making a low, slow clucking noise. 'You and me both,' Edward continues. 'What a state we're in … Have you been in a scrap? Cyril, was it? Or one of the new birds? We don't like change, do we, old girl? But what can we do? We have no choice. Got to adjust … Move with the times … Go with the flow. That's what Marianne says … Marianne … No, you don't know Marianne. She says it's no good fighting back if you want a quiet life.'

The microwave pings and he puts Helen back in the box.

Marianne … So many questions.

Why had she been at the museum? Had she come to see him? What had she wanted? Will she ever forgive him? Should he write to her now? *What a bloody mess …*

After the pie, he takes a second glass of wine up to the office and turns on the computer.

To: Marianne Hayward
From: Edward Harvey
Date: 22nd May 2003, 22.46
Subject: Emailing in Hope

Dear Marianne,
What must you think of me? I am having enough trouble thinking of me. It was all a mistake. It isn't the real me. Hope what you said to Taryn was just the result of shock and that in time you will be able to forgive me – and her.
It all seems so ironic when only the week before you

were telling me you thought I was wonderful! Felt guilty
even then. But what could I say? Once it was done, there
was no going back.
Were you coming to see me? A surprise, perhaps?
Ordinarily, I would have been so pleased.
Know you were upset by what happened. I'm sorry
beyond words.
love
Edward

After clicking the send button he deletes all trace of the email
from his computer and once again castigates himself for being
in such a reprehensible position.

Felicity is sound asleep when he goes up to bed, lying on
her front, head turned to the side, hair sprawling across the
pillow in curling tendrils. He undresses in the bathroom and
creeps stealthily back to the bedroom, draping his suit on a
hanger on the side of the wardrobe. The trouble with living in
an old property is that the floor boards squeak. Some he knows
to avoid, but tonight they all seemed out to get him.

Felicity stirs. 'That you, Ted?'

'I hope so. Shhh. Go back to sleep.'

Felicity is blessed with a sound constitution and a calm
temperament that means she could sleep on a washing line,
and is seldom disturbed, even by family strife. The outdoor
life and added responsibility are making her even more resilient
and it isn't long before her breathing becomes deeper and
audible.

He hasn't told her yet about Patrick Shrubsole's offer. There
may be no need. He doesn't know if he fancies spending so
much of every week away from his country idyll even if it
doesn't seem so idyllic at the moment.

He wishes he could discuss it with Marianne.

Come Saturday morning, there is still no word from Marianne. Edward decides he will try very hard to involve himself in Felicity's schedule so that at least he can't be accused of not making an effort. He has been so wrapped up with London visits and keeping on top of his university workload that he almost hasn't noticed that spring is turning to summer, that the days are becoming balmy and that Felicity's little seedlings have graduated from the greenhouse to the garden and are beginning to grow into something distinctly edible.

Rick's raised vegetable patches allow ease of picking, improved soil quality and good drainage. They and the traditional plots are now under full production and the first of the home grown produce is being harvested – mostly in the form of salad vegetables and leaves. Much goes to the restaurant, but already Felicity has found an outlet for surplus at a grocer's on the edge of Exeter, as well as in Broadclyst village shop. In addition, they have joined the three-weekly cycle of Farmers' Markets at Silverton, Whimple and Topsham, James and Rachel taking responsibility for getting up early to do the necessary transportation and selling. Usually James's girlfriend, dim Kylie, is persuaded to help. The only problem is that although she can cope with selling single items, adding up has never been her forte and she becomes muddled and flustered if anyone asks for more than two items. For this reason all the prices have zeros on the end.

The old tangle of previously untended strawberry plants is cropping well despite minimal attention, and Gianni has been creating some delicious mousses, sorbets, ice creams and soufflés. Rick has said to Felicity that next year they might consider polytunnels, but Edward is concerned over the environmental impact, not least the views from the air. Rick has also suggested raspberry canes because buying fresh is exorbitantly costly. Edward would like to object to this too, but he likes raspberries and agrees that it would be cost-effective.

Meals are taking on an altogether more interesting tone as Felicity practises dishes that may find themselves on the menu at the Retreat, and leftovers from both her efforts and Gianni's make their way back to the house. Home grown animal produce is still limited to eggs, and soon chickens, but James and his friend Paul have been joining Len Molwing and his son Peter when they go out shooting rabbits, and Felicity is often using the resultant haul in fancy starters or stews.

Soon after breakfast there is nearly a diplomatic incident between Olivia and Felicity, the former having been habitually popping round in the hope of acquiring a particular vegetable or a few eggs. Edward has just brought the dogs back from a walk and can't help but overhear.

'Olivia,' says Felicity, 'much as I would like to hand out veggie freebies to all my friends, I am trying to run a business and at the moment we are nowhere near breaking even. If you'd like to borrow some wellies and help us with the picking, then we could discuss some sort of edible recompense.'

Olivia glances at her long nails and shakes her bird's-nest hair. 'Darling, I couldn't possibly risk ruining these. Couldn't you spare just a teensy-weensy lettuce?'

Felicity stands her ground. 'We sell them for sixty pence at the market, but I'll settle for fifty as it's you.'

Olivia looks decidedly put-out, but rummages in her Prada bag for some change. 'I never thought of you as parsimonious before,' she says a shade huffily.

Edward rushes to Felicity's defence. 'Be fair, Olivia. We have to treat all our friends the same and Flick can't just keep handing over our produce as if it was nothing. Rick has to be paid ...'

'It's a lettuce,' says Olivia.

'And last week it was eggs, radishes and spring onions,' says Felicity.

'And they were sooo delicious. How about swapsies, then? I could bring you something you don't have in exchange. A bit of old fashioned bartering.'

'Swapsies would be most acceptable,' says Felicity and the crisis is averted.

After Olivia has gone, Edward asks Felicity if there's anything in particular she would like him to do. James and Rachel are selling at Silverton Market, and Harriet and Christopher are collecting eggs and strawberries.

'There are four rabbits waiting to be skinned and cleaned, if you're offering,' she says. 'And if you're up to some DIY, there's a flat-packed hen coop waiting to be assembled. We need to move Helen, Amy and Sarah into the orchard. They refuse to mix with the others and I don't want any more injuries.'

He wishes he hadn't asked. Minutes later he is up to his elbows in fur and intestines and after that he is in the orchard with a toolkit and some dodgy instructions. He is out of his comfort zone but refuses to be beaten. Of course he could have said no, but he needs the Brownie points. It is at times like this when Rick's presence would be most welcome.

Two more days pass and Marianne still hasn't replied, despite Edward trying to will a response. He wonders if she has gone away for half term, searching for an explanation for her silence other than the obvious one: that she meant what she said about wanting nothing more to do with him. He finds it difficult to contemplate life without her emails – both mad and sensible – and now that he has met her, she seems an irreplaceable part of his life. Come Wednesday, he has almost given up hope when her name appears in the Inbox.

To: Edward Harvey
From Marianne Hayward
Date: 28th May 2003, 20.19
Subject: Re: Emailing in Hope

Edward,
Sorry for the delay in replying, but I have been at a loss
to know what to say, or even if I want to say anything.
I know you are sorry you were caught out. Were it not
for my being on a course near Russell Square, I wouldn't
have come to see you and would have been none the
wiser. It was meant to be a surprise because soon the
exhibition will be over and I thought it would be good
to meet again before it becomes more difficult – and
hopefully have a chance of the guided tour round the
mazes as you promised.
One of the reasons I've been so candid with you is
because I believed 100% in your integrity. I've said to you
before that male-female e-relationships are fraught with
difficulty but I believed we had transcended the potential
problems because there was no hidden agenda.
I know it's not your fault that Taryn is my friend, but
even if it was someone else, I would feel the same.
Marianne

Ouch! This is not what he wanted to read.

To: Marianne Hayward
From: Edward Harvey
Date: 28th May 2003, 21.02
Subject: Re: Emailing in Hope

Dear Marianne,

Have let you down big-time. Have let myself down.
There is no hidden agenda, I promise I can be trusted!
This was a temporary aberration due to forces that at
the time seemed beyond my control. Am going through
some kind of midlife crisis. Have never before had to
face problems with Felicity. Have been unsure how to
deal with it. Am dismayed by not seeming important to
her any more and that my wishes are not being taken
into consideration in anything that she does. Don't
want to sound like I'm making excuses, but perhaps
these might be considered mitigating circumstances?
Taryn has the same dominant manner as Felicity and
for a few hours of complete madness (fuelled by
alcohol) I fell under her control. Pathetic! Am wiser
now.
As ever, in the continued hope of friendship.
love,
Edward

To: Edward Harvey
From Marianne Hayward
Date: 29th May 2003, 20.40
Subject: Re: Emailing in Hope

There are no mitigating circumstances in this situation.
You have been luckier than most in having such an easy
passage through the matrimonial maelstrom thus far. If
the solution to problems is to leap into bed with the
Taryns of the world (and I'm assured there are many of
them out there), then we would all be playing the game
and there would be no hope for trust.
Marianne

So harsh, thinks Edward. *So judgemental … Probably because of the business with Johnny and that Charmaine woman.*

He is hurt and considers a response.

To: Marianne Hayward
From: Edward Harvey
Date: 29th May 2003, 23.05
Subject: Re: Emailing in Hope

Believe me when I say that I agree with your sentiments.
All I ask is that you forgive my transgression.
Edward

Days go by, a week, then two; it is almost mid-summer, and there is no further word from Marianne. He decides he will continue to send her emails every so often and hope that eventually she will relent.

22

Meanwhile Taryn is also preoccupied by thoughts of Marianne. After the fracas at the museum, she tries at first to pretend that nothing serious has happened and that she and Marianne will carry on as normal. At work, when she is not teaching her classes she returns to the staffroom and manically sorts out folders and files, throwing away accumulated piles of old photocopies and worksheets that lie in half a dozen cardboard boxes under and around her desk. When an anxious thought surfaces, she swats it away. After all, Marianne knows what she's like when it comes to men and this hasn't so far had a detrimental effect on their relationship.

Half term arrives and Taryn waits expectantly for contact. Usually Marianne would phone either to chat, or to arrange a walk in the park or a game of tennis. When by Friday she hasn't called, Taryn acknowledges that she should act fast if her friendship is to be saved.

She has just come home from a shopping trip to the Glades in Bromley and is sitting on a stool in the kitchen, drinking a cup of coffee and sorting through her post. Late morning sun is streaming through the window and she relishes the idea of swinging a racket in the open air. She sends a text message to Marianne suggesting they meet, but receives no reply.

Taryn becomes thoughtful. When she was a teenager, her mother said that friends need to be nurtured just as much as boyfriends because when the boyfriends disappear, the friends will still be there to pick up the pieces. Now Marc is gone, she needs Marianne more than ever. Throwing herself at Edward (and at least she admits to that particular verb) has been a Very Unwise Thing to Do and she must consider her strategy carefully if she wants to put things right. Marianne is no fool and she also finds forgiveness difficult – as demonstrated over the business with Johnny and Charmaine which took a considerable while to resolve.

On the following Monday evening she calls Marianne by landline, thinking that a direct approach will be the best policy. Johnny answers and tells her Marianne is not at home. Taryn doesn't believe it.

'She's probably told you we had a bit of a disagreement a couple of weeks ago. I want to put things right.' She tries to sound light and casual, but inside she is uncharacteristically worried.

'Taryn, I don't know what the problem is, but I can't force her to speak to you.' Johnny's tone is one of mild exasperation.

'But you could persuade.'

'She's quite adamant.'

'P-l-e-a-s-e, Johnny.'

Johnny pauses. 'Okay, I'll see what I can do. Are you at home all evening? I'll try to get her to phone you back.'

Taryn doesn't for one moment think that Johnny will try very hard to persuade Marianne, so it is no surprise when the hoped-for return call doesn't materialise.

She decides to write a letter, by hand, to send by snail mail. Thankfully she has some writing paper left over from a Christmas present given to her the previous year. It is white with a spray of primroses in the corner. A bit twee for her tastes, but it will serve the purpose. It is years since she's written an old fashioned letter and it takes her several attempts before she is satisfied with the result.

Dear Marianne,

We have been friends almost forever. We've had our ups and downs and always come through them. I've always been rash and silly and thoughtless. You know this and you've put up with me and helped to keep me on track. If you and Edward hadn't known each other and I'd told you about him, you would have persuaded me not to lead him astray. You see without your guidance, I am a moral bankrupt!

I can't turn the clock back, but how I wish I could. Please give me another chance.

Already I miss our chats. I had hoped you'd want to play tennis soon. I still hope.

A million sorries,

Taryn

xx

Short, but it says what she wants it to say. She folds the paper carefully, pops it in an envelope, seals it and adds a first class stamp. She will put it in with the school post tomorrow.

Two days later she is once again doing playground duty with Kimberly Edge. The sun is blazing and they stroll languidly round the perimeter of the playground.

'You look different,' says Kimberley. 'Are you okay?'

'I met a man, a kind and thoughtful man who taught me *love*,' says Taryn.

'Is that a poem?' says Kimberley. 'I like that. I feel that about Jase.'

'Yes, kind of. "He took me on a journey across vast blue oceans, to an island where the seas were warm ... Where mermaids lay on rocks and sang ... And now he's gone and I am changed."'

'Beautiful. Who wrote it?'

Taryn smiles wistfully. 'It was written by a foolish woman about a man called Edward Harvey.'

'I don't think I know him. What did he do?'

Four days later, she receives a reply from Marianne through her letterbox.

Dear Taryn,

I appreciate your writing and at least recognising the enormity of the damage that exists between us.

I am calm now, but no less shocked. I cannot believe what you did. It was despicable and totally against the grain of friendship.

Time and again I think that it shouldn't matter, but then I realise it does. My friendship with Edward is so important to me. He links my past to my present; he healed my soul. I worry that without him I will lose my confidence again. He has been like a good luck charm since I found him. But all that is changed now. I don't trust him any more. There's no point in continuing the contact.

Just now I don't want to see you either. I will get angry again and it will serve no useful purpose. Maybe in a few weeks I will have calmed down, but I don't know if we can go back to before after such a break of trust.

I miss you too. Already I wish we could be chatting about the things that we've been doing this week. But even if we did meet up, the chatting wouldn't be like it used to be, so I would still be feeling a sense of loss.

They say that each moment of forgiveness is a karmic step forward. I'm not big enough to take that step.

Marianne

*

Taryn sighs and scratches her head. She has stopped moussing and blow-drying her hair and she is unaccustomed to it feeling flat and limp. She will write again, this time by email.

To: Marianne Hayward
From: Taryn Danielli
Date: 10th June 2003, 16.12
Subject: Trying to Build Bridges

Dear Marianne,
Thank you for your reply. You've always had a bigger heart than me. Please, please, forgive me. I promise I won't compromise our friendship again.
Love and hugs,
Taryn

She wishes, she hopes, but nothing comes back in return.

Where should she go from here? Will Marianne relent under pressure, or is it best to leave her in peace? If Marianne was a man, she would know what to do: retreat and wait.

But Marianne is not a man.

She remembers when she fell out with Katrina. It was over something and nothing, yet the rift lasts to this day.

Usually she says, *'What's the matter with them? I am the wronged one; I am the victim. They are the bitch, the betrayer, the incompetent, the gossip, the unreliable one.'* But not this time; not with Marianne.

Katrina was half-American, and tiny like herself but with long brown hair and a soft almost cherubic face with round eyes spaced wide apart. Katrina and she were friends just after university, both teaching in the same school when Marianne was in the full throes of love with Johnny and didn't have so much free time as before. Taryn and Katrina partied and dated and slept their way out of boredom as an antidote to the newly-acquired professionalism they were expected to portray during their working days. They went to pop concerts and writhed and bounced close to the stage with blue-streaked hair and wild black eyes. Once at some rock band gig they were invited to the party afterwards, where a hotel suite was awash with half-naked girls and drugs and sex and whole pineapples balanced on every available surface. Taryn and Katrina surveyed the scene, assessed the talent, looked at each other, winked, and homed in on suitable targets. It was like an orgy. It was an orgy; such fun to be had before the threat of Aids.

And so it went on for a year or two until Taryn invited Katrina round one evening and Katrina phoned about two hours before she was due to arrive saying she was out of sorts, was tired and could they give it a miss. Taryn went all cool and frosty, telling Katrina she had refused another invitation for the evening and that she hadn't planned to be on her own. 'I expect you to honour our engagement,' she had said curtly. She was in one of her slightly manic phases and craved company.

When Katrina still said she wasn't coming, Taryn went into a sulk and didn't call her again. Ever. Katrina didn't call her either, and that was it.

Something and Nothing.

But big consequences.

Afterwards she told Marianne that Katrina had let her down, but in a more rational mood, she assented that perhaps she had been unreasonable. She has since regretted her pig-headedness. That is why she acted so swiftly with Marianne. Before it is too late. Or is it already too late? She won't yet give up.

Gloom sets in. It isn't grey like ordinary gloom, but black and navy blue with lightening streaks of yellow and orange. Her head hurts and her legs are leaden. She feels slightly sick and doesn't want to eat. On Sunday morning she stays in bed all day in a trance-like state playing over recent events.

She recalls her night with Edward and the new feelings it stirs. She wishes so much to experience the thrill again, but he made it pretty clear that he didn't want her, even before Marianne's untimely appearance. That hurts. She wonders if it's Edward she wants, or someone like him. After all, she hardly knew him and after delving into archaeology in order to impress, she knows she isn't all that keen on his subject – all that dust and death gives her the heebie-jeebies. Marianne is genuinely keen on the ancient world. No wonder they are friends.

Someone like Edward … That's what she needs.

By evening, the sickness has waned a little and hunger forces her to the kitchen. She throws together some pasta with tomato and basil. *Always pasta …* It reminds her of childhood and home. She sits eating it in front of the television, but the screen is blank. There is enough drama going on in her head.

She hasn't seen her father since her mother's funeral eighteen years ago. He sends her cards on birthdays and Christmases and occasionally a cheque which she always sends back without a word of acknowledgement. He used to phone sometimes and she used to hang up. It's almost like this now with Marianne, but the opposite way. She doesn't like being on the receiving end. *What goes round comes round,* she thinks, pessimistically. Someone like Edward wouldn't want a bitch like her.

She hears how her father is keeping from her sister Louisa who still lives in Leeds, a mile or so from Carlo. Louisa is a nurse, married to Ian who manages a local store. They have two frighteningly well-behaved girls, Emma and Tamsin, who write Auntie Taryn thank you letters almost before they have opened their presents. She can relate to them better now they are teenagers and within the zone of her teaching experience. Louisa is always inviting her to stay, but Taryn believes it is a conspiracy to reunite her with Babbo. Louisa says Carlo no longer drinks and is riddled with guilt. He wishes more than anything that Taryn will make peace before he dies. So far she has been unable to forgive. *Like Marianne!*

What goes round comes round …

When she looks in the mirror with her flat hair and no make-up, she sees the little girl she was, looking distinctly middle-aged, and it scares her. What would her father think of her now? She doesn't like what she sees on the outside or what she feels within.

I am a bad person. She says this twice to herself and then once out loud. Before, other people were the bad ones.

Before what?

Before Edward.

Edward is a good person. She is sure of that, yet together they did a bad thing. She hears the nuns from her school talking about her childhood sins and making her say Hail Marys and Our Fathers until she was cleansed. And her sins were only little sins in those days.

Thinking vindictive thoughts about Lynne Beacham.

Arguing with Sister Concepta about the nature of the Holy Ghost.

Hiding Terry the gardener's spade – only because he was rather dishy and she wanted him to notice her.

Bunking off from a games lesson because Sister Thomas always made them have showers and she hated the lukewarm water, the feel of the chilly white tiles under her feet and exposing her young body to the scrutiny of the other girls.

Now she doesn't believe in God and reckons it will take more than a few prayers to get her out of her current mess.

As well as losing God, she has also lost her spirituality and the latter, she believes, can exist without the former and be found again.

Why am I bad if Edward's good? We both sinned. What makes us good or bad?

Her mind blanks and darkens again. She takes her plate to the kitchen, but adds it to a growing pile of unwashed dishes from the day. She might go to bed and hide under the duvet until this mood goes away. But what if it doesn't go away?

Intention is the key to goodness and badness, she thinks. *I did not mean well; my intentions were bad. Edward didn't mean to sin. I am bad ... I made him do a bad thing, but he is not bad.*

She is soothed by the child-like repetition, the familiar feelings of Catholic Guilt and the untangling of her confused thoughts.

Why am I bad? Was I born bad, or made bad?

She knows the answer to this. All in the space of a night when she was so young and she lost her faith in her father.

She wonders if she should try to get some help. Not so much with the hypomania or depression, but with her fear of loving and the destructive force that comes with it.

She remembers Dr Woodcock and his eagerness to recommend drug treatment. Times have changed. And she knows that there are many other forms of therapy that might be helpful.

This time she wants the best and someone not too close to home. She returns to the living room, boots the computer, Googles 'Harley Street Psychotherapists', checks a couple of sites and scribbles down a number.

23

To: Marianne Hayward
From: Edward Harvey
Date: 22th June 2003, 22.01
Subject: Still Emailing in Hope

Dear Marianne,

Your silence suggests you haven't forgiven me. Will never forgive myself ... Will live in hope that in time you will believe my sincerity and regret, and will continue to mail you unless you say not to. You have said before how easy it is to lose touch ... Would be a pity after all the memories we've shared. Only beginning to know the real you!

Lectures at BM finished; exhibition dismantled and Henrik and I are going to collaborate on a book about mazes. Already have interested publisher, so it's just a question of meeting the deadlines.

Hope things okay with you.

love,

Edward

Edward has always been extremely disciplined and personal matters have rarely been allowed to distract him from his work. Since the Taryn incident he has been restless and less focused and now that Marianne has found out, he finds it even more difficult to concentrate.

At the university he is uncharacteristically devoid of

enthusiasm and would be in danger of forgetting appointments were it not for Gemma's efficiency. He can tell by her furrowed brow and the way she keeps trying to reduce his workload that she knows all is not well. She doesn't ask, and he believes it would be unwise to tell her. If she thought his marriage was going through a difficult time, she may harbour false hope.

The students have completed their exams and are trickling home for the summer. The annual calmness has fallen on the university as buildings and open spaces are reclaimed by staff, who now have time for idle chatter and reflection instead of constantly rushing between lectures, seminars, tutorials and meetings.

It is the time of year when the research aspect of the job cranks up a gear. Papers that have been promised and put on hold are at last written, and in the fertile soil of a student-free campus, new theories are germinated and ideas cultivated. But Edward's thoughts are clouded by Felicity's continued distance and the seeming loss of Marianne. Guilt taps away at his sensibilities like a sculptor chiselling through a piece of stone, leaking contentment, leaving a hollow space of emptiness and finality. If she were to forgive him, then perhaps he would feel absolved for his transgression.

To: Marianne Hayward
From: Edward Harvey
Date: 5th July 2003, 10.38
Subject: Book

Dear Marianne,
Often wonder what you are doing and how things are progressing with your book. Are you still writing? You said you wanted to show me some of the Brocklebank

chapters. I would be very pleased to see anything you
have written.
Edward

Felicity's ventures are in full swing. The Retreat is gaining an
excellent reputation, the menus detailing ingredients and the
decision to offer a two-tier portion size and pricing being very
popular with customers. The potato harvest is well underway
thanks to her forethought in chitting some even before she
gave up her job. Rick planted them out in March and they
have been cropping since June.

Tired of rebuff, Edward is very cautious about approaching
Felicity for sex. Occasionally it is she who initiates, but he
suspects it is out of duty rather than desire, as she is less than
enthusiastic and seems keen to hurry the process along with, he
believes, faked climaxes. He wonders if this is the pattern of the
future until they cease having a physical relationship altogether.
He hadn't planned for early celibacy. Perhaps if all other aspects
of the relationship were good, then it wouldn't matter so much.

He is surprised that he is becoming fond of the sheep.
They are so calm and non-judgemental and he spends much
time watching them at dusk. He will be sad when the growing
lambs have to leave, though Felicity says she will hang on to
the girls to expand the flock.

To: Marianne Hayward
From: Edward Harvey
Date: 15th July 2003, 18.13
Subject: Still Emailing in Hope Despite Having Nothing
to Say

Dear Marianne,
Hope you are surviving these crazy temperatures! We

215

are slightly cooler down here today, but London looks monstrous.

Realise now how much I have depended on you coming up with conversation topics! It is easier to respond than to initiate. Now I find it hard to know what to write. Perhaps I lack imagination?

Sorry to be so brief. Still hope you will reply one day.

I am sad that you've gone … Just sad …

love,

Edward

After sending this email he blinks and takes a deep breath, struggling for composure. He leaps from his seat and calls the dogs for a walk. He needs to get out. He doesn't want any questions about his state of mind.

Rachel comes running after him. 'Dad! Dad! Can I join you?'

Edward never says no when his children want to walk. For years he has encouraged them away from the computer or the TV and out into the open air where, he tells them, real life begins.

'Are you okay, Dad?'

She floats by his side in a summer skirt and skimpy vest, and with retro '70s fashion very much in vogue and her long flowing hair, she reminds him so much of the young Felicity. He nods, giving a half smile. It is always a shock when the young begin to ask after the welfare of parents; an acknowledgement of adulthood, responsibility, a changing of the order. He doesn't know what to say. Rachel can read him too well.

'It's all this stuff of Mum's, isn't it? I know you don't agree with everything.'

Rachel matches him stride for stride. He likes a brisk pace

and where as Harriet always moans at him to slow down, Rachel often pushes him faster. 'It's not that I don't want her to do these things. It's her turn. Your mother has stood by me since we met. Entertaining the right people; looking after you lot; making sacrifices. Perhaps I didn't realise how much.'

'She doesn't ask you any more, does she? Like about what she wants to do. I heard her telling Olivia. She said if she asked you and you said no, then she wouldn't be able to do whatever, and that would be that. I think it really matters to her.'

'I know. It's taking me time to adjust. It's a new way of life.'

'Will it get sorted?'

'It's normal for married couples to hit sticky patches. We've been unusually lucky to be free of them thus far.'

A sticky patch … Is that all it is?

'Do you tell Fanclub about it?' fishes Rachel.

'I haven't heard from her for a while,' says Edward.

Rachel gives him a lingering stare as if checking for validity.

They cut through the paddock and walk down the lane that borders the Molwings' land, Felicity's sheep in the nearest field are mostly lying down and gazing skywards. The air is humid and hazy. Edward wonders if it is going to thunder.

Rachel picks a strand of long flowering grass from the verge and swishes it as she walks. 'James and Kylie are really into the markets. I mean Kylie! Who would have guessed? And Mum says she makes a good waitress.'

'Is James serious about her?'

'Serious as in shagging, or serious as in potential marriage?'

Edward cannot believe how open his children are about sex. He never discussed such things with his parents and is disarmed, embarrassed. He gives her a shocked look.

'Hey, Dad; it's cool,' she says and scampers after the dogs, turning and grinning over her shoulder.

Soon she will be gone. With James being nearly the oldest

in his year, and Rachel one of the youngest, they are only an academic year apart. In fourteen months, two children will have flown the nest, a family halved in the blinking of an eye.

To: Marianne Hayward
From: Edward Harvey
Date: 20th July 2003, 7.49
Subject: Crossroads

Dear Marianne,
Am at a crossroads in my life.
When does it happen that the future becomes predictable? When do people stop saying, 'You have your whole future ahead of you'? Your future is always ahead of you and in truth, always uncertain. When does a whole future become half a future?
Have a choice to make – a radical one. Do I settle for maintaining the status quo, or make a few feathers fly by taking the job in London and commuting back here for long weekends and holidays? This is probably the last chance for something different. I haven't discussed it with Felicity yet – I don't want to unsettle her unless I decide to take up the offer. Am I more likely to preserve my marriage by staying or going? Would 'absence make the heart grow fonder'? I am an outsider here now, despite best efforts to adapt.
I always appreciate your psychological take on such matters.
As ever,
Edward

By the end of July there is still no word from Marianne and Edward is losing hope.

To: Marianne Hayward
From: Edward Harvey
Date: 31st July 2003, 6.47
Subject: Losing Hope

Dear Marianne,

Tomorrow am off to Scilly, and home on Monday
evening. Let's hope this year's holidaymakers are
interested in mazes! May hire a bike on Tresco. Looking
forward to being there and getting away from all the
activity that now goes on at home! No peace to be had
here any more. There are always people everywhere and
am noticing it more now since end of term when I
spend far less time at the university. When I try to work
I am constantly disturbed or being badgered into helping
pick things, skin things (rabbits!), or dig things up. But it's
great that Felicity is making a go of this and that the
children are each finding a role in which they can be
useful. There are also positives with regard to the quality
of meals!

A pattern is developing to Felicity's week. On Mondays
when the restaurant is shut, she spends an hour in the
morning with Rick establishing what fresh produce will
be available that week and what needs to be planted and
harvested. In the afternoon she meets Gianni the Italian
chef (who is rapidly acquiring a Devonian accent!) and
plans the week's menus. Of course there's a fairly
standard menu that is tweaked every month or so, but
each week they add new dishes depending on what's in
season or what we are growing. (I say 'we', but as you
know, I play virtually no role in this!)

The restaurant is open Tuesday – Saturday evenings and
now Wednesday and Friday lunchtimes when 'Women

who do lunch' seem to flock there in droves. (Excuse agricultural metaphors!) Already it is popular. Felicity's concept was spot on and Gianni can cook very well. Word is getting around and people are travelling from quite far afield. She has had to take on more part-time staff (mostly friends of the kids while it's holiday time!) and it seems to be paying for itself, which is a relief. One or two mornings a week she makes or paints rustic pots. (Did I tell you she has had one of the outhouses turned into a kiln?) The rest of the time is looking after the children, animals or cooking. Another month or so and our home-reared lambs will be ready for slaughter. Will be sad to see them go, but already they are losing their sense of fun.

We are rarely in the same place for long enough to speak – except at meal times when there's always at least one child present, or in bed when she's too tired. Have tried so hard in the last few weeks to mould into her new way of being, but am not succeeding. Perhaps age has made me less pliable!

love,

Edward

Tomorrow, Scilly. Once Marianne would have been so swift to wish him well. He has written early in the evening to give her time to reply. Surely if she is ever going to reply, she will reply to this. He has written more than he has ever done in one hit. She will know how much effort it has cost him.

Outside it is still warm and balmy and is only just beginning to get dark. Felicity is outside watering plants, checking the kiln, putting the hens away, counting the sheep and lambs.

Marianne … Saviour of my troubled mind … Where are you?

He knows she checks her mail regularly and if she's working

on her book, she'll be on the computer late in the evening. Before he retires to bed, he checks his email again.

Nothing.

A dark thought occurs; a thought that seems to extinguish joy from his life. Perhaps when he returns it will be time to let her go.

24

Behind closed doors in a flat just off Harley Street, Taryn is buried in a squashy mustard armchair in a room that looks very much like a small sitting room, but without the homely clutter. A desk and computer are in the corner and there are prints of Klimt's *The Kiss* and Monet's *Water Lilies* on the off-white walls. Taryn notices a box of tissues discretely placed on the lower shelf of a central table with a glass top. There's a sofa and another chair. No *chaise longue*; how disappointing. She is unusually nervous and picks absently at the stitching of her denim jeans.

In the second squashy chair, Shaleenie Velandran looks decidedly more relaxed. She is an elegant woman, probably in her late thirties and dressed flamboyantly in a long Indian-inspired print skirt with gold embroidery and sequins, and plain pink top. Copper-coloured bangles jangle on her forearms. With her long dark glossy hair, she might have stepped out of a Bollywood movie.

First she asks Taryn about necessary administrative details and background information, then she asks if Taryn understands about how confidentiality works.

'I'm not going to top myself,' says Taryn.

Shaleenie smiles and sits back in her chair and crosses her legs. 'Have you had any counselling or therapy before?'

Taryn explains about Dr Woodcock and the suspicion that she has borderline bipolar disorder. 'But I didn't do any tests, or anything like that. We just talked.'

'Tell me why you are here,' says Shaleenie in a quiet

unthreatening voice, notepad almost hidden in the folds of her skirt.

Taryn's first instincts are to lie, to pull the wool, to deceive, to fake. Then she remembers exactly why; that she is looking for answers about the person she has become; an explanation of how she has stooped so low as to cheat on her best friend (for that's how she sees it). She remembers it's ninety pounds a session and decides to come clean.

She begins at the end with a distraught Marianne, on the steps of the British Museum, and as if the events were connected by a coloured rope, she traces them back to Edward, hesitantly, hanging on for dear life lest she lose her way.

It is difficult telling Shaleenie about him. She blushes; she is ashamed and frightened of being judged. She tells of the almost wild compulsive need to track him down and break through his defences; how their first meeting evolved with flirtatious repartee, and how she followed it up with cunning and guile that now horrifies her when she thinks of the damage it has caused.

'And afterwards – after that night – I felt something … Something different, compared with the others.'

'How would you describe this feeling?' asks the quiet voice with no hint of judgement.

'Warm and safe. I didn't want him to leave.'

'And do you never remember feeling like this before?'

'Not since I was a child.'

Shaleenie tilts her head, saying nothing. Taryn waits for her to ask *when?* and *who?* Like a friend would in the games that friends play when they want to tell, but want to keep the suspense; teasing, holding back, making the friend work for the information.

Then she remembers it isn't a game; that it's ninety pounds an hour.

'My Babbo used to make me feel safe until—' She stops, again waiting for the prompt that never comes. 'He was great at first, when I was very young. Lots of love and cuddles. Then this guy Gino opened a rival ice cream business and something snapped,' she laughs. 'I mean, it sounds crazy that such a little thing … but to them it was Ice Cream Wars. Imagine that! I suppose with Babbo it started out as stress, and that led to the excessive drinking, and the drinking led to him beating up my mum.'

'How often did this happen?'

'Once or twice a week.'

'And you were how old?'

'Eight or nine.'

'Where were you when this happened?'

'Mum used to send us upstairs when he was in a mood. That's me and my little sister, Louisa. *"Take Louisa upstairs,"* she would say. *"Take Louisa upstairs."'* Taryn is back in the little terraced house, a small defiant child facing her father, the man she once loved so much it hurt. 'We used to hide behind the bedroom door waiting for the shouting and the crashing, holding on to each other, shaking.

'One night I went downstairs and tried to stop him. I thought he wouldn't hurt me, his little darling; his *Bella*.' Taryn says this last word with a sarcastic sneer in her voice. 'But he was a different man. Crazed. He shouted and called me names and hit me as well. Yeah, he apologised the next day; said it wouldn't happen again. But I'd heard him make such promises to my mum. I didn't believe him.'

'And did he hit you again?'

'When he was drunk. It was as if he couldn't help himself. I started to hate him.'

'Are you sure?'

Taryn licks her lips and furrows her brow. *Am I sure?* Everyone knows that love and hate are closely related, yet once she'd decided to hate her father, she never thought that she might still love him. Thinking back, it had been a struggle; an effort requiring huge determination not to be seduced by his offers of chocolate and other treats. 'I wanted to hate him, but I had to try really hard to make it happen, to stop feeling love.'

'And do you think you succeeded?'

'At a conscious level.' Taryn smiles, aware that she is offering her own analysis.

Shaleenie smiles back in acknowledgement. 'You have mentioned several things: your falling out with your friend; your father; your night with Edward. Which of these is the most important?'

'My relationship with my father made me determined not to love any man. So I dated the ones I didn't respect. The bastards.'

'In what way are they bastards?'

Taryn glances down but doesn't see. Shaleenie won't let her get away with anything even though Taryn is sure she knows the answers. 'The usual things. They're sexy and entertaining when you meet them and they make you feel a million dollars. They have to have you. They say they've never met anyone quite like you; that you're special and funny and beautiful. What girl doesn't want to hear that? Eventually they wear down your defences. You sleep with them. Then the games start. They back off and approach, and back off again until you don't know where you are and your head's in a spin. But I never allowed myself to love them. They're untrustworthy and unreliable; they let you down; they probably don't like women very much.'

'Why do you think you're attracted to such men?'

Taryn thinks: *because I am susceptible to bastards. Because I am a bastard magnet.* She considers a way of phrasing this in a way more acceptable to Shaleenie.

'I've had good times with bastards.'

Shaleenie waits, then widens her eyes at Taryn and juts out her chin, inviting more.

'Stops me getting too close; liking them too much – in case they let me down. I did to them what they did to me. But I did it better and they came running. And that is why this guy, Edward, was different. He wouldn't normally have strayed. He was the ultimate challenge and I made it almost impossible for him to resist. I'm good at getting men to want me. Physically, that is. After Marc, my most recent relationship, I wanted to prove that I was still good. Clearly I am!' She hears herself sounding conceited, the manic side of her personality coming to the fore, *delusions of grandeur,* and she shrugs and grins as if she doesn't really believe what she has said.

For a moment there is silence. Shaleenie waits, then asks, 'Do you see your sister nowadays?'

'Not much.'

'How often?'

'Twice a year, perhaps. Phone calls every month or so.'

'How did you feel about her when you were small?'

'Protective.'

'Did he hit her too?'

'No.'

'How do you feel about her now?'

'She's always trying to persuade me to get in touch with Babbo, but I have nothing to say to him.'

'What would the child Taryn have wanted to say to him if she'd had the words?'

'That he hurt me both physically and mentally. That I was too young to understand why; that it wasn't fair; that it's ruined my life.'

'How would you feel about telling him that now?'

For an intelligent woman like Taryn it is easy to make the connections now that she has been pointed in the right direction.

Looking back on the session, she can see that her case was easy-peasy for a professional like Shaleenie to unravel.

Marc fallout plus feeling middle aged equals need to prove attractiveness. The bigger the challenge, the greater the reward from success and the greater the self-esteem. Edward equals the biggest challenge possible. Over-excitement brought on by hypomania leads to blinkered vision and failure to take anyone else's feelings into account.

Edward not being bastard material leads to feelings of love long buried, and elevation of him to a level of importance beyond that which was reasonable and rational after such a short acquaintance – and especially given their respective interests. Also peeved that he still favoured Marianne despite wild sex with Taryn. Voila!

Ninety pounds to discover what I already knew. Hmph!

Taryn knows deep down that she wouldn't have come to these conclusions so quickly – or admitted them – without the expert help from Shaleenie. However, now that she has been provoked into facing truths, she is clever enough to run with it and progress, at least in part, on her own. She will see Shaleenie again, but she is too expensive to drag the whole process out for an unnecessarily long time.

She will talk to Louisa and possibly, just possibly, arrange a meeting with her father.

25

Many who discover the Isles of Scilly wish they had found them earlier in their lives. Photographs show a tropical archipelago in a turquoise sea, yet the islands are only twenty-eight miles south-west from the tip of Cornwall, usually hiding behind the weatherperson on TV, which is probably why many people are unsure exactly where they are.

Edward sits in the open stern of the catamaran *The Spirit of St Agnes* which is ferrying him across from the main island of St Mary's where he arrived via plane from Exeter. His mind has been racing since leaving home, thoughts tumbling over each other as if they are in an Olympic dash. He tells himself to stop, to slow down, to remember where he is and that for the next few days he will have some time for calm.

The boat is lurching on a choppy, blue-black, white crested sea, its engine droning noisily. Voices of other passengers are very much middle-England and Home Counties. Ages are varied, but the adults are probably between thirty-five and seventy, while the children seem mostly pre-teens.

St Agnes is the most southerly of the islands, only a mile across in each direction. It is a country in miniature with many different moods; a wild and rugged perimeter around a patchwork of tiny hedge-bordered fields. The lighthouse shines bright-white from the centre, still an important day-mark, but the light is no longer used at night and resides in the museum on St Mary's.

The boat's engine changes into a less urgent key as it chugs into The Cove between St Agnes and its partner island Gugh (pronounced as *you* with a G in front of it and attached by an umbilical sandbar except at high tide). *Spirit* manoeuvres against the quay, protective buoys on the side thumping and scraping as they contact the stones, water slapping and slurping and splashing. The ropes are tied and passengers are helped ashore by a smiling, sun-bronzed young man in denim cut-off shorts and a red vest top. As Edward steps up onto the sloping quay he feels he has truly escaped from his Devonian life, if only for a few days. He hopes the distance will enable him to think clearly about his future. Nothing is simple any more. The life plan that was once so pleasantly predictable has recently been through a shredder.

A flaxen haired gentleman of imposing stature is waiting to greet him with a few other accommodation owners, all looking slightly anxious lest their visitors have missed the boat. He is Julian Beresford-Smith, the owner of the Parsonage where Edward is staying overnight. Hands are shaken and pleasantries exchanged about the journey and the weather.

Edward knows from previous experience that he should make his own way up the half mile or so of track to the Parsonage, and that Julian will fetch his luggage from the quayside and transport it in the back of a small truck. Other visitors are also met by their hosts and a convoy of tractors, trailers and buggies are waiting in line. Cars are strictly not allowed and holidaymakers need to be prepared to walk.

Edward passes the Turk's Head pub on the right, making a mental note to come back down for a late lunch. Sparrows hop around the picnic tables that overlook the tiny harbour, pecking at crumbs, so tame like all the garden birds on Scilly. He wonders why they have no fear, for even though there are no wild predators, there are cats. It is a twitchers' paradise, with a wide variety of both resident and migrant birds. Johnny and Marianne said that when they last holidayed here, the visitors' log at the Parsonage noted an excess of a hundred and forty different species spotted in the garden.

As he walks, dimly conscious of the noise from a group of gulls arguing over territory on the rocks below the pub, his mind wanders back to home and he recalls his last conversation with Felicity. It wasn't so much a conversation as a series of grunts from her as he tried to provoke an emotional response to his departure. He was in desperate need of reassurance as to his continued significance, and having come to expect a family fuss when he was going to be away from home for more than a couple of days, he considered this indifference to be a measure of how much things had really changed.

The previous year, prior to his leaving for the dig, Felicity had insisted they go out for a meal and then she pampered him with champagne and leisurely sex. Now she is hardly the same woman. Tending to the animals until late the previous evening, she fell into bed, announced she was *'knackered'* and turned her back. In seconds he could feel the tremors and hear the deep breathing of early sleep and he had closed his book, all remnants of hopefulness gone.

In the morning she asked for a reminder as to when he was returning. James slapped him on the back and said, 'Rock on, Dad.' Rachel gave him a hug. Harriet, who had never been too keen on hugging, proffered an embarrassed half-wave from a safe distance of three metres, and Christopher bolted past him on some vegetable-related mission dreamed up by Rick whom he worships with the zeal of a pop star fan.

Now on St Agnes with its wild beauty and emptiness, Edward feels small and insignificant and alone. The isolation of Scilly is a stimulus for facing truths and confronting the demons. There is no escape. Here one's emotional guts are on display, a bared soul to be cleansed by the fresh salty winds; for sadness to give way to gladness; to renewed hope and optimism.

Agapanthus flowers the size of grapefruit spring from the verges and over garden walls; vibrant blue lollipops, exuding an evocative scent, the summer scent of the island. The path is narrow and he has to squash into the pittosporum hedge to allow the passage of a tractor and trailer conveying baggage across the island to Troytown camp site. Each few hundred metres of path has its own character, built by different islanders in sections according to the materials available and their differential skills. In places there are muddy patches and potholes and he treads a zigzag line where the path has deteriorated. It could do with a grant from English Heritage or the Lottery Fund. He will put in a word next time he bumps into the West Country Director.

Tomorrow morning he will limber up his lecture series with a talk and walk here on St Agnes, including the Troy Town maze. He passes the island stores, a small multi-purpose shop and post office. Outside there is a blackboard where chalk scribblings tell of boat trips and cancellations, and notices of upcoming events. A single yellow wellington and a green fleece are laid out on the rock beneath it; lost property.

He reads: *'Saturday 2nd August: Dr Edward Harvey tells us about his discovery of our original maze, of mazes in general, and the archaeology of Scilly. Meet at Phone Box at 10.30. for walk to Castella Down. All welcome.'* In a place as small and remote as this, where the inhabitants are generally responsible for their own entertainment, a visiting speaker of any sort, let alone a published and highly respected university don, is the cause of great anticipation.

He isn't being paid for his efforts but his accommodation is being provided at no cost, and in any case he sees it as some recompense for the hospitality he received last year and the freedom that allowed the discovery to be made and his archaeological career to be given new impetus. Perhaps the publicity will be of some benefit when he and Henrik publish their book, though with such a small population – even with the addition of holidaymakers – this seems overly optimistic. Either way, it is a break of a sort, and with Felicity being so busy, the only one he is likely to have this year. He wonders if, with all the new animals, they will ever go away together again.

The Parsonage is a sizeable white building tucked snugly among mature trees below the lighthouse. As well as offering the bed and breakfast facility, it has been extended for self-catering and Julian has built more holiday accommodation in the orchard at the back. On Scilly, it pays to be multi-skilled and resourceful. From its elevation, when the weather is clear, Edward has views across a plush green mattress of tree-tops to all the other main islands.

Julian is married to Pam who was a Hicks. It seems nearly everyone on the island is related to a Hicks, as evidenced by the memorial plaque in the church remembering those who died during sea-rescue missions, and the inscriptions on the tombstones in the graveyard.

Pam greets him like a long-lost friend. She asks about his journey and the family and shows him to his room which overlooks their well-stocked garden. Every available nook bursts with agapanthus and perennial colour. Lawns are divided by cordyline palm trees, their yucca-like leaves and nests of creamy flowers adding an exotic touch. Huge hydrangea bushes border the pathways leading from the house, and gnarled fruit trees heavy with developing apples, rise from the orchard.

He unpacks and settles down on the double bed for a short power nap before walking back down to the Turk's Head to indulge in a steak. Then, after a pint of beer and a word or two about tomorrow's walk with a couple of windswept women of a certain age, he decides to visit the maze on his own; to run through what he plans to say; to savour the atmosphere.

He strolls back up the road again and past the shop. Outside a cottage, a basket has been left with *50p* written on a wooden cover. He lifts the lid and looks within where there is a tin and half a dozen live crabs which twitch a little when he prods them.

Further up the hill past the lighthouse there are small stone cottages, more agapanthus, and a trolley on which organic vegetables appear throughout the day, as if delivered by fairies. Items are individually priced and a plastic ice cream container houses the money. Edward takes a closer look and finds a jar of ruby chard, bags of courgettes, boxes of cherry tomatoes and bunches of herbs. He is comforted in the knowledge that there is still somewhere in England where old-fashioned values and honesty prevail. Had he been self-catering, he would have made use of all of these offerings.

He continues past the line of coastguards' cottages with their misplaced watchtower. Previous visits to Scilly have acquainted him with the knowledge that the islanders tend only to divulge information when asked. They therefore did not interfere when the builders of the watchtower constructed it at the wrong end, facing away from the sea.

Just beyond, at almost the highest point on the road, he turns through a gate to the left and bounds down towards the sea, feeling the springiness of the turf beneath his feet. Ahead there is the stunning spectacle of the natural rock known as the Nag's Head. From his high vantage point it looks like an angel with huge wings. Up close the shape of a horse's head is clearly distinguishable, towering above Edward, carved from the granite over hundreds of years of extreme weather conditions, and covered on the eastern side with a thick mat of healthy grey-green lichen. He runs his hands across outcrop, feeling its roughness and fissures and the different textures of the lichens.

At the Nag's Head, he turns sharp right, heads through a

gate and down a hedge-bordered track, dodging many old and new cow pats, before entering Castella Down with its majestic rock formations rising up in grandiose piles, all naturally created, yet with the artistic balance of a Tate Modern installation. Between the rock-piles are little coves, one with dozens of pebble towers, the granite sparkling with mica crystals as if filled with tiny stars. He never ceases to be awestruck by the geology and wonders if this is what attracts Marianne's husband Johnny to the islands.

Sadness seeps out of him and hangs in the wind, enveloping him with grey mist despite the luminosity of the sky and sea. He is filled with a sense of his own mortality, aware of unfinished business and an urgency to make the right decision that will shape the years to retirement. This time last year he was happy. How quickly things change. For so long he led a life of clear direction and purpose, much of it orchestrated almost imperceptibly by Felicity in the background. If he is honest, it was she who decided when they married, where they lived, when they had children. She fed these notions to him often during the aftermath of some night-time intimacy, and happy to have someone else make the decisions while he focused on his career, he gave her free rein.

Now he is paying the price for all that freedom. Perhaps he shouldn't blame her for her lack of consultation over the restaurant and the animals; it is little more than has been the norm throughout their marriage. Only the sex has changed; the lack of sex. And while this was often in the past the gateway to some revelation, its absence, in her mind at least, might suggest a consequent lack of suitable opportunity to tell him things.

He continues on the undulating coastal path and quite suddenly comes upon the 1980s' maze, built by dowsers who believed the original had been put in the wrong place. There are no signs of warning to announce its presence; it is just there. Unobtrusive, cobble-sized stones marking out a path of seven concentric circles; except they are not circles, but a labyrinth following the traditional pattern of a Troy Town maze. Nearby are the fading scars of the old maze, now largely overgrown with short tufted grass, and directly beside it, freshly excavated the previous year and more deeply sunk into the earth, an ancient maze he found by chance when an inspirational whim caused him to suggest digging to the side of the old one.

The area is well known for its energising properties and, after walking the maze, he sits on a grassy patch, breathes deeply, closes his eyes and tries to think of nothing.

But nothing won't come. Instead are images of home; imagined conversations with Felicity about Stancliffe; the face of Marianne when she saw him with Taryn at the British Museum. He pushes them away but they return bigger and bolder, making more noise, competing with the seabirds and the wind.

What had Marianne written in her email? *I believed 100% in your integrity.* Clearly she didn't any more. That hurt. His thoughts buzz back and forth like trapped bluebottles: Scilly; lecture; Marianne; seabirds; Felicity; mazes; Taryn (No! Block the thought! *Out, out damned thought!*); Stancliffe Uni; Devon Uni ... Marianne ... Felicity ... Lecture ...

He has never contemplated a life without Felicity, and if he were to take on the job at Stancliffe then it might be a sign heralding the death throes of his marriage. It was unthinkable. Or was it? Until recently he had felt cherished, translating her support as love. But if he took a cynical standpoint, every action of their relationship, from the moment she approached him in the student refectory to their moving in together, to the children, could be seen as cold calculation to ensnare a man with good prospects, who was kind and dependable. Seen in this light, her so-called love seems contrived, and the speed with which she has withdrawn her affections now she is a woman of independent means with hormones on the slide, begins to fill him with suspicion.

And what of the progression of his feelings for her? She entertained him with witty repartee, created a comfortable home, cooked like a professional and allowed him to discover the magic of sex. She was confident and attractive, convincing him that she could have married any man she wanted and that he was special because she had chosen him. When the children came along, he felt privileged and blessed, and whenever she mentioned her restaurant dream, he never took it seriously, convinced she was completely content in their family idyll. She was the woman behind the man, and he loved her for it. Now when he looks over his shoulder, she is nowhere to be seen, but in her place is a shadowy figure that has been increasing in clarity in recent weeks; the figure of Marianne.

The sun is fierce and the ground hard and dry. He scans the horizon. In the distance the Bishop Rock lighthouse stands sentinel like a hazy, elongated pawn. He takes off his jacket and making a roll for his head, lies flat against the earth trying to feel the pulse of the ley lines, the energy to help the decision he must make about whether or not to take the offer of the professorship at Stancliffe. Gradually, the negative images recede and the cooling wind licks his face and all he can hear are waves and sea birds crying.

He drifts into a light sleep and when he wakes and sits up, he thinks he sees a woman with long dark hair in loose ringlets down her back standing a few metres away on the rocks. She is unsuitably attired in a long white dress and she has ribbons in her hair. He thinks he hears singing, but it could be the gulls and the wind. His head is still dulled by slumber. He blinks and rubs his eyes, looks again and she has vanished. He has heard of the ghost of St Agnes, but doesn't believe such things. She must be a lone and eccentric camper taking a stroll before supper.

Scilly is not a place for dressing up, the wild winds, the walking and the boat travel playing havoc with any attempt at sartorial elegance. Strong footwear, shorts, jeans, t-shirts and sweaters, mostly in muted colours, are the most practical uniform. Layering is essential as the weather can turn in minutes from bright sunshine to a darkening sky with chilly Atlantic breezes. A cagoule lies waiting in most rucksacks.

Felicity used to pack for Edward before he went on any trip longer than a day or two. She claimed he had no idea of practicalities. This time she was picking herbs for the restaurant when the time came.

For his lecture round St Agnes the following morning, the sun is warm and he is wearing a pale blue open-necked cotton shirt with the sleeves rolled up, and a respectable pair of denim jeans. The wind blows his hair even more tousled than usual, and the more mature women in the waiting audience by the phone box sneak appreciative glances as they catch up on the local gossip with their fellow islanders.

At events like these, most of the island's adult inhabitants capable of self-propulsion will show support. A significant handful of holidaymakers have also joined the group, keen to learn more about the archaeology of the islands that many of them visit year on year.

He wishes Marianne was among them; his fan club, his childhood admirer, his friend. Recently she has provided solace and advice in ways that were once offered by Felicity. But now even she seems to have given up on him, and he feels an emptiness commensurate with the expanse of nothing beyond the south-western rim of the island where there is only the Atlantic Ocean for hundreds and hundreds of miles.

By teatime, Edward has left the Parsonage, returned to St Mary's on *Spirit* and is transferring to Tresco on *Firethorn of Bryher*, a single hulled, open boat with twenty or so people on board.

Tresco is the second largest of the Scillies and independently leased to the Dorrien-Smith family. It exists very much as a commercial enterprise, mostly of holiday timeshare properties and two hotels, and unlike the other islands where visitors are secondary and merge with the community, on Tresco they seem to be its life-blood. Some have described it as a glorified holiday park, but that is to devalue its wealth of history, its silver-sand beaches and views reminiscent of an ocean paradise.

The approach to Tresco is glorious, and on the calm turquoise sea, gazing upon the Monterey cypress trees rising high in the middle and forming an exotic skyline, Edward imagines he might be in the south Pacific heading towards a treasure island of wrecks and pirates and skulduggery.

Opposite, a young couple gasp at the view, kiss and hug each other and delight in their romantic holiday. Again Edward is aware of absence – Felicity's, not so much in the physical sense, but the spiritual.

When he wakes the next day at the luxurious Island Hotel, he is disorientated. Sun streams through long flimsy curtains in front of the French windows of his room and he is aware of being hot under a sumptuous white cotton covered duvet, his head enveloped in squashy pillows.

Through the curtains is his private balcony with rustic stairs leading down to the garden and a view across to some of the Eastern Isles and St Martin's. *This is the life,* he thinks, but wishes he had someone to share it with and that Felicity had torn herself from her garden, her animals and restaurant just for a couple of days. It is odd that in the past he has relished such solitude. It may be 'the life', but he is lonely without the emotional connection.

He has arranged for a bicycle to be delivered to the hotel and after a leisurely breakfast of cereal, toast and poached egg with smoked haddock, he locates it among the many others in the cycle racks and sets off for the Abbey Gardens at the southern end of the island. The day is his until the evening lecture, after dinner.

The air is sweet and balmy with hints of ozone, and the sun is trying hard to break through the mists. He sets off, struggling up the hill past the church then, with growing confidence, free-wheeling down the other side, past the New Inn.

He stops off at the island shop to buy ham, cheese, crusty bread and some juice for a picnic lunch. It is refreshing being able to leave the bike leaning against a wall without any fear that it will be taken.

Then back on the narrow roadway he passes tractors pulling strange green contraptions, open at the sides, and in which visitors sit helplessly as they are ferried from the heliport or quay to their accommodation, as he was the previous day. It reminds him of *The Prisoner*.

To the right across a narrow channel is the small island of Bryher. At very low tides he knows it is possible to walk across. *Not for the faint-hearted,* he thinks. Tresco feels less isolated than St Agnes, snuggled between the crooked arm of St Martin's and Bryher's shadowy hills. The protection afforded from some of the fiercest winds is one of the reasons for the most incredible and diverse array of sub-tropical plants in the Abbey Gardens.

Edward parks the bike, pays his entrance fee, consults the map and plots his course. The gardens are described as 'spectacular', and they don't disappoint. Of course he has been there before, but it is impossible to see everything in one visit.

He strolls, he stops to admire, he strolls some more, and round each corner, along each path, extraordinary examples of vegetation jostle for attention. When he came with Felicity, she reeled off many names that he had never heard before. She was his guidebook and he remembers being impressed and wondering when and how she had committed to memory so many complex Latin names. Eventually he settles down on a lawn in a more open area and eats his lunch; then a cup of tea in the tearoom and back to the hotel, following a track across the middle and round the other side of the island.

All the while his thoughts flit from the scenery to home. He stops by the magnificent Monterey cypress trees on the hill in the centre of the island. From a distance they give Tresco its uniquely tropical contours and close up they seem to stretch to heaven. He touches the immensity of one of the trunks and gazes upward into the never-ending canopy. He loves trees; he knows his trees, and perhaps if Felicity had wanted to manage a forest, he would have joined in the adventure wholeheartedly.

Back on the bike his thoughts turn to the question of the professorship at Stancliffe. Perhaps he has been selfish? Perhaps it is Felicity's turn to do what she wants and perhaps he should accept her unilateral decision-making without question because in many ways it is what she has always done. If he didn't like it he should have stepped in before twenty years had elapsed and habits had been formed. He will say *no* to Stancliffe; *no* to being Professor Edward Harvey; *no* to the long weekly commute that would have effectively told Felicity that he wanted nothing to do with her plans. He will try to show more interest in the day to day running of the restaurant, he will accept that his time is over and edge graciously towards retirement in his job at the University of Devon, writing the occasional paper, perhaps giving the occasional lecture elsewhere – and skinning the odd rabbit in between.

He has behaved abominably with Taryn and if he is to suffer, then so be it. He will even give up trying to persuade Marianne to forgive him because she, too, is a distraction and he doesn't deserve her friendship. He will compromise for the first time in his life.

In the evening, boatloads of holidaymakers are ferried from Bryher and St Martin's for dinner at the hotel followed by his slide show and lecture about the archaeology of the Scillies. This lecture will be repeated on St Mary's the following evening before he returns home.

The lecture takes place at the back of the dining room which has been hastily set out with a semi-circle of chairs and a screen. Edward had already sorted the slides and the projector. Twenty-eight islanders and visitors have come to hear him speak, and next morning Edward accompanies some of them, plus additional trippers, back to St Agnes for a repeat of the archaeological walk, taking in the maze. Judging by their questions, they seem enthusiastic and appreciative. Then it is a return to Tresco, bags packed, boat to St Mary's, another very comfortable hotel, and the whole process repeated.

The walks and talks are a success and when he climbs aboard the plane to journey home, he feels the sense of satisfaction that comes from a job well done. He has also managed to lay the foundations for possible excavations on Tresco the following summer, accompanied by his students.

As the plane takes off and the islands become fast retreating specks of land in the vast Atlantic, he drifts into a light snooze where images of agapanthus and the Parsonage garden become tangled up with Felicity and the hens ... And a woman walking on the cliff edge near the Troy Town maze with her hair blowing free. A woman they say is the ghost of St Agnes. Or is it Marianne?

26

'Gordon Bennett! What's with the new style, sis?'

Add a foot or so of long dark hair, remove make-up, snappy clothes and high heels, substitute ill-fitting jeans, oversized t-shirt and trainers, and Louisa Claypole is a carbon copy of her sister. The basic framework is identical; the finish is as far removed as it is possible to be.

In temperament too, the sisters are not the same. Where Taryn is wild storms and burning sunshine, Louisa is misty drizzle and at best low cloud with cool bright patches as the sun tries hard to penetrate. A dour Yorkshire husband with a penchant for wearing women's underwear, is possibly the reason. Ian is also – in Taryn's opinion – frightfully dull, conversing at length about the psychology of trapping shoppers into buying goods with astute product placement and cunning aisle displays. As far as Taryn knows, Louisa never suffered abuse from their father, so her inclination towards pessimism can't be blamed on that.

On the positive side, Louisa is warm-hearted and compassionate and possessor of more than a fair share domesticated genes.

It is Friday lunchtime in mid August, Taryn having gone straight to Kings Cross station after breakfast and hopped on a train to Leeds. She touches her new silky-smooth hair and grins. 'How's things?'

'So-so,' says Louisa with a downward turning of the mouth, giving Taryn a hug before ushering her into the living room and onto the only chair devoid of pending ironing. 'Excuse the mess. Kids, eh! Tamsin won't wear anything twice before it's washed. I think she takes after you. Emma's more of a slob, like me. They're out, by the way. McDonalds and the flicks with a couple of friends. Thought we might need some privacy.' She has the same dusky voice as Taryn, but with a more obvious northern accent.

Taryn glances at Louisa's clothes but thinks better than to affirm what she has just said. Instead the new more diplomatic Taryn says, 'You should get them to do their own ironing now they're teenagers.'

'It's easy to see you haven't got children. Anything to keep the peace … Y'know, it's years since I've seen you with your hair flat.'

'I'm having an overhaul. What do they call it when snakes shed their skin?'

'Ecdysis,' says Louisa, who is a nurse and studied biology at A level.

'Yes, that's the chap. Ecdysis … I'm reinventing myself like Madonna. And not just on the outside.'

'Don't tell me you're having that colonic irrigation?'

'You must be joking! I'd not be letting anyone anywhere near my backside with a bloody hosepipe.'

'What then?'

'Psychotherapy.' Taryn feels pleased as she says the word. As if giving it to another person to play with makes it real. It's an admission that she has a problem and needs sympathy not judgement; that she is trying to do something about it like an alcoholic standing up and announcing it to a support group.

'"Bout time too, if you don't mind me sayin'. So what's brought this on? Why now? I'll get you some food while we chat. Pasta okay? I saved some sauce from our last night's supper.'

243

'Pasta would be great.' Taryn follows Louisa into the chaotic kitchen and tells her about Marc, Edward and Marianne.

'You've excelled yourself this time, I must say.' Louisa shakes her head, puts a pan of water onto the cooker to boil and breaks open a new box of tagliatelle. 'Always thought Marc was bad news and I knew there must be something funny going on when you said you wanted to come and stay for the weekend. Ian thought you might have some terminal illness. You haven't, have you?'

'Not as far as I know.'

'Marianne's been your friend for donkeys'. I liked her. That time when I came down for your twenty-fifth. She was interested in me and what I wanted to do.'

'That's Marianne. She's not a selfish, egocentric bitch like me.'

Louisa raises her eyebrows.

'I notice you're not contradicting me. You're supposed to pat me on the head and tell me not to talk crap.' Taryn sniffs and then starts to cry.

Louisa looks shocked and offers her a tissue. 'Hey, sis! Where's this comin' from? You're always sayin' you don't do cryin'.'

Taryn blows her nose and apologises. 'It's this therapist woman, Shaleenie. She's opened the floodgates. Or she's made me open the floodgates.'

'I think it's *you* who've made you open the floodgates,' says Louisa, who knows a little about psychotherapy from her nursing training. 'You wouldn't have gone to see her in the first place if you hadn't wanted to change things.'

'Not at ninety pounds an hour.' Taryn wipes her eyes and gives a hollow laugh.

'Coo, is that how much it costs down there?'

'Yup.'

'And this Edward bloke – will you be seeing him again?'

'I am the pits as far as he's concerned. He is a really nice guy, you know, and I've stuffed things up for him as well as me.'

'It takes two to tango.'

'I caught him at a weak moment.'

Louisa pauses and folds her arms. 'There are other Edwards. Other nice men. Granted they're likely to have an ex wife and a kid or two.'

'Edward is different. Intelligent, sensitive, nice-looking; but he had something special that you don't find every day. Even Marianne said he wasn't a run-of-the-mill guy. She didn't believe he was capable of adultery either. Said she felt safe emailing him. That's why he was such a challenge for me.'

'Oh Taryn!' Louisa says it in a voice that is used to saying it; a voice that expects disappointment; that despairs of her sister ever doing the right thing. There have been many '*Oh Taryn's*' over the years, uttered first by their mother Daisy, and later by Louisa.

'I know. I'm such a disaster area when it comes to men.'

Then while eating the pasta, she tells Louisa about her mania and depression and Louisa nods as if she has known all along.

'Might you see our dad?' she asks.

'I might, but not this visit. I want to talk to you first and then just maybe I'll see Babbo another time. But I'll need you to prepare the ground. Don't want him going into shock and having a heart attack.'

'You don't want to leave it too long. He's not in the best of health as it is. I think it's his liver. Even though he hasn't drunk anything for years – so he says – the old habit has caught up with him.'

There's a flutter of concern in Taryn's abdomen. Is this new, or would it have happened despite the therapy?

Later when the washing up has been done and the kids have returned, been fussed over and gone out again, Louisa and Taryn take a cup of coffee into the living room.

'How's your relationship with God these days?' Louisa is still staunchly Catholic and a regular attender at Sunday Mass.

Taryn laughs. 'Don't, Louisa. Just don't.'

'He will listen if you ask,' says Louisa.'

'Nothing will persuade me back to the Catholic fold,' says Taryn with emphasis.

'But you don't have to go back *into* the fold. Just wander round the outside and peer over the wall. There are ideals that might be helpful.'

This sounded a little like how her spirituality might be re-awakened. 'And how do I peer over the wall without getting sucked back in?'

'How about a retreat?'

She'd never thought of that.

Louisa continues, 'There's an abbey in Sussex that does retreats. I wanted to go myself, but couldn't leave the girls.'

Taryn feigns disinterest, but makes a mental note. Monks would be easier for her to deal with after suffering at the hands of nuns. *And they're men!* Then she castigates herself for impure thoughts.

The following week, Taryn tells Shaleenie of her visit.

'And how do we feel now?' asks Shaleenie. Today she wears a long, purple cotton dress with a gold chain belt worn low on the waist.

'Relieved to have said everything I've been bottling up for years. I never realised how much resentment I felt towards Louisa. I resented the fact that she's not had to suffer what I did, yet it was me who protected her from it at the time. How logical is that? I'm going to see my father next time. Soon. I'm looking for closure before he dies.'

'This is excellent news,' says Shaleenie. 'You have come a very long way in a short space of time.'

'But I keep slipping back. The old thoughts are still there. I'm constantly fighting them.'

'It takes more than a couple of weeks to learn new patterns. The thing is not to be disheartened when you slip up.'

'And there still remains the problem of my friend Marianne. What do you think I should do?'

'What would you like to do?'

'To tell her what we spoke about last time. About the mania and the depression. About Babbo drinking and hitting me. About my fear of loving.'

'Would she understand?'

'She teaches psychology.'

'Why do you think this might help your situation?'

'It would explain why I wanted Edward. If she understands that, then maybe she will see it as less of a breaking of the sisterhood vow. I never thought she would find out. And I never stopped to think how she would feel if she did.'

'And if she hadn't found out?'

Taryn sighs. 'A month ago I would have said that would make it okay; today I say of course it wouldn't. My sister asked me about God. When I was little I used to pray that Babbo would stop getting drunk and stop hitting Mum. When it seemed God wasn't listening, I gave up on him. I was a good child until then. A bit strong willed at times, but essentially good. I felt I didn't deserve what happened; that if God was fair, he would see that and protect me. What I'm trying to say is that while my moral decline might be linked with disillusionment and lapsing as a Catholic, it doesn't necessarily follow that in order to regain a more principled way of living, I have to rediscover the church.'

'Quite so,' says Shaleenie.

'But I will try to rediscover my spirituality.'

By the end of her second session, Taryn believes she has enough tools to continue the treatment herself – at least for the time being. Louisa was right in identifying that the cure comes from within; that the desire to be healed is an essential precursor to the success of any therapy. However, she believes that this process might be supported by a retreat at the abbey that Louisa mentioned and she resolves to look into the possibility. When she steps back into the sunshine in Harley Street, it feels as if the burdens she has been carrying for almost forty years are beginning to fall away.

Meeting up with her father will be traumatic, and she doesn't yet know what she will say, but she hopes that the end result will enable her to forgive and move on.

She also intends to visit Marianne.

Both can wait until she's been to the abbey.

27

After his trip to Scilly, Edward is met at Exeter station by James, not Felicity. His hopeful optimistic heart sinks, but he is still very pleased to see his eldest child. It is gratifying to have the taxi roles reversed.

'Hiya, Dad!'

Edward slaps his son on the back. 'Only a week to go until the results. You okay?' Despite the approaching evening, it is still very warm and he removes his jacket.

In the car James cuts short Edward's ramblings about the wonders of Scilly. 'Look Dad, before we get home there's something you need to know.'

'Nobody's ill, are they?' He turns suddenly cold.

'Nothing to do with health or anything.' James hesitates. 'We have a new acquisition.'

'Your mother's?'

'Yeah.'

'Spending more money? On what this time? More animals?' The cold feeling is replaced with a different anxiety.

'No, not animals.'

'What then?'

'You'll see in a moment. She said just to warn you to be prepared for a surprise; not to tell you what it was.'

'Oh God.' Edward had hoped his homecoming, and decision to make peace, would be uncomplicated.

They turn into the road that leads to the Deer Orchard.

'Oh bloody hell, James. What the fuck is that?'

'Dad!' reprimands James; more role reversal.

'I do not believe this! Has your mother gone stark-staring mad?' Edward is horrified by what he sees.

A huge bright white structure rises from the farthermost corner of the orchard, clearly visible above the trees; a central cylindrical tower and three angled blades at the top rotating slowly in the breeze.

'It's only a wind turbine. Don't you think it's cool?'

'I think …' Edward daren't repeat what he really thinks, but already his thoughts of peace and calm have evaporated. He grits his teeth and James gives him a worried sideways glance before turning into the drive.

Christopher is the only member of the family waiting in the house to greet him, unless you count the dogs who bounce delightedly at his feet, the spaniels making low woofing noises, tails like metronomes. According to Christopher, the girls are at a barbeque in Silverton and Felicity is down at the beehives.

Edward strides through the garden towards the orchard wondering what he should say. He is incensed, and although there is a part of his brain telling him to calm down and that nothing can be achieved by going mad, the other part feels he has been calm for too long and that this will provide an excellent opportunity for catharsis; for releasing all the anger that has been backing up over the preceding months. Felicity – he presumes it is Felicity – is bending over a hive, attired in her bee-suit, her face hidden from view.

'Okay, Flick, how much?' he says before he has quite reached her.

Felicity jumps back from the beehive. 'Ted! It's brilliant, isn't it? Have you had a good time?'

Edward is not sure whether she is oblivious to his anger or using cunning tactics to distract him. 'How much?' he asks again.

'Forty-three k,' she says through her beekeeper's space

helmet, wafting a bee with a thick white-gloved hand and replacing the lid of the hive.

Edward gasps. He daren't come too close because already there are stray bees flying uncomfortably close to his face. 'You have spent forty-three grand on a bloody windmill without asking me? I'm sorry but it's not on. You've gone too far this time.'

'Aw Ted! Don't be such a bore. Think of the advantage: free electricity. And we'll be able to sell some back to the Grid. Estimate is that it'll pay for itself in nine years.' Felicity says all this calmly. She is expert at averting rows with cheerfulness and measured responses.

'Nine years! And that's supposed to make me feel better? I might be dead in nine years.' He feels his anger bounce back at him from her protective clothes. 'Look, can we talk properly? I can't see your face.' He backs away from the hives and Felicity follows.

'Statistics would suggest we'll still be around to benefit.' She takes off the gloves and the helmet and shakes out her hair in which there are bits of hay. They walk back to the house.

'Don't you need planning permission?'

'You were too busy with the exhibition. I didn't want to bother you. It's all sorted.'

'Killerton and the council?'

'Killerton think it is a great idea. They may follow suit in a few years.'

'You knew I'd say no. This is really underhand and shabby. I'm bloody cross, Flick. I suppose it's too late to send the damned thing back?'

'But it's beautiful! Look, Ted. Clean energy and far enough away not to be noisy for us or the neighbours.'

'And no objections on the grounds of spoiling the view?'

'We are lucky to be surrounded by people concerned over

the wellbeing of the planet. Only the Pavals have been a bit sniffy but they get sniffy over anything. You can't even see it from their house.'

'You could have bought a smaller one.'

'Small might not be enough for our eventual needs.'

He wonders what these eventual needs might be and how far Felicity intends to expand her enterprise. He doesn't want to know the future, yet irrationally feels left out of the present. 'We should have discussed it.'

'And you tell me everything, Ted?' she says.

He begins to panic. Taryn? Marianne? What does she know?

She continues, 'Patrick Shrubsole ring any bells? Some Dean or other at Stancliffe?'

'Ah.'

'Yes, "*ah*,"' says Felicity.

Why is it that she always seems to finish with the upper hand? 'There was no point in worrying you about it when the likelihood was that it would be dead in the water, for practical reasons if no other.'

'Ditto wind turbine.'

'Not the same thing at all. Wind turbine very much happened unless I'm seeing things.'

'And Stancliffe?'

'I thought I'd think about it a little more while on Scilly.'

'And what have you decided without consulting me,' says Felicity, still in measured tones, making him feel like a naughty child.

His resolve to decline the offer and to become involved with her enterprise suddenly seems a much less attractive possibility. 'I've decided to see if it can be accomplished.' The words escape from his mouth almost without him being aware that they have.

'Oh,' says Felicity.

The power pendulum swings back in his direction. 'It's a good enough train service to London. I became quite used to it while the exhibition was on.'

'That was once a fortnight, not three or four times a week – which would presumably be the case if you were working in London.'

'Ah,' says Edward again. 'Perhaps I could stay somewhere during the week. We could buy a flat with your bottomless pot of money.'

'Buy a flat! Even the price of a shoebox up there is exorbitant.'

'Forty-three k on a wind turbine is exorbitant. James will probably be in London. We could share.'

'Are you mad? James won't want Daddy cramping his style.'

'Only for part of the week. And the space might do us good. You and me.'

'Space? What do you mean space? We've enough space here, haven't we?'

They stop in the corner of the orchard to put the old hens away in the small coop assembled by Edward. He is privately pleased that it hasn't collapsed.

'I've told you how I feel,' says Edward. 'I've tried to become more involved, but this is just not my thing. Patrick's offer is too good to refuse. I've been too long in the same institution. I'm stale – I need a new challenge.' The justification was easy once he started.

'Stancliffe isn't exactly Oxford – or even Exeter. Not sure what the attraction is.'

'They have a very good archaeology department and their head of department is retiring. They're expanding and need to keep their reputation. They want someone with experience to lead the team. They've got funding and are offering a chair. The status would be good for my writing – among other things.'

'And more money?'

'Yes.'

Felicity is thoughtful. Edward knows she has always been attracted by status – hence her pursuit of him at university.

'I'm used to you being away for odd nights, but to abandon us on such a regular basis, I don't know.'

'I am the one who feels abandoned. I may as well not be here for all the attention I get.'

'Stop being so petulant. You know there's been a lot going on for me. I thought you understood.'

'Not when it excludes any time for us.'

'Don't you think about anything except sex?'

Edward hates being made to feel like some kind of deviant and goes silent. Needless to say there is no welcome-home activity between the sheets that night.

The following morning he is up early with the intention of dealing with his emails. His inbox is almost overflowing and he scans the two hundred or so names in hope. But the longed-for reply from Marianne isn't there. Perhaps she has computer problems; perhaps she is away; perhaps she has no intention of ever mailing him again.

He wants to tell her about Scilly and how the lectures were received; about the wind and the sea and the weird, almost visionary, experience he had down at the maze. He has told Felicity about all the key happenings, but her head is full of vegetables and menus and she listens to him without hearing what he says. It is better that he takes the job in London and spends time away during the week. He will fell less resentful about being excluded. Maybe they can then have quality time at the weekends. He visualises welcoming arms and her old enthusiasm, but not with conviction.

In the afternoon, he calls Patrick Shrubsole and says he is interested in the job. Patrick is delighted and says that the

Stancliffe department will manage with an acting head for one term.

'I've a particular harridan in mind,' he says and laughs. 'Fiercely ambitious, but too tyrannical in style for permanent leadership. She'll make them jump until you arrive.'

'Can I come and look round the place again and finalise details?' asks Edward.

Patrick suggests he spends a week in early September, staying in one of the nearby student halls, and meeting the department so that he is up to speed on new initiatives and can input on planning.

Afterwards Edward takes a tour of his property, perhaps acting out some primitive territorial behaviour of checking the boundaries. Following the line of the house to the right of the back entrance, he comes to the out-buildings containing the kiln, Felicity's new office, the animal food store, the lambing pen and the old stable that sometimes houses the goats. A sharp left turn takes him down a gravel path bordered on either side by raised beds of green vegetables which, he has to admit, have been a great success and are still cropping superbly thanks to Rick's skill. To the side of these is the new greenhouse, and running the length of the back of the property are the larger flat vegetable plots, the remaining lawn and the long-established blackcurrant, redcurrant and gooseberry bushes and the new raspberry canes.

At the bottom of the gravel path, he passes through a gate into the paddock where the new hens and the goats roam. Beside this is the orchard with fruit trees, the old hens, the two bee hives and now the wind turbine. Beyond the orchard and paddock is the lane, and on the other side of that, the Molwings' field where over a dozen sheep and lambs are grazing. As Edward walks he marvels at what Felicity has achieved in a relatively short space of time. She seems happy tending to the animals, organising rotas, harvesting the vegetables, cooking for the restaurant, learning more about animal husbandry and horticulture and, of course, throwing her pots. She has worked hard to make a success of each enterprise. No wonder she has little time for him. In a strange kind of way he feels proud of her. He will tell her. Maybe that will restore communication – even sex.

When they are in bed together reading, he makes a peace offering.

'Flick ... I'm sorry I didn't tell you about the Stancliffe job and discuss it with you first.' He waits for her to say the same regarding the wind turbine and then they could perhaps have a hug and who knows what else, but she says nothing. He continues, 'I was thinking this morning about all you've achieved these past months. It's very impressive. I may not agree with everything, but you've shown real guts and determination. I am proud of you, you know, even though it may not seem like it.'

At last there is a response, a smile. She puts down her book.

Edward moves closer and gives her a kiss on the mouth. She doesn't object or pull away, but neither is she enthusiastic. The love-making that follows is so lacking in passion it might be from a step by step guide.

28

Taryn is on the doorstep of Marianne's house in Beechview Close. It has taken some considerable courage to arrive here unannounced, unsure of the welcome she will receive. Days of weighing up the pros and cons convinced her that there is nothing but pride to be lost, and much to gain if she can somehow persuade her erstwhile best friend to forgive her.

At the abbey deep in the Sussex countryside, she was reminded that pride is a barrier to contentment and that she should replace it with humility. A kindly and elderly monk called Father John had taken her through the teachings of the Desert Fathers and Mothers, aware that her faith was at best fragile and probably non-existent. He spoke quietly and patiently that the loss of spirituality – or *Acedia* as he called it – is something that is commonplace in the busy modern world. He agreed with her that rediscovering her spiritual self would be a good place to start, and that she should be open minded about what might follow. She knew he meant God and decided not to argue.

Over two days she roamed the abbey grounds, attended prayers, group sessions and one to one discussions. She felt the tug of her childhood; the rituals and the seemingly mindless chanting. But this time she listened to the meaning of the words, tried to believe their power and absorb them.

In the Quiet Garden she sat on a rock among the trees by a pond, lost in thought. All around her were long grasses, birds singing and the soothing trickle of water. At the start, her thoughts were like a bag of jumbled knitting wools and she wondered if the noise in her head would ever stop. But hour by hour the strands became clearer and it was possible to separate the yarns into their different colours and rewind them into balls.

It is now Tuesday, the 9th of September. She has purposely selected a day when Johnny is likely to be at his weekly departmental meeting, because to have him hovering in the background would make what she has come to say impossible. Of course Holly might be home – it still being the university holidays – but that's a risk she'll have to take.

Marianne's car is in the driveway. She is back from college and likely to be in. One of her two tabby cats sits on the windowsill in the sunshine, eyes half closed, and end-of-summer roses drop their blooms in a velvety pink carpet in the front garden, smelling like an exotic boudoir. How many times has Taryn walked up this path with never a thought for details?

She has purposely dressed simply in black jeans and a white vest top that shows off the natural pale bronze of her skin. She has tied a black cardigan around her waist. Her hair is still flat and has grown longer, restyled in a rare visit to a salon so that it frames her face in a way that works with gravity rather than against it. It is now coloured a deep brown shade which is less severe than the black and closer to its original natural shade. She wears a hint of mascara and peach lipstick, presenting a picture of innocence and vulnerability. Vanity, it seems, is a sin too far gone to extinguish.

Marianne seems not to recognise her at first when she opens the door. She folds her arms as if greeting a pushy salesperson intent on getting their foot in the door. She is lightly glowing and looks well rested.

'May I come in and talk with you?' Taryn asks quietly. 'I know you're probably busy, but ...' She shrugs and waits.

Marianne does a double take and her jaw drops. 'You!'

'Please?'

They exchange glances, eyes meeting. Taryn thinks she detects the hurt she has caused. Marianne hesitates then steps aside and gestures her through to the kitchen where she appears to be preparing something Chinese. Piles of finely chopped spring onions, mushrooms, red and yellow peppers and pak choi wait in glass bowls on the counter. *So predictable,* thinks Taryn, *me and my pasta; her with the Chinese.*

'I'm sorry to disturb you,' says Taryn wishing so much to return to the informality of old, where either could drop in upon the other without a moment's notice, never fearing that they would be unwelcome. They each accepted whatever state they found the other in, be it bleary-eyed from sleep, damp and towel-wrapped from being dragged from the bathroom, or up to the elbows in vegetable peelings. And Taryn wasn't like this with anyone else. 'How have you been?' she smiles. 'Have you had a good summer?'

'We're all okay,' says Marianne, coolly putting the kettle on out of old habit. 'We went to Brittany. It was great. We'd go again. Coffee?'

Then there is an uncomfortable silence while Marianne mixes the instant with water and adds some milk. It is clear to Taryn that Marianne intends to make no conversational effort whatsoever. And Taryn doesn't want to waste words while there are distractions. When they both sit down at the kitchen table, Taryn begins her story.

She tells Marianne of the counselling with Shaleenie, her drunken father, the abuse, her borderline manic-depression, her suspicion of men, her fear of love and the consequent collection of bastards. She omits telling of the visit to the abbey and the stripping down of her mind and heart and soul as she began to embrace the teachings she had rejected; rejected before she was old enough to truly understand the meaning.

Marianne nods and shakes her head at appropriately empathic moments, but otherwise it is difficult to know what she is thinking. Once Taryn believed she always knew.

'So when I met Edward and he was just as sweet as you said, I couldn't help myself.'

'Do you realise how pathetic that sounds coming from a mature woman? I'm sorry about all this baggage you've been carrying around. And, if I'm truthful, a tad hurt you didn't feel you could tell me about it. Especially as I've told you virtually everything.'

'Virtually,' says Taryn, slowly taking a sip of coffee while she considers what to say next. 'You never said you had a thing about Edward. Whenever I asked, you claimed it was innocent and platonic.'

'It is. It was. I don't have a thing.'

'So it shouldn't matter what I did.' Taryn knows she's on shaky ground but will try anything to shift the blame.

'I don't understand why you went to meet him in the first place. Without telling me or seeing if I'd mind. That was really cheap.' Marianne's tone is accusatory.

'After Marc, I was seriously depressed and insecure. I know I put on a brave face and I *was* glad to be rid of him, but the thought of someone new wasn't exactly appealing.' Taryn wonders how much of her insecurity she should divulge. Perhaps this is a time for honesty.

She continues, 'When you've been married almost all your adult life like you, you can't possibly understand what it's like to keep on having to start again from the beginning. It may be fun at first, but after thirty odd years, I'm tired; tired of finding out all the likes and dislikes: food fads, music, films, sex and so on.' Then she pauses and takes a deep breath. 'I'm tired of being disappointed. After Marc, I decided to have a break from men, but when I swung back into a manic phase, I had this mad idea of seeing what the wonderful Edward was like, not with any particular plan in mind, but just because I was bored. He seemed familiar after all you said, like someone with whom I could start further down the path – cut the preliminaries. And I didn't tell you because I knew you'd go mad. And if you'd gone mad I wouldn't have pursued it. But at that time I just had to. Like being possessed with wild uncontrollable intention. I might not have liked him. I was prepared to be unimpressed, but when I realised I was attracted to him, it snowballed into a seduction offensive. It was unfair on him and out of order as far as you were concerned, but when I'm like that I lose all sense of perspective. I believe everything is possible and to hell with the consequences. You know what I'm like.'

'What happened to trust; to sisterhood? All the things I thought you valued?'

'I hate myself,' said Taryn. 'The person I was. But I've changed. It's never too late to change and I'm facing up to my past. Surely I'm worth a second chance?'

'Mere words,' says Marianne. 'How can you change something that's wild and uncontrollable?'

'A different mind-set should change the desire; the intent. Then the wild and uncontrollable will be directed in a more suitable direction. That's the theory, anyway.'

'I see.'

'I've missed you very much,' says Taryn. 'You are the steady one. You stop me doing stupid things.'

'Yeah, if you tell me what's going on.'

'It's such a waste of all the years it takes to build up a friendship like ours.'

'Quite.'

'It doesn't have to be.'

'I think it probably does,' said Marianne.

There is a formality in the atmosphere that was never there before.

'Have you heard from Edward?' asks Taryn.

'I'm not sure that I want to discuss him with you. That's the difference between before and now.'

'I'm the only one who really knows about you and him.' Taryn shuffles through her pack of options, seeking to give Marianne no choice but to relent.

'There is no him and me.'

'So you keep saying. Have you heard from him at all?' Taryn persists.

Marianne sighs and clutches her mug of coffee with both hands. 'Many emails of apology immediately after you were caught, but he's not been in touch since the beginning of the summer holidays. After the first email I said I didn't want any further communication, and I haven't replied to any of the others. I guess he's given up. I don't expect I'll hear from him again now. And that's such a waste too; dozens and dozens of emails building a unique and irreplaceable relationship.'

'I can understand your continuing hostility toward me, but don't punish Edward too. Next time he writes, arrange to meet. Hear what he has to say. You can always back off if you don't like what you hear. If you can't forgive me, forgive him.'

'You have a nerve telling me what I should and shouldn't do.'

'It's only old friends who can tell you.'

Marianne hesitates.

Taryn persists. 'He deserves forgiveness more than me. I led him on; I cast a spell … Really. With *Love-in-idleness*.'

'What are you talking about?'

'You know, in *Midsummer Night's Dream*? I had some on my windowsill. I use it with the kids just to add drama to our lessons. *"Flower of this purple dye …"* So I squashed some up and dabbed it on his eyes when he was dozing.'

'What? You're completely mad.'

'It worked!' Taryn reconsiders. 'Something worked. So perhaps he couldn't help himself. And if that was the case, it would be a pity to punish him.'

'I don't think he'll write again.'

'Write to him. Say you've had time to calm down.'

'I can't.'

'You need him; he needs you.'

'I don't need him now I've got Johnny back. I miss him because he adds another dimension to my life, and because he understands the past; our schooldays; the bullying. He's got Felicity; he doesn't need me.'

'I doubt their relationship will survive in the long term – unless he is prepared to live a life he doesn't want.'

'I can't offer him more than friendship,'

'It's all he wants from you.'

'You know that?'

'He likes you, Marianne. I think in the same way you like him.'

'And what's that?'

'A kind of innocent love, I think.'

'You cannot presume to know how I feel, I don't even know myself. Love is too strong a word. How can I love him?'

'But you do, don't you?'

'Did … Maybe … As a friend.'

'Exactly. Nothing need be any different.'

'It feels grubby now.'

'Thanks!'

'Truth hurts.'

'You idealised him and he's fallen short. That's real life. That's you and me and every normal person in the world. None of us is perfect. Even if this hadn't happened, there would have been something sometime that would have sullied your snowy-white image of him. Time for a reality check, Marianne. Most men wouldn't have put up the resistance he did, or backed off afterwards like he did. He's a very decent person. He likes you too – and, okay it may not be in quite the same innocent way as you feel about him, because men are men – but he would never take advantage. In any case you wouldn't see each other often enough for there to be a problem. He's not a sleaze, Marianne, and I can recognise sleaze from twenty paces. I've got a PhD in sleaze-analysis!'

Marianne looks pensive. 'I thought we'd be friends for always.'

Taryn wonders if she means Edward, or is talking about her. 'You still can,' she says, meaning either or both.

'This doesn't feel right, does it? Can't you feel how stilted we are with each other? You are afraid of offending me. I'm holding back because I don't trust you any more.'

The front door opens and Holly bounces in with youthful vitality. A skimpy, blue-striped top shows off her slim waist above low-cut flared denim jeans, and long dark hair worn loose completes the retro hippy style. 'Auntie Taryn! Haven't seen you for ages. You look … different.'

Taryn wonders what Holly knows about the fallout with her mother.

'And you are as pretty as ever,' she says. 'And less of the Auntie. It makes me feel old.'

With the arrival of Holly the conversation takes on a more general tone and Marianne resumes her supper preparations. Taryn takes the hint and gets up to leave.

When they part on the doorstep, Marianne gives no indication that she wants to meet up again and Taryn decides it is best to say nothing more at this stage. It is progress that they have managed to speak at all.

29

It is mid September and Edward is in London for a week of talks and meetings at Stancliffe University, in preparation for starting his new job in January. He wants to be involved with strategic planning, final staffing and timetabling, and the administrative mountain that precedes the onset of the academic year. One of the senior lecturers will be acting head of department for the autumn term, overseen by Patrick Shrubsole. She is called Essie Fairway, a crow-faced woman with black Cleopatran hair. Edward perceived hostility when they were introduced; a forced smile that didn't cause the natural bulge under the lower eyelids, and clipped tones through too-red tight lips. Clearly she would like the job on a permanent basis. He would have to practise some serious diplomacy but, if his experiences in Devon and Scilly were anything to go by, he was good with women of a certain age and a charm offensive should thaw the ice in due course.

Following a departmental meeting, he and Patrick have been in private discussion, firstly at the university and now at a nearby pub where they adjourn for some food and drink. Time moves on as they chat, alcohol loosening their professional reserve. They toss around a few thoughts on the long-term direction of the new archaeology department then, as the evening wears on, they find they have common interests in the history of Britain and in population and migration patterns. Another couple of pints and they are generating ideas for a radical proposal regarding the future sustainability of the country, modelled on the Isles of Scilly.

'All we need is a serious drought or other major climatic malfunction and we'll be in the shit,' says Patrick, smoothing his forelock. 'Our agricultural systems are stretched as it is and if one or more of them fail, then supply will not be able to meet demand and we could have a disaster on our hands. The larger the country, the longer it takes for the tipping point to be reached, but we'll get there one day if we carry on as we are. If the problems are global, importing our way out of the mess will be impossible and only countries that have had the foresight to work with nature will survive.' His enthusiasm is infectious.

'You sound just like my eldest son,' said Edward. 'I don't disagree. But all the solutions are unpopular. Successive governments are too afraid to take meaningful action.'

'Attenborough mentions it periodically.'

'And few take any notice.'

'Saw this fellow on TV saying that they have to control red deer numbers in Scotland, "for their own benefit". Eventually the same rationale may need to be applied to us.'

'Can't see it in our lifetime,' says Edward. Of course education may help. Create awareness.'

'Maybe we should write a paper based on the Scilly experience,' says Patrick.

This is a reference to the 1800s when life on the islands became unsustainable due to over-population. Ever smaller packages of viable land were passed on to descendants and many of the islanders were starving. When Augustus Smith became Lord Proprietor of Scilly in 1834, he forced evictions to the mainland, a radical move that in the long run saved the islands.

Patrick continues, 'We could present a catalogue of worst case scenarios from leading experts; make 'em take note. Good publicity for the department and for your maze book.'

And the discussion proceeds with ever wilder suggestions

as to how the UK might evolve towards a more sustainable future.

Consequently it is late when they leave the pub and the evening has turned into night. Patrick turns in one direction and Edward in the other. It is only a few minutes' walk back to Darnley Tower, the hall of residence in which he is staying. Perhaps because it is later than on the previous days, the short cut is ghostly, quiet and dark. Edward notices with a twinge of sadness, an empty takeaway container in the gutter, disgorging leftover chips and a half eaten hamburger. His footsteps echo and he hears the rhythm of his stride, the slip of shoe soles on pavement, the click of his right heel where he must have trodden on a drawing pin. He quickens, reminded of old monochrome movies of London's treacherous fogs and the eerie shapes and the strained violin music. There is a chill in the air, heralding the approach of autumn, but nothing extraordinary to signal impending doom. No shrieking owls or magpies or black cats or broken mirrors.

He is still thinking about the meeting, and the massive responsibility that he will be undertaking in January when he is officially released from his current job and can begin the weekly commute to London. It is far removed from the cosy department in which he has spent most of his working life. He will miss knowing that he is trusted by his colleagues; the years of credit he has amassed that means he doesn't have to try so hard and can make the odd mistake without being harshly judged.

And he is concerned about the logistics of his term-time living arrangements, as yet undecided. Commuting is a possibility, but he believes that staying in the city for three nights per week would lead to a more focused induction into the job. Family life wouldn't be the same, but already it has changed beyond the familiar.

Then it happens in a blur and he gasps as from a shadowed alley a large hooded figure jumps in front of him. There is a flash of white teeth and then an ugly grunting noise. He tries to sidestep and propel his body forward at speed, but too late. He sees a glint of steel a millisecond before it slashes down his cheek. His left hand flies up in protection and that too is on the receiving end of a second swipe with the snaking blade. He is aware of stinging pain.

He hears his voice, 'Hey!' and swings his briefcase at his attacker, trying to knock him off balance. Then there is a sharp jab in his chest that makes him draw breath, but no sound comes and he is sent plummeting. Once again his left hand tries to protect, this time to break his fall, and it contacts the edge of a step and he hears a crack and feels more pain as he collapses onto the ground, his face cold against the pavement. He is dimly aware of his briefcase being prised from his hand, wallet and phone taken from his jacket, a final kick to the ribs and then footsteps running down the road.

His breathing is fast and shallow and he tries to move but he can't raise himself off the ground, agonising pain making him give a strangled yelp and slump back down again. He can feel stickiness under his hand and taste blood as it pools beside his cheek. The pain is beyond anything that he has ever known and his brain dulls in response. He is drifting quickly towards unconsciousness and he gives fleeting thoughts to Broadclyst and home, to Felicity, the children and Marianne.

There are so many things I still have to do … I have a book to write … I am not ready for this, he thinks.

Is this how it will end, alone in a dark street in the greatest capital in the world?

30

Two days after her visit to Marianne's, Taryn is so preoccupied while she parks her car outside her flat in Coppercone Lane that she fails to notice the black BMW a little bit further down the road. As she turns to lock her car she is startled by a voice.

'Hiya, Taryn! What's with the Barnet?'

It's Marc, familiarly be-denimed and with a black leather jacket slung over his shoulder. He is looking very tanned and swarthy, and is smiling benignly as if he has no recollection of their last encounter when his Scrabble board went whizzing through the air as Taryn effectively ejected him from her flat.

'What do *you* want?' she asks gruffly, giving him a scowl, nonetheless registering his familiar smell of expensive aftershave as the breeze blows in her direction. She faces him on the pavement with hands on hips, her jaw jutting upwards as she meets his gaze.

'Thought the dust would have settled and we could have a friendly chat over a cup of tea – and a sticky bun. Don't want to part on bad terms.' He shakes a paper bag as if he might be offering goodies to a child.

Taryn grits her teeth and narrows her eyes. *Don't want to part on bad terms?* This was almost exactly what she said to Edward. It is also a familiar scene, played out at regular intervals throughout her two-year relationship with Marc. Granted, their finishing was more dramatic this time, and more weeks than usual have elapsed since they have seen each other, but his tone is essentially the same as on previous occasions. His presence doesn't surprise her.

Taryn stands her ground. 'I don't still have any of your possessions, do I?' The retrieval of a few CDs or a misplaced item of clothing was often an excuse to make contact.

Marc shakes his head. 'Or even better, you wouldn't have a beer, would you? I'm a bit parched. Work's been chaos this week.' He swaggers past her and heads down her path, nodding at her to follow.

Bloody cheek! Taryn pauses and contemplates giving him a piece of her mind. This would be how the old Taryn would react, loudly and with much indignation. She decides instead to be civil. 'You may have a cup of tea, and that's all.'

Previously it didn't take much for her to lower her guard and the next minute they would be tearing off each other's clothes and heading for the bedroom. The monk at the abbey said that the antithesis of lust was chastity and that this means sticking to the chosen path with regard to sexual behaviour, whatever that chosen path may be. By the abbey pool with the water lilies and the orange carp she decided she must reject affairs and flings and relationships empty of emotional feeling. She must open her heart to the possibility of love, and then hope for it to strike. Marc was now a no-go zone; he didn't fit the new checklist; he wasn't a man like Edward.

Surround yourself with impenetrable light, girl!

But old habits have been strongly conditioned and her physical response to his appearance is one that could quickly break her resolve. She can sense rippling muscles under his shirt. The scent of sex emanates from his every pore. She must tread carefully. She follows him towards the flat and is shocked when he produces a key, unlocks the door and strides into the kitchen.

'Er, I'll have that key now if you please,' she says.

He dangles it in front of her face and then as she reaches for it, he pockets it in the front of his jeans. 'We can play *hunt the key* if you like.'

She doesn't respond, busying herself with mugs and kettle, tea bags and spoon.

Marc puts his bag of buns on the counter, opens a cupboard, takes out a couple of plates on which to put them, and asks how she's been.

'Do you mind!' she says.

He grins, exposing his super-straight, super-white, cosmetically enhanced teeth.

They move to the living room and he flops in her favourite chair, the chair he commandeered for himself during the few weeks they were living together. Taryn places his mug on a coaster before sitting on her other chair, clutching her tea to her chest. She leaves her bun on the table. 'So, what's happened to the floosy?'

'Pippa? Aw, that was something and nothing. Intellectual lightweight. Not like you, Babe. And useless at Scrabble.'

For Scrabble read sex, thinks Taryn, unable to stop herself from sneaking a quick glance in the direction of Marc's upper trouser department. 'There's no going back this time, Marc. The old Taryn is on her way out. Can't you see?' She touches her hair.

'Nice,' says Marc lasciviously. 'Touch of class. But then you always were a classy bird.'

'Nothing you say this time will persuade me to give our relationship yet another chance.'

'That white top is extremely sexy.'

'So you've said, many times before.'

'Aw … How about, "I think I'm in love with you"?'

'Such a cliché and I don't believe you.' Yet her heart patters faster all the same.

'No-one makes love like you do?'

'I know. But still a cliché.'

'And you say I'm the arrogant one.'

Taryn can't help but smile.

'See, I can still make you laugh.'

It would be so easy to weaken, but it's not what she wants any more. *I don't want this … I don't want him … I don't want the games and the rows and the high maintenance life.* A deep breath. 'Yes Marc, but that's not enough any more. I don't love you and I'm looking for some stability.'

'I could get you a little set of wheels. Or a zimmer?'

She gives him an acid glare.

'You're not getting any younger, you know.'

This touches a nerve and Taryn's mood rapidly hardens. 'Right, that's enough. Meeting suspended.' She gets up and gestures towards the door.

'I do like a masterful woman.' Marc hasn't moved a muscle and is still sitting relaxed with his legs wide apart.

'I mean it! Come on. Out!'

'No chance of a quick shag then?'

'Marc!' This time she isn't laughing.

'What about my tea?'

Taryn stalks out of the room to the front door.

At first she thinks he's going to refuse to move, but she waits … and waits. After a couple of minutes he appears with his jacket, taking fast sips of tea, shaking his head and bearing a sulky expression. 'You might never get a better offer. I won't ask again.'

'Have a nice life,' she says, not really meaning it, but glad she has maintained a level of self-control this time. He thrusts his mug at her with half the tea still in it splashing up and over onto her white vest.

'And the key.'

He drags it out of his pocket, flings it at her and it lands on the floor at her feet.

As he saunters down the path, he looks over his shoulder

and grins. She knows he will be back; that he will ask again. It has happened before; first the resistance and then the gradual weakening under pressure.

But this time it will be in vain. The encounter with Edward has changed her opinion of the likes of Marc forever.

She closes the door and returns to the living room, settling herself on her sofa, now taking the bun she left earlier and sinking her teeth deeply into its scrummy softness. Shaleenie has helped her unravel. And most of the yarns are now in orderly balls. Now it is just the loose ends to tie, one by one, bow by bow. She's tried her best with Marianne and can do no more at present. The short-shrift treatment of Marc was the best response for now and when he returns – which he will – she must be equally resolved. She thinks about her father. This is the big one; the most unravelled and the longest string. If she meets that challenge head on, her whole life will change. She's nurtured the resentment for over thirty-five years and all she has achieved is further hurt.

She swallows a mouthful of bun, wipes the crumbs from her lips with the back of her hand and picks up the phone, needing a friendly voice to say, '*Good onya Taryn*'. The phone hovers while she decided who. She sighs. Once it would have been Marianne, no hesitation. She dials Neil's number but is greeted by the answerphone. Unusually disappointed, she hangs up. What about Isabelle? Isabelle would say the right things. But Isabelle isn't at home either. Perhaps these are signs that the time for procrastination is over. She fetches her old address book, lifts the phone again and punches in the number of her dad.

31

There is a bleeping noise and a mask over his nose and mouth. The air smells so pure and it is effortless to breathe. He's not sure where he is and he doesn't care. He feels like he is floating in the clouds, but a radio is playing vaguely familiar music and he hears them say, 'What is your name?' and 'Do you know who you are?' And he thinks, *Of course I bloody know who I am,* and he tries to speak, but no sound comes and his throat hurts. They say other things too, but he doesn't listen. He wonders who *they* are, but his eyes won't open even though he strains his eyelids, and when he twitches his mouth there is something in his cheek that feels like the time he stapled his finger by mistake when he was twelve, only worse.

The voices recede as he is pulled back into sleep again, and nothing.

When the voices come back again, and the sleep from which he is being drawn falls away more easily, he manages to open his eyes a fraction, peering through millimetre slits and absorbing brightness and a crisp white uniform, an out-of-focus, sweet young black face with braided hair and a white hat.

Still the rhythmic bleeping, the face mask, the radio on in the background; music interspersed with DJ chatter, strangely soothing when normally it would drive him mad.

Hospital, he thinks, and then a dim recollection of darkness and pain and damp and cold. *I am alive … I think I am alive …* He checks for signs. Breathing, hearing, feeling … His eyelids are so heavy they don't want to open, but he forces another fleeting peek and sees the white uniform and the black face again. He licks his teeth in an exploratory way … plays with the saliva in his mouth … swallows …

His brain begins to chug like an old generator gradually gathering momentum. He remembers … he doesn't want to remember. *How hurt am I?* His legs seem slightly elevated and he checks them for feeling, starting with his toes. His feet respond as he tenses and relaxes his muscles. He does the same all the way up past his knees to his hips. *Not paralysed; not broken.* This is a good sign, but an unpleasant sensation that he is peeing all the time suggests that he has been fitted with a catheter. His right hand, the one he uses most, seems to be attached to a needle which he presumes is linked to a drip, but his fingers move in the way that fingers do, though one is in the grip of a heart monitor. Not so with his left hand, which feels encased in something tight, along with his lower arm.

He blinks properly and moves his head a fraction. The nurse takes off the mask and straight away he misses that purest of air and notices a pain as he breathes.

'You're going to be fine,' says the nurse with a Jamaican lilt. 'You've been in a spot of bother. Do you remember what happened?'

He tries to think, and he recalls the glint of a knife and being face down on a cold pavement and the taste of blood, unbearable pain, believing he was going to die and never see Felicity or the children again. *Or Marianne.* The name comes to him from nowhere. *Who is she? Who is Marianne?* He pulls away from the thought, letting it recede and fade.

'Tell me your name,' she tries again.

'Edward Harvey,' he says huskily, without a pause.

'Well, Edward Harvey, you're in hospital and we've had to give you an anaesthetic to patch you up. That's why you're a bit woozy.'

Anaesthetic … patch-up. He registers the information, wondering at the truth, afraid of what it might be; the pain in his chest, the pricking in his face, his left arm. 'I'm so thirsty. May I have some water, please?' The words come out in a croaky whisper.

She hesitates and frowns. 'I'll see what I can do. But in the meantime, we could do with some information.' She speaks very slowly as if to a child. 'Where were you going? Where do you live? Who should we contact?'

He finds it difficult to reply. 'My wife. Felicity.'

'Does she live nearby?'

'Devon.'

'That's a long way.' The nurse looks thoughtful as if she's not entirely sure whether to believe him. 'You're in London, Edward. Do you have any family here?'

'Am I going to die?'

'Unlikely now, but someone will be missing you.'

Unlikely, now. That's good. What about before? It must have been touch and go. 'My wife's in Broadclyst, Devon,' he says, every word a struggle, understanding how the alert elderly must feel when treated as if they are idiots. 'I've been working here this week. At Stancliffe University.'

The nurse straightens up and smoothes her uniform. The next time she speaks she is less condescending. 'It's a long way from Devon and it'll be a fair while before she can get here.'

Images of home flutter through his mind and fill his vacant brain with his world. It is like blood pumping life into the shrivelled wings of a newly emerged dragonfly. *Felicity … children … animals … restaurant … If she comes at all.*

He tells the nurse his home phone number. 'What day is it?'

'Friday morning, 12th September.'

Nearly two days lost …

'She wasn't expecting me home until later today.'

'That's good. Hopefully she won't have been worried.'

Once she would have worried if he hadn't spoken to her for a day.

'How did I get here?' It is such an effort to speak, but he wants to know.

'I believe a young couple were passing in a car. They called an ambulance.'

'What's happened to me?'

He sees something in her face that alarms him.

'The doctor will explain everything soon.'

Now he is even more alarmed.

The nurse disappears and returns after about fifteen minutes saying that Felicity said it would be difficult to leave the house immediately, but she will come tomorrow. 'And the police would like a word if you're up to it,' she adds.

The surgeon is an Asian man in his fifties with steel-grey hair and a strong jaw. He has the type of face that gives confidence; the type of face that all medical professionals and airline pilots would have if they could choose.

After a brief introduction during which he asks about Edward's work, he then moves on to explain the nature of the injuries and the treatment required. It is grim news, but it could be worse; he could be dead.

In addition to massive blood loss, he has also suffered a cardiac tamponade. The point of the knife blade nicked the pericardium surrounding the heart, causing blood seepage into the space between it and the heart muscle. This is a life-threatening condition if not treated quickly. He has much for which to thank the young couple who came to his rescue.

His left hand and wrist were lacerated when raised to protect his face after the initial slash to his cheek. In the case of

277

the former he was lucky that the radial artery hadn't been severed, but there is severe ligament and possibly significant nerve damage, compounded by a fracture to his wrist which it is likely he bashed on the edge of a step as he fell, reaching out his hand in a reflex to save himself. As for his face, he was lucky not to lose an eye. In both cases he is unlucky in that he will be scarred for life in two conspicuous parts of his body. He has a fleeting thought about losing his looks; about Felicity not finding him desirable any more – assuming she still does, which he has begun to doubt. He imagines the embarrassment on other peoples' faces as they try not to stare, but are compelled towards the injuries like magnets. It is bad enough facing the usual range of age-related deteriorations. A knot of fear twists in his stomach, but he isn't a slave to vanity; he supposes he will survive.

Another twenty-four hours pass, during which time he becomes used to the rituals of being woken frequently by nurses for purposes of taking measurements and invading his person in other ways that he doesn't like to think about. He is moved first to a high dependency ward and then to a room on his own. As his condition improves and he requires less rigorous monitoring, he feels lonely and neglected and wonders about the merits of private healthcare which he and Felicity have been arguing about since her mother's inheritance came through, but never got round to organising. At least it is quiet.

When Felicity arrives late Saturday morning he is fast asleep.

'Ted!' says a voice with a certain amount of urgency.

He opens his eyes. 'Hi, Flick.' He tries to be as upbeat as his face will allow.

'What a state.' She plants a kiss on his mouth and he smells her familiar soapy scent as if she has recently showered. Her hair is loose and he recognises her dress from a few seasons

278

back. He hasn't seen her in a dress for months, jeans being her preferred uniform at home, and a smart suit at the restaurant.

'You look nice,' he says, meaning it, feeling the old love, more valued because it was so nearly lost, wanting some sign that she feels the same.

'Can't say the same about you,' she laughs and turns the chair so she can see him when she sits down.

He tells her what happened as far as he can remember. The same details he told the police. He is still wired up to machines, still sprouting the catheter and various other tubes and drains.

'The only things he didn't take were my keys,' he says. 'So no need to change the locks. Did they tell you what happened to me?'

'Broadly. Are you in much pain?'

'Yes, but they keep giving me painkillers. I'm sleeping like a cat.'

'How long will you be here?' She sounds mildly concerned. If he expects her to be more so then he should give her all the gory details. But they can wait. He doesn't even know all the gory details himself and he would like to know. He has yet to look in a mirror.

'A week or two.'

'I can't stay.'

'I don't expect you to.'

'Now I've seen for myself that you're okay. And I've brought you some pyjamas, wash stuff and other things. Money.' She nods towards a carrier bag.

'Thanks. Have you told Mum and Dad?'

'I thought it best to play it down until I'd seen you. Didn't want to worry them. I've booked into a hotel for tonight and I'll see you again tomorrow but then I think I need to leave.' She looks for reassurance that he is okay with this. He knows she hates hospitals and has never been the most sympathetic of people when it comes to illness. The children are always packed off to school unless they have a temperature.

'I understand,' says Edward. 'You can't leave the kids and the business. I'll be fine.'

'Perhaps James and Rachel can come down next weekend. I was wondering if there's anyone we know in London who would come to see you. I'd feel less guilty if someone could pop by. How about that old school friend of yours? The one the girls call Fanclub. The one you stayed with earlier in the summer? Is she nearby?'

Marianne … That name again … He remembers … remembers why he wants to forget. Would she come to his rescue despite what happened between them? Or might she tell Felicity about Taryn?

Edward's damaged heart beats a little faster and the monitor registers the rise. He hopes Felicity doesn't notice.

'Would you inform Patrick Shrubsole at Stancliffe and Gemma at UD?'

Felicity nods. 'I've already told Patrick. He said he thought he hadn't seen you around, but as you hadn't arranged to meet again, it didn't cross his mind that anything was wrong. I've arranged to pick up your stuff from the room you've been using. Some of it I'll bring back here tomorrow, the rest I'll take home.'

Edward had forgotten about his temporary accommodation in Darnley Tower, and how efficient Felicity is in contacting people and sorting things out.

Felicity persists, 'It's Marianne, isn't it? Your classmate? Is her number somewhere at home?'

He swallows. He doesn't have the strength to explain that they've lost touch, or to argue. He'll have to take the risk that Marianne won't mention what really happened. 'It'll be in the diary on my desk – around the time I stayed over at the beginning of May.' He swallows again and tries to calm his breathing.

'I'm sure she'd want to know. Is she compassionate? She might bring you some grapes.'

How can you be so flippant when I'm in this state? Perhaps it's nerves, he thinks generously.

He asks about the restaurant and the latest on vegetable production. Felicity appears excited by the onset of autumn and the orchard fruits that she is using to make jams and compotes and pies. Her face lights up as she talks of organising the pickers and packers – mostly friends of the children – and the successes at the farmers' markets.

'Gianni makes some delicious plum sauces to have with duck or game,' she says. 'And Rick has a mate who can shoot so that's our supply chain. James is still bringing in rabbits from the Molwings' land. Not sure what we'll do when he leaves for uni, but Peter Molwing might let us have a few if we pay him. I've been interviewed by *Good Food Magazine* about the dietary aspect of my menus and now BBC South West has been in touch about a possible feature. It's all happening, Ted. So exciting!'

He finds it difficult to concentrate on what she is saying and notices that she doesn't ask how his meetings have gone with Patrick and the Stancliffe team, or even about his pain levels or state of mind. It is all about her life now.

Two days later, when reluctantly he begins to drift from sleep towards consciousness, he is aware of nagging discomfort and uneasiness. The hospital is deliberately reducing his pain relief and he tries to sink back into the relative comfort of sleep. He senses the presence of someone sitting by the bed. He doesn't know who. Perhaps Felicity has come back, or one of the children.

Sleep claims him again and he is bothered by dreams. He is at Brocklebank Hall, his old prep school … in the large shed that was their classroom … and Marianne is telling him about a play they are rehearsing … and her voice seems so real.

'Edward … Edward … Speak to me Edward.'

He opens his eyes and there is a blur of white walls and lights and a person sitting by his bed, fleetingly touching the back of his hand, the hand that doesn't hurt.

Gradually Marianne's face comes clearly into view. She gives a half smile. 'You're back,' she says.

'Is it really you or am I dreaming?'

'It's me. Felicity said she couldn't stay and wondered if I might drop by.'

'That's very good of you.'

'No problem.' She says this as though it a mere nothing that she should be sitting by the bed of someone that only four months earlier she said she never wanted to see again.

'God, I'm thirsty,' says Edward. 'They don't have decaf tea here. When I asked, this dragon of a nurse said, *"This is the NHS, honey,"* in a really cross voice. Like I was asking for something exclusive. Wouldn't you think they'd have decaf in a hospital?' He struggles to prop himself up, and she helps and offers him a drink of water. The touch of her arm across his back sends a pleasurable shiver through him.

'Oh, Edward,' she says gently with a furrowed brow, before sitting down again.

Her dark hair is loose on her shoulders and a silver bangle shines on her arm. He notices the tight jeans, the eye make-up, the lip gloss, the nail varnish, the perfume. She has made an effort to look as though she hasn't.

'Thank you for coming, I didn't think you would. It was Felicity's idea.'

There is a long pause during which Marianne looks deep

into his eyes. He holds her gaze and again is mesmerised by the sea green of her irises and the fathomless expanse of belladonna pupils. She inhales audibly before speaking.

'I owe you a favour,' she says as if she might be offering to feed somebody's cat.

'How come?'

'Helping me to flee the Brocklebank ghosts.'

'So this is just a dutiful visit?'

Marianne shakes her head in an ambiguous way. 'I'll do what I can, but when you're back on your feet …'

'I don't want your pity,' says Edward. 'Just your friendship.'

'That is something I can't promise.'

Edward decides not to pursue this line of conversation. He has no strength to navigate the rock-strewn waters of a difficult discussion. Instead he enquires about Johnny and Holly and work.

She says they are fine and work is busy, but doesn't elaborate.

He wants so much to recapture the tone of her crazy emails and of the conversation they had during his visit, but she has subtly reintroduced a formality.

Then she says, 'Do you want to talk about what happened?' But she says it like a psychologist would say it and not like a friend.

He tells her what he can remember, which isn't much. She nods, but doesn't comment. Suddenly he feels so tired and is struggling to keep awake. There is a long pause.

She fishes in her bag. 'I've brought you grapes. Is there anything else you'd like food-wise?'

'I feel sick most of the time. Painkillers.' Then he closes his eyes and sleep takes over. When he wakes, she's gone and he wonders why he didn't ask her to bring him something to eat; to ensure he would see her again.

The following Saturday, soon after tea time and now on a

ward with three other men, he is surprised by James and Rachel. He notes the look of horror on their faces, quickly disguised. He is sitting up in the chair by the bed, doing a Sudoku puzzle.

'We wanted to check you were okay,' says James. 'Ma's got a big thing going at the restaurant tonight; a party from Killerton Estate.'

Rachel parks herself on the bed. 'When Fanclub rang her after she'd seen you, Mum like asked if we could stay over with her if we came down.'

More guilt-assuaging tactics. 'And?'

'Fanclub's coming here to see you again – in about an hour – and she'll take us back to her place. I'm having the spare room and she said James will have to like sleep on the sofa or an air bed – but he's used to that.'

Edward feels that he might be blushing. 'And you will have to stop calling her Fanclub.' His head is clearer. He remembers all the details of the encounter at the museum. At least it gives him more opportunity to try to make amends and recreate the camaraderie of old.

'Tomorrow we'll come and see you again on our way back to the train,' says Rachel.

'All sorted,' adds James. 'So, how are you Dad?'

'At least I'm allowed out of bed now.'

Rachel says, 'We've brought you a new mobile and it's all set up for calls. We can text you and stuff.'

Edward has never been a lover of text messaging, but can see the advantages of it in a situation such as this.

By the time Marianne arrives, he is tiring and the children are running out of upbeat things to say. It is with some relief that he greets her, noting that this time she is wearing a long skirt. He hasn't yet been able to pigeonhole her style. She fascinates him. Is that the attraction?

'I've brought you some decaf and some peppermint tea bags and some more grapes,' she says.

Rachel laughs. 'Mum said you were the grapes type.' Then she looks embarrassed as if perhaps this wasn't a wise thing to say.

Marianne appears to take it in good spirit and smiles. She introduces herself to the children and says that Holly is looking forward to meeting them. 'And how are you today?' she asks Edward, pulling up another chair. There is warmth in her voice, but he isn't sure whether this is a genuine thawing, or an act for the benefit of the kids.

'Improving, thanks. They say I might be fit to leave on Tuesday – but are concerned about the journey all the way to Devon so that might delay things.'

'How would you like to come back to Beechview Close for a few days until you're well enough to travel further? Felicity said she might find it difficult to leave everything if you're released midweek.'

Edward is annoyed that Felicity has imposed on Marianne again, even though he would much prefer to leave the hospital as soon as possible. 'I really don't want to put you to any bother.'

'It's Johnny's suggestion,' adds Marianne. 'I think you're in his good books after being so enthusiastic over his rock collection. Holly's still at home for another week, but you can stay in the spare room again if you don't mind being with all the clutter.'

Edward is almost overcome with gratitude at this kindness, contrasting sharply with Felicity's tough-love approach. And to stay again with Marianne would be just the therapy he needs.

'And you don't mind?'

'I wouldn't have agreed to it if I minded.'

Still Edward is not sure how she feels but James and Rachel are following the conversation intently so he doesn't ask. This time when the three of them leave, he relaxes into the best natural sleep he has had since the accident.

32

It is almost half a century since Taryn was born and now city skylines glint with tubular steel and glass, the modern and sometimes bizarre rising up between the spires and domes of old. Leeds is no exception. It has changed since Taryn was young, but here and there in the old part of the city there are still back-to-back terraces, lost in a time warp. It is to one of these streets that Taryn takes a bus.

Louisa offered to drive her but she said she wanted to do the journey alone. She didn't add that she was frightened; that this was one of the hardest things she had ever done in her life. When she phoned Carlo to say she was coming to visit, she was at first greeted with silence and then the croaky voice of an old man.

'Is my daughter, Taryn? Is really you? Ma Bella? After all this time?'

She was expecting the strong, resonant, heavily accented tones that she was accustomed to hearing as a child, and her stomach rose and her throat tightened as realisation dawned that he was a fading shadow, weak, diminished, sad. Nothing Louisa had said prepared her for the reality.

Now she is metres away from seeing the face to go with the voice. She must expect to be shocked, but must hide it. September rain stings her cheeks and the east wind makes her eyes water and her nose run. It is colder up here, the onset of autumn already showing on the trees. She fumbles for a tissue, not wanting the wetness on her face to be misconstrued.

She bangs the old brass knocker, now tarnished and dull:

rat-ta-ta-tat, such a familiar sound, stored in her memory from when friends came round to play. *'Is Tarie coming out?'* They used to call her Tarie and the knocker used to be shiny bright: *the first thing people see; make a good impression.* Her mother's words. *Daisy ...* Daisy, with the soft curls and the innocent face. *I miss you, Mum,* she thinks. She notices the green paint peeling from the door. Could it be the same paint from when last she visited all those years ago when her mother died; when there were cold stares and harsh words exchanged with her father and vows never to step across the threshold again? She hears shuffling and then the clink of a chain.

Carlo isn't quite seventy but has the stoop of a ninety-year-old and his cheeks are sunken and ghostly. He holds the door frame while giving a half smile, white hair wildly arranged by the brush of an arthritic hand. His nose is purple and larger than Taryn remembers. He mutters, 'Ees good to see you, Bella,' fixing her with such a strong glance that she flinches and has to look away. Still that piercing stare behind the clouded eyes of age.

Taryn steps over the threshold and back in time, and is immediately aware of the smell of decay; of mustiness, stale sweat, and lingering monosodium glutamate from packet soups and microwaved dinners. Once Carlo would have scorned such eating habits, but now she supposes he hasn't the energy to construct the fresh dishes of old.

Long ago this was her home and she recognises many familiar objects; the large wooden hat-stand in the passage, always in the way; the multicoloured Venetian glass bowl on the hall table, brought by her father from his mother's house in Italy and used for collecting keys and other odds and ends. Even the carpet on the stairs is the same, though worn and frayed on the treads, the edges piled with papers and junk mail, a pair of socks, a packet of digestives. She wonders if this tendency towards clutter is the reason for her need for tidiness and cleaning. Obsession was what Marc called it. Were the seeds sown here?

Carlo leads her into the back room where he has always lived, where the family always lived; the front room empty, cold and sterile, for guests that never come any more, a cold stale smell of neglect permanently in the air. The back room is full of un-ironed washing and unwashed crockery, more junk mail and old newspapers. He waves a hand at the mess.

'Your ol' Babbo, he live like a tramp,' he says with some attempt at humour, his smile exposing missing teeth.

'Do you have any help?' She doesn't know why she asks this because she already knows the answer.

'I no want some busy-body nosey-parker in my house.'

'You should let Louisa help.'

'Louisa? Baah, she has family.'

Taryn wonders if this is a dig at her. If the expectation is that she as the single daughter should give up her independent life and come and look after her father. It is what they did in the old days. She is aware of tears forming and breathes deeply through her mouth, sickened by the old cooking smells and worse. She decides to take charge. 'Shall I make us a cup of coffee? Do you have coffee?'

'Cappuccino, Bella.' he gives a wry smile. 'Some things your ol' Babbo still remember 'ow to do.'

She moves into the kitchen and is amazed to find everything where it used to be. The pleasant aroma of ground coffee greets her when she opens the cupboard. She automatically goes to the cutlery drawer and even the spoons are the same spoons, old Sheffield steel.

They sit facing each other across the parlour table, with its discoloured oilcloth cover, pock-marked with cigarette burns on Carlo's side even though he gave up smoking years ago.

Taryn looks at her father and regresses to the child she was when he hit her and beat her mother. The prepared speeches disintegrate like sand castles in the face of the incoming tide. She blinks back tears.

'So how my Hun' bunch? You smart grown-up woman now. Still so pretty. Why no husband snap you up, eh Bella?'

Taryn bristles inwardly at the assumption that she, along with all women, is incomplete unless married. 'I'm happy to be single, Babbo. Honestly.'

'I give bad impression of life with husband, of marriage, eh?'

'Not just you.'

'Am so, so sorry,' says Carlo. 'I cannot turn back clocks; I cannot make it all right with your mother. I have big regrets. Daisy was good woman; no deserve me. Was drink done it. And that bastard Gino Gambero and his god-awfulness pizzas.' He gives a harsh laugh. 'But I no make excuse. I will die soon. Too late for your mother, but you, Bella?' He looks at her with sad eyes.

She notes the faded irises that were once so clear and feels a twinge of the old love that was once so strong.

'Say you forgive me and I die in peace.'

'You can't die yet,' says Taryn.

'Look at me,' says Carlo. 'Everything an effort. My liver is no good now. All those bad years of drinking. I was bad father then. But not always. You remember, eh, Bella? When you were little girl and we play football in the yard? And I teach you to make pasta? I think you like the football best. You were tom-boy.'

Taryn remembers. Her sessions with Shaleenie have enabled her to open the box of happy times that she kept hidden away for all of her adult life. Not just the football and the games, but the hugs and cuddles and abounding love that evaporated when the drinking started.

'They were good times, Babbo. That's why it was so hard for me when you changed.' She remembers what Shaleenie said about going back to the person and telling them how you felt. 'You became a monster. I was scared for all of us. I thought if you could change like that, then so could any man.'

Carlo sighs. 'I hate myself. Even then, I hate myself.'

'Why didn't you stop?'

'No easy, Bella. I quickly become alcoholic. Must 'ave been in me always. In Italy I had glass of wine, but no more. I come to England, fall in love with your mother. She so beautiful, like you. We no much money for drinking. Then Gino come and I get stress so bad. I drink to feel better and I drink too much. My body – it had cravings. I promise to stop, then I say, *"Just one, Carlo. One is okay. One help to calm down after hard working day."* Then I have another one, and another, and I no care any more an' I drink till I forget about Gino and the business and your mother nagging. Was like … how you say? Anaesthetic.'

'But you stopped eventually. Why not sooner? When it mattered? When it would have made a difference?'

'Because I was a fool, Hun' bunch. A middle aged, sad-bastard, fool. And I regret all these years. All these lost years.' He hangs his head and his white hair straggles over his forehead.

Taryn hesitates, then reaches forward and touches his hand. She feels the bones through the thin dry skin and he clasps her fingers. Onion layers peel away and she reaches out as an adult who at last understands that just like she isn't perfect, nor is anyone else.

It will be all right now. The years of closed doors and refusal to acknowledge him melt. It wasn't that he hadn't cared; just that he was flawed, as she is flawed.

Afterwards Taryn walks to the second bus stop from her father's house, needing to feel the air on her face and to smell its sweetness. Her eyes water again, but this time with overwhelming emotion and she chokes and sniffs. Is this what life comes too? Trapped in a dark, smelly house with dust and everything old and shabby, too tired and stiff to clean and sort things; too overwhelmed by the mountainous challenge of a lifetime of acquisitions. So distanced has she been from elderly relatives that she has been able to delude herself from the realities of life's end. She is guilty of selfishness; of looking after her own interests and believing the world owes her some comfort for all that she suffered as a child. Now she realises it's not so simple.

By the time she reaches Louisa's, she has regained her composure. Louisa wants details but she refuses to answer questions, biting her lip and finding difficulty in keeping her emotions under control.

'Would you like a drink?' asks Louisa.

'I didn't know you kept any in the house?' Taryn is under the impression that as a reaction to their father, Louisa is virtually tee-total and keeps temptation well out of the way.

Louisa opens the cupboard above the bread bin, removes copies of Delia Smith's *Summer* and *Winter Collections* and reveals bottles of vodka and tonic tucked at the back. 'For emergencies,' she says.

Taryn raises an eyebrow in surprise, but decides not to castigate. She is grateful, but wondering if Louisa is on the same road as Carlo was, all those years ago. The thought makes her stomach churn. Why does she hide it if she's not? Taryn knows Ian wouldn't approve. Though enjoying a night out with the lads himself, he always makes disparaging remarks when Louisa is under the influence of drink. Taryn wonders if he is frightened of a genetic tendency.

The vodka soothes her. *Pots and kettles,* she thinks. *Just like Edward said.* She is not above drinking too much herself and knows this is yet another vice that she should tackle – but not today. And she can't be the one to probe Louisa about whether she has a secret drinking habit. Not now, not yet, maybe never. She tries to banish the thought.

Later in bed, in Louisa's spare room with its old-fashioned chintzy curtains and floral wallpaper from the 1970s, she replays the events of the day, her muscles tensing in response. She grits her teeth and thinks of other things: of world rivers, American states, Wimbledon champions; anything to keep her mind off the smell of decay and age, with undertones of urine and stew. In her world of disinfectants, bleaches and obsessive-compulsive cleaning regime, this could not be worse. The negative thoughts creep between Yangtze and Rubicon; between Texas and Wyoming; between Jimmy Connors, Roger Federer and Manuel Santana. She tries to push them away, to stop her brain from analysing and worrying about what to do.

It is only when she is safely back in her flat in Coppercone Lane the following day that she relaxes and allows the tears to flow again. Only then does she decide she will visit again soon, stay with Louisa and try to help clear up their father's house.

33

Edward is already dressed when Marianne arrives at the hospital after work on the following Tuesday. He is pleased to see her, but feels awkward that she rather than Felicity should be offering such support. She asks how he is, but is uncommunicative while helping gather his few possessions into various carrier bags, perhaps embarrassed by the intimacy. Although capable of walking, he doesn't object when a small Asian man appears with a chair to wheel him to the dispatch lounge. He feels weak, old and vulnerable and, when the effects of the tablets wear off, is still in considerable pain. He has virtually no use of his left hand, which remains plastered half way up his forearm, and is alarmed by what he is unable to do, yet thankful that it is not his right hand; his preferred hand. The next few weeks will be a carousel of hospital visits in Exeter; dressing changes, and when the cast is removed, 'aggressive' physiotherapy.

They take a taxi back to Beckenham, speaking little. Edward is conscious of every bump in the road jarring his injuries and is thankful he isn't yet travelling all the way to Devon. He tells Marianne of a visit from Patrick Shrubsole the previous evening.

'Checking that I'll still be taking up the job after Christmas,' says Edward. 'Hate it when work people see you stuck in a hospital bed. He brought me a book he's written about the history of Saffron Walden. Why should I be interested in that?'

'And are you taking up the job?'

'Already handed in my notice at Devon. Not that they've

appointed anyone else yet and they'd probably have me back despite all this.' He touches his face and makes a gesture with his plaster cast. 'But I've grown stale there and I need a change – especially with Felicity being the way she is.' He waits for her to ask him to elaborate, but she doesn't. Although she is being perfectly pleasant, there is something he can't quite identify that confirms his suspicion that she is still upset about the business with Taryn.

Later in his room at Marianne's in Beechview Close – the spare room with its mishmash of assorted furniture from previous lives and its computer in the corner – he feels like a displaced person. He is used to hotel rooms and days away from home, but always by choice, and always with the secure line back to his family. Now that line is broken and he is drifting like kelp fronds in the Sargasso Sea.

He dares to look in the mirror again and his unfamiliar face stares back, the beginnings of a beard. He doesn't like it; doesn't suit it. Despite his mostly dark hair, the beard is coming thorough with patches of grey and it ages him, the red scar clearly visible underneath, tight and hurting. He also notices how much his hair has grown, although next to Johnny's it is still relatively short. He thinks he looks like an axe murderer.

He muses on his luck or lack of luck; such far-reaching consequences from being in a particular place at a particular time. A moment longer on the phone to Felicity and the kids, a visit to the loo, an extra gulp of beer, even a pause to tie a shoelace, or sneeze, or watch a squirrel loping along the branch of a tree above the pavement. Any one of these things could change the future by a few seconds, enough to change a life.

Every day millions of things happen because it's six, not seven minutes past; because of check-out delays, traffic lights, a pause to exchange a word or two; because of the smallest of decisions; because of timing. Change just one of the links in a chain of events and the future will be different. The pleasant things are taken for granted, the unpleasant lead to castigation and many *if only's* in the succeeding years. He knows about the agony and futility of soul searching in the aftermath, and he will try very hard to resist.

There is the sting of tears behind his eyes, but he doesn't cry. A legacy from the prep school life: crying is for girls. Observable emotion to be obliterated otherwise the bullies noticed and a price would be paid. He remembers Barnaby Sproat and his gang; remembers being held under water in a sink in the boys' toilets, unable to breathe, thinking he would drown, then being left humiliated in a soggy heap on the floor. Lessons learned: boys don't cry. He shudders. It's all too much. Like a child he curls up on the bed, hugging the pillows with his good arm, and gives way to momentary self pity and longing for old comforts.

When Marianne, Johnny and Holly have all retired to bed, he emerges to face the slow process of undressing and ablutions, one-handed. Even if he was at home, he doubts Felicity would help, or that he would want her to. At the hospital they gave him a leaflet advertising a plastic cover for broken limbs, complete with a watertight seal. He must order one online.

The following day, when Marianne and Johnny are at work, he is left in the capable hands of Holly who fusses around him as if she has been charged with his life. He doesn't mind.

'Mum says I have to make sure that you move at least once every hour,' she says in an authoritative teacher voice, which he expects she has learnt from her parents.

It is nice to be the centre of attention for once. He notes that Holly's hair is a similar dark brown colour to Marianne's but about a foot longer and glossy straight. They sit at the table in the kitchen, while he eats scrambled eggs then toast, and talk about his children who she says she enjoyed entertaining at the weekend. He has already had several text messages from Rachel gushing compliments about everything 'Holly'. He supposes that any attractive go-getting young woman, three years senior, is going to engender hero worship in someone of seventeen.

He asks her about her course and offers advice on how to deal with an inappropriately attentive lecturer. 'And if he doesn't take the hint, don't be afraid to report him. Such behaviour isn't tolerated these days. Have you told your parents?'

'Dad would go spare, and Mum would tell Dad.'

'I see. So you trust me to say nothing.'

'Why worry them.'

On the second day she tells him about her boyfriend Dylan, who was killed in a car accident the previous summer.

Edward knows about this from Marianne's emails at the time, but being confronted now by the person most affected by the tragedy moves him in an unexpected way. He is reminded of when he and Felicity met, both still very young, both at college. He remembers how bowled over he was by her forthright patter, her seduction techniques and the doors she opened to a world of intimacy that he had never known. If anything had happened to her at that time he would have been broken. He would be even now, despite their differences.

'I haven't wanted to see anyone since,' says Holly, bringing him back to the present. 'Of course I go out and meet people and I have male friends, but I don't want to go through the ritual of playing at romance after having found the real thing. I think I'll know it when I see it again.'

Edward is impressed by her maturity and unnerved by her certainty. It is as if he is seeing what Marianne was like when she was a young woman, though remembering Marianne's early emails about the fallout from her time at Brocklebank

Hall, he suspects Holly has much more confidence in her attractiveness than her mother did at the same age.

Holly continues, 'I get mad sometimes about how unfair it all was. Just a few seconds later or earlier on the road and it would never have happened. Do you think that about what happened to you?'

Edward loves the directness of the young and wishes that age didn't lead to caution and reticence and having to guess what other people are thinking.

'Yes, but it serves no purpose. You have to try to look for positives; see it as a learning experience. But you can't help wishing that it hadn't happened. At the moment I'm finding it hard looking in the mirror.' *Hard to a point of being unbearable.*

'You're even more like Harry Potter now.'

Edward looks puzzled.

'Didn't Mum tell you? When I first saw your school photograph, I said you would have made a good Harry Potter.'

'Indeed,' says Edward with a wry smile.

'Gosh, is that rude of me? Meant in a good way. And now you have a scar like Harry, even if it's in a different place.'

'I could do with some wizardry at the moment.' But as soon as he says it, he realises that wizardry is exactly what he has in being here with Marianne and her pleasantly distracting family.

He notices how Johnny almost always calls her Mari with an intimacy he envies. Of course it's no different from Flick; what is different is that it is Marianne and he wishes he knew her well enough to do the same. He also notices how Johnny shares the chores – something he, Edward, only does in spasms when the mood takes him and he's not in the middle of writing up some paper. Maybe Felicity has built up years of resentment for all the times she has vacuumed and cooked and ironed when he was in his office, rattling away on his computer.

Johnny and Marianne seem companionably close. There is no hint of irritation, no remnants of the bumpy patch of the previous year. It is how he and Felicity were until the money and the menopause. Perhaps they can come through it too.

He likes Johnny and thinks that if they lived closer together they would have the potential to be good friends. Their respective interests in geology and archaeology seem to complement each other, and they each have similar views on education. Johnny is going to Dorset at the weekend, staying in a caravan and walking the Jurassic coast. The plan is that he will take Edward along in the car to be picked up by Felicity at Charmouth, a village between Bridport and Lyme Regis.

'It'll be easier than struggling with trains,' says Johnny. 'And not too far for your wife to drive.'

Edward is relieved and grateful. Although he is gaining strength each day, he is still sore, and self-conscious of his plastered arm and wounded face.

On Thursday night Johnny goes out to play snooker, Holly is visiting friends and Edward finds himself alone in the house with Marianne for the first time since coming out of hospital. He is in the living room reading one of Johnny's books about the geology of the West Country when Marianne appears having completed the after supper chores.

She sits down and he glances up and smiles. 'Tell me more about that book that you're writing.' He's been meaning to ask her for ages, wanting to hear again about how wonderful she thought he was when they were at school and about the way that she has spiced up the plot of her novel in order to make it more enticing. He is still unsure how much of it was the truth. And since the Taryn business, her manner would indicate different emotions now.

'It's all but finished.'

'You were going to let me read some chapters.'

'I was, but now I'm too embarrassed.'

'You've already told me that you've exaggerated.'

'I'll leave it to you in my will,' she says. 'You can read it when I'm dead; when I'm beyond embarrassment. If it doesn't get published – and that's a probability given the way mainstream publishing is going and the luck that would be needed – I think it would find a good home with you and your family. You'd look after it. You'd know what to do with it.'

He doesn't know if she's being serious. 'But I nearly died. And I could still die first. Then I'll never have read it.' He says this lightly, almost teasingly, so if she was joking, it doesn't matter. 'You could always self-publish.'

'Expensive and viewed with suspicion.'

'Increasingly more respectable and possibly, or even probably, the favoured option in the future.'

'I have a sequel to work on before I go down that route. It's more commercial; less constrained by the sensibilities of people like yourself.'

People like myself … Is that what he has become to her? *People* … So cold compared with how she was; so remote, so distant. 'Don't worry about my sensibilities. I know it's fiction …' He hesitates. 'Especially now.'

'Well, whatever,' says Marianne. 'And tomorrow, I thought you might like a change of scene and a breath of fresh air in the local park – if you feel up to it. The weather forecast is good.'

'But it's Friday. Aren't you at work?'

'I've reduced to four days a week since the start of term. I want to focus more on my writing. It's hard with full-time college commitments.'

'When did you decide?' Edward is hurt that he didn't know; that she hadn't mailed him about it as she had mailed him about so many of her thoughts in the past couple of years.

'Near the end of term. After I found out about you and my best friend.'

He hears the ice in her tone and decides not to pursue it. But he likes the idea of a walk, although concerned about the effort involved.

'If I park near the gates, there's just a very short walk to the lake where we can sit on a seat and watch the geese. You'll like it; it's a real oasis.' Again she speaks without a flicker of the warmth that they shared when they first met. It is as if she is a carer, making the suggestion out of duty.

He agrees that this would be therapeutic on several levels.

The following day is warm, and after a leisurely breakfast they leave Holly – who's going on a shopping expedition in town – and go in the car to the ornamental park that Marianne says she often frequents.

They stroll slowly from the main gates, through an avenue of magnificently tall pines: Corsican, Scots, Weymouth and an enormous Wellingtonia, the giant sequoia. Edward stops to check the names and read the information on the plaques. Very tame squirrels run relays up and down, legs outstretched sideways, hugging the broad trunks, making flattened square shapes of grey fur. The path splits around carefully manicured flower beds and they follow the branch to the right in the direction of the lake, sitting on one of the many wooden seats that have been donated to the park in memory of deceased partners or family members. From the island there is a cacophony of sound from the herons. On the water, Canada geese squabble, their honking echoing in the autumn air.

This may be the last time they are alone together before Edward leaves for Devon. Maybe the last time for always, he thinks. There are many things he wants to know, and if he doesn't ask now it will probably be too late.

'Why did you come to the hospital?'

'Felicity would have wondered why not.'

This was true. He could imagine Felicity phoning Marianne, her managerial tone guaranteeing compliance with any request she might make.

'You didn't have to invite me back to your home.'

'It was Johnny's idea. He would have wondered if I'd said no.'

'So what you said in the hospital about owing me a favour – is that all it was?'

There is another of Marianne's long pauses and he can almost hear the neurons firing as she ponders her response. He waits.

'Nothing is straightforward. I am not straightforward. If you had known me for longer, you would realise.'

Edward remembers the slightly crazy emails when she pondered the meaning of the Burgess Shale, the demise of the Y chromosome, and so much more. Of course he wasn't dealing with an ordinary woman. 'So are you going to give me the chance to know you longer?'

'You are Androcles and I'm the lion,' and she smiles an enigmatic smile that could mean anything.

'I see. Actually, I don't.' *Nothing is straightforward.*

'You pulled the thorn of Brocklebank from my soul. Now it's my turn.'

'And I thank you.'

'But don't assume this means we can carry on mailing in the same way as before.'

Edward's new hope suddenly diminishes.

'You are one of very few people who know the extent of what is under the surface,' she continues. 'All the mad emails … The philosophising, the butterfly mind, I keep it under wraps for most of the time. Not many people know that part of me – I only shared because I trusted you.'

'I'm sorry.' Again the realisation of how much he has hurt her. Realisation, and deep regret.

'Of course a few people catch a glimpse now and then when my guard is down and I am carried away by some thought or other. Then they realise I'm not quite the same as they are.'

'Different is good.'

'Different can be a curse. I don't know whether it was being at a boys' prep school that's caused it, or whether it would have happened anyway. What most people see is an attempt at conformity.'

'You mean you're acting?'

'Not totally. I've become so used to my public persona that it's now a very real part of me.'

'And Johnny?'

'Johnny has known me since I was a teenager, when I was most definitely out of synch with the rest of the world. I'm lucky that he loves what I am.'

They sit watching the comings and goings of the geese, enjoying the late September sunshine. Edward notices the leaves beginning to turn. Marianne might feel she is different from others, but to him, she seems in tune. Perhaps it is their shared history ... And this midlife crossing of paths. He wonders about Twin Souls.

After a while he asks if she's seen Taryn. Neither of them has mentioned her name thus far and he knows it is a risk.

'Yes. It was she who persuaded me I should relent. She even said I should write to you again.' Marianne doesn't meet his eyes, but stares across the lake with a sad, faraway expression.

'Is she forgiven?'

'She's told me a lot I didn't know about her that might explain or excuse, but the whole dynamic of our relationship has changed. The easiness has gone, along with trust, and joy.'

'I am so sorry to have been partly responsible for this. It would be a pity for you to lose such an old friend.'

'I didn't lose her; she lost herself.'

Edward is thoughtful and they sit in almost companionable silence for another ten minutes or so before taking a very gentle walk by the lake to the rose garden and back.

'That looks like a Turkey oak,' says Edward, gesturing towards a tree in the centre of the lawn and circled by wooden seats at the base. He loves trees and this park seems to have been planted with variety in mind. He wishes that he could have more such walks when he is feeling well, but suspects this is a unique moment that he will treasure for the rest of his life.

Early on Saturday morning, as Edward is being driven along the Dorset coast for the rendezvous with Felicity. Johnny says, 'I've already run this past Marianne – and Holly – so see what you think … When you start your job in London after Christmas, would you like to lodge with us? You said you would stay in London from Monday to Thursday, so it's only three nights per week. I know it's not the most convenient location, but the transport links are good and Mari goes to work later than me so she could take you to Beckenham Junction on her way to college. You could have Holly's room during term time. It can be until you find something more suitable or – if it works – for as long as you like.'

Out of bad things, good things can happen, thinks Edward.

34

Taryn spends another two weekends with Louisa during the first half of October, and together they visit their father's house to tackle the mess and the grime. At first he protests angrily and as loudly as his thin voice will permit. 'Is no your jobs to clean up after me. Go away! I no want bothered. I tired. Bugger off, daughters. No interfere. When I die, then you come.'

But though Louisa looks hesitant, Taryn marches into the kitchen, snaps on some Marigolds and amid much clattering, begins to wash the dirty dishes. She calls through to him, eyes misting, 'We're not going, Babbo. How can we leave you to live like this? Mum would turn in her grave.'

'You happy enough to stay away before. Now I tell you I no want you here. I no deserve.'

Taryn chokes back tears. 'When I was little you did so much for me. We're not going and that's final.'

Tentatively, Louisa comes through to help; Taryn washing, Louisa drying and finding homes for all the dishes.

'I'm ashamed I let him carry on like this,' says Louisa.

'You had no choice. You had to respect what he wanted until it's clearly not possible. Like now.'

They find mould growing in mugs and on plates, and half consumed packets of ham and bacon left to rot, hidden among the debris of junk mail. On the stairs is a box of eggs, three months past its sell-by date, and upstairs a festering pint of milk that has Taryn retching as she pours its lumpy contents down the sink. No wonder the place has a peculiar smell.

As they work they hear Carlo's periodic outbursts, but he

remains seated in the adjoining room, slumped like a stuffed dummy, too weak to make too much of a fuss.

At the end of the first morning the worst of the kitchen has been cleared and cleaned, but there is so much more to do.

The next day, and the following weekend, they return each morning and deal with one more room at a time. Louisa shrieks when she finds a dead pigeon half hidden beside a worn leather pouffé, both exuding feathers and almost indistinguishable in the dark corner of the back room.

'Next door's cat,' says Carlo by way of explanation. 'He come for scraps; he bring me presents.'

When the little house is at least in a habitable state, Taryn tells Carlo that they have arranged for him to have a woman come in for an hour, three times a week, to clear up and keep it tidy.

'I no want,' he says feebly.

'You no choice,' says Taryn, mimicking his accent, trying to make light of it, to jolly him along. 'She's called Wendy; she's nice; you'll get to like her and she will keep an eye on you. She can speak a bit of Italian and she said it will be good to practise. Louisa will bring your shopping twice a week and we'll get you a microwave.'

'I no want microwave. Radioactive. I no trust.'

'You are having a microwave,' says Taryn determinedly, and you will learn how to use it. They are completely safe – and in any case, a few microwaves aren't going to make much difference, the state you're in. You'll be able to get yourself some easy meals.'

Carlo looks defeated.

'I will pay for whatever support he needs for the time being,' says Taryn to Louisa. 'But we must contact social services and see what he's entitled to in the way of an attendance allowance. I think we should try and arrange a carer, at least once a day.'

'He won't accept help.'

'It's either that or a home.'

And back at Louisa's, Taryn is less self assured but in a stronger state than when she made her first visit. Once again the vodka is extracted from its hiding place behind Delia Smith, and until Ian comes home from work, and while the girls are occupied elsewhere, Taryn tells Louisa more about Edward, Marianne, and her visits to Shaleenie, and Louisa tells Taryn about Ian raiding her knicker drawer and about the vodka in the recipe cupboard.

'I'm not an alcoholic,' says Louisa, gazing into the depths of her glass, 'but sometimes I feel it wouldn't take much more to tip me over the edge. Perhaps some therapy would do me good too.'

35

Meanwhile back in Devon recuperating, Edward finds the first four weeks are full of pain and self pity as the initial gratitude of being alive is replaced by self-castigation, of carelessness at being caught out late at night in a quiet London street, and incredulity at how a moment in time can radically change a life. At first each waking second is consumed by his injuries. He is constantly aware of pain management – prepared to suffer moderate pain rather than take the cocktail of tablets with which he has been left. Anything with codeine in it makes him feel hot and sick, almost as if he has a fever. After about four hours sleep each night he wakes and is restless for the duration. Felicity sees this as a reason to move into her office next to the kiln where she has installed a bed-settee. The old outside toilet has been replaced with new conveniences, including a washbasin, principally so she and Rick don't need to tramp through the house when they are working outdoors. She let it slip that she *'needs to go more often'*. Yet more evidence that she is going through the menopause. Edward hopes this defection is temporary. If she is trying to avoid sex then this is a waste of time as sex – at least the having of real-life actual sex – is far from his thoughts at the moment.

His hand and wrist are still shrouded in plaster although he has had to have the cast changed now that the swelling has gone down. When he is on the move, his arm is immobilised and protected in a sling but when sitting, or watching TV, he has been advised to keep it free, resting on a cushion. Four times a day he exercises his elbow and shoulder, following instructions to the letter, determined to do whatever it takes to regain full function.

He taps away on his computer with his right hand, struggling with capital letters until he becomes more dextrous with the shift key. It is a laborious process sending emails and keeping up with as much work as he can. He can't cook – not that he did much anyway, but now he is unable, he wishes he'd done more. He can't peel potatoes or carve the chicken or even use a knife and fork. Felicity prepares him meals he can eat one-handed, and when they have a roast, she cuts up the meat into bite-sized portions as she once did for the children. He hates this level of dependency and the pitying words from their friends. Olivia and Alexander come to peer at him, offering sympathy, bringing wine. He isn't sure if this is especially for him or part of the bartering arrangement with Felicity. Either way they leave with a bag of newly pulled parsnips and a swede.

He ventures outside for fresh air but is nervous of being alone in the lanes down which he has walked hundreds of times. It isn't London, but he knows that bad things have happened in lanes such as these. Even the presence of the dogs does little to calm his fears. The Josie Lawrence case springs to mind: a country lane, a dog and a nutcase with a heavy implement; lives lost, lives changed. He cannot drive, so he stays at home, lonely when Felicity is at the restaurant and the kids are at school. He tries to catch up with some of the novels he feels he should have read. He orders Booker shortlisted titles from Amazon, but most of the pile remains untouched. It is difficult both to balance the novel and turn the pages one-handed and he often breaks off, staring into space. He would progress with the maze book, but finds it difficult to concentrate. Mostly he is bored.

He has shaved off the menacing beard and the injury to his

cheek is clearly visible, an angry red arc about three inches long with parallel pin-pricks either side where the stitches have been. On rare visits to the supermarket with Felicity, check-out staff and people in the street give sideways glances when they see the scar. He feels for them, knowing their uncertainty about where to look. He wants to tell them what happened, deal with the curiosity, get the questions out of the way.

His mother comes to stay for a long weekend, *'So I can see the damage for myself. Make sure you aren't playing it down.'*

He has been playing it down and she is aghast. They share a rare lingering hug and he notices how small and bird-like she has become.

'I won't tell your father the details,' she says.

Edward's father has heart problems and is not fit to travel.

James left for UCL almost as soon as Edward returned and it is clear that Felicity misses him. *One of her boys, gone,* he thinks. He also thought he saw tears on her face; a rare thing. He's hardly ever seen her cry – not even when her parents died.

The kids come and go, offering words of encouragement, but Edward knows they don't understand exactly how he feels. Their lives move on in the fast lane, highlighting his torpor. Only Christopher and the dogs seem to show genuine sympathy, keeping him company and looking for affection. Perhaps the young and animals really do have a sixth sense of intuition. At least it gives him the opportunity of spending some quality time with his youngest son.

Rachel has had a series of short-term boyfriends in recent weeks. Since she met Holly and heard the tragic story of Dylan, she is searching for her soul mate with a vengeance. Geeky Damien was sent packing as she decided she needed to see what else was out there.

310

Edward tells her it doesn't work like that. 'These things just happen when you least expect.' *Don't I just know!*

'That's such a cliché and so not true. Just because you and Mum met that way. What about all the personal columns; the dating agencies? All I'm doing is cutting out the middle person and saving a bit of cash.'

'Has it never occurred to you that you may be meeting the wrong kind of blokes?'

'Why would that be?'

How can he tell her that because she is so pretty she will attract the best looking guys who will see her as a conquest before they see her as a person? They will be the first to move in while their friend – possibly their much more suitable friend – hangs back for the pickings; for second best. (This was something he learnt from a conversation with Marianne.)

Marianne …

He misses her. Even though he was only at Beechview Close for a few days; even though he is more comfortable recuperating in his own familiar surroundings; even though she was so cool when he was there. It is illogical. He is hopeful that with time she will return to her former self, sure that this coolness is manufactured because she believes it is what he deserves.

He writes to her every week or so and is always hopeful for a lengthy reply. But her emails are short and remote. Any chance of total reconciliation seems far away. All he wants from her is friendship and what he took for granted for so long, now seems as elusive a snow leopard. Nothing has been said about Johnny's offer of lodgings, and as this seems to be the most sensible solution to his accommodation problem in the short term, he knows he must broach the subject sometime.

In late October, three weeks after starting uni, James meets a fellow biologist called Kate. She leads him through an underwater world of seals off the Kent coast, and a sandbank far out to sea witnesses the beginnings of a relationship based on mutual interest and respect. James brings her home on a fleeting visit to check on his father's progress. Kate is windblown and outdoorsy with a natural glow of health and inner wellbeing. Not for her a preoccupation with tints and dyes, fake tan and lip gloss. She is up early in the morning and out with James and the dogs before anyone else has stirred. Later in the day she helps Rick, digging over one of the vegetable patches with gusto.

'He's well fit,' she says to Felicity afterwards with mock London accent.

Edward notices Felicity blush.

Meanwhile James visits Kylie to tell her that their relationship is over. Edward knows there will be tears enough in which to wash one of her skimpy camisoles. When James returns he looks as if he has been crying too. He has a soft empathic heart and cannot bear to see any living being in distress. Kate tactfully keeps out of the way, charming Felicity with enthusiastic chatter about the restaurant and the plans for the following year, and making a few suggestions for recipes that would please the young.

Edward wonders if there's something in the ether with all this breaking up going on. He fears where it will stop.

Afterwards Kylie hangs around the family, sad and hopeful. She continues to waitress in the Retreat and says she will help Felicity with the Farmers' Markets through the winter. She tells Edward that she knows James will come back to her. 'He was so upset when we broke up. I know it's only a fling with this other girl.'

Edward knows it isn't and is blunt. 'He won't come back to you Kylie. He's in another phase of life now. Let him go. You'll find someone much better for you in time.'

312

Kylie sniffs, hesitates and sniffs again. 'He's so clever and I'm just an ordinary Devon girl. But I can change. D'you think I should go to evening classes?'

In bed later, Felicity says that much as Kate is eminently suitable, the longer Kylie's mooning over James, the longer she will help with the business for very little money.

'You've become so mercenary, Flick,' says Edward.

From the early November, Edward makes weekly visits to the physiotherapy department at the hospital in Exeter. It is peopled by young men and women in short white fitted shirt-overalls and blue trousers. Some wear tracksuit tops when they are not treating patients and they dash about in trainers, leaping up the stairs two at a time, exuding fitness. *What happens to physiotherapists when they are over thirty-five?* His physio is Hebe Keeble, a lean young woman with an Anglo-Indian complexion, a high black ponytail and a brisk but kindly manner.

When he first sees her, after his cast is removed for the second and last time, he is alarmed to find that his wrist is almost immovable.

Hebe asks him many questions about the accident and his general state of health. She pulls at his wrist with firm definite strokes. She kneads the back of his hand which feels as if the bones have become fused, and she pushes his fingers into a fist until he yelps. The scars, she says, must be massaged firmly lengthways and crossways with oil or cream to try to keep them supple. She is the first to tell him this.

After the session he mourns the lost use of his non-preferred hand; a hand he has always felt was inferior and at times relatively useless. He hadn't appreciated it enough; this hand for steadying pans while the other stirs; this hand for opening doors while the other carries shopping. This incapacity is a lesson. It is now incapable of sufficient force on the handles of a tin opener, on taps, on the toilet flush, on tubes of toothpaste, on opening the fridge door, even on the buttons of the remote control. He struggles with his shirt buttons, his flies, and starting the zip on his outdoor jacket is impossible.

Painful exercises follow and he measures progress with a set of dividers, a protractor and a couple of rulers.

'The Poles are reached by tiny steps,' he says to Felicity, smiling through the pain, laying his hand on a towel and forcing it over the edge of the table.

'You'll get there,' says Felicity. 'You always do.'

And he wonders what she means by this and decides not to ask.

From eBay he buys therapy balls in different colours and different degrees of softness. He is soothed by the jelly-like feel in his hand and he squeezes fifty, then a hundred, then two hundred repetitions, once, then twice, then three times a day. Hebe recommended Aqueous Cream for his flaking skin and Bio Oil for his scars and he stacks up his collection of lubricants and medicines on a shelf in the bathroom.

One evening he catches Harriet staring at him when he is plastering his arm in cream before settling down in front of an episode of *Silent Witness*.

'Does it hurt much?' she asks.

'Never stops,' he says, deciding to be truthful. She winces and he wishes he'd lied.

'What kind of hurt?

'No, Harriet, you don't want to know.'

'I do. Tell me how it is.'

'It is as if someone else's hand and wrist have been attached to my arm. Like you see when people have their arm severed in farm machinery. It feels like a lump of rusty metal with joints in need of oil. When I stop moving it for more than fifteen minutes, it seizes up and I have to begin the process of un-seizing, one finger at a time. When I move it, it is so tight the knuckles are sore. The scars sting and prickle every time my shirt or jumper touches them and now the weather is getting colder, it takes longer to get it moving. Do I need to go on?'

'Does Mum know? Have you told her?'

'She hasn't asked.'

'Tell her.'

'She really doesn't want to know.'

Suddenly Harriet bounds over and throws her arms around his neck, giving him an awkward hug across the arm of the chair, taking him by surprise. Then she's off, embarrassed, but the gesture was so unlike Harriet and so heartfelt it makes him choke.

To: Marianne Hayward
From: Edward Harvey
Subject: Rehabilitation
Date: 10th November 2003, 22.15

Dear Marianne,
Back to work this week. Short days; easing in gently – if such is possible in the teaching world! All my lectures moved to this half term! Should be back in swing before move to Stancliffe.
If still okay with you and Johnny, I would be pleased to lodge with you for at least the first few weeks. Will be easier to make decisions about where I want to be when I am physically there and doing the job.
Physio going slowly and painfully, but each week I can move my hand more. The ligaments were badly damaged too and will take ages to heal so am hopeful for continued improvement for perhaps as long as the next couple of years. Have started driving, but not distances as hand seizes up. It was fantastic to get behind the

wheel again and regain some independence rather than
relying on lifts. Now I know how the kids feel!
love,
Edward

Now he is back at work, occasionally there are brief stretches
of time when he is sufficiently distracted to forget what
happened; to forget the attack and the associated fear. Then
follows the realisation and the remembering and it is like each
time he has to face it anew. His students are shocked and
sympathetic, grateful for his return, keen to cooperate.

To: Edward Harvey
From: Marianne Hayward
Subject: Re: Rehabilitation
Date: 11th November 2003, 17.28

Dear Edward,
Glad to hear you are back at work and progressing.
These things take time.
Johnny is enthusiastic about your lodging with us. He
wouldn't have offered otherwise.
Marianne

Johnny is enthusiastic. Not 'I'. Not Marianne. Such has been the
nature of her replies to his emails since the resumption of
contact. Always polite, but short and impersonal. Nothing
about her, even when he asks specific questions. It saddens
him. She used to be so consistently effusive in the days before
the Taryn episode.

Outside the wind turbine reminds him of diverging paths. The
noise follows him when he is out with the dogs such that even
when beyond range, he swears he can hear the turning blades.

36

Re-installed in Beckenham and a couple of weeks after the visit to Leeds, Taryn's front door bell rings and she glances at the clock. It's Sunday, and six in the evening. She wonders who would be calling unexpectedly at such an hour. She has completed her preparation for the following week and has almost dozed off in front of the television. People generally don't call on Taryn unannounced because they know that she doesn't like to be taken by surprise.

On the step is Neil, casually attired, hair flopping over his face.

'Would you like a pumpkin? Allotment's gone wild with all this rain.' He waves a sizeable orange object in front of her face. 'Haven't seen you properly for yonks. You've been keeping very quiet at work. Thought with Mr Bad-News out of the picture, we might get back to checking out the odd play.'

'God, it's huge!' says Taryn.

'That's what all the girls say,' says Neil, with a wink.

Taryn takes it from him, dropping her arms under the weight. 'Just the job for some winter soup. Are you coming in? I haven't eaten yet. I can offer you pasta?'

'Such a wide repertoire.'

'Now don't tease. I can cook other things, but pasta's quick.'

'Pasta would be lovely.'

'Wellingtons!' she says accusingly.

Neil removes his muddy boots and leaves them on the doorstep before following Taryn into the kitchen and parking himself at the small table in the corner.

Taryn scurries around chopping onions and tomatoes, filling Neil in about her father while he sits at her kitchen table. She's never mentioned this to him before, but now she finds she can talk easily and objectively about her past and the current situation.

Neil listens with a degree of amazement. 'You never cease to surprise me, Taryn. All this going on, and you never said. Why the sudden spilling of the beans?'

Is that what she is doing? *Spilling beans?* Taryn is not a spiller of her own beans even though she is inclined to fling around a few belonging to others. Of course she told Edward, but that was Edward. And she told Shaleenie – but that was different to the tune of ninety pounds an hour. And she told Louisa because she's family and Marianne because she was trying to restore their friendship.

But why is she telling Neil?

She realises she is pleased to see him. 'You're a good man Neil,' she says, frying the onions, suddenly aware that good men are no longer off her radar. 'Too good for the likes of me.'

'I think you have potential,' he says with a wry smile. 'Potential to be good.'

Taryn pauses with spoon hovering in mid air. She is struck by a thought, and as she stirs in the tomatoes and adds some torn up basil, the thought begins to gather momentum. *A man like Edward* … What if? The thought grows and balloons. *What about Neil?*

While they eat, she decides to tell Neil the rest of the story of her father; the early years. And of Marianne, and Edward; the whole sorry tale. Neil listens, half-closing his eyes when hearing about the night of passion.

Taryn pauses, unusually sensitive. 'You never bothered about Marc.'

'I knew you didn't love him. This was different, I can tell. It hurts because – well you know why – I wish it was me.'

'Oh Neil, you daft bugger!'

'You know Taryn, this is the first time you've let me through your defences. What's going on?' His look is direct and pleading.

'I've always liked you, Neil.'

'Liked, but not more than that.'

'I've changed.'

'You hate me now?'

'Perhaps, I more than like you. But there would have to be rules.'

'Rules?'

'Joking!'

Taryn feels herself flushing. It is an unaccustomed heat and she averts her eyes quickly. *I don't do embarrassed.* She loses her nerve. 'I am a relationship disaster, Neil, and you know that.' She gets up with the plates and loads them into the dishwasher. 'Marc says I'm obsessive-compulsive about cleaning. And I'm set in my ways.'

'We don't have to move in together,' says Neil. 'Even if we tried and it works out. Quite a few couples are choosing to live apart nowadays. There may even come a time when living apart is the new living together – particularly if kids aren't involved.'

This is going places Taryn hasn't intended. 'Some strawberries?' she asks, changing tack.

Neil appears to take the hint and nods.

After Neil leaves, no more intimacies having been exchanged, Taryn phones her father and has a reasonably convivial conversation with him, apart from him objecting to one of the carers who now comes to get him up in the mornings. *'She is ol' bossy-boots, Bella. She drag me out of my bed; she insist she wash me. I can wash self. I no like old woman looking at my privates. And she has face like rat.'* Then she speaks to Louisa to ask her to check that the carer respects her father's dignity and lets him do as much as he can by himself. She makes a shopping list, does a few yoga exercises and finally curls up in front of the TV with a mug of tea.

She thinks about Neil again. He is pleasant looking, even if a little on the chunky side. He is honest and reliable and has many similar interests to her own. He thinks she's fabulous – despite her known flaws – is solvent and grows his own vegetables. *What more could a girl want?* The problem: he doesn't excite her enough.

The solution: *does it matter?*

37

Edward begins his job at Stancliffe University on a cold damp January day with frost on the pavements and air that hurts when he breathes. He starts all his lectures with Holly's Harry Potter reference and an explanation of how he came to be scarred. The students warm to him, sympathetic, smiling. It breaks the ice and he finds he can laugh along with them, even though in private moments he continues to be self-conscious.

Four months have passed since he was attacked and he is now restored to a reasonable level of fitness. The bruises have faded, his pericardium has healed and he has reasonable mobility of his damaged left hand and wrist, though it throbs if overused. The visible scars are still very evident, and meeting new people is always an ordeal as he wonders what they are thinking and how much information he should divulge.

His psychological wounds are less obvious to the outside world, but he is keenly aware that he is not exactly the same person as before. He is more cautious and constantly scans the environment when he is on the streets of London. He knows he is lucky that it wasn't worse, and he feels guilty about not always appreciating that luck. In mirrors, he looks but does not see; dealing only with necessary concessions to vanity such that hair is appropriately combed, tie straight, face free from detritus like crumbs or smears of jam. Once he thought he was quite good-looking because Felicity said so and the trail of students outside his office door suggested the same. Now he cannot see beyond the lurid boomerang on his cheek.

Essie Fairway, the dragon with the Cleopatran hairdo, who

was acting as head of department for the previous term, is very cool in her manner towards him. He pretends to ignore it and sets about a serious charm offensive, seeking her advice on matters both practical and intellectual, and affirming many of her decisions while secretly intending to change most of them as soon as a respectable settling in time has passed. He is not of the opinion that it is wise or necessary to go into a new job and straight away make a mark by sweeping aside the old and bringing in a host of new initiatives. No, he prefers a quiet and stealthy approach, gathering information, seeing what works and what doesn't; seeing who works and who doesn't. By the time he is ready to launch any proposals, he will already have allies and know from whom he needs protection.

He has noticed how the cynical and dyed-in-the-wool spend as little time with students as possible, scurrying off to their offices as soon as their lectures are over and adopting a closed door policy with limited time for consultations. That was not the way at Devon and would have to stop. Research is important, but without the students, many of their jobs would be dust.

His life begins to swing backwards and forwards between Broadclyst and Beckenham, and so focused is he on his physical and mental recovery and the demands of the new job, that he has had little time to dwell on his relationship with Felicity. He settles into the rhythm of the commute to Stancliffe and the pattern that is Marianne and Johnny's working week. They are predictable and they don't fuss. They leave him to his own devices.

Marianne continues in her emotional retreat from him. She has been guarded in her conversations and he wonders how much is due to resentment over the Taryn incident, or if she is protecting herself from her feelings which, since her appearance by his hospital bed, they both know exist, even though she never says. It was Johnny who invited him to stay and Johnny who seems most overtly enthusiastic about his presence, enjoying engaging him in conversation after supper and once persuading him to visit the Jolly Woodman for a beer and a convivial debate about the relevance of archaeology in today's world and the legacy of Tony Blair, whom Johnny admires and Edward despises in equal measure.

Johnny says he is amused to find that Edward, like Marianne, has a similar dislike of creamy mashed potato, and when probed they each reveal that it is probably caused by the lumpy offerings at Brocklebank Hall that made them retch. Butter beans, large fat-exuding sausages, overcooked cabbage, milk puddings and custard are also off menu for both of them, probably for the same historical culinary reasons. Edward finds these similarities comforting.

When he returns home on Thursday evenings, Olivia has been found sitting in the newly extended conservatory with a gin and tonic, waiting for Felicity to pull up some winter vegetables for her. Conscious of their earlier disagreement, Olivia now always brings a bottle of wine in exchange. Edward learns that she and Alexander are not getting on. Alexander has befriended a woman from work and Olivia is Not Happy. The woman in question is ten years younger with immaculate mirror-shine straight hair and neat small teeth. Apparently she makes Olivia feel like a caricature. Edward can understand why, but decides not to comment. *Another couple in crisis,* he thinks, wondering if it goes with the territory of middle age and menopause.

He and Felicity have evolved into companions of a different sort, sharing a bed physically since the weather turned colder, but not emotionally and rarely sexually. The last time they had sex was after watching a late night film on Channel 4, when scenes of nudity unexpectedly fired some desire in Felicity and

323

she approached him in the bedroom with a waft of his favourite perfume, some silk-satin lingerie and more than a little enthusiasm. Afterward, he noted it was she who pulled away first and escaped to her side of the bed, reluctant to share the post coital afterglow, seeming embarrassed to have broken her apparent resolve of celibacy.

They also managed a meal together at the Retreat, where Edward was expected to admire the latest display of pots for sale, expound on the service provided by the teenage waitresses, order three courses, rave about the food and pay for the privilege.

'It wouldn't do to be seen to be having freebies,' said Felicity. *Indeed no!*

During Edward's second weekend back home from Beckenham, Felicity has organised a wassailing ceremony in the orchard. It is on the night of 17th January – the old Twelfth Night according to the Julian calendar. Such a ritual is primarily aimed to awaken the trees from their winter sleep and provoke them into providing bountiful fruit later in the year, but as Edward has just begun his job at Stancliffe, she says the party is also in his honour. It is a rare moment of recognition, made all the more special by an unexpected visit from James and Kate who have come down from UCL especially for the occasion.

All the preparations have been going on while he has been in London and he is surprised when at dusk, friends and neighbours appear sporting home-made, brightly coloured rag jackets and the most amazing array of hats sprouting twigs, flowers and feathers. They bring pots and pans, some carry fire torches, including Rick who also wears a grotesque fox-like mask.

Edward has attended other such events in the locality so he knows what to expect, but having one on his own property is a new and not altogether welcome development, not least because Mr Versatile is leading the proceedings and making him feel usurped.

Felicity is glowing as she dishes out mulled cider and canapés in the kitchen, courtesy of Gianni. After the rituals outside, there will be a barbeque on the patio with guests moving into the kitchen if cold.

'Simply stunning,' says Olivia, helping herself to a tiny crab cake followed by a miniature beef wellington, eyes apparently checking the whereabouts of Alexander relative to the woman from Killerton about whom there are rumours.

As with the restaurant menus, all the food items have an accompanying card of ingredients and notes about suitability for those on special diets. Although time consuming, it has been one of the best of Felicity's decisions, many people coming to the Retreat when for years they have avoided the awkwardness of eating out.

Rachel is the wassailing queen and she follows Rick through the French windows and into the night. Edward tags along at the back having shut the dogs in the living room and locked the doors. Being in London and seeing how security conscious Johnny and Marianne are, not to mention his own salutary experience, has made him extra cautious, much to the annoyance of Felicity who likes an open house policy.

As darkness falls, they troop down to the orchard where a bonfire is already roaring and providing an eerie light among the trees. The men light their torches and it is as if the years have turned backwards to a time when such Pagan rituals were an essential part of life.

The wassailers gather around the largest of the apple trees, Rick standing before them and addressing the tree, *'Health to thee, good apple-tree. Well to bear pocket-fulls, hat-fulls, peck-fulls, bushel-bag-fulls …'*

It is the most Edward has ever heard him speak.

Bells are rung; pans and buckets are bashed with spoons. There is much shouting and blowing of whistles. Peter and

Len Molwing fire a couple of shots into the sky and a group of half a dozen Morris men start clashing their sticks together.

Rick taps the tree on the branches and the roots while Felicity pours cider round the trunk. The friends and neighbours each hang a piece of toast on the lower branches for the robins and then throw cups of cider into the tree. A circle forms and they all join hands. Edward finds himself between two of the women who work in the shop at Killerton House, while Felicity is opposite between Rick and Gianni, her face full of smiles, the perfect hostess. Harriet is looking after Christopher and showing him what to do. Rachel, on the other side of Rick, looks beautiful in the firelight, just like the young Felicity, and Edward's heart feels heavy. Don Blackett, a local teacher, picks up his accordion and Rick leads the singing:

> *'Here we come a-wassailing among the leaves so green,*
> *Here we go a-wandering so fair to be seen ...'*

The Morris men dance, the circle sways, and the singing becomes louder and louder. Gradually the wassailers peel away from the circle and dance around the other trees, the alcohol loosening their inhibitions. Felicity sashays over to Edward and gives him a hug and a kiss, but there is no love in her eyes and he believes it is a gesture for the guests and not for him. Soon she drifts back to Rick and Gianni, swinging girlishly between them, and Edward remembers when he first met her and how she said she was done with Jack-the-Lads. She must've dated countless Ricks in the past. Perhaps Rick was her 'type' and Edward merely good husband material. No-one can see his eyes misting over in the darkness.

The twelve weeks of term fly by and it is only when the Easter vacation is upon him and he returns to Broadclyst for an uninterrupted period, that he has time to think clearly about all that has happened, and of the future.

Plenty of time, but no answers.

A year into her project and Felicity's life is one of ceaseless action as she prepares her seedlings for planting. She revels in it and her latest venture has involved Rick clearing the most overgrown and underused corner of the orchard in which to plant a few grapevines and an olive tree. It was something she and Edward had talked about long before her inheritance.

'Must be prepared for climate change,' she said. 'Won't it be fab if we could offer our own Deer Orchard wine as the house white at the Retreat?'

The goats, Margo and Barbara, each have a kid, a female who will be kept for milk and breeding, and a male whose unfortunate fate will be in a stew to excite the palates of Felicity's more adventurous restaurant clientele. An incubator has been installed in the kiln room, and free range Deer Orchard chicken is now also on the menu.

The restaurant continues to be talked about in glowing terms and Felicity basks in the success with an 'I told-you-so' expression.

'You must be so proud of her,' says Lyn Wade from the village post office when Edward goes in with a birthday parcel to post to his sister in Kendal. He smiles in what he hopes is a proud kind of way, castigating himself for being so negative about the enterprise. Then he wonders: perhaps he should be proud. It is an amazing achievement after all. But Versatile Rick is responsible for much of the hard labour in the garden, and Gianni's food is the critical factor on which the success of the restaurant depends. Nonetheless, Felicity has worked nonstop. It is as if she was born to this life of animals, vegetables, cooking and making pots and her previous job as a university administrator was merely making do. It probably was.

Edward wonders how she showed no hint of resentment when he was pursuing his career. Perhaps she knew her current life would have been incompatible with raising the children. He hopes so, otherwise the guilt might be unbearable.

Now that he has some time away from Stancliffe, he is able to draft chapters of the maze book and send them to Henrik for editing. Henrik does likewise in return. They hope to be able to start the publication process by the end of the summer holidays.

Patrick Shrubsole phones him regarding their discussion the previous September about the burgeoning UK population.

'What discussion?' says Edward. In view of what had occurred immediately afterwards, he had blanked most of that fateful evening.

Patrick says he has been in touch with a producer he knows at the BBC and persuaded him that a documentary using Scilly history as a predictor of future problems on the mainland would provide some cutting-edge television and ruffle a few feathers.

'If we can get Attenborough interested,' says Patrick, 'it will happen, no question.'

So there is much going on in his own professional world, but not enough to distract him from personal concerns.

He misses his midweek sleepovers in Beckenham. Without the camaraderie that came with his existence at the University of Devon, he realises how short of male friends he is. All his life he has easily picked up acquaintances, but most of his evenings socialising have been with Felicity's friends and their husbands.

Feeling bereft, he phones Conrad and they arrange to meet at the Three Tuns in Silverton. Conrad is already there when Edward arrives and they greet each other warmly. They haven't met since Conrad paid a visit shortly after Edward's return from hospital.

First they discuss Edward's old department and the fact that Gemma seems lost and far grumpier.

'Has Fanclub tried to get into your pants yet?'

Edward shakes his head in disbelief at the question.

'Disappointed, mate! Sure you were in there after she came rushing to your bedside.'

'I have more conversations with her husband.'

He isn't expecting to speak to Marianne or Johnny until he is due to return for the summer term and it is therefore with some surprise that he receives an email from Marianne, written in the friendly tone of old.

To: Edward Harvey
From: Marianne Hayward
Date: 14th April 2004, 18.25
Subject: The Earth's Revenge

Dear Edward,
We have become used to you being here midweek and even though it is the holidays and Holly is here, there is a feeling of being one short! Holly would have liked to see you again. She sends her love and hopes you continue to feel better. Perhaps she will still be here when you begin your next term? She says if so she will move to the spare room. You are honoured!
I am having a phase of Earth concern and wondering if natural disasters are its way of fighting back against over-population and plundering of resources. If the Earth were a conscious being, then it would be searching for cunning plans to save itself.
I suppose there are those who would say that God is doing it on the Earth's behalf ...
love,
Marianne

Love, Marianne … It's been a while since she signed herself off in this way. Perhaps he should tell her about Patrick's proposal. Maybe she could be involved too. Maybe this would help to improve relations. This email is the nearest she has come to the old Marianne and he wonders if she is missing him like he is missing her. He doubts it. *And women are not like men,* as Conrad is so fond of reminding him. What she might miss will not be the same.

To: Marianne Hayward
From: Edward Harvey
Date: 16th April 2004, 22.38
Subject: Re: The Earth's Revenge

Dear Marianne,
How charming of Holly! It would be good to see her too.
Rachel says that as far as the environment is concerned, we at the Deer Orchard are the ones having the cunning plans and that if Felicity gets her way there will be a snowball effect and everyone will have a wind turbine in their back garden! She hasn't got a leg to stand on re the population question as we have overstepped our entitlement by 1.6.
love
Edward

To: Edward Harvey
From: Marianne Hayward
Date: 16th April 2004, 20.21
Subject: Re: The Earth's Revenge

Asked Johnny about wind turbine but he says

Beckenham not ready for radical ideas yet!
However, if you add yours and my kid entitlements
together then we are only .2 over quota so no need to
feel bad!
Marianne

Edward is heartened by her linking them both together in this
way. But when he returns to Beechview Close, Marianne again
pulls up her emotional drawbridge and he is once again baffled.
He can only guess it is a means of self-protection. But from
what exactly, he cannot be sure.

38

One sultry Monday evening at the beginning of May, Taryn goes round to Marianne's. She has not spoken to her since September and hopes enough time has elapsed for her to relax hostilities. Marianne's car is not outside, but she rings the doorbell anyway. One of the tabby cats comes out of the bushes and weaves figures of eight round her ankles in a token of recognition. She does not bend down to stroke it.

When Edward answers she is completely taken aback and gasps on two counts.

First she sees Edward, and that is surprising enough. There is no reason to expect him to be standing on this doorstep looking like he lives here.

And then the arching scar, raw and red, like a tribal mark.

Her jaw drops and she shakes her head and frowns as if she has come to the wrong house, but realises this is not possible. In milliseconds she makes the assumption that Johnny has scarpered and Marianne is now shacked up with Edward. *You dark horse, Marianne!*

'You!' she says wide eyed. 'How? Why? What's happened to your face?' A scenario of a confrontation with Johnny and a knife flits through her mind. But surely not! Yet sane men have been known to become crazed when cuckolded.

'Hello Taryn,' says Edward. 'I am lodging here midweek, that's all. And as you see I've been in a bit of trouble.'

Of course it had to be a sensible explanation for his presence. She is aware of a fast-beating heart and a strange tugging in her stomach; of unaccustomed weakness of knee. She listens with mounting horror as he tells her an abridged version of the attack.

'Not one of my best experiences,' says Edward.

'And have they caught the bastard?' she asks, trying to compose herself.

'Alas, no. My description was virtually non-existent and I don't hold out much hope after all this time. If I'd died, then they might've put in more effort.'

She shakes her head and says how sorry she is; that it is chilly on the step as she didn't bring a cardigan, and can she come in. His story has shocked her and she feels faint. She never was good at the thought of blood. Particularly the streams of it she now visualises pouring down the pavement, with Edward's life ebbing into the gutter. She can't believe she didn't know; wasn't told about something so important. Once she would have been the first with whom Marianne would have shared the news.

'Marianne isn't here,' says Edward, looking over his shoulder into the house.

'Oh … Well, perhaps I could tell you, and you could tell her. Put in a good word.' She shrugs and folds her arms. If she can sit down with a cup of tea until her head clears. If she can show him how she has changed in the intervening months …

'Tell me what?' He hesitates.

'Tell you what I was going to tell Marianne. Promise I'll be on my best behaviour. Promise. Promise. Promise. If I explain. Hey! Please?'

He holds the door for her to step through and she ducks under his arm.

She follows him into the living room. He gestures towards a chair and takes up position on the edge of the sofa. He doesn't offer her coffee.

'Gosh, Edward,' she says, settling back into her seat, wishing he would do the same, smoothing her hair, still unaccustomed to its sleek soft feel. 'It's good to see you again. Really. Despite everything. I've so much to thank you for. I was such a cow. Sorry, an' all that.' She pulls an apologetic face. 'What I did was so despicable it forced me to confront myself, God-awful woman that I was.' Her father's phrase. 'A real bitch; a tart. Not pretty things. Decided it was time to change, so I've had a couple of sessions of therapy, been on a retreat, re-invented myself and – would you believe it – spoken to my father for the first time in decades.'

At this news, Edward appears to relax a little. 'And?'

'Once we began talking, I wondered why I had stayed away so long. Seeing him looking so old and vulnerable, I was shocked. All the bad things that kept me away suddenly seemed less important. I remembered how it was when I was very little and he treated me like a princess.'

Edward nods.

'You were the only person I'd told about Babbo. And you listened and didn't judge me. Nothing terrible happened afterwards. Well it did, but not because I told you. It just made it easier to tell someone else. Now I need to try to persuade Marianne that I'm no longer such a scheming hussy.' Taryn looks up and smiles, trying to catch Edward's eye; wanting him to hold her gaze like he once did on that magical night that was their undoing.

Edward looks down. 'Marianne is difficult to shift when she gets an idea into her head – as I'm learning.'

'Might you put in a word for me?'

'A word in your favour from me might be misconstrued.'

'She and I have both lost so much. Surely you can see that?'

'Marianne's not good at taking advice unless she asks for it.'

Taryn is hurt that someone else should now know her once best friend as she does. 'I know,' she whispers.

'Of course you do,' says Edward.

Taryn changed tack. 'So how do you come to be at Stancliffe?'

'Felicity bought a forty-three grand wind turbine while I was in Scilly last summer.'

'Imagine that!'

'It's no laughing matter, believe me.'

'You're still together?' Taryn is seized with a flicker of hope that he might now be a free man, all thoughts of her new resolve temporarily suspended.

'We were happy for twenty years. It takes more than a wind turbine and a few sheep … '

'Will you stay together? I'm still available should the right man come along.' She laughs, trying to make it sound like a joke.

'You're so direct, Taryn.'

'Always better to cut to the chase.'

'Look what trouble that landed us in last time.'

'I don't regret it. Despite what happened with Marianne. It's because of what happened that I'm a new woman.'

'I can see you're changed on the outside, but what about the inside?'

'I have to start somewhere. I have to be allowed an occasional lapse like an alcoholic.'

'Taryn, you must see that we can never, ever, have a relationship of any sort. We're different people with different ideals. It wouldn't work long term and I'm not on the market for a quick fling. Indeed, I'm not available at all.'

'I know. I'm joking.' She isn't, but deep down, she does know. Edward may seem to be her new type of man, but she knows even the new Taryn could not be his type of woman. This in itself evidence that a consummate shift has occurred. Once she would never have given up until she had worked her way through her whole repertoire of wiles.

Later, back in Coppercone Lane, Taryn pauses by the mirror, a gin and tonic in her hand. It is late, after eleven, and she has been drinking since she returned from Marianne's. All evening she has been brooding over Edward's words, and from being buoyant after the achievements in Leeds, her mood is now plummeting. It is hard to admit defeat. Even the new Taryn still believes she is the complete seductress. *And now he's just five minutes away. What a waste!* She also believes in her drunken state that she has fallen in love with him.

You are a self obsessed, ridiculous middle-aged woman. MIDDLE AGED! Get that! And he will never want you ... Never! Never! N-E-V-E-R.

She flops on the sofa with her knees raised and a cushion on her stomach. She cannot get him out of her mind. The night they shared, the preliminary flirting in the pub, the game she played back at the flat when all her tried and tested moves worked like a dream. Would she ever feel normal again? *If this is what love means, you can keep it.* Perhaps she should sue Shaleenie for opening her heart. She laughs hysterically and then her eyes fill and she catches her breath as the tears fall. She has cried more in the past few months than in the whole of the rest of her adult life. *What is left for me now?*

The following morning, after Johnny has gone to work, Edward is left with the uncomfortable dilemma of whether to tell Marianne. He had promised no more deception and he knows breaking that promise is a recipe for doom. He considered that he handled the meeting with Taryn very well. What a woman! He was amazed by her cheek, but her new vulnerability had brought out his compassionate side and he had treated her far more gently than he thought she deserved. He was aware of her manipulative strategy. How quickly she forgot his wounds and focused on herself. *A woman incapable of empathy,* he mused.

Johnny asked him once if he knew what the Taryn story was and why Marianne had broken contact with such a longstanding friend.

'She won't tell me,' said Johnny.

Edward was uncomfortable in denying all knowledge.

'I've never liked the woman,' continued Johnny. 'A flighty piece. Sees herself as a *femme fatale,* thankfully not my type. She's a bad influence on Marianne. I'm not sorry she's out of the picture.'

Edward isn't sorry either. Yesterday was just a blip.

Marianne's reaction is to start visibly, to frown and then to try unsuccessfully to rearrange her face in an impassioned manner.

Edward persists, 'She wants to see you.'

'Well she can jump.'

They are in the kitchen, Marianne making sandwiches, and Edward washing breakfast dishes. It is of some regret that Marianne doesn't have a dishwasher, though he privately admits to enjoying the shared domesticity of this morning ritual, especially since their conversations have become so stilted.

'I believe she's changed. She's seen a therapist, seen her dad.'

'You let her in?'

'Yes.'

'Very brave.' Marianne seems focused on cutting her sandwiches into triangles.

Edward feels the need to justify. 'I didn't wish to be rude. She means nothing to me. You must know that?'

Then silence.

Virtual silence for the rest of his week in Beckenham. Edward is alarmed and unable to find Marianne alone until the following Wednesday when Johnny has gone to play badminton and they are sitting watching the end of the news and the weather forecast.

'I'm sorry if my letting Taryn in has upset you.'

'It's nothing.'

'I have learnt that when women say nothing, they mean something.'

Marianne sighs. She looks like a wounded animal that is almost too weak to run away. 'I lost my best woman friend and you in the space of five minutes. Two of the most important people in my life apart from Johnny, Holly, Mum, Dad and Louis.'

He registers what she has said. 'You haven't lost me.'

Marianne continues, 'We had one meeting since. Me and Taryn … She came over. I suppose it was an attempt at reconciliation. I told her how hurt I'd been, and she apologised. But it wasn't enough. There was something hollow. We were so guarded for fear of offence. She asked me about you and I realised I couldn't talk to her about you any more because I didn't trust her. In that instant I knew I would never trust her again – especially not now you're here.'

'She is – was – mentally unwell. Can't you forgive that?'

'Even if I could forgive, I'm not sure if I can trust. And that trust is necessary if we are ever going to be friends again.'

'Would you like me to leave? I don't want you not repairing things with Taryn because of me. In any case, there's a tension between us when I'm here. You haven't said you've forgiven me. When you wrote at Easter, it was like the old you. But now … Is it me being here? Is it because of what happened? I don't want to make you unhappy.' He dreads the thought that she may call his bluff. That she will say, *Yes, go!* What would he do without her now that Felicity is on Planet Restaurant? But he has to ask.

There is a long pause with searching glances exchanged.

'I don't know,' she says finally, not looking at him.

He feels the fragility of the situation. He cannot bear the tension.

Finally she looks up and meets his eyes. There is so much sadness there. She doesn't speak but holds his gaze until he can't endure it any longer. He goes upstairs to his room – Holly's room – and looks around at the mixing of his things with her teenage paraphernalia. Is this the time for a dramatic gesture; throwing his meagre possessions into a case and walking away, not just for the weekend, but for always?

He hears footsteps on the stairs, a presence in the doorway.

'I'd miss you if you went,' says Marianne, arms folded. 'I know I'm a bit cool. But it has to be that way – I'm sure you understand why,' and then she floats out of the room leaving him wondering.

I'd miss you ... What does that mean? An awareness of absence? A wish for presence? More than a wish?

39

On the train back to Exeter for the weekend, Edward considers his dilemma. Once he only wondered about excavations, artefacts, stratigraphy, middens, mazes, lectures and issues of departmental significance at the university. Relationship issues were off radar until Felicity's inheritance and he is therefore unskilled in their resolution and unused to devoting hours to their contemplation. He often makes lists in his professional capacity, so he sits back in his seat and mentally tabulates the plusses and minuses of each available course of action.

Plan A. If he stays at Marianne's there will be possible or even probable continuing atmosphere – but it might improve with effort, and if so lead to a revitalisation of an important friendship. On the downside – if it is a downside – he might become more emotionally involved with her than is prudent.

Plan B. A flat in London will remove him from the tricky situation, but it will be less spacious, more costly, more lonely and probably have no garden in which to while away summer evenings. He will also have to cook more or exist on takeaways which are bad for health.

Plan C. If he 'retires' to Broadclyst at the first respectable opportunity, he can become a kept man and pursue his own hobbies in order to avoid being drawn in to Felicity's business. He can devote more time to writing and to giving lectures around the country. He can take up cycling or fishing and develop his golf game, wrist permitting. But Felicity will resent him being free and not supporting her in the business, so leading to Plan D, where he can become front-of-house in the restaurant and kowtow to the paying customers; or run the farmers market stall during term times when James is at uni, and freeze in winter for the privilege. Or he can help with the gardening and compete with Mr Versatile.

Looking at it like this, it is a no-brainer *(ghastly modern phrase).* His mind feels clearer; the most attractive option is clearly staying with Marianne and Johnny – assuming he can do something to improve the atmosphere at Beechview Close. If it doesn't work out, he can always revert to Plan B or, God forbid, Plan C or D.

When he arrives home, no one seems to be around but there are numerous Post-it notes on the table with scribbled messages in the diverse handwriting of the different members of the family. Felicity is cooking at the restaurant because Gianni is in Italy visiting his parents; Christopher is having a sleepover at a friend's; Rachel is on yet another date with another different suitor; Harriet is waitressing with Kylie who is persistent in hanging round the family even though James is mostly in London entertaining Kate. Edward is secretly pleased that Kylie will now be unlikely to be instrumental in helping to carrying on the male line.

In a moment of spontaneity he decides to go to the restaurant and surprise Felicity, cynically supposing that as usual he will be charged for the meal.

Seated at a table with its red tablecloth, he notes the growing number of glazed vases and bowls on the shelves around the room, each with a clearly visible price beside it and some bearing a red dot to signify that they have been sold. An odd-shaped urn with a grinning cat painted on the side seems out of place. He surmises that this is one of Olivia's works.

Harriet gives him the menu and he decides to order a Mediterranean fish stew.

When it appears, Harriet says, 'Mum hopes you enjoy your meal. She also said we mustn't forget to give you the bill.'

The meal is excellent, and judging by the happy faces of the other five groups of diners, the restaurant continues to please.

Later, leaning on a fence post in the paddock at dusk, gazing across the lane and through the sheep into the middle distance, he registers Felicity beside him.

'Thanks for coming down tonight. You don't come enough. It's nice to show you how things have progressed. What did you think?'

'I think it's great.' It isn't like Edward to be unimaginative with adjectives.

'Sold two bowls and a vase to some tourists from London,' continued Felicity.

'Indeed.'

'And have you noticed how keen Christopher is to get involved? At first I thought it was a phase, but he helps in the garden as much as he can. Rick has built him a raised bed of his own to grow what he wants. He's not as academic as the others. Clever, yes, but in a more practical way. I can see this being his future. Ted, are you listening to me?'

'Yes. "Christopher; raised beds; his future".'

'You don't seem yourself,' says Felicity quietly, searchingly.

'I haven't been myself for some time,' he says, 'even discounting the obvious problems.' He flexes his wrist. 'This new life of ours. This life in two separate parts of the country. It's strange.'

'It was your choice to be away. But then you've always been away a lot. I'm used to being a part-time, academic's widow.'

Edward considers this statement carefully. This is why Felicity has made so many plans without him; because she has always had to; because he has always let her. He begins to understand and to take some of the responsibility; some of the blame. *Even for the wind turbine.*

'But when I used to come home, it was us and the children.

We did the family thing really well. Being away seemed to enhance that. Now I come back and there's a void.'

'You should get more involved.'

'I've tried, but it's not me.'

'I'm sorry.'

It is all becoming clear: he loves interacting with the animals and the notion of the Good Life, but he doesn't enjoy the physical work involved. He is a theoretical being, not a practical one; a writer; an orator; living his working life through his mind rather than through his body.

'Are you happy, Flick?'

'More fulfilled than for a long time. I remember when we first moved down here and I took any work I could just to help us with the cash flow. My favourite job was being an apple grader; that wonderful smell and learning all the names. I used to stand at my workstation dreaming up recipes for them. It wasn't a mundane job for me but an opportunity to be inspired. Then James arrived and the apples were gone. Until now. They say the perfect job is something that makes you smile. What I'm doing now makes me happy all day. I no longer dread Monday mornings. Now I have purpose beyond you and the kids; something for the future.'

He suspects as much, but it still hurts to hear it. He searches her face, flushed with energy and health and regaining the bone structure that has drawn admiring glances in the past. This outdoor life is helping her to shed the excess pounds and despite their differences, he finds the old desire stirring once again. But her constant rejections are taking their toll. A question that has bothered him for weeks begins to surface.

'Am I still important in this scheme?'

'Of course you are, you silly fool!' She sounds shocked. 'This is our home, you and me. I know this seems a bad thing to say, but you're just not the centre of my world any more. As I'm not yours; have never been yours.'

'*What?*' He cannot understand why she should say this. She has been everything that is good about his life. 'You are.'

'No, Ted, I'm not. I've never been more important than your work. The kids and I have always fit in around your job.'

'No.'

'You took the job at Stancliffe.'

'Nothing mattered more than you and the family.'

'Past tense?'

Shall he contradict her? Or shall he admit he made a mistake, come home, settle for the rustic life. Accept it will no longer be the joyous existence of his young adult life. Will it be enough?

Instead, he says, 'Where do you see this going?'

'The restaurant? Fifteen-year plan; then sell up. It could be a pension provider. But who knows what the future holds? We might want to retire to the coast.'

He is reassured that she still considers him in her schemes.

'I'd miss this place,' says Edward.

Felicity appears calm in the silence that follows.

Edward taps his fingers on the fence.

Eventually Felicity speaks. 'Life has its ups and downs; relationships don't run smoothly all the time. We've been luckier than most and maybe now it's our turn to deal with difficulties. We'll be fifty soon and to have got this far with comparative ease is a bonus. You've been spoilt – getting your own way all this time. You must learn to compromise.'

'It would be easier to compromise if …' he decides to be blunt, 'if our sex life hadn't gone AWOL.'

'Is that all that you think about?'

'It's important to me – to men. You've changed. Even when the kids were young, you were enthusiastic.'

'So, weren't you the lucky one? Due some time off I'd say.' She pauses, looking into the far distance. 'I think I'm at an age where the hormones are playing up and I can take it or leave it. Simple biology. I'm not as randy as you any more. Perhaps if you made more effort to persuade me, I might …'

'Then tell me how,' he says.

She gives him one of her looks that means he should know the answer. 'This middle age thing is a bit of a shit. I don't feel very well most mornings and I'm still upset about what happened to Mummy. I know it wasn't exactly unexpected, but you forget, then you remember. You reflect; you wonder what's happened to your life. I'm an orphan now. You still have both of yours. And I've no siblings. I know there's you and the kids, but it's just a strange feeling of finality.'

'Yet you seem so happy doing all of this stuff.'

'I am happy doing it; because it distracts me from feeling old. And I don't stop, because when I stop, the reality sinks in.'

'At the wassailing, I thought you seemed so young and beautiful.'

'Did you really, Ted? That's the nicest thing you've said to me for ages.' And she puts her arm around him and leans her head on his shoulder, and for those few minutes that they are standing close he wonders that perhaps there is hope and that what was lost will be found.

Then she walks away leaving him gazing at the sheep.

Compromise. Marianne once wrote in an email that it was only the women who compromise. Perhaps she was right and perhaps it is his turn. But at what cost? Is this what he wants? Only this? A flat in London perhaps, or Marianne's, and this at the weekends? These are the alternatives.

Such a colourless existence without Marianne. But will her proximity become too much to bear if he stays?

Questions, questions …

Taryn meanwhile wakes in a better mood the day after her unexpected encounter with Edward. Sober, there are fewer terrors and the negativity of the night before puzzles her. *Chemicals,* she thinks. *Everything we stuff through our mouths is inevitably going to affect what we are. I should become tee-total. There's a thought! And a new challenge.* She ponders this idea, wondering at the strength of her will. It would be tangible proof to present to Marianne in a few months time. *I am on the wagon; haven't touched a drop since May.* But Edward would be there. Could she face him without wanting him? Would Marianne trust her intentions?

And if she is honest, it is Marianne's rejection that has wounded her more. Despite the realignment of her mental state and her romantic aspirations, when it comes to her ex-best friend it is as if she has returned to a child. She is desperate to heal the rift, and Taryn doesn't *do* desperate.

She wonders about Marianne's novel and how near it might be to completion. Marianne had asked her to edit the book when it was finished, saying she valued Taryn's knowledge of literature and expertise in correcting English language and spotting the clichés. Might a reminder of this help to open the door? But the book was inspired by Edward, and anything remotely *Edward* might be counter-productive.

Perhaps she should demonstrate her integrity by getting involved with someone else. Like Neil.

Neil has been attentive at work, but hasn't pushed things since the previous autumn when he came with the pumpkin and she offloaded about her father. He's made no suggestions that they meet and nor has she. It is as if he is waiting for her to make the first move. She knows that she gave him hope when they last talked about it; perhaps he doesn't want to hear that she has changed her mind again. If Taryn is totally honest, she has missed him.

She has been celibate since the night with Edward, fulfilling her vow after her visit to the abbey that any future physical relationship must be accompanied by genuine feeling. Even another visit from Marc did nothing to tempt her. She is beginning to trust her new self; to feel the sense of a permanent change.

Neil … She's mulled over the possibility for months. She's prevaricated; talked herself into a relationship and then out again. She's thought about the lack of excitement, dismissed it as no longer important, revived it as being essential, wondered that it can be created in other ways, and that having a steadying influence in the background might be just what she needs. She thinks again, picks up the phone and then replaces it.

The following Monday, after her final lesson of the day, she watches her GCSE group leave the classroom.

'Krystal, make sure you have that homework tomorrow, yeah? No excuses. No, "I've left it on the bus". This is an important year for you. You can achieve great things if you focus. Yes?'

Krystal grins over her shoulder. 'Yes, Miss.'

Taryn gathers up her folder and a pile of essays but instead of heading for the staffroom, she goes in search of Neil.

She walks down one flight of stairs and along a grey tiled corridor, stopping at the end and knocking on a wooden door bearing a Head of History plate.

Inside, Neil is behind a desk that is covered in piles of exercise books, paper, red pens, paper clips and half a salad sandwich in a plastic box. The sight of all the mess nearly makes Taryn change her mind. *But he did say they didn't have to live together.*

'Well Taryn, what are we after this time? You don't usually pay me a visit at the end of the day unless you want something.

More archaeological advice?' He seems rather curt, not his usual self.

Taryn closes the door behind her and clears her throat. 'I've come to ask you out.'

'What and when? I'm pretty busy at the moment.'

'I mean "Out" out.'

There is a long, long pause. 'No can do, Taryn. After that evening of the Pumpkin, I had such hopes. But then nothing; absolutely nothing. I've wanted to be more than just friends for ages. Thought we'd be good together. Always hoped you'd relent in the end and settle for someone steady and reliable rather than your usual choices. But you were always adamant. Never gave me hope until that night. I thought you were going to give us a chance, but a man can only wait so long. Didn't you hear about me and Lesley?'

Taryn's heart drops an inch or two. She hadn't expected this. She has long depended on Neil being there, if and when she needed him. The thought of another woman stirs her newly discovered jealousy again. Her look is crestfallen. 'I've given up drinking. I wanted to be sure I could stick to it; that I could be more reliable.'

'Kidding,' says Neil. 'Needed to know you meant it; can see by your face that you do.'

Taryn doesn't like it when the joke is on her. Her instinct is to turn and march out. But that is the old Taryn; the Taryn that always had to have the upper hand. The new Taryn drops her shoulders and grins. 'So, are we going to give it a whirl?'

Neil gets up from behind his desk and after closing one of the blinds, he chivvies her into a discrete position by a filing cabinet and gives her the warmest of hugs.

The new Taryn allows herself to relax into his embrace and they stay there rocking silently while the clock on the wall marks a new beginning.

★

In Beckenham the following Tuesday morning, after Johnny has left for school, Marianne reaches for the kettle at the same time as Edward does and his hand clasps hers. He doesn't let go. He didn't plan it, but now he feels his palm against her skin, and the warmth like an electric surge reminds him of the urgent feelings of his youth. It triggers the opportunity he has been waiting for.

'I will never abuse the hospitality offered by Johnny and you. You don't have to be so guarded.'

He keeps hold of her hand as the seconds pass, feeling the beat of time during which all the possibilities spin like a carousel. She doesn't pull away.

She half turns towards him and he catches a flash of green eyes and widely expanded pupils, quickly averted. She opens her mouth and closes it. She is breathing quickly.

He continues, 'I don't want you to be so cool. It's not right; it's not you. This is your home, your world, your life, and you must feel relaxed here. I want to stay, if you're still happy to have me, but I need you to forget the Taryn thing. I have put it down to experience; a temptation that although not resisted in the first instance, I have resisted – have wanted to resist, ever since. There are personal issues between me and Flick that it would be unfair on her to reveal, but which could be used in my defence regarding Taryn. We're having a difficult time. But it's the first time. It may pass. I'm not without blame. She's made me realise that I've never had to work at the relationship before; never had to compromise. I don't know how to. But perhaps these are things I can learn, and I'm going to try. We have too much history and I believe we do still love each other. But even if it doesn't work out for me and Flick, I won't look to Taryn as an alternative, and nor would I make life awkward for you. I promise.'

Marianne remains tense; listening. She flexes her fingers, but still does not remove her hand from his grasp.

'Why don't you ring Taryn and patch it up. Put it behind you; forgive us. I want us to be friends and this rift is getting in the way.' He gives her hand a final squeeze before releasing it.

Marianne looks at him again with a mixture of regret and compassion. She sits down at the table. 'I'm sorry about you and Felicity and you mustn't give up hope. That's something I learned last year. When you get to our age, you think you know how to do relationships, but while the rules for teenagers seem pretty universal, the ones for us are not. All the good years stack up like credit against the bad. Twenty years is a massive investment for friends as well as lovers. But I don't think Taryn and I can ever get back to how it was. I'm shocked at how little I really knew her. So many secrets; so calculating. That's not what I expected from such a good friend. I know she's changed and I know she's had more psychological baggage than I ever imagined, but what we had is lost.' Marianne sighs. A long, drawn out sigh. 'I don't want to lose you too. I want you to stay. I'll try to be less … edgy.'

Edward is persistent, 'Ring her. I know it won't be easy but in punishing her, you are punishing yourself.'

'Suddenly so wise.' says Marianne with an edge of sarcasm. 'Sorry, I shouldn't say that. Forgiveness isn't always possible.'

'Arrange one of your games of tennis. Even if it's nothing more than that to start with. You've nothing to lose and so much to gain.' He is aware first of resistance, then a weakening, a hesitation. 'Ring her; text her. She's paid the price and I do believe she is trying to change. She needs you, Mari.'

'Only Johnny calls me Mari.'

'Sorry! I think of you in my head as Mari now, because of Johnny. Do you mind?'

'No.' Marianne picks up her mobile and turns it over in her hand. She puts it down.

'Do it now or you may never do it, Mari.'

'I can't. I just can't. Maybe sometime; maybe not. But I do forgive you. I know you didn't mean to do what you did.'

'All I want is your friendship.'

'You have it. I expected too much from a mere mortal. It isn't because of Taryn that I've been distant. Not recently, anyway. You've just alluded to it. But I'd like you to stay. And you've been through such a lot. I know it will take a long time for you to heal.'

He smiles, relieved. 'Do I look terrible?'

'I like the designer stubble.' She laughs and then looks serious. 'I look at you and all I see is Edward. If I look really hard, I see a trace of Edward at eleven, and I also see the Edward at forty-seven that I met last year, if a little bruised.'

It's what he wants to hear, but he doesn't know whether to believe her. 'I dare say the scar will fade a little in time and I'll get used to it. Felicity says I should grow a beard again – and I know many archaeologists do – but I've never been the bearded type and I looked awful when I came out of hospital.'

Marianne is laughing, a sound that reminds him of bells. He wonders why this should be so funny.

'Scars can be quite attractive on good-looking men.' Her eyes twinkle. She turns to the fridge and extracts a pack of bacon, waving it at him. 'Would you like a buttie?'

The highly-charged moment is gone, but she is smiling again with something of the old friendliness and warmth. He lays the kitchen table with plates and cutlery and cuts some bread. So much that is unspoken. So much that is understood.

Minutes later they are sitting at the table opposite each other, Marianne scribbling on a pad, notes of shopping reminders and things she has to do at work, and he wonders if

351

this is a snapshot of the future. Workaday mornings at Beechview Close where they flit from one scene to the next in sound bites, rarely completing one thought before another more pressing one kicks in. Pomegranate juice – Marianne is on a health kick – and bacon sandwiches and a *frissant* of something that is never realised but that will help to prop the faltering midlife ego. He has yesterday's newspaper to hand, but the bylines are a blur and the news items far less distracting than the woman in front of him.

Pomegranate juice and bacon sandwiches, he thinks, shaking his head wistfully. It is enough for now. It might always be.

ALSO BY LINDA MACDONALD

Meeting Lydia

"Edward Harvey. Even thinking his name made her tingle with half-remembered childlike giddiness. Edward Harvey, the only one from Brocklebank to whom she might write if she found him."

Marianne Hayward, teacher of psychology and compulsive analyser of the human condition, is in a midlife turmoil. After twenty years of happy marriage, she comes home one day to find her charming husband in the kitchen talking to the glamorous Charmaine. All her childhood insecurities resurface from a time when she was bullied at a boys' prep school. She becomes jealous and possessive and the arguments begin.

Teenage daughter Holly persuades her to join Friends Reunited which results in both fearful and nostalgic memories of prep school as Marianne wonders what has become of the bullies. But there was one boy in her class who was never horrible to her: the clever and enigmatic Edward Harvey, on whom she developed her first crush. Perhaps the answer to all her problems lies in finding Edward again …

Meeting Lydia is a book about childhood bullying, midlife crises, obsession, jealousy and the ever-growing trend of internet relationships. It is the prequel to *A Meeting of a Different Kind* told from Marianne's perspective.

Paperback: 9781848767126   *Ebook: 9781848768574*